DESERVING RYLEIGH

The Refuge, Book 7

SUSAN STOKER

Edited by Kelli Collins

Cover Design by AURA Design Group

Manufactured in the United States

CHAPTER ONE

"Isn't this exciting?" Alaska asked Ry with a huge smile, just before she hurried across the room to talk to Henley.

She managed to smile at her friend and nod, but as soon as her back was turned, Ry's lips turned down again. She was in no mood to celebrate the imminent birth of Henley and Tonka's baby.

Everyone was gathered at the lodge at The Refuge, and Robert and Luna had made a huge cake for the impromptu baby shower. The mood was festive, anticipation in the air. This would be the first baby born among the close-knit group of friends, but there would be more to come in the near future. Reese would be next, due in another month or so. Then Lara a few months later, and Maisy had recently learned she was pregnant too. Not to mention Cora and Pipe's first foster child, who would arrive in the next week.

It was a joyous time at The Refuge...for everyone but Ry.

She shouldn't be here. Unfortunately it was too late. She should've left way before now.

1

But first Jasna had gone missing...then Reese was taken. And she couldn't have lived with herself if she hadn't done what she could to help rescue Lara. But her real downfall was Stone. She'd been determined to do what she could to find him—ultimately using a computer that wasn't protected.

She'd had the best of intentions but that didn't matter...not to a man like her father.

She sighed.

"If you're that unhappy, you can leave, Ryleigh."

Ry stiffened. She didn't have to turn her head to see who'd approached. There was only one person who used the name she'd been given at birth. She was "Ryan" until she'd admitted to the owners of The Refuge that she'd lied about who she was, and why she was here. Now she went by Ry, which she actually liked better than Ryan.

But Spencer "Tiny" Denny refused to call her anything but Ryleigh.

Besides the use of her given name, she'd recognize Tiny's voice anywhere. The low, rumbly sound of it slid down her spine and sent shivers through her body. Once upon a time, she'd dreamed about having a fling with him. But she'd blown any chance of that the moment she admitted she'd been lying to not only Tiny, but *everyone* at The Refuge. She'd done it for very good reasons, but she had no doubt this man would never forgive her.

After all...he'd told her so.

Everyone else seemed to take what she'd done in stride. She hadn't done anything that would bring harm upon The Refuge or the people living here...yet. She'd done everything she could to help, when and where she could. And yet, Ry had a feeling even if she saved the place from burning to ash around them, Tiny still wouldn't forgive her.

She didn't really blame him. The things she'd done here were just the tip of the iceberg. If Tiny or the rest of the men who owned the world-renowned retreat knew who she *really* was, what she was capable of, the things she'd done...she'd be kicked out so fast her head would spin.

And Ry had a feeling Tiny knew she was hiding so much more than she'd admitted. Which was probably part of the reason why he was so curt with her.

"Did you hear me?" he asked.

Ry nodded.

"You either need to stop looking like you'd rather be mucking out Melba's stall and smile, or leave," he told her.

She took a deep breath. She might not like being around Tiny all that much now, but he was right. She did her best to relax her muscles and even managed to smile at Alaska, who was staring at her and Tiny from across the room with a worried look on her face.

Ry glanced toward the man and studied him for a long moment. He was taller than her by a few inches, and she wasn't exactly short. At six feet, he seemed to tower over everyone simply because of his confident presence. It was no secret that the girls and others compared him to the iconic Jake Ryan from the movie *Sixteen Candles*, but Ry didn't think he looked like the actor. He was way better-looking. The stubble on his jaw and cheeks made her want to run her hand over it to know what it felt like.

He had the most amazing turquoise eyes she'd ever seen, longish hair, and what she thought was a permanent furrow in his brow. One that lately seemed to be getting deeper. Because of *her*.

He was muscular and intimidating, and being around him somehow made Ry feel safe. It was a dichotomy that made no sense. He didn't even like her, and yet she knew if the shit hit the fan, he wouldn't hesitate to protect her. Simply because the others considered her their friend.

He was loyal, a hard worker, and very observant. From the outside looking in, one might think he was laid-back and a big teddy bear, but Ry knew the truth. She'd lived in his cabin for a few months now, and the second he walked through his door at the end of each day, the polite veneer he wore for the world sloughed off, and he became the man he *really* was.

Tough. Hard. Unforgiving. Suspicious.

And Ry was probably the biggest idiot on the planet—because she liked him even more, now that she'd seen the real man underneath. Yes, he could be mean, and Ry had been on the receiving end of his venom more than once since she'd admitted she'd lied to everyone. But she'd also seen him in action. His background as a Navy SEAL had given him the tools to act under pressure. To know instantly and instinctively what needed to be done, and he never hesitated to throw himself into any situation if it meant keeping his friends safe.

Ry rarely allowed herself to think about her future, because she suspected her time on earth would end sooner rather than later if her dad had his way...but when she *did* allow herself to dream, Tiny was at her side. They worked together as a team, taking out bullies and making their corner of the world a little safer, better.

However, that was a *pipe* dream. With the way Tiny was shooting daggers at her right now, it was obvious he'd never feel anything but suspicion toward her.

Staying was like having a knife thrust into her side over and over, and coming back for more. But she couldn't leave. Not now. Not when she was sure her father had found her.

After all the precautions she'd taken. After all the sacrifices she'd made...one mistake was all it took for him to track her down. But she didn't regret using Brick's computer just that one time. She'd been as desperate as everyone else to find Stone, Owl, and Lara. Using the unsecured computer to do a few searches was all it took for dear ol' dad to grab onto the thread she'd left in cyber space...but it had also helped them find their friends.

"What's *with* you today?" Tiny asked gruffly.

Ry swallowed hard. "I don't know what you mean?" she fibbed.

Tiny snorted. "Right. I'm not sure why I expected you to do anything but lie again."

Wincing, she turned to face him, suddenly exhausted. Overwhelmingly tired of lying to the people who'd come to mean the world to her. Tired of walking on eggshells around the man next to her. Just...tired.

"You want to know what's *with* me?" she asked in a low tone.

"Yeah, Ryleigh. I do," Tiny responded, looking her in the eye.

"I'm terrified. Every moment I'm here brings more danger to everyone and everything I've come to know and love. But I can't leave, because if I do, there won't be anyone here to protect all of you.

"I lied to everyone. I lied to get the job, but you know what? I'd do it all over again if I had the choice. Because I *like* it here. I'm thrilled for Henley and Tonka. I love the

5

stupid goats who try to eat my shirt every time I go into the barn. I love chatting with Jasna about her days at school. Working with Carly and Jess was the highlight of my mornings before I was forced to give up my job as a housekeeper. I can't wait to see how this place flourishes with the addition of the helicopter.

"The Refuge is an amazing place. Serene and calm and healing, and it does so much good for the men and women who come here. And I know if I stay...it could all be destroyed. But if I go, it will *definitely* be destroyed.

"I'm sorry I lied. To you, to the girls, to your friends. I'm sorry you're stuck with me in your cabin when you hate me so much. And I'm *damn* sorry being around me makes you so unhappy. But I'm going to fix this. Somehow, someway. Then I'll leave and you'll never have to see me again.

"Now, since you correctly pointed out that I'm being a downer, I'll head back to the cabin. Tell everyone whatever you want as to why I'm gone. It doesn't matter. Nothing matters anymore."

With that, she spun on her heel and headed for the door. Tears swam in her eyes as she made her escape. She probably shouldn't have blurted all that out, but she hadn't lied. About any of it. She was terrified out of her mind, and so scared and sorry that her presence here was a threat to the only people in her life who'd treated her as if she wasn't a freak.

She made it out the door and had taken only four steps toward the forest, and Tiny's cabin, when her elbow was gripped and she was spun around.

Ry acted on pure instinct. With thoughts of her father front and center in her head—and what he'd do to her when he finally made his move to get back what she'd taken from him—she threw herself to the side, landing hard on her hip. She didn't hesitate when she hit the ground, using her momentum to roll away from the threat.

"Jesus, Ryleigh! It's me. Are you all right?"

Once again, she immediately recognized the voice. Tiny had followed her.

Of course he had. He liked to get the last word.

Feeling off-kilter, Ry scrambled to her feet and faced her nemesis.

"What the hell happened just now?" he asked.

"I didn't know you'd followed me. You startled me, that's all," she said with a lift of her chin.

"You actually think I'd hurt you?" Tiny asked in a low, gruff tone.

Ry didn't know how to answer that. Did she think he'd do something to bruise her skin? *Physically* hurt her? No. Not really. But he *had* hurt her. Every time he glared daggers at her. Every time he refused to talk to her when they were alone in his cabin. Then every time he deigned to open his mouth, and his disdain for her poured out loud and clear, he hurt her.

"Fuck!" he exclaimed, pacing away, running a hand through his hair. When he faced her again, Ry could see the determination in his gaze. "We need to talk."

"No," she said without hesitation. "We don't."

"You can't expect to lay everything you just laid on me back there and then *not* explain what the hell you meant."

Ry sighed. She was so exhausted. And things were just going to get more difficult from here on out. She hadn't held her tongue like normal. She'd blabbed way too much to Tiny.

7

"The time to talk to me was when I told you who I was. When I admitted that I got the job here under false pretenses. But you didn't want to hear what I had to say then, and I'm not too inclined to explain myself now. Believe me, if I could leave, I would. You'd have your cabin back, wouldn't have to see my face every day, and wouldn't feel the need to hover over me, trying to make sure I'm not doing anything that will hurt The Refuge. News flash, Tiny—I'd never do *anything* to intentionally put this place in jeopardy. Not when I've worked so damn hard to help it prosper. But there are people out there who'd like nothing more than to see this place burn to the ground. Simply because it means something to *me*.

"And that's why I can't leave. Because I screwed up. But I'm going to fix it. I don't know how, but I am. You want to know all my secrets? Too bad. I might've told them to you before...but now? No. It's too late for that. Just please know that I'm going to do whatever I can to make The Refuge stronger than it's ever been before. For all the babies that will be born in the upcoming year, for you and your friends who served our country bravely and without hesitation, and for each and every guest who needs this place to heal."

"Ryleigh," Tiny began, but she was done.

She turned her back on the only man who had the ability to tear her to pieces with a simple look and headed for his cabin. If she had any other place to go, she would. But she'd moved out of her apartment in Los Alamos when Stone was missing so she could share whatever scrap of information she found in a more timely manner. The small guest room in Tiny's cabin was her home for the moment, and while she was grateful for the roof over her head, every second spent with Tiny was torture. Because he hated her. He'd made that clear.

Thankfully, he didn't follow her back to his cabin. Ry let herself in and went straight to her room. She lay down on the bed and curled into a ball on her side. Closing her eyes, she tried to think, to strategize. But even though she desperately needed a plan, she couldn't think about anything but the confusion and worry in Tiny's eyes after she'd stupidly overshared.

She'd never seen those expressions on his face before in regard to *her*. Usually he looked at her with suspicion and contempt.

Confused and weary from the stress she'd been under, Ry fell into an uneasy sleep. One punctuated with her father's face, laughing manically, and Tiny shaking his head and telling his friends, "I told you she was trouble."

CHAPTER TWO

Tiny stared at Ryleigh as she disappeared into the trees, headed for his cabin. He was confused. The things she'd said...they blew everything he'd thought he knew about the woman out the window.

He'd be the first to admit that he'd been hard on her. He wasn't sorry. She'd lied to them over and over. Not only that, but it was obvious with her computer skills being what they were, she could easily steal The Refuge blind. The thought of anything happening to this place made Tiny's blood run cold.

He couldn't imagine not living here. Not being in the mountains of New Mexico. If this place failed, he had nowhere to go. Had no idea what he'd do. The Refuge had saved him, and he was so grateful to Tex for hooking him up with Brick and the rest of the men, and to all of his friends for deciding to make a go of the unique retreat.

And after years of much-needed healing and calm at the place he'd help to build with his own two hands...the truth of the matter was, Ryleigh made him feel things he'd thought were dead and buried.

She infuriated him, frustrated him…and yet a part of him, buried way down deep, worried about her.

He *hated* himself when he yelled at her. He didn't miss the way she flinched from him and seemed to withdraw every time. And yet, he hadn't been able to make himself stop. He was so *angry* that she'd deceived them all, and he simply didn't trust her. Sure, he didn't trust many people in his life, but the one thing he couldn't tolerate was lies, and Ryleigh had lied her ass off from the second she'd stepped foot on The Refuge.

But it was finally dawning on him that maybe, just *maybe*, she'd had damn good reasons for those lies.

Just like some of his friends had suggested might be the case. But he'd refused to listen.

She'd said a lot of things tonight, things he needed to think on and share with his friends and Refuge co-owners…but the thing that bothered him the most was the fact that she was scared. No. *Terrified*. Of what, he didn't know, but it didn't sit well with him. Not at all.

Tiny turned and went back into the lodge, realizing quickly that he was in no mood to socialize. He found Tonka, who was standing away from the group, watching his wife with a small smile on his face.

His friend turned to Tiny as he approached.

"You leaving?" Tonka asked without preamble.

"If that's okay with you," he said with a shrug.

Tonka's lips twitched. "I think I, more than anyone, understand when someone needs space."

Tiny chuckled, then sobered. "The changes in you are, frankly, amazing. The man I knew when we first arrived wouldn't have been able to cope with being around this many people for as long as you have tonight. Would've especially hated being the center of attention like you are."

Tonka shrugged. "Don't love it, but I *do* love Henley. And seeing how happy she is, how she thrives being around her friends...it makes what I want immaterial."

"Doesn't it worry you? How much your life has changed because of a woman?" Tiny asked, genuinely curious to hear his friend's response.

"No. Here's the thing...I wasn't actually living at all before I let Henley in. I was stuck in the past and what happened to me. I allowed it to guide my life, instead of dealing with what happened and moving on. Thanks to her, I've learned that life doesn't stop when bad shit happens. We either have to find a way to get past what life throws at us, or we stop living altogether."

"That sounds like something a shrink would say," Tiny said cynically.

"Maybe, maybe not. And I don't even care that you're talking shit about my wife's profession. I've learned a lot from Henley. It's not as if her life has been all sunshine and roses. If she can come out the other side of the horrors she's lived through, why can't I? I'll always miss Steel. There will always be a hole in my heart for my dog, but life goes on. And to answer your question...I'll never enjoy being the center of attention, but for Henley, I'd do anything. Same goes for our unborn child and Jasna. They're my everything."

Tiny was happy for Tonka. He really was. Even if he couldn't understand that kind of devotion. It required trust, and he didn't have it in him to trust a partner that way. Not again. He'd been burned too badly. "Right. Anyway, I'm headed out."

"Saw Ry leave a little bit ago. I'm guessing she's not going to plan The Refuge's downfall if you take your eyes off her for two minutes," Tonka said dryly.

"Now that Stone's back and she doesn't have anyone else to rescue...I wouldn't be so sure about that," he retorted.

"The women like her. They'll be sad if she leaves," Tonka said.

Tiny shrugged. "They'll be all right. They have their husbands. And all the soon-to-be-born babies."

The look Tonka gave him made Tiny want to squirm, but he held firm. Holding eye contact with his friend for a long moment.

"I think out of all of us, you're the most...broken," Tonka finally said.

He wasn't wrong. "I'm good," he lied.

"And she needs a friend," Tonka persisted.

Tiny was done. He didn't want to hear Tonka defend the woman he didn't trust as far as he could throw her. He'd seen up close and personal what she could do with that computer of hers. She was ten times as deadly as a terrorist with an RPG. He had no doubt she could take out a country with her fingertips and a keyboard. If everyone wanted to stick their heads in the sand and refuse to see how dangerous Ryleigh could be to The Refuge, that was on them. He wouldn't be fooled so easily. It was why he'd taken it upon himself to watch her like a hawk.

"Well, it won't be me," Tiny said firmly. "Congrats on

the baby. Henley's going to the hospital in a few days to be induced, right?"

"Yeah. Friday."

Tiny nodded, then clasped his friend on the shoulder and gave him a squeeze of support before turning and heading for the door. Looking at his watch, he saw that Ryleigh had left fifteen minutes ago. His heart rate sped up. She could do a lot of damage in fifteen minutes.

He hated that he felt that way, but he couldn't help it.

As he walked through the trees toward his cabin, he tamped down the feeling of guilt he felt for thinking the worst of his houseguest. He purposely thought about some of the things she'd lied about since she'd been at The Refuge.

She'd gotten Alexis to quit so she could have a shot at getting her job as housekeeper. She'd lied about her name and her background. Her experience.

Then there were the lies by omission. He was grateful that she'd had the ability to help Jasna and Reese. But he couldn't help but think if she'd come clean sooner about who she was and what she could do, they might've been found even quicker.

She'd only told the truth about who she was—and what she could do—when she'd no longer had a choice. When they were desperately trying to find Owl, Stone, and Lara.

Despite trying to remind himself of all the times Ryleigh had lied to him and his friends, he couldn't help remembering those two simple words he instinctively knew she hadn't meant to blurt out less than thirty minutes ago.

"I'm terrified."

She hadn't lied about *that*.

Tiny had seen her face when she'd said it. Could see the fear in her eyes. He didn't know exactly who or what she was afraid of, only that she claimed she wanted to leave but couldn't. He didn't understand what that meant... but the thought of her not being around bothered him in a way he'd never admit to anyone.

She'd also said something about protecting The Refuge, and that she thought her being there put the place in danger. It didn't make sense. And Tiny didn't like not knowing what threat might be coming for them—or where it was coming *from*.

He needed more intel, and the only way he'd get it was by talking to Ryleigh.

Determined to make her tell him outright what was going on—whether she wanted to or not—Tiny hurried the rest of the way to his cabin.

When he entered, the lights were off and Ryleigh was nowhere to be seen.

For a moment, his heart skipped a beat. Had she left after all? She'd only been out of his sight for a short time, but it was possible she'd fled. Moving quickly, he went to the room where she'd been staying and without bothering to knock, pushed the door open.

His muscles relaxed when he saw Ryleigh on the bed. She hadn't left. Tiny didn't even want to question why he was so relieved...but then he frowned as he continued to stare at the woman who'd turned his life upside down.

She was on her side, facing the door, knees drawn up and curled into a tiny ball. She looked...vulnerable. He couldn't see her mahogany-brown eyes, since they were closed tightly, but her straight black hair fell across her cheek, the ends pooling on the pillow under her head.

Running his gaze over her slowly, it registered then that she'd notably lost weight in the last few months. He hadn't thought much about when or what she ate, but he felt a deep flash of guilt, because he knew when they *did* share a meal, it was spent in complete silence, usually with Tiny glaring at her, resenting her presence. Ryleigh always left the table quickly.

He'd been a colossal ass. He could admit that. But he wasn't sure how to be anything other than who he was. Ryleigh made him uneasy and nervous at the same time. The others might not admit it, but this woman was a threat. All he'd done was try to keep an eye on her, to make sure she didn't do anything that would hurt his home and sanctuary.

And yet...

He leaned heavily against the doorjamb as it hit him like a ton of bricks that even if she *did* try to do something to harm The Refuge...he wouldn't have the first damn clue how to fix it. He didn't understand computers the way she did. Didn't have a single idea what he was looking at when she manipulated code as her fingers flew over a keyboard.

He'd watched as she used her knowledge and contacts on the dark web to try to find Stone. And what she did...it was genius. The woman was smarter than anyone he'd ever met. So far out of his league, it wasn't even funny.

Her confession tonight also made it clear he'd been kidding himself—he wasn't forcing her to stay so he could keep an eye on her. She was here by *choice*. She'd chosen to remain at The Refuge. Moreover, she'd *chosen* to stay in his cabin, even though he treated her like total shit.

Like some kind of self-imposed penance.

Tiny noted the way she flinched every time he spoke to

her harshly. How she stayed in her room as often as possible to avoid any kind of conflict. And yet it hadn't made him curb his behavior toward her...and hadn't made Ryleigh accept the offers from any of her friends to stay in their cabins.

For the first time since she'd admitted she wasn't who they'd all thought she was, Tiny felt a bit of remorse for the way he'd treated her. That didn't mean he suddenly *trusted* her. Just that he could acknowledge he'd been a jerk.

Seeing her now, vulnerable and obviously stressed, if her body language while she slept was any indication, Tiny sighed. *He'd* done that. Made her feel unwelcome, on edge, and probably unsafe, if the way she'd thrown herself to the ground tonight was any indication.

And yet...she still hadn't left.

If he was in her shoes, he would've been gone the moment Stone was securely back at The Refuge. But here she was.

Remembering more of her words from earlier, how she'd said it was too late to leave, Tiny's lips compressed in a hard line. He wanted to wake her up, insist she tell him what was going on, what she wasn't telling him or the others.

She was still keeping too many secrets, but reluctant as he was to admit it, Tiny wasn't as angry about it as he'd been even two hours ago. She was trying to protect them, that much seemed clear. From what or who, he had no idea —but he'd find out.

Standing upright, he eased the door to Ryleigh's room closed, leaving it open a crack so he could hear if she needed him—which was ridiculous, because it wasn't as if she'd ever cried out for him in all the time she'd been here, but still—and went into the living area. He poured himself a large glass of water and went to the sofa and sat, staring into space as he tried to work through his next steps in his mind.

Ryleigh was scared of something, didn't feel as if she could leave, even though it was obvious she wanted to, and whatever was frightening her involved The Refuge.

Shivers of dread shot down Tiny's spine. Something was coming. Something big, if it terrified a computer genius like Ryleigh. He didn't know what, or who, or when, but it seemed clear the key to The Refuge coming out unscathed on the other side was the woman sleeping in the next room.

Tiny had joined the Navy to protect and serve. Had loved being a SEAL. He hadn't done much protecting or serving Ryleigh...but starting tomorrow, that would change. He might not trust her, but he could admit that nothing she'd done had actually hurt him or his friends. On the contrary, she'd done everything in her power to help.

He'd ease up on her, do his best to get her to confide in him. Once he knew what the threat was, he could mitigate it. Then Ryleigh could leave. Get on with her life. And he could do the same.

Now that Tiny had seen the fear in her eyes, he had a hard time maintaining the animosity he'd felt toward his houseguest for so long. She wasn't faking that emotion. He'd bet his Budweiser pin on that. What was the saying? Honey drew more flies than vinegar. Starting tomorrow, he'd do what he could to help shoulder whatever burden Ryleigh was bearing.

Feeling better than he had in months, though not fully understanding why—beyond reluctantly admitting it had been slowly becoming harder and harder to be curt to his houseguest anyway, even without tonight's revelations—Tiny chugged the rest of his water and stood. He took the empty glass to the kitchen sink and headed toward his bedroom.

Tomorrow. A new day, a new plan.

And Tiny wouldn't fail. It wasn't an option. Not when the hair on the back of his neck was standing up. He never ignored that feeling when he was on missions as a SEAL, and he wouldn't ignore it now. If Ryleigh was the key to keeping The Refuge safe, he'd do whatever it took to get her to confide in him.

CHAPTER THREE

Ry was increasingly uneasy. Over the last two days, Tiny had been...different. And it was freaking her out. When she'd gone into the living area of the cabin the day after Henley's baby shower, he'd actually said "good morning"... as if he hadn't spent the last few months grunting and growling at her at the start of every day.

Then he'd handed her a mug filled with coffee, fixed exactly how she liked it. He'd *never* done that before. She'd always made her own coffee each morning. She'd stared down at the drink, wondering if he'd poisoned it, and he'd chuckled. *Chuckled.* And told her, as if he could read her mind, that he hadn't put anything in it...other than the sugar and cream she normally liked.

And things had just gotten weirder from there. He hadn't glared at her once. Hadn't insisted she tell him exactly what she was doing online. Hadn't made any snide comments about her dark web contacts she sometimes used when she needed intel.

He wasn't acting like the Tiny she'd gotten to know

over the last few months, and she had no idea why. And that made her incredibly nervous.

Tiny wasn't a gentle man. He called things as he saw them. Didn't beat around the bush when he was pissed about something. He abhorred lies—which, she understood, was why he hated her—but he was acting as if all the untruths she'd told since arriving at The Refuge no longer meant anything to him. Which she knew wasn't the case, as he'd told her time and time again that he didn't trust her *at all*.

But in the last two days, he'd left her alone more than he ever had before. He didn't hover over her as she scoured the web, trying to find out what her father had up his sleeve. Didn't demand she tell him where she was going each morning, who she'd be hanging out with. It was as if something had happened the night of the baby shower, but she wasn't sure what that might be.

Yes, she'd blabbed some things she wished she hadn't, but he hadn't asked questions after she'd made it clear she wouldn't be sharing any more of her secrets. Hadn't demanded she tell him why she couldn't leave—or worse, insist she go, since Stone had safely returned to The Refuge.

It was bizarre. And frankly, Ry didn't like it. Was waiting for the other shoe to drop.

But hopefully that wouldn't be today, because everyone was currently heading to the hospital. Henley was being induced, and no one wanted to miss the birth of her and Tonka's baby. They'd opted not to find out the gender, so everyone seemed twice as excited.

Of course, Ry hadn't been able to resist. She'd hacked into the hospital database and found the sonogram pictures, so she knew the gender. But she wasn't about to share a secret that wasn't hers to share. Her need for information, to not be surprised, was a big fault. Ry knew it, but she couldn't seem to stop herself from digging for information she knew was out there for the taking. It made her an awful person, but her father had hidden so many things from her, she had a deep compulsion to investigate for intel. It was the only way to keep herself safe.

She was currently sitting in the back of Brick's Rubicon between Cora and Lara. Alaska was in the front passenger seat. The others were either on their way to the hospital or already there.

"Do Tonka and Henley have names picked out already?" Lara asked as she ran a hand over her own pregnant belly unconsciously.

"I think so, but they aren't telling what they are," Alaska said with a shrug.

"It's a girl. I know it!" Cora exclaimed happily.

"No, definitely a boy," Lara disagreed. "He's really low in her belly."

"How someone carries a baby doesn't have anything to do with gender," Cora told her with a snort.

"Yes it does! I read it on the web!"

"I read a story yesterday about a woman who was kidnapped by Bigfoot and had his love child...so that means it has to be true, right?" Cora retorted.

Everyone chuckled.

"Okay, good point. I just...I want them to have a boy," Lara said.

"Why?"

"I don't know. I mean, a boy would be awesome. He

could follow Tonka around and help feed the animals and stuff."

"And a girl can't?" Cora huffed.

Ry bit her lip to hold back the smile that threatened to escape. Being around the two best friends was always a hoot. They argued and bitched at each other like sisters, but the love between them was easy to see. The fact that Cora had gone to such extreme lengths to find her friend when Lara had disappeared wasn't something Ry understood. Intellectually, she could appreciate it, but she'd never had that kind of relationship with anyone...blood-related or otherwise.

Lara sighed dramatically. "Okay, true. I'm being sexist. And now that I think about it...seeing Tonka with another daughter wrapped around his little finger, the way he is with Jasna—and his dogs Wally and Beauty—would be equally as awesome."

Ry saw Brick smiling as he drove, but he didn't interrupt the conversation. All too soon, they pulled into the parking lot at the small hospital in Los Alamos. Ry knew from talk around The Refuge that Tonka had wanted Henley to go to Albuquerque to have their baby, since the hospital was bigger, but she'd put her foot down, insisting she wanted to give birth right there at "home."

Brick pulled up to the hospital doors to let the women out before parking. Ry walked with her friends through the doors and they headed toward the waiting room down the hall. It wasn't hard to figure out where everyone was, as Reese's laughter rang out to their right.

The second they walked into the room, it felt as if everyone started talking at once. Ry had gotten used to how...*exuberant* The Refuge gang was, but it still sometimes took her by surprise. She'd grown up in a home that was extremely quiet. She was expected to be that way too. Her mom had tried to encourage Ryleigh to laugh more, to get outside and play, but her dad was in charge of their home, and he preferred she sit behind a keyboard and learn everything he had to teach her.

Thinking about her mom made Ry sad, so she purposely turned her thoughts to the people around her.

"We didn't miss anything, did we?" Alaska asked no one in particular.

Maisy giggled. "No. Although you were cutting it close."

"I know. The last guest to check in had a hundred questions. And then I had to make sure Robert, Jess, and Hudson had things under control."

It wasn't often that all the owners of The Refuge left the property at the same time. But as this was a special occasion, no one had wanted to stay behind. Ry felt uneasy about leaving, especially with her father out there, no doubt watching and planning, but she hadn't known how to bow out without explaining why.

The time was coming when she'd need to tell not only Tiny, but *all* the guys what she suspected was going to happen soon...but she kept hoping and praying she was wrong.

"You okay?"

The two words came from her right, and they surprised Ry so badly, she jerked in surprise.

"Whoa, easy."

Looking up at Tiny, Ry could feel herself blushing. How she'd missed him approaching her, she had no idea. He looked good today. He had on a pair of well-worn jeans and a checkered button-up shirt, which seemed molded to his arms and chest. And he smelled amazing, like usual. She figured it was whatever body soap he used, because Tiny would never be the kind of man who bothered with cologne.

When he lifted a brow at her, Ry realized she'd been staring at him instead of answering his question. "Oh, yeah, I'm fine. Is Henley all right?"

He didn't answer right away, simply stared at her. Ry wasn't comfortable with being on the receiving end of such scrutiny. Had gone out of her way to keep from being noticed for most of her life, both in person and while she was fiddling around online. But this man *saw* her. She didn't feel as if she could hide anything from him, especially now that they were basically living together.

"She's fine," he finally said. "Tonka's been coming out and giving us updates when he can. The last we heard, she was fully dilated and ready to push."

It felt a little weird to be discussing the birth process with Tiny, but he didn't seem uncomfortable in the least discussing dilation and what it meant. She shouldn't have been surprised. He was amazingly unflappable—most of the time.

"That's good," Ry said after a moment. She felt awkward and uneasy around him. Always had, because she was all too aware of her attraction toward him. Though, after she'd admitted her name wasn't really Ryan, that she'd finagled herself into the job at The Refuge, the previous few reciprocal looks he'd given her had disappeared completely.

Which brought her back to the last two days. Now when he looked at her, it seemed as if he was trying to read her mind, figure out what made her tick. And despite how nervous that made her feel...she couldn't deny the attraction she'd felt for him during her first several months at The Refuge was sparking back to life.

It scared the crap out of Ry. Because Tiny didn't like her that way. And if he was changing tactics, trying to be nice to her or—God forbid—seduce her for some unknown reason, there was a high probability she'd fall for it.

Tiny continued to study her, and it felt as if they were the only two people in the world at that moment. Ry could drown in his turquoise eyes, and it took every ounce of control she had not to lean into him. She didn't hear the excited chatter of their friends in the small room. She was lost in the magnetism of the man standing next to her. Had he leaned closer? Ry inhaled, and his scent filled her senses.

Yeah, he'd totally stepped closer.

"You know the gender, don't you?" he asked quietly, seemingly out of the blue.

Swallowing hard, Ry considered hedging, but she'd lied enough to him. She simply nodded.

Instead of his jaw tightening, and the disapproving look he usually had on his face when he realized she'd used her computer skills to find out something she shouldn't, he actually smiled.

Ry wondered if she'd entered some sort of alternate dimension.

"I figured you probably did, because every time a discussion came up about whether they were having a boy or a girl, you never volunteered your opinion."

The realization that Tiny paid a *lot* more attention to

her than she'd realized should've been alarming. Should've had her itching to grab her beloved computer and get the hell out of New Mexico. But instead, it made her feel... protected. Knowing he was there, watching out for her, made a yearning she thought she'd pushed down to the recesses of her being flare hot and fast.

She wanted what her friends had.

Every time Brick went out of his way to check on Alaska when she was working the front desk, that yearning flared. When Tonka met Henley at her car as she arrived back at The Refuge after her shift at the mental health clinic in town...when Spike let Reese babble to him in the few Spanish phrases she was learning...when Pipe called Cora "love" in his sexy-as-hell English accent...when Owl stood behind Lara with his hands resting on her baby bump as if he could keep them both safe with that simple touch...when Stone looked at Maisy as if she was the center of his world...

Ry yearned to have what they had.

It wasn't jealousy, per se. She was as happy as could be that her friends had partners who clearly loved them. She simply wished she could experience the same. She'd been on her own for years. Doing what she could to stay two steps ahead of her father, who'd used her for his own despicable schemes since the day she was born.

It had taken a very long time for Ry to understand that her father didn't love her. Had *never* loved her. To him, she was merely a means to an end. Someone who could take the fall for everything he'd done, if it came to that.

She was thirty-one years old and had never felt wanted or loved...until she'd arrived at The Refuge.

She'd researched the retreat online and liked what

she'd seen. Better yet, it was far off the beaten path. Her dad would've never expected her to be hiding out in such a place. It wasn't that she'd needed the money from the housekeeping job she'd applied for all those months ago—she didn't—it was a place where she could hole up while she continued giving away as much of the money her father had acquired over the years as she could.

It wasn't as easy as people might think to spend thirty million dollars. She couldn't bring attention to herself, and she had to be careful about where she stashed the money until she could give it all away. The more bank accounts she opened, the more ways her father had of finding her. But if she put too much in any one account, questions would be raised and tax ramifications would have to be dealt with.

Ry felt a touch on her arm, and once again, she jerked, startled. Tiny was standing even closer now, blocking out the rest of the room with his body as he stared down at her. He was running his fingers up and down her upper arm. He hadn't said a word while she'd been lost in her thoughts.

"So many heavy thoughts running through your head," he mused.

Okay, this almost-gentle Tiny was *totally* freaking Ry out. She was used to him sniping at her, making her feel guilty and ashamed of who she was, what she did.

"Just worried about Henley," she told him.

"One of these days, you'll feel comfortable not lying to me," he told her. Then with one last touch, he dropped his hand and stepped away from her.

Just when he was about to turn away, Ry blurted, "That wasn't a lie."

Tiny's eyes narrowed a fraction. "No?"

She shook her head. "I *am* worried about Henley. Tonka would be devastated if anything happened to her. I know they both want their baby, but not at the expense of her health. I was just thinking about what it would be like to be loved like that. To know someone would do anything and everything to keep you safe."

As soon as the words were out, Ry regretted them. She should've let Tiny walk away. Shouldn't have cared that he thought she'd lied to him yet again.

"You've never felt that? Even as a kid?" Tiny asked.

The urge to laugh off his question, to lie and say of *course* she had, was strong.

Instead, Ry forced herself to hold his gaze. She shrugged and shook her head.

"I'm sorry. I didn't have a fairytale childhood, but my mom did her best. She loved me. My brother though...he was my best friend. We did everything together. He always had my back, and I had his. He would do anything and everything to keep me safe...just as I would for him. Anyway, I'm sorry you didn't have that. Also...I want to apologize for my behavior."

Ry's head spun. Who *was* this man? It couldn't be the guy she'd lived with for the last few months. Who glared at her every day, never let an opportunity pass to let her know he didn't trust her as far as he could throw her, and had no problem taking out his every frustration on her.

"I don't trust easily." He snorted. "Actually, that's an understatement."

"Yeah, I've noticed," Ry told him without rancor.

His lips twitched. "Yeah. Anyway, I've taken out my frustrations on you. You lied to me, to all of us, and that didn't sit well with me. I abhor lies. But after our chat a few days ago, I tried to look at your situation from...a more objective standpoint. I don't know why you did what you did, or what you're very obviously running from, but the lies you told us...they weren't malicious. Yes, you used your skills to find information you shouldn't have, but you also used them for good too. So...I'm sorry for being an ass."

Ry's hand came up and before she could think better of it, she poked Tiny in the chest. Hard.

"Ow! What was that for?" he asked, grabbing her finger before she could poke him again.

"I'm trying to figure out if I'm dreaming this or not," Ry told him.

He chuckled.

And she could do nothing but stare at him in disbelief. Laughing around her twice in as many days? Because of something *she'd* said? Yup, definitely dreaming.

"You aren't dreaming. I'm not saying I'm going to magically start trusting you, or *anyone* for that matter. Just that...I forgive you for what you've done in the past, and I'm sorry for anything *I've* done or said that's made you feel as if you don't fit in here at The Refuge. Because you do. More than me, most days."

Tears threatened. But Ry held them back. She loved the pseudo-family she'd found. But she couldn't stay. Not after what she'd done. Not with her father out there hunting for her. Looking for any way to make her pay for double-crossing him.

"It's a girl!"

Ry jolted yet again, and she didn't miss the way Tiny steadied her before stepping away, giving her some room.

At Tonka's announcement, cheers rang out in the waiting room. When everyone had settled down, he went on.

"Henley's fine. They're getting her settled and when they're done with all the weighing and evaluation of the baby, they'll let her have some visitors."

Everyone started talking at once, giving Tonka their well wishes and letting him know they'd wait as long as it took for their turn to meet his new daughter.

Tonka turned to Jasna, who was under his arm, snuggled against his side. "You want to tell them your little sister's name?"

The teenager beamed up at him and nodded. She turned to the group and announced, "Elizabeth Ryleigh Matlick!"

Ry's mouth fell open in shock. No. They couldn't have named their daughter after her. No way, not after she'd lied to them all.

"Elizabeth because we like the name. And Ryleigh for obvious reasons." Tonka's gaze met hers from across the room. "Because without you, we would've lost Jas."

This time it was impossible to keep the tears from forming. Ry closed her eyes even as she felt herself surrounded by her friends. They comforted her and congratulated her. The mood was joyous, but all Ry could think of was how generous and loving these people had been.

She didn't deserve it.

Her presence was putting them all in danger. If they knew...

Of course, they *didn't* know, because she hadn't told them. Was afraid the friendship they'd extended to her would dry up faster than she could blink. And once again, she'd be alone. On the run.

But as she stood there in the middle of their friends, thinking about how Tonka and Henley had actually given their baby *her* name...she realized that she'd badly misjudged the men and women from The Refuge. If they knew her history, they wouldn't turn their backs on her. They'd go out of their way to do what they could to help. Because that was the kind of people they were.

Tonka took Jasna with him when he left, so she could see her mom and meet her baby sister. They would spend some time alone together before everyone started shuttling in and out of the room to meet the newest addition to The Refuge family.

Ry got hugs from everyone as they impatiently waited to be able to meet little Elizabeth. Tiny didn't approach her again, but every time she looked around, Ry saw him nearby. Instead of feeling as if he was watching over her because he didn't trust her to be out of his sight, she felt... comforted. Her head still spun with the changes in his behavior. She didn't really understand how or why he'd made the switch, but she couldn't deny she much preferred this Tiny to the one who was curt and downright mean.

Ry let the others take their turn going back to Henley's room to see her. She suddenly felt shy about seeing her friend. She'd had no idea Henley and Tonka had plans to honor her the way they had. This was why she didn't like surprises. She didn't know how to react to them.

Finally, it was her turn. To Ry's surprise, Tiny escorted her down the hall toward Henley's room. She was tongue tied and didn't have any idea what to say to him. Thankfully, he didn't seem to expect her to say *anything*. He walked by her side, only moving behind her when they passed someone in the hall. Even then, she could feel him at her back, a larger-than-life presence that made her not feel the need to keep her head on a swivel. Which was practically a miracle, because for ten years, since the day she'd snuck out of her father's house, she'd done nothing but look over her shoulder.

When she entered Henley's room, she noticed right away how tired her friend looked. Happy, yes, but also exhausted. And it was no wonder. She'd been in labor for hours, gone through the pain and excitement of giving birth, and had been holding court with their friends for at least two hours now.

Little Elizabeth Ryleigh was sound asleep in the crook of Henley's arm, and Tonka stood at the side of her bed, staring down at his wife and daughter with a look of awe.

"Hey," Ry said, unsure what else to say.

"Get over here," Henley ordered, holding out her free hand.

Ry stepped forward and gave her friend an awkward hug.

"Sit," Henley ordered, gesturing to a chair that was pulled up next to the mattress.

Ry sat obediently.

"Finn, I love you, but can you please give me and Ry a moment. You can take Jas to get a snack. She hasn't eaten all day, and I've been listening to her stomach growling for the last hour."

"I don't want to miss anything," Jasna whined.

"Honey, you aren't going to miss anything. Elizabeth is asleep, and she's gonna stay asleep for the time it takes you to eat and return. And I'm going to take a nap as soon as

Ry heads out. You'll come back, kiss me good night, then go back to The Refuge with Finn because the goats are probably eating the wood of their stalls by now, and Melba is probably mooing up a storm, and I'm sure Scarlet Pimpernickel misses you something fierce. Not to mention it's past Beauty and Wally's dinnertime."

"All right. But don't let Elizabeth do anything cute until I get back!" Jasna told her mom. Then she leaned over the bed, kissed her mom, and headed for the door.

"We'll be back soon. Then you can sleep," Tonka told her before giving her a long and heartfelt kiss. "Love you so much. You have no idea the gift you've given me today."

Ry felt like a third wheel, but she stayed completely still, as if that would make her invisible.

"Go," Henley ordered. "Oh, and bring me back a large order of tater tots. I'm *starving*."

Tonka chuckled. "Yes, ma'am."

As soon as Tonka was gone, Tiny approached the side of the bed and smiled down at Henley. "Congratulations, Hen."

"Thanks, Tiny."

"She's beautiful," he said, gesturing to the sleeping baby.

"She's a baby, of course she is," Henley said. "I need you to give me and Ry a moment as well."

Tiny nodded. "Of course. I'll be down the hall if you need anything."

Henley rolled her eyes. "I don't know what I could need, but thank you."

Tiny's gaze met Ry's, and she wasn't sure what she was seeing in them. She had so many questions, but knew she'd never ask any of them. It still felt as if she was in an alternate universe. She'd gotten used to the status quo, of Tiny treating her as if she was a spy who needed constant super-vision. And now he was...

She didn't know *what* he was doing.

The second Tiny was gone from the room, Henley sagged against her pillows.

"You're tired," Ry said. "Maybe I should go too."

But Henley's hand shot out and gripped her arm tightly. "Please, no. Stay."

"Why?" Ry blurted.

"Because you're even-keeled. You have an aura that always seems to calm me. I love our friends, they're all amazing. But all that enthusiasm can be exhausting. With you, I can relax. I don't have to pretend with you."

Her words floored Ry, and she shook her head in disbe-lief, still having a hard time wrapping her brain around what this woman had done. "I can't believe you gave your daughter my name."

Henley smiled. "You saved Jasna, Ry. What you did...I have no words. I don't even know *all* that you did, just the basics, but still. No one has ever done anything like that for me before. You risked your life for my daughter, and it meant something. Means *everything*. You haven't let me thank you, not really, and I wanted to make sure you knew how important you are to me and Tonka. And Jas. Without you, we..." Her voice cracked.

Ry's chest felt tight. She hadn't even thought about what she was doing more than a year ago, when she'd gone out looking for Jasna. She'd just acted. Had done what was right. What she'd needed to do to atone for all the sins of her past.

"Will you tell me the story? All of it?" Henley asked.

"I'm not sure—"

"Please," Henley interrupted. "I need to know what happened to her. What she went through. What you saw, what you did. How you found her. I haven't pushed before now, but today, on Elizabeth's birthday...I find that I want to know. If Tonka knows, he would never tell me because he wants to protect me. I don't *want* to be protected. Not when it has to do with Jasna. Please, Ry. I need to know."

Ry nodded. She understood that need. She felt it every day of her life. If there was information out there, she had to find it.

"First, you should know—I knew you were having a girl before today," she blurted.

Henley chuckled. "I'm not surprised."

"You aren't mad?"

"No. You didn't let the secret out. Didn't let on that you knew. To anyone. I don't care that you hacked into the hospital records to find out. Not in the least. Just as I don't care if you broke laws to find Jas, or Reese, or to do anything else you did. You're a good person. To the core, Ry. No matter what's happened in your past, or how you came to be at The Refuge, I won't believe anything else."

Ry was overwhelmed yet again. What had she done to deserve this woman's support and loyalty? Yes, she'd found Jasna, but anyone would've done what she had, if they had the skills.

Taking a deep breath, Ry began talking.

CHAPTER FOUR

Tiny stood quietly outside the hospital room, leaning against the wall. He wanted to be nearby in case Henley or Ryleigh needed anything. He hadn't meant to eavesdrop, but he couldn't pry himself away now if his life depended on it.

Hearing Henley's support for Ryleigh made him feel even more guilty than he did already. She didn't sound in the least worried about what Ryleigh could do, about the hacking. And her words about how she thought Ryleigh was good to the core...

She was right.

With that knowledge slowly sinking in, Tiny needed to hear the story about how Ryleigh had found Jasna as much as Henley did. He'd gone over the incident in his head again and again, and because he wasn't some computer genius, he couldn't figure it out. How she'd discovered where Jasna was, who had taken her.

He held his breath as Ryleigh began speaking.

"As you know, we were in my car when you got the call

that Jasna was missing," Ryleigh said. "You mentioned Christian Dekker's name. So after I dropped you and the others off at The Refuge, I went back to my apartment and immediately started looking into him."

"Looking into him?" Henley asked.

"Yeah, hacking into the police database and seeing if he had any kind of record, first of all."

"He was a minor," Henley said, sounding confused.

"And?"

There was silence in the room for a beat, then Henley snort-chuckled. "Right, sorry. Continue."

"There had been some complaints against him, but nothing that the cops could arrest him for. I probably shouldn't admit this, but...what I do isn't exactly a secret anymore. I also read *your* reports on him, and your boss's thoughts on him too. Read all the things his parents had said when they were in therapy. I realized that you had a *very* good reason to be worried about him. To think he might be behind Jasna's disappearance. So I tracked his phone.

"And before you ask, yes, I thought about calling the police, but they need probable cause and a search warrant. By the time they got all that, Jas could've been hurt, or worse. So I did what I do best, and I found him. Discovered he was at that cabin out in the middle of the woods. And I went to check it out."

"Ry! That wasn't smart or safe!" Henley exclaimed.

Tiny agreed. His fists clenched, and it took all the control he had to not burst into the room and...he wasn't sure what. He wasn't mad at Ryleigh, per se, but he couldn't believe she could be so stupid! To take such reckless risks...

Ryleigh didn't respond for a long moment, and Tiny wished he could see her face. She sucked at hiding her emotions, and if he could see her, he'd have a better idea of what she was thinking.

"Oh, Ry," Henley finally said, her tone full of emotion. "Hasn't *anyone* worried about your safety before?"

"No." Her tone was flat. Matter-of-fact.

He took a deep breath, and his anger faded into sorrow. He felt bad for Ryleigh. She'd obviously never had anyone care about her. Not as a daughter, a friend, or anything else. His heart hurt for her...doubly so after the way he'd treated her.

"Anyway, it doesn't matter how unsafe it was, because if there was even the slightest chance he had Jasna, I had to find out. The cabin looked pretty deserted, and it was in the middle of nowhere. There weren't any neighbors to come running if I screamed for help or anything. There was a car parked outside, and the license plate matched the numbers I saw in Christian's files, so I knew he was there. And there was only one reason he would be at a place like that...and it wasn't good. I didn't know what to do," Ryleigh said in a shaky tone that made Tiny once again want to burst into the room and comfort her.

"I'm not a commando. I'm a computer nerd; good with my fingers on a keyboard, not so good when it comes to fighting."

"You don't like conflict," Henley said.

Tiny blinked out in the hall. It was such a simple statement, but now that he thought about it, Henley was absolutely right.

"I hate it," Ry agreed. "I couldn't ever do anything right growing up. I got yelled at...a lot. Told I was stupid for the tiniest mistakes. And every time I made one of those mistakes, I was punished by having food withheld, my electronics taken away, wasn't allowed to go to school. I had to redo whatever I'd messed up until it was done correctly."

"Like what?" Henley asked.

There was a brief pause. "Once, after I'd hacked into the state's treasury database to change tax information for my dad—and I messed up—the cops came to the house. My dad threw me under the bus, ranted and raved about 'kids these days,' and he let the police take me to the station. I truly thought I was going to be put in jail, and I was terrified. When they finally took me home, after spending hours telling me about all the awful things that could happen to me if I ever did anything like that again, I was a complete mess."

"How old were you?" Henley asked gently.

"Eleven."

Tiny's jaw dropped in a silent gasp. Eleven? She'd hacked into a state database—on her father's orders, from the sounds of it—when she was *eleven*? What the hell?

"That's really young." Henley's tone was even, and Tiny couldn't help but be in awe of her skills. She was a talented psychologist, and it was obvious why she was so popular at The Refuge with the guests.

Ryleigh didn't respond, but Tiny could imagine she'd probably shrugged off Henley's comment before she continued. "Anyway, as I was standing in the trees, staring at the cabin, wondering if I should call Tonka, or maybe Tiny, Christian came out of the house. By himself."

Tiny couldn't help but feel good deep down that she'd wanted to call him for help. Ryleigh seemed so self-assured. So confident. But to know when push came to shove, she'd thought about reaching out to *him* for help, made satisfaction bloom deep in his chest.

"I watched him leave and was itching to find out where he was going, but I needed to know if your hunch that he'd taken Jasna was correct. I waited until he was gone, then carefully approached the house and looked in a window. Jas was there, asleep on the floor. I mean, I figured she probably wasn't *actually* asleep. She wasn't moving. I didn't see any blood or anything, so I hoped that was a good sign. I took a moment to go online and check to see where Christian was—I'd sent a link to myself before I left my apartment, with his cell phone trace. I saw he was still headed toward town, and I figured I had enough time to get Jas out of that cabin.

"I went inside and was able to rouse her enough to get her off the floor. I got her to my car and drove away from that cabin like a bat out of hell. I was on my way to The Refuge, but I pulled over before I got there. I checked where Christian was again, and saw he was at that fast food place. The bastard had kidnapped a young girl and was getting a *burger*? It disgusted me. I called the cops through their tip-finder line and told them where they could find him. I knew the police were looking for him; I'd heard them talking on an emergency scanner app I have... which is completely legal, by the way. Anyone can download it and listen."

"I'm not judging you, Ry. Not even a little. How could you even think that after all you've done for me and my family?" Henley asked.

"I just...I know what I do isn't legal. But it's been a

41

long time since I've done anything that would hurt someone else," Ryleigh admitted quietly.

Tiny thought about that for a moment, and while he didn't know exactly what it was she did on her computer, since she'd admitted that she wasn't who everyone thought she was, the things she'd done had been nothing but helpful. Yes, she'd hacked into places she shouldn't have, but she'd done so because she was trying to find Lara. Then Stone.

"We're lucky to have you on our side," Henley said gently.

He heard a sniff, then Ryleigh was speaking again. "Anyway, I told the cops where Christian was, and where the house in the woods was located, just in case they didn't act on my intel soon enough to get him while he was still in Los Alamos. I got back on the road to bring Jas to The Refuge, but I realized how many questions there'd be for me if I did that. I *love* The Refuge. Actually liked my job. I knew if I just waltzed into the lodge with Jasna, everyone would have questions and I'd have to leave. And I know it was really selfish of me, but...I decided to leave her in one of the bunkers, then anonymously text Tonka where she was, so he could go get her."

"Ah yes...the bunkers," Henley said.

Tiny pressed his lips together. He was aware Tonka had told his wife about their hidden bunkers on The Refuge property. He'd even brought her to the one Jasna had been put in for safekeeping, so she could see it for herself. For closure. Alaska also knew about them, because Brick had stashed her in one before going hunting for the asshole who'd been trying to kidnap her again. They weren't quite the secret they used to be, that was for sure.

"You know about them?" Ryleigh asked. "They're not common knowledge."

"I know about them," Henley confirmed. "But not where they're all located. Can you tell me more about them?"

"No, I can't," Ryleigh said somewhat firmly. "It's not my secret to tell. I'm sorry."

Ryleigh had managed to surprise Tiny once more. The woman obviously knew a lot of information about many different things, including The Refuge, and probably the men who owned the place. But the fact that she wasn't going about disclosing that information willy-nilly impressed him. He still wasn't comfortable with the level of knowledge she possessed, and he wondered what else she was keeping a secret, but he had to admit that she'd surprised him by not telling Henley everything she knew about the bunkers.

"It's okay. So you brought Jasna back to The Refuge?"

"Yeah. She didn't seem to be having any trouble breathing, and I couldn't find any injuries on her. I didn't think it would take Tonka long to get to her, so I figured it would be okay to leave her alone for a little while. I made sure she was safe where I left her and went back to my car. On my way back to Los Alamos, I listened to what was happening at the cabin on the scanner, then sent Tonka the text letting him know where he could find Jasna."

"And you went home," Henley said flatly.

"Yeah."

"By yourself."

"Uh...yeah?"

"Oh, Ry," Henley said, once more in a heartbroken tone.

Tiny felt the same way. He'd known what Ryleigh had done for a while now, but hearing it from her own lips put everything in a new light. She hadn't sought out approval for her actions. Hadn't wanted any kind of thanks or kudos. She'd saved Jasna's life, stolen her right out from under a killer's nose, then went back to her apartment, alone, and kept quiet about the whole thing.

"And Reese?"

"What about her?" Ryleigh asked.

"You tracked her and told the guys where she was, then went on with your days as if nothing happened?"

"It wasn't a big deal."

"Not a big deal? Ry, it's a *huge* deal. You saved her life too! Who else have you saved over the years and refused to take credit for? How many other people have you been a guardian angel for, and they don't even know?"

Tiny understood Henley's bewilderment. He felt the same way. He'd thought the worst of Ryleigh, and he was just now beginning to grasp how solitary her life had been.

"Not enough," was her response. "I've done bad things. Used my skills to destroy people's lives."

Tiny's brow furrowed. The Ryleigh he knew wasn't a bad person. But then again, it was becoming more and more obvious that he didn't really know Ryleigh at all.

"Bullshit!" Henley exclaimed heatedly.

"I have," she insisted.

"Well, if that's true, then you didn't *want* to. Someone made you."

And just like that, clarity hit.

Her talk of being scared, of needing to protect The Refuge and everyone who lived there, of "fixing" things, her claim that she'd done things to help The Refuge prosper, and "people" who would like to see the place crash and burn because it meant something to her...it all made a little more sense now.

There was someone out there who hated Ryleigh. Enough to want to hurt her...maybe even anyone and anything she showed an interest in.

He'd suspected for a while she'd been hiding. Running. Though for how long was anyone's guess. And given the things she'd let slip in the last few days...it sounded like whatever or whoever she was hiding from had most likely found her.

She'd protected Jasna, and Reese, and exhausted herself trying to find Stone. There had to have been an immense amount of pressure on Ryleigh's slender shoulders—and what had Tiny done? Made it worse. Given her the cold shoulder, treated her as if she was a pariah.

And yet she'd stayed. Because she was continuing to protect them. All of them.

He felt like shit.

Having some insight into her actions didn't make his distrust of her disappear, but it put a large dent in the shield he'd wrapped around his heart for sure.

"W-What? Why would you say that?" Ryleigh asked.

"I've spent my life studying the human psyche," Henley told her. "The hows and whys behind people's actions. You're a good person, Ry. Down to your little toes. If you did bad things in the past, it wasn't because that's who you are—it was because you had no choice. I wish I'd known it was you who'd helped Jas back when it happened. I wouldn't have let you sit in your apartment by yourself after that ordeal. I'm kind of mad at you for doing that. But...I understand. You were doing what you thought was right. Well, I hope you understand that you're a part of us now. The Refuge. You're our friend. And I have never felt more sure in the decision to name my daughter after you than I am now."

"Henley," Ryleigh protested in a watery tone.

Tiny took a deep breath and pushed off the wall he'd been leaning against. He quietly walked away from the hospital room, needing some air. He didn't feel bad about eavesdropping. Ryleigh had shields thicker than his had ever been. The thought of *why* she had them made Tiny want to rage. But he couldn't do anything to help her until she opened up about her past.

Someone was out there, threatening her. He had no doubt about that. And not only threatening *her*, but The Refuge too.

She'd said it herself, she didn't feel as if she *could* leave now, because whoever was out there knew how important The Refuge was to her. That alone told Tiny that she was a good person. Anyone else would've fled long before now to save their own skin. But not Ryleigh.

He felt horrible for the way he'd treated her. As if she was a criminal. Someone who had to be watched twenty-four/seven. And all along, she'd had nothing but the best of intentions for his friends and his home.

Did she still break the law with the things she did online? Undoubtably, yes. But now that he thought about it, Tiny wondered what else she'd done to help The Refuge. She'd all but admitted there was more the other night, when she'd blurted out those things she probably never meant to say. Something about how she hadn't worked so hard to make the place prosper, only to see it get hurt now.

The thought that Ryleigh could be a modern-day Robin Hood made him even more ashamed. Not that The Refuge needed charity, they were definitely doing all right. But even as he had the thought, Tiny had to admit that the last year had been their best yet. They'd expanded, bought a helicopter, had more business than they could handle...he had to wonder if that was at least partly due to Ryleigh and her computer skills.

The doors to the small hospital opened automatically as Tiny approached, but he barely noticed as he took a deep breath as soon as he was outside. He headed for a bench situated in a small green space near the entrance, and sat. He leaned over and rested his elbows on his knees as he stared at the ground.

Thoughts swirled through his head. Everything he'd heard Ryleigh telling Henley, things that had happened at The Refuge over the last several months, things he'd said to Ryleigh, knowing they would hurt her.

He'd been such an ass. He'd be the first to admit that. But Ryleigh had gotten under his skin even before they knew who she really was...and he didn't like it. So he'd used her admission as an excuse to distance himself. To bolster the shields he kept around his heart.

As brave as Ryleigh was—she'd been willing to go toe-to-toe with a *killer*, for God's sake—she was also reckless in a lot of ways. And naïve...

It hadn't escaped Tiny's notice that she liked him. The side glances, the way her cheeks heated when he caught her staring at him. But that was *before*.

Before she'd admitted she'd been lying to everyone.

Since then, there'd been no more glances. No more blushing. Just a lot of wary expressions, a lot of nervousness, and as much avoidance as she could manage. Which wasn't much, considering he rarely let her out of his sight. But she hadn't left. She'd stayed to do whatever she could to help find Owl, Lara, and Stone. And when Lara and Owl had returned, she'd continued to take whatever Tiny dished out, because Stone was still missing. And she'd worked tirelessly to help find him.

Tiny sat back on the wooden bench and stared into space, remembering the past. Another woman who'd lied to him. But Sonja hadn't been anything like Ryleigh, who wore her every emotion on her face. No. Sonja was an amazing actress. Sure had *him* fooled. He'd thought they were soul mates. The day she'd accepted his proposal had been the happiest day of his life. Didn't have the slightest doubt of her love for him. He'd gone on missions secure in the knowledge that his fiancée was waiting for him at home, as worried about him as he was her.

The reality would make an excellent true crime show. Betrayal, a lover's triangle, a fiancée who secretly hated her soon-to-be husband. Who didn't want to be a Navy wife. She'd convinced her lover that Tiny was abusing her. That he'd never let her go. She'd claimed she was scared of him...and that the only way they could be together was to kill him.

And the stupid kid bought her lies hook, line, and sinker.

Then again, Tiny'd had no idea she was anything other than the loving fiancée who'd seemed so happy to see him every time he'd returned from a dangerous mission.

She and her lover were so dumb, even if they'd succeeded in killing him while he slept, they wouldn't have gotten away with it. The texts they'd sent back and forth, the internet searches she'd done, the receipts from the hotel trysts...they would've been caught within days of his death.

But they'd failed to kill him, obviously. Sonja had plunged a knife into his chest and miraculously missed hitting anything vital—like his heart, which she'd been aiming for.

The fight afterward had been swift, brutal, and over very quickly. Tiny had knocked out his fiancée with one punch, and it didn't take much more to subdue her lover, who'd been waiting next to the bed to help finish him off after she'd made the first strike.

But now that he'd had some time and distance, and he was actually allowing himself to think about what had happened, Tiny realized he was more embarrassed that he hadn't known his fiancée was cheating on him and plotting his death, than hurting over her betrayal. If she'd broken things off with him to be with that other man, he wouldn't have been happy, but he would've let her go. Would've moved on fairly quickly.

Instead, she'd left him with the inability to trust. He hadn't slept next to a woman since that night. Hadn't trusted anyone enough to be that vulnerable again.

Yes, Ryleigh slept in his house, but always in another room, and his door was always closed. He'd been a light sleeper all his life, but he was even more so now. The smallest creak of the floorboards had his eyes flying open and Tiny racing out of his bedroom to see what Ryleigh was doing. She was always surprised by his appearance. No matter how quiet she tried to be, he still heard her.

Sonja had done that to him, and he resented her for it.

She and her lover were still behind bars, but they

wouldn't be forever. He'd vowed to be there for every one of their parole hearings, to make sure they stayed locked up for as long as possible. But now that he was settled at The Refuge...he found his need for revenge had dried up, at least.

Besides, he had something more important to concentrate on now.

Ryleigh.

Did he trust her? No, not really. But now that he understood there was more behind her actions than duplicitous intentions, Tiny found himself not *quite* as distrustful as he used to be.

"Everything okay?" Tonka asked as he approached the hospital. He had a fast-food bag in one hand and was holding Jasna's hand with the other.

"Yeah," Tiny said as he stood.

"Ry still in there talking with Henley?"

Tiny nodded.

"You think it's safe to interrupt them?" Tonka asked. "Want to get these tots to her while they're still semi-warm. Then get Jas back to The Refuge so we can check on all the animals."

"You coming back here after?" Tiny asked, already knowing the answer.

"Of course."

"Me too?" Jasna asked. "I don't want to miss anything!"

Tonka chuckled. "You aren't going to miss anything but crying and pooping."

"Ew, gross. Don't say poop," Jasna complained with a grimace.

Tiny and Tonka both chuckled.

"You can muck out a barn without blinking, but talking about your sister pooping grosses you out?"

"Seriously, stop!" Jasna demanded.

Tonka was smiling so big, Tiny couldn't help but stare at him in wonder. Tonka had always been the reticent one. But ever since marrying Henley, he'd definitely opened up. Still, he didn't think he'd ever seen his friend so...carefree.

"All right. Come on, let's go see your mom and sister. Then we'll get some stuff done back at the barn, make sure you're all settled with Alaska and Brick."

"And you'll have more pictures for me so I can show them to my friends at school next week, right?" Jasna asked.

"Of course. Come on, let's go give these tots to your mom."

Tiny followed the duo back into the hospital and down the hall toward Henley's room. When they entered, Ryleigh and Henley were laughing about something.

"Yay! Tots!" Henley exclaimed when she saw her husband.

"Trade ya, Elizabeth for a large tater tot," Tonka told her with a grin.

"Deal. Gimme!"

Everyone laughed.

The sight of the teeny little baby in Tonka's arms made Tiny's heart skip a beat. It wasn't as if he'd thought about having children very often. He wasn't even sure if he *ever* wanted any, but seeing his friend so besotted, so happy, made him feel all mushy inside.

"I'm gonna go," Ryleigh told Henley.

"All right. Thanks for the talk. You belong here, Ry.

Who else will teach Elizabeth how to be a computer genius like you?"

Ryleigh gave her a small smile, then an awkward wave —which Tiny found adorable—and headed for the door.

Since she'd arrived at the hospital with their friends, who'd already left, he quickly said his goodbyes as well and hurried to catch up with Ryleigh.

"What's the rush?" he asked as he came up next to her.

"Oh...you didn't have to leave just because I did," Ryleigh said.

Tiny frowned. "You need a ride," he told her, something she obviously knew.

"Yeah, but I was going to catch an Uber back to The Refuge."

"Absolutely not," he said with a shake of his head.

It was Ryleigh's turn to frown. "I know you don't trust me even a little, but I already told you that I'm not leaving yet. You don't have to worry that I'll hire a taxi to drive me to the airport or anything."

Tiny sighed. "I wasn't worried about that. But we're going to the same place. I can take you home."

"You aren't responsible for me," she countered.

"And you aren't responsible for everyone who lives and works at The Refuge, or what happens there either," Tiny blurted.

Ryleigh stopped in her tracks in the middle of the hallway and stared at him. "What?"

"You heard me. You worked your ass off to find Stone, but he's back now. Everything's good. You can stop worrying so much."

To his surprise, Ryleigh laughed. But it wasn't a

humorous sound. "Right," she said cynically, then started walking toward the exit once more.

Tiny ground his teeth together. He hated that she was still keeping secrets from him. "I'm not your enemy," he told her as they walked.

"Could'a fooled me."

As soon as they stepped outside, Tiny stopped her by gently grabbing her arm. She looked at him in surprise.

"I realize I've been an ass, and I'm trying to apologize. I'd like to start over."

Ryleigh stared at him with an expression he couldn't interpret.

"Start over? New leaf? Whatever you want to call it. No more hovering over you while you work. No more insisting to know where you are and who you're with or who you're talking to. I want to go back to how things were when you first started working at The Refuge."

"Really?" she asked skeptically.

"Yes."

"Why?"

"Because."

"That's not an answer," she said, one brow hitching up.

Tiny shrugged.

She sighed, looking away. "All right."

Tiny felt as if he'd hit the lottery. It was a start.

"Are you tired?" he asked as they started walking toward the parking lot. He was surprised how hard it was to drop his hand from her arm.

"Exhausted."

"Me too. I thought I'd make hamburgers for dinner instead of going to the lodge. That work for you?"

She looked at him a little suspiciously this time, but nodded.

They were silent as they climbed into his car and headed back toward The Refuge. But it was a comfortable silence, not like the ones fraught with underlying tension that they'd suffered through for the last few months.

Tiny had no idea where this new start would take them, but he was determined to discover all of Ryleigh's secrets. Not because he thought she'd use them against him or his friends, but because he had a feeling if he didn't, she'd disappear into thin air...and if that happened, no one would ever find her again. Not if she didn't want to be found.

CHAPTER FIVE

Ry couldn't help but be suspicious about Tiny's abrupt about-face. She was very thankful that he wasn't hovering over her all the time, but she was desperate to know what had changed his mind.

And now that he was being nice to her, another issue had cropped up...namely, that she liked being around him *way* too much for her peace of mind. A grumpy, suspicious Tiny was easy to dislike, to block out of her head. But a nice, respectful, and thoughtful Tiny? He was impossible to ignore.

And the more she was around this Tiny, the more she *wanted* to be around him...which wasn't good. She was leaving. As soon as she figured out what her father had up his sleeve, she was out of there. She'd already decided to head to the northeast. Maybe the Boston area.

The thought of leaving New Mexico and The Refuge made her head *and* her heart ache, but it was for the best. She'd become too attached to the people here. And getting close to people opened the door for her father to use them against her.

The only indication she'd had so far that her dad had found her was that small ten-cent withdrawal from The Refuge's bank account. She'd been monitoring the account to make sure her dad didn't drain it dry, simply because he could. She'd thought for sure that ten-cent deduction was a sign of things to come. Her dad's way of fucking with her. But it had been weeks since then, and nothing else had seemed out of the ordinary.

Ry was paranoid, she'd be the first to admit that, but apparently this time...maybe she'd been wrong. It was both a relief and a blow, because it meant she probably *could* leave, *should* leave, as soon as possible. If her dad hadn't yet found her, every day she spent at The Refuge was one more day that passed when he *could* find her.

But the small niggling at the back of her neck that still insisted her dad was simply messing with her couldn't be ignored.

There was a very real chance he was waiting for her to bolt, to leave The Refuge vulnerable, so he could strike without her there to mitigate the damage. Yes, she could defend The Refuge remotely, but she knew her dad. Knew how his mind worked. Being there, seeing firsthand what was going on, gave her an advantage. Her dad's strikes could be so subtle, or seem so legitimate, her friends might not even know there was a problem until it was too late.

Ry sighed. She was sitting on the small front porch at Tiny's cabin. He'd left earlier to go on a hike with some of the current guests. They were going out to Table Rock, then continuing on for a longer, more strenuous hike. He'd made them a delicious egg and vegetable dish that morning for breakfast, told her all about his schedule for the day, and afterward, said he'd see her later.

Then Ry had held her breath when he'd walked toward her, leaned in...

And kissed the side of her head as nonchalantly as if he'd done it every day that she'd been living in his cabin.

She'd stood there in the kitchen, frozen in confusion for several minutes after he'd gone.

Ever since asking her if they could start over, he'd started touching her all the time. Brushing against her when they passed each other in the hallway—her arm, her back—and now, that morning, *kissing* her.

It was a friendly kiss, nothing that would make her uncomfortable. But a kiss nonetheless. The scariest thing about it was how badly Ry had wanted to turn her head slightly so his lips could touch her skin and not just her hair.

She was falling for this Tiny. The one she'd met when she'd first arrived. Not the one who'd intimidated her with his anger and frustration and animosity.

But she *couldn't* fall for him. She was leaving. Period.

With that thought in her head, Ry got to her feet and headed toward the lodge. She'd already spent some time online this morning searching for signs her father had found her, and not finding any. She'd also distributed around two hundred thousand dollars to various charities, money her father would literally kill her for spending.

Now she needed a break. Visiting with Robert and Luna up at the lodge would provide one. The father and daughter had been making lunches and dinners for Tonka, Henley, and Jasna, so they could spend as much quality time as possible with their new family member, and because being a new parent was exhausting. Maybe she'd offer to bring the noon meal to their cabin...so *she* could get some quality time with little Elizabeth herself.

She still couldn't believe Henley and Tonka had named their daughter after her. No one had ever done anything like that for her before. Hell, she'd never even had friends before. Not really. Leaving New Mexico and not being able to see Elizabeth grow up would be the most painful thing she'd done to this point in her life, but the alternative wasn't an option. She couldn't stay. If she did, everyone here would be in constant danger. There was no telling what her father would do to anyone helping her.

Some people might think Ry was being overly dramatic. Would question what her father could *really* do to anyone. But she knew. Harold Lodge wasn't a man who let bygones be bygones. And it wasn't as if she'd stolen just a couple bucks from him when she'd left.

A smile crossed her face, thinking about what his reaction must've been when he realized what happened. That the daughter he'd painstakingly trained in his craft, the girl he'd thought was firmly wrapped around his little finger, who would never *dare* step out of line because of the very idea of the punishment she'd receive if she did, had disappeared into thin air—taking his entire fortune with her. The money he'd illegally stolen from nonprofits, banks, millionaires, corporations, towns, and even the scariest drug cartels around the world.

He'd never give up trying to find her, trying to get his money back.

Ry had no doubt Harold Lodge would've stolen plenty more money by now. He wouldn't be hurting, living on the streets and having to rely on the kindness of others. No, he would've immediately started recouping the loss of his fortune. But he wouldn't forget what she'd done. No, he'd want revenge. Which was why Ry couldn't stay at The Refuge.

She opened the door to the lodge and smiled at Alaska, who was standing behind the reception desk. There were a few guests sitting in the comfortable leather chairs in the lobby area, but they didn't pay any attention to her after looking up curiously to see who'd entered the building.

"Hey," Alaska said in a chirpy tone.

"Morning," she replied.

"What's up? Everything okay?" Alaska asked.

Ry smiled at her. "Everything's good. I thought I'd come up and see if I could bug Robert and Luna for a while."

Alaska leaned forward. "They're making cookies this morning. I think that's why they're sitting in *here* reading, instead of at their cabins," she said, gesturing to the guests in the expansive lobby.

Ry chuckled. "Don't blame them."

"So, if you sweet-talk Robert...will you grab me a couple? They're so good straight from the oven."

"You know if you went in there, Robert would give you whatever you wanted," she said dryly.

Alaska wrinkled her nose. "Probably. But I'm trying to watch what I eat."

"Why?"

She frowned. "Because I could stand to lose a few pounds."

"No," Ry said firmly.

"No? No what?" Alaska asked, sounding confused.

"You're perfect exactly how you are. And I know Brick

would say the same thing. You get plenty of exercise running around this place. Helping guests, going on hikes, playing with Jasna, taking Mutt for walks...you're *healthy*, Alaska. You want a cookie, eat a cookie. Life's about balance."

"That's...wow."

"Women are way too hard on other women...including ourselves. We nitpick every little thing. Look down our noses at others when we don't know a damn thing about them. We're willing to let men get away with just about anything because they're easy on the eyes or simply because they're guys. But we're super judgmental toward each other. I hate it. You're beautiful, Alaska. You're hard-working, you keep this place running so smoothly, you're the one everyone looks to when they need help with something."

"Ry," Alaska said, blinking furiously to keep the tears in her eyes from falling.

"All I'm saying is, don't think you need to lose weight because you don't look like the people in magazines. You could weigh eight hundred pounds and I'd still think you were the most beautiful person I've ever met because of your personality, your goodness. Because you didn't even blink when you found out I'd lied to you, that I'd finagled myself a job here. You stuck up for me, supported me—and don't think I missed every time you glared at Tiny when he was being...well...Tiny."

"He was being mean," Alaska said with a sniff.

Ry couldn't help but smile a little at that. "He was being *protective*. Of the place he and the other guys built with their blood, sweat, and tears. I don't hold that against him."

"Well, I do," Alaska said stubbornly. "But I've noticed he hasn't been quite so mean lately."

For some reason, Ry blushed. She shrugged. "He said he wanted to start over."

Alaska wiped the rest of her tears away and smiled. "It's about time."

"About time, what?"

"He got his head out of his butt and saw what was right in front of him. We were all pretty excited when he moved you into his cabin. Even though he was being a jerk, we still thought it would ultimately be a good thing." Alaska grimaced. "But then he got meaner toward you, and we were all *pissed*. I'm relieved he's finally figured his shit out before the guys had to intervene."

"Intervene?" Ry's head was spinning. She'd had no idea Alaska and the others even thought that way.

"Yeah, knock some sense into the man. Threaten him if he didn't start treating you better."

It was Ry's turn to struggle with her tears.

"Oh, I didn't mean to upset you."

"You didn't. It's just...I haven't had friends before," Ry blurted, then immediately wished she hadn't. Who admitted something like that? It was pathetic.

Alaska came around the desk and pulled Ry into a huge hug. "Me either," she whispered before she pulled back. Her hands stayed on Ry's shoulders as she met her gaze. "When I was kidnapped, I was vacationing in Russia. *By myself*. Because I didn't have anyone to go with me. When I was in high school, I was too weird and too poor for other girls to feel comfortable around me. I admit that I didn't try very hard to befriend them myself, because my mom was too unstable. Anyway, that continued when I got older. I switched jobs a lot, so it was hard to make true friends. Moving here to The Refuge was the best thing that ever happened to me."

It was on the tip of Ry's tongue to agree. But she wasn't staying. So she simply nodded instead.

"Right, so...cookies. You'll see if you can swipe me a couple?" Alaska asked.

Ry was glad for the reprieve from the intense moment. "Of course."

"Thanks."

The two women smiled at each other for a long moment, then Alaska squeezed Ry's shoulders before letting go and heading back behind the desk. "I've got a little more paperwork to do, then I'm done for the day. The new guests have all checked in and I've answered all the email inquiries. I just need to update the schedule with the newest bookings."

She nodded. "Cool." Alaska worked really hard and was good at what she did. She thrived on making sure the guests were happy and on keeping everything organized. She was an amazing admin, and The Refuge was lucky to have someone as skilled and friendly as her manning the front desk.

Ry turned to head to the kitchen but didn't get two steps before the door to the lodge opened. Looking to see who it was, she stopped in her tracks when she saw Tonka. He looked spooked.

"What's wrong?" Alaska asked. She'd obviously seen his distress as well.

Ry stayed where she was, unabashedly eavesdropping. She didn't like it when her new friends were upset, and something had definitely upset Tonka. Her thoughts immediately went to the animals he cared for. Had something happened to one of them?

"Do you know where Brick is?" he asked Alaska.

"I think he's down at the hangar with Stone and Owl, discussing helicopter things. Why? What's going on?"

"I got a letter from Tricare. I don't know what's happening, but something's wrong. I need his advice."

Ry's blood ran cold. She wasn't sure why, she had no reason to feel uneasy, and yet a cold breeze felt as if it ran down her spine at Tonka's words.

"Maybe I can help? What'd the letter say?" Alaska asked.

Ry stepped closer to the desk, needing to hear Tonka's response.

"They claim something's wrong with my insurance. And that they aren't going to pay for Elizabeth's birth *or* Henley's hospital stay. I don't understand what's gone wrong. I tried to call them, but of course there's like a three-hour wait to talk to someone."

"Don't panic," Alaska said firmly. "Let me call Drake and get him up here. He'll know what to do."

"Can I see it?" Ry asked, holding out a hand for the letter.

Both Alaska and Tonka turned to her in surprise, as if they'd forgotten she was there.

Tonka didn't hesitate to hand her the letter. Ry read it quickly, realizing it was a form letter of sorts, informing Tonka that his medical benefits were in question because of "anomalies."

Anomalies. Yeah, right. Deep down, Ry knew this was her dad's work. This was how he operated. He was sneaky, dirty. Liked to poke at people, hurt them a little bit at a time until they were completely broken.

She'd wanted to think that ten cents was nothing, but her instincts had been right.

It was him. Testing the waters.

"I can fix this," she told Tonka firmly, her mind already spinning with what she needed to do and her fingers itching to get to her computer.

Tonka's expression cleared, some of the panic he'd been feeling literally fading away before her eyes. "You can?"

Ry nodded.

"I'm not sure Tricare will talk to you."

Ry lifted an eyebrow slightly and met Tonka's gaze head on. "I'm not going to call them."

Understanding dawned in his eyes.

"But if you're not comfortable with that, you can talk to Brick. I'm sure he'll have some ideas about how to fix this." Ry doubted that, but she had to make the offer.

"I trust you."

Ry had to swallow hard so as not to burst into tears.

Tonka had no idea what those three little words meant to her. He knew some of what she was capable of—not all of it, because she hadn't opened up to anyone about her past and the things she'd done, and what she could *still* do. But enough that he was well aware she was going to use her computer skills to figure out what was going on with his insurance.

"Will you need my social security number? And Henley's?"

Tonka was kind of cute in his naïveté. "No."

"But you'll need them to—"

"I'm sure she can find them," Alaska said, interrupting.

"Oh...yeah. Right. Okay, well...I'm going back to the cabin. Elizabeth is a little fussy this morning and Henley didn't get much sleep last night. If you need anything, don't hesitate to come over. Okay?"

Ry had no idea what she'd done to deserve friends like this. Frankly, she *didn't* deserve them. But she was doing her best to make up for her past sins. "Okay. I'll come over when I've figured out what the issue is."

"Thanks, Ry. I mean it. I'm sorry if I panicked for a moment there. I just...I don't want Henley to worry about anything, and this would definitely make her worry."

Ry nodded—and blinked in surprise when Tonka stepped toward her and gave her a brief but tight hug. Then he gave her a chin lift and turned to leave.

"Did Tonka just chin-lift you?" Alaska asked, sounding awed.

"Yes?" Ry said, a little confused.

"And he *hugged* you. The change in him from when I first got here is like night and day. Between Henley and Jas doing their magic, the animals, and now Elizabeth, he's a completely different person. I'm so happy for him."

Ry nodded, but her brain was already focused on the steps she needed to take to figure out what her father had done, and how to fix it.

"Right, I can tell you're anxious to get to work. How about *I* go visit Robert and Luna and get *you* some cook-ies, then bring them down to Tiny's cabin?"

Ry would normally kill for Robert's chocolate chip cookies fresh from the oven, but even thinking about eating right now made her feel nauseous. "It's okay. I want to figure this out. I'll come up later and grab some."

"Do you need any help?" Alaska offered.

"Thanks, but no, I got this." The last thing she'd do was involve anyone else in the clusterfuck that was her life.

"Okay, but if you need anything, just yell."

"I will." She totally wouldn't. Alaska didn't need to know that.

On autopilot, Ry made her way to the front door of the lodge. She still held the letter Tonka had received, and she read it again while walking quickly toward Tiny's cabin.

Upon entering, she went straight to the kitchen table, where she'd left her laptop. It was her baby, her most prized possession. Without it, she was nothing. A high school dropout with few discernable skills in the real world. The computer defined who she was. It was *all* she was.

With a deep breath, she opened it and put in her password. As easy as breathing, Ry put in several more passwords to access the dark web. She needed to be very careful, she didn't like hacking into government databases. They'd gotten more sophisticated over the years about security, and the last thing she needed was to get caught.

But more than that, she had no doubt her dad was out there watching and waiting. He'd set the bait and she was responding, as he knew she would. He was probably gloating and laughing wherever he was right now. The only positive was that it wasn't as necessary to try to hide her location anymore. Her father knew where she was, and he was fucking with her. This was simply the beginning, they both knew it. The game of cat and mouse had started.

Ry had no doubt her dad would continue to mess with The Refuge until she gave in and talked to him. Gave him back the money she'd stolen.

Gritting her teeth, Ry concentrated on the screen in front of her. He wasn't going to win. Now that The Refuge was in his sights, he'd never stop. Even if she left, he'd continue with his games until he'd destroyed the PTSD retreat. He wouldn't feel even an ounce of remorse either.

It was up to Ry to stop him, once and for all. She'd have to use all her skills to lock down The Refuge electronically. To safeguard the money, the various accounts, and the online footprints of employees who worked there.

But she couldn't possibly cover everything and everyone. Her dad would always have a way of getting in, of causing havoc.

Feeling sick that she'd done this, that her presence was a threat to everyone, she took a deep breath and concentrated on the task at hand. She needed to fix Tonka's records—*all* of them. Lock them down. And everyone else's too. Because if her dad could mess with Tonka's health insurance, he could also fuck with all the guys' retirement accounts, benefits, and even service records.

No way would she allow that.

* * *

Three hours later, Ry sat back in the chair with a heavy sigh. She'd done it. Found where her father had messed with Tonka's records and fixed them. The insurance claim for Elizabeth's birth was in the works...was actually being accelerated. Tonka should receive notice that the insurance payment was being processed immediately.

"Here."

Ry startled so badly, she would've knocked over the

glass of water Tiny had placed next to her elbow if he hadn't moved quickly enough to lift it out of the way.

"Easy," he soothed.

Looking up, Ry blinked in confusion. She didn't even remember Tiny coming back. Had no idea how long he'd been there.

"You were concentrating so hard, you didn't hear me come in," he said, as if he could read her mind.

"Oh, sorry."

"It's fine. Tonka called Brick, who sent me a note while I was out hiking. We came back early because I wanted to check on you. You good?"

This new Tiny was so hard to get used to. For so long, all she'd gotten were scowls and distrustful glares when she was on her computer. And questions. Lots of questions. Tiny always wanted to know what she was doing when she was working; it took her out of her head and made it hard to concentrate. But today, he'd managed to not only come into the cabin without her hearing, but had obviously puttered around the kitchen getting her a drink as well. It was disconcerting.

"Ryleigh?"

Hearing her given name should've brought back horrible memories. Of her father threatening her. Yelling at her when she screwed up something. But instead, coming from him, it was...nice. He was the only one who called her Ryleigh, and it made her feel special.

"Right, sorry. I'm good."

"Did you figure it out?"

She nodded. "Yeah."

"Awesome. Tonka will be very relieved. You have to be

hungry. It's past lunch, and I'm assuming you didn't stop to eat anything. I made us some sandwiches."

Ry blinked at the plate that suddenly appeared next to the glass of water. It was a turkey and cheese sandwich. Made with mustard and lettuce and tomatoes. Heavy on the cheese.

Exactly how she liked it.

Looking up at Tiny, she blurted, "I'm not sure I like this nice you."

To her surprise, instead of getting irritated, he actually *smiled*. "You'll get used to it."

But Ry wasn't sure she would. "Don't you want to ask me what I did? How I fixed Tonka's records? If what I did was illegal, and if it could come back and hurt The Refuge?"

Tiny surprised her by turning her chair toward him as if she weighed nothing, then leaning over, caging her in by putting his hands on the armrests. She should've felt hemmed in, threatened, but surrounded by Tiny's masculine scent, seeing the muscles in his arms ripple as he braced himself over her, and staring up at his stubble-covered jaw, it was all Ry could do not to throw herself at him.

"I *did* ask what you did...you said you fixed the problem. I wouldn't understand anything you told me about *how* you did it, and I already know what you did was illegal...and I don't give a shit. I also already know you wouldn't do anything that would come back to bite The Refuge in the ass."

All Ry could do was blink up at him. This was such a big turnaround from how he'd been acting for the last few months, it didn't seem real.

"Look, I've been an ass. I know it, and I've promised to be better. Am I comfortable with the things you can do? Not really. But in all the time you've been here, you haven't done anything to screw up our business. I'm thinking you've probably done a lot of stuff that has made things *better*, not worse. You found Jas and Reese and didn't want any recognition for doing so. You worked your ass off to find Owl, Lara, and Stone. And Tonka told me that you didn't even hesitate to volunteer to help him."

He sighed, looking away briefly before locking his gaze on hers again.

"You want to know the *real* reason why I was so horrible to you, Ryleigh?"

Ry didn't need to ask. She knew. Because she was a criminal. Did illegal things that could definitely hurt The Refuge if they were discovered. And because she'd lied to everyone.

But he blew her mind when he spoke.

"Because I was so goddamn attracted to you—and the last woman I thought I was in love with tried to kill me."

She stared at him with huge eyes, shocked at his admission of attraction toward her and literally *dumbstruck* that someone had tried to kill him.

But as soon as his words sank in, anger rose within her, hot and fast. "What was her name?"

Instead of telling her, Tiny grinned. "Nope, not happening."

"What's not happening?" Ry asked.

"If I tell you her name, you'll find her with that computer of yours and do who the hell knows what. She's paying for her sins, you don't need to take retribution against her."

The hell she didn't. "What happened?"

"Not now. I'll tell you the whole sordid story, but you've been hunched over that computer for so long, your back has to hurt. And you have to be hungry. How about you eat, then get changed, and after we go tell Tonka he's good to go, we can take a walk. Maybe we can take Wally and Beauty with us. Let them get some exercise. Tonka told me both dogs have been glued to Elizabeth's side as her new bodyguards. Maybe we'll see if Jas wants to come too. It'll do everyone some good to get some fresh air."

Ry didn't want to walk. She wasn't exactly an outdoor kind of girl. She'd never really had a chance to enjoy nature while growing up, and besides, she liked being on her computer. Liked being a nerd.

What she *really* wanted to do was find whoever the bitch was who'd tried to kill Tiny and make sure her life was a living hell. It wouldn't take much to drain her bank account, get her fired from her job, and make sure everyone she came into contact with knew she was an attempted murderer.

"I probably shouldn't admit it, but I like that blood-thirsty look in your eye," Tiny said, palming her cheek and lifting her head, so she had no choice but to meet his gaze. "She's in jail. Comes up for parole in a year or so. We can worry about it then. For now, she's reaping what she sowed. You didn't comment on the first part of what I said, though."

Jail. Even better. That's all the info Ry needed to find the bitch. She could search databases for Tiny's name and figure out where she was.

"Ryleigh? Are you listening to me?"

Blinking, she focused. The hand on her cheek was

calloused and warm, and it took all her control not to tilt her head into his touch. "I'm listening."

"I haven't felt an attraction toward a woman in years. And when I realized that you weren't who we all thought you were, it sent me spiraling. I let my bitterness overwhelm my common sense. You don't deserve the way I've treated you, and I'm done thinking the worst. You're scary as fuck with what you can do with that computer of yours, but since you've been here, you've done nothing but look after us. It's appreciated, but you don't have to protect us all by yourself anymore.

"Let us in...let *me* in. Let me help you with whatever it is you're scared of. The Refuge is all of ours. You don't have to shoulder the responsibility for this place by yourself."

"I do if it's my fault the place is threatened," she whispered.

But Tiny shook his head firmly. Then he crouched in front of her, and she was no longer looking up, but instead looking down at him between her legs. His hands were resting on her thighs now, not in a sexually suggestive way, but a comforting hold.

"If I screw up and one of the guests gets hurt, no one would blame me, they'd all work together to make sure that person is cared for. If Tonka messes up and leaves a gate open and Melba gets out, we'll all pitch in to get her back home. If Savannah makes a mistake on our taxes, we'll work to fix it. We're a team at The Refuge, Ryleigh, and you're now a part of that."

She wanted to cry. She *wanted* to be a part of Team Refuge, but the hellfire she could bring down on this place wasn't like a cow escaping its pen or a simple mistake on taxes. Her being there could literally get people hurt. She had no doubt her father would do whatever he felt was necessary to get his money. Including killing people she held near and dear, if that's what it took to get her to transfer the cash back to his account.

But it wasn't that easy. Not anymore.

"I have one more question before I let you eat and we head out to get some fresh air," Tiny said.

Ry held her breath as she waited to see what he was going to ask.

"Before...well...*before*, I thought you were feeling some of the same things for *me* that I was for you. Have I ruined that? Has my shitty attitude toward you killed any chance I might've had of being more than your friend?"

Ry literally thought she was having a heart attack. Was shocked that he was coming right out and asking what she thought about him.

"I'm a virgin," she blurted—then immediately closed her eyes in mortification. She couldn't believe she'd said that.

"Ooookay," Tiny said slowly. "You think that matters?"

Ry forced her eyes open. "It *doesn't*? I'm thirty-one and haven't ever had sex. That's *weird*. I mean, I'm not ashamed of it. I just haven't felt the urge to do it with a guy."

"Do it," Tiny echoed with a small chuckle.

Ry frowned. Was he making fun of her?

"You being a virgin doesn't change how I think about you. You're mysterious, smart as hell, compassionate, self-less. You're also a nerd, too pale because you spend way too much time inside, and somewhere along your life's journey, you've learned that it's better to lie than to tell the truth. None of that turns me off. I admit that the lying thing is a tough one for me, with my past, but the lies you've told haven't been malicious, so I can overlook them...for now. But I need you to do what you can to try to curb that. There's no need to lie to me. About anything. If you don't want to tell me something, just tell me you need time. I'll give it to you. But please, no more lies."

Ry swallowed hard. Tiny was being...overwhelmingly awesome. She didn't expect this. She almost preferred his scowls.

"Guys like women with experience," she said, once again blurting out what she was thinking.

"No, they don't," Tiny countered. "Men like women who are into them. Period. How much experience she does or doesn't have isn't a factor. It's about the emotional connection between them. Learning what they like to do together. Your virginity has no bearing on my feelings about you one way or the other. You could've supported yourself on the streets by taking money for sex, or you could've been a nun, and I'd still feel the same way about you."

Ry swallowed hard.

"You never answered my question," Tiny said gently.

"Which one?"

"Did I kill any interest you might've had in me by being an overbearing asshole?"

Ry was at a crossroads. She could lie and say yes. She had no doubt Tiny would back off. Wouldn't kick her out, would continue to be her friend, while keeping his distance as she did her best to figure out how to deal with her father.

Or she could suck it up, find the courage to tell him

that she was still just as attracted to him now as she'd been before her true identity was revealed. She had no idea what that would mean. She would still probably have to leave, and it would hurt a hundred times worse if she got involved with him.

Tiny stayed crouched in front of her as she contemplated how to answer him. He'd asked her not to lie to him again. Begged.

"No."

It was one word, but the relief she saw in Tiny's posture and expression told her everything she needed to know.

"Good. I'm going to do better by you. I'll do my best to get you to trust me, tell me what has you so scared, so we can fix it. Okay?"

It wouldn't be that easy, but she nodded anyway.

"Eat," Tiny ordered as he stood.

Ry blinked in surprise. She didn't know what she'd expected him to do, but she thought maybe he'd kiss her. Or at least give her a hug. Instead, he ordered her around as if she were ten years old.

He chuckled as he stood above her. Again, as if he could read her mind, he leaned down and kissed the top of her head. Then he reached for her computer and looked at her as he asked, "May I?"

Ry nodded.

Tiny closed her laptop and scooted it to the center of the table. Then he pushed the plate with her sandwich and her water closer.

"What about you? Aren't you hungry?"

"I ate my sandwich while you were still working. I'm good."

"Oh...okay."

He smiled down at her. She hadn't been on the receiving end of many of his smiles, and Ry had to admit, she liked it. A lot.

"The faster you eat that sandwich, the sooner you can have the chocolate chip cookies Alaska gave me to bring to you."

"Cookies?" Ry asked, sitting up straighter.

"Yup."

"Gimme," she ordered, holding out her hand.

Tiny chuckled. "Not until you eat your sandwich. You'll need more than sugar and empty carbs for our hike."

"Mean," Ry grumbled, but she dutifully picked up the sandwich he'd made. Even when Tiny was upset with her and treating her like crap, he'd still gone out of his way to make sure she ate. He was never so selfish that he made himself dinner and didn't let her have any.

Of course, the silent meals were so uncomfortable, she'd frequently abandoned her plate in favor of fleeing to her room, leaving half of her food behind.

The sandwich was delicious and it hit the spot. Ry hadn't realized how hungry she was until she'd started eating. She ate every bite and washed it down with the water, then smiled at Tiny when he placed two chocolate chip cookies on the table as a reward. They were warm from the microwave and melted in her mouth.

Tiny put her dishes away as she ate the dessert. Then Ry changed into a pair of comfortable boots and some layers for their hike.

CHAPTER SIX

Tiny was extremely pleased and relieved that things between him and Ryleigh seemed to be mostly back on track. She'd forgiven him for being a jerk readily enough... which honestly didn't surprise him too much, considering how kind she was. He'd had the evidence right in front of his face for months, and he'd stubbornly continued to think the worst.

But she'd proven over and over that all she wanted to do was help. Even when she'd been working as a house-keeper, she'd gone out of her way to assist others. Always volunteering to stay longer if needed, and to help Jess and Carly after she was done with her rooms if they were still working. Even now, he sometimes found her shadowing Joshua, the newest housekeeper, helping out when needed.

Now, all his animosity had turned to worry. She'd admitted that she was scared, said she needed to protect everyone at The Refuge, but she still wouldn't open up to him about why. When she'd told Tonka that the thing with Tricare was a simple misunderstanding—Tiny had a feeling she was *hugely* downplaying the incident—Ryleigh had seemed extremely uncomfortable with his effusive gratitude.

Though she hadn't actually said a word, Tiny strongly suspected she thought it was *her* fault there'd been an insurance mix-up in the first place. Which was crazy... wasn't it? He couldn't think of any reason *why* it would be her fault. The government insurance they all carried thanks to their military service was known to be glitchy, just like any insurance company.

But ever since Tonka had brought the issue to her attention a few days ago, Ryleigh had seemed...jumpy. The first thing she did every morning was open her laptop, her fingers flying across the screen as she searched for God knows what. Tiny had no clue, but it was obvious she was looking for...something. Someone? He didn't know, and she wasn't talking.

It was frustrating that she wouldn't talk to him, but he knew better than anyone that he couldn't force her to confide in him. She wasn't an over-sharer at the best of times. Hell, he'd been as shocked as Ryleigh when she'd blurted out that she was a virgin. If he hadn't surprised her so thoroughly with his admission that he was attracted to her, she probably would've *never* shared something so intimate.

Tiny was secretly relieved to have that vital information. It told him something important—that he needed to go slow. He didn't care that she hadn't had sex before. It didn't turn him off...though he *was* mindful of the fact that taking her virginity came with the weight of certain responsibilities. But for now, he was just proud of her for knowing what she wanted—an emotional attachment to someone before she jumped into bed with them. If they got to the point where she wanted to be physical with him, he'd make damn sure she knew that he valued her decision to let him be her first.

In the meantime, and until she trusted him enough to talk about her fears, he'd learn as much about Ryleigh as he could through observation. He already knew how little she liked the outdoors, and it amused him. She didn't mind walking around the grounds of The Refuge, but going out into the woods where there were—gasp—bugs and wild animals, wasn't her thing. It was pretty cute. And it reinforced the fact that she was more comfortable with her computer than anything else, and had clearly grown up that way.

Today, Stone was taking him and Ryleigh up in the helicopter The Refuge had purchased. The former Army Night Stalker pilot wanted to scope out the best routes for sightseeing tours of the area, and he'd invited them both to come with him.

"I'm not sure about this," Ryleigh said nervously as they walked toward the newly built hangar on the property.

"What aren't you sure about? Stone's an amazing pilot. I have more confidence in him than I do in the pilots who fly commercial jets."

"It's not that. I know he's good. I've seen his— Er..." Her voice trailed off.

Tiny couldn't help but laugh. "You've seen his records?" he guessed.

"Yeah. But I didn't mean to," she added quickly. "I was trying to find out more information about his background, so I could maybe find him that way. They kind of just jumped onto the screen without me doing anything."

Tiny laughed harder. "Uh-huh. Just jumped onto your screen, huh?"

She gave him a sideways glance and seemed to relax when she realized he wasn't upset.

"What about mine?"

"Your what?" Ryleigh asked.

"My records. They just happen to appear magically on your screen as well?"

She shrugged.

Tiny nudged her with his shoulder. "It's okay if you saw them, it's not as if I did anything every other SEAL hasn't."

Ryleigh stopped in the middle of the trail and stared at him. "You swam three miles into the ocean, dragging your injured teammate behind you, while being shot at from the shore, and then avoided terrorists who were searching for you by boat, getting to the rendezvous point that you didn't even know would still be there or not."

"SEALs don't leave SEALs behind," Tiny said with a shrug. The incident she was talking about had been hell. He still had nightmares about it. But he'd saved his teammate, and while they were being hunted, acting as a distraction for the terrorists, the rest of his team had killed the target they'd been sent in to find and eliminate. A win-win in his book.

Ryleigh simply shook her head and continued toward the hangar. "Whatever," she mumbled, nudging him back, making Tiny smile.

Every now and then, his arm would brush against hers as they walked, and every single time, a surge of what felt like electricity shot down his body when they touched. It was a little disconcerting...but also a massive turn-on. He couldn't even imagine what being with her skin-on-skin would do to him. Or being deep inside her body. He didn't know if they'd ever get to that point, but he could dream about it.

"Anyway, as I was saying, this is gonna be fun," he told her. "We'll both get to see The Refuge from the air. There's so much more than just the land around the cabins."

"Filled with wild animals. And cliffs to fall off of. And bugs. Lots and lots of bugs."

Tiny grinned.

"You know, I was content to see that stuff through the lenses of the cameras you guys put all over the property. I've seen all the mule deer, squirrels, and coyotes I ever want to see through my computer screen. Not to mention foxes, raccoons, sheep, cougars, and if I'd known there were *bears* here, there's no way I would've taken this job."

"Why did you? Take it, I mean?" Tiny couldn't help but ask. He wasn't sure Ryleigh would answer him, she was very good at evading his questions...but to his surprise, she didn't hesitate to speak.

"I wanted somewhere off the beaten path. I was tired of the noise of the city. And all the people. I saw an ad online for this place, and read a review from someone who'd stayed here and claimed it changed her life. I looked up the website and was impressed with what I saw. It was rugged, but somehow still charming and quaint, and you guys do a lot of good things for people. I especially liked that." She shrugged. "And when I saw it for the first time, when I was here for my interview, it just had a...*safe* feeling."

Tiny nodded. "Yeah, I felt the same way when I first arrived. I mean, there weren't any cabins or anything yet, but just being out here soothed my soul in a way I hadn't felt anywhere else."

"Except for the bugs, it's perfect," Ryleigh said with a grin.

They approached the hangar. Stone had left the bay door open and they could see the chopper inside.

Without thought, Tiny reached for Ryleigh's hand. He wasn't sure why, just that he needed to feel connected to her at that moment. Hearing she'd felt the same about The Refuge as he did the first time she'd stepped onto the property, made him want to be even closer to her.

They walked hand-in-hand into the hangar—but as soon as Tiny saw Stone, he knew something was wrong.

"Got bad news. We can't go up today," Stone told them.

Ryleigh dropped his hand, and Tiny let her go. "Why not?" he asked.

"The fuel we ordered wasn't delivered this morning. I'm not sure why. I called the place, and they said they had no record of our order, which is bullshit because I personally verified it with them last week. It wasn't on their schedule, which is super weird. Anyway, we got it straightened out, but they can't come out for a few days now."

Tiny was disappointed, as he was looking forward to seeing the property from the air, but he understood that sometimes glitches happened. But when he turned to Ryleigh, he stiffened. She was staring at Stone intently, and she looked...guilty, for some reason.

"What? What's wrong?" he asked quietly.

She turned slowly to look at him, then blinked. "Um...nothing."

Tiny's lips pressed together. It wasn't *nothing*, not if her reaction was anything to go by. He watched as she took a big breath and got control over her emotions. "Maybe we can do it next week then?" she asked Stone.

"I've already rescheduled," he said with a nod.

"Cool," she said.

Just then, Stone's phone rang. He smiled apologetically at Tiny and Ryleigh, and answered. "Hey, *Stellina*, what's up? What? Fuck. Okay, I'm on my way up there. Take a deep breath, she'll be fine. They'll *both* be fine. I know...all right. I'm coming."

Stone hung up and didn't wait for Tiny to ask what was wrong. "That was Maisy. Something's wrong with Reese. She's bleeding. She thinks it's the baby. Spike's taking her to the hospital as we speak and everyone wants to head over to be there for her."

"What do you need us to do?" Tiny asked.

"Can you get the hangar closed up? Everything's good in here, I locked the chopper down when I realized we wouldn't be going up."

"Will do. Go. Get to Maisy. She doesn't need to be stressed this early in her pregnancy."

"That's what I keep telling her, but she won't listen to me," Stone said with a wry grin. Then he sobered. "Thanks, man. I'll see you later?"

"Absolutely, yes," Tiny told him.

He and Ryleigh worked together to close the huge hangar door, then he once more took her hand in his as they made their way back up the trail toward the cabins, much faster than their earlier stroll.

It wasn't until they were on their way to the hospital that Tiny realized he hadn't pressed Ryleigh about her reaction to the fuel delivery mix-up. But now wasn't the time. She was worried about Reese, as was he.

He made a mental note to ask later though. He didn't like when she kept things from him, and while he didn't think she'd lie to him, since he'd asked her not to, not talking about something that was clearly bothering her was almost just as bad.

A couple hours later, everyone was back at the lodge at The Refuge waiting for word about how Reese and the baby were doing. She'd been airlifted to Albuquerque to their level-one trauma center, so they could better treat her and the baby.

Brick's phone rang, and everyone immediately hushed as he answered it.

"Brick. Hey...yeah, okay...uh-huh...glad to hear it. I'll tell them. When? Good. We'll be waiting. All right. Later."

"So? Was that Spike? What'd he say? How's Reese? And the baby?" Alaska asked her fiancé impatiently.

"Yeah, it was him. Reese is okay. It was touch and go for a while, she lost a lot of blood, so they'll be keeping her in the hospital in Albuquerque for a few days to make sure she's really all right."

"Oh, thank goodness," Lara breathed.

Tiny let out his own breath of relief. He had no experience with pregnant women and the things that could go wrong, but he was glad Reese was okay.

"And the baby?" Henley asked, holding her own newborn in a carrier against her chest.

"Premature, but breathing on his own."

Everyone gasped.

"Wait—she gave birth?" Cora asked.

"Apparently," Brick said with a grin. "Dylan John Fowler was underweight, but the doctors think he'll be just fine. He's in the NICU, but Spike said it was a precaution, not because anything was majorly wrong."

The worry in the room bled away. No one expected the second baby of The Refuge to be born so soon after the first, but the occasion was just as joyous as when Henley's little girl arrived.

Everyone began to talk about moving up the baby shower they'd planned for next week, and deciding who would be going down to Albuquerque to see Reese, Spike, and Dylan first.

Everyone except Ryleigh. When Tiny looked over, she had her head buried in her phone, thumbs racing over the screen.

"What're you doing?" he asked as he sidled closer to her.

She didn't even look up. "Ordering food for Spike. And clothes for all three of them. They left here so fast, they didn't have time to pack a bag. When Reese feels better, she'll want some soft PJs to wear. And hospital food sucks. Reese will probably be too exhausted to eat right now, so I'm making sure they have good stuff delivered to her room for later."

Her compassion made Tiny feel guilty all over again about how he'd treated her.

"And I'm making sure their insurance is good to go," Ryleigh mumbled under her breath.

Tiny smiled at that. Should he be worried about what databases she was hacking into as they stood there? Probably. But since she was looking out for one of his best friends, he couldn't seem to dredge up any concern whatsoever about what she was doing.

Lunch was a celebration of sorts. Even though the people they were celebrating were down in Albuquerque, it didn't take away from the happiness of the moment. Everyone was excited about Dylan's appearance in the world and very relieved Reese was all right.

Tiny overheard Owl and Stone talking about the problem with the fuel delivery for the chopper, and how that could be a huge issue if, in the future, someone needed evacuation because of an injury or wildfire.

It took a moment for Tiny to realize Ryleigh wasn't eating. She was picking at the food on her plate and pushing it around. "What's wrong?" he asked softly, for her ears only.

She looked up at him. "Nothing."

Tiny pressed his lips together in frustration, reminding himself that her reluctance to talk to him wasn't a surprise. He'd been a dick to her for a long time. It wasn't as if she was going to open up and tell him her deepest, darkest secrets just because he'd apologized. He'd have to prove to her that she could trust him, that he wouldn't go back to being the asshole he'd been up until this point.

He opened his mouth to tell her as much, when sounds of a ruckus came from the reception desk.

Someone had arrived after lunch was served, and Alaska had gone over to help the man. Nothing seemed amiss...but now the new arrival was yelling and waving his arms in the air.

Brick was moving before anyone else had even noticed, but Tiny and all the other guys were quickly on their feet. Some of their guests were volatile because of the traumas they'd experienced. No one judged them for it, but at the same time, it wasn't acceptable for that anger to be taken out on Alaska, or any other staff or guests at The Refuge.

"I don't care what your computer says, I have a reservation!" the man shouted, his face turning red. "See? It's right here! This is why I printed off my confirmation, things always get fucked up!"

"I'm sorry, sir, but there's no record of that reservation number in the system. It must not have gone through," Alaska said in a calm, steady tone.

"How could it not have gone through when I have a freaking reservation number and an email telling me what time check-in starts?"

The man had a good point, but Tiny wasn't interested in that at the moment. He was more concerned with how angry the guy looked. While Brick circled the desk, heading for Alaska, Pipe was the first to reach the guest, and he didn't pull any punches. He stepped into the newcomer's personal space, forcing him to take a few steps back from the desk.

"We'll figure this out, but you need to relax, mate," he said firmly.

"You can't tell me—" The man's words abruptly cut off when he got a good look at Pipe. The man could be intimidating, with all his muscles and tattoos, and he was using both to his advantage at the moment. The angry man probably also thought better about whatever he might have said next when he saw all the remaining Refuge owners converging on him.

Brick gently pushed Alaska behind him at the desk, but she refused to completely back off.

"Mr. Henderson has a reservation number, but there's no record of it in our system," she told Brick unnecessarily. "I'm not sure how that happened."

"Do we have a cabin available?"

Alaska bit her lip and wrinkled her nose. "We're booked up tonight. Tomorrow, cabin four will be empty because we had a cancelation, but not tonight."

"The friends and family cabin?" Owl asked from beside Tiny.

Alaska took a moment to consider his suggestion, then nudged Brick aside so she could reach the computer. She clicked on the mouse and typed something, then nodded.

"That should work," she said. Looking at the guest, she took back control of the situation, as if she wasn't surrounded by six very protective men. "Sir, I'm not certain how this happened. The cabin you reserved isn't available, and tonight, everything is sold out. But we have a special cabin that's reserved for friends and family that's available. It's smaller than the one you reserved, but you can stay there tonight, and tomorrow move into cabin four. To apologize for the inconvenience and the mix-up, we'll give you fifty percent off your stay, if that's acceptable."

Tiny could hear the stress in Alaska's voice, but she was as professional as ever.

"Yeah, I guess that'll work. I was really excited to come here and couldn't believe my luck when I was able to get such a late reservation. I'm sorry if I...uh...if I was too harsh a moment ago."

"It's okay," Alaska assured him.

"Can I see the confirmation email?"

Tiny glanced over and saw Ryleigh standing to his right. He wasn't sure when she'd appeared at his side, but he wasn't particularly thrilled she'd put herself in range of a potentially dangerous man. Nine times out of ten, their guests were polite and calm, but a PTSD episode could flare at any moment, and the last thing Tiny and his friends wanted was for someone to get injured.

Mr. Henderson shrugged and held out the piece of paper he'd been clenching in his fist. She took it, and Tiny grasped her elbow and gently moved her off to the side. She dutifully shuffled where he wanted her to go, her mind occupied with examining the piece of paper.

Tiny heard Alaska talking to the man, and he vaguely noted some of his friends heading back to the lunch tables and the impromptu celebration of Spike and Reese's newest arrival, but his attention was riveted on Ryleigh.

Her brows furrowed, and she frowned as she read the email Mr. Henderson had received. From where he was standing, it looked legit. It had The Refuge's logo on the top and the signature line looked authentic as well. He had no idea how a mistake as big as sending someone a confirmation *without* a reservation could actually be made, but he knew Ryleigh and Alaska could figure it out.

Owl volunteered to show the man where his cabin for the night was located, and as soon as he and Mr.

Henderson had walked away from the desk, Alaska began speaking.

"I don't know what went wrong. That's never happened before. There's no way he should've gotten that confirmation without the number being generated by our system. And if he had a confirmation number, it should be on the schedule!"

"Easy, Al, it's okay," Brick told her.

"It's fake," Ryleigh said firmly. Her voice wasn't loud, she was being cautious so the other guests eating nearby wouldn't overhear, but she sounded completely confident in her assessment.

"What? *Fake*? How is that even possible?" Alaska asked in confusion.

"Look—the email address is correct, but it's spoofed. See the a? It's different from the one in our default email font. Ours is a circle with a straight line drawn down on the right side. But this one is a Cyrillic a," Ryleigh said, pointing to the email address.

"That makes a difference?" Brick asked.

"Absolutely."

"But...why? *How*?" Alaska asked.

Tiny kept his gaze locked onto Ryleigh. She knew what this was about, of that he had no doubt.

Alaska took the piece of paper and studied it. "Wow, this is really good. The picture at the top, the way it's set up, the signature—everything is exactly like what we send out."

"I'm sure that was done purposely," Ryleigh said.

"So did Mr. Henderson actually pay for his stay? Where'd his money go?" Brick asked.

Anger rose within Tiny at the realization—someone

was stealing from them. Had spoofed their confirmation email and taken the guest's money. Not only was The Refuge out the cost of the man's stay, but they would also essentially *pay* the guest to stay there, since they were refunding half of his charge.

"Tiny?"

Turning, he saw Luna standing behind him, looking concerned. He hadn't even heard her approach, which he mentally kicked himself for. "What's wrong?" he asked.

"Dad's having a meltdown...I think...can you come to the kitchen and talk to him?"

Tiny nodded, on Brick's heels as his friend also headed toward Robert and the kitchen. He wasn't sure what was happening *now*, but his gut was screaming that something was very wrong.

When they entered the kitchen, they walked into chaos. The weekly delivery of food had obviously arrived while they were eating and dealing with the reservation issue, but it seemed twice as big as normal. There were boxes of food on every available surface, and Robert was checking off items, muttering swear words under his breath.

"What's wrong?" Brick asked, interrupting the chef's rantings.

"Everything! This order is all wrong!" Robert exclaimed. "I ordered twenty dozen eggs and instead got twenty. *Twenty* total, not twenty dozen. The flour's missing entirely. I got baking chocolate instead of semisweet chocolate chips. If I used that in my cookies, you'd all revolt. The asparagus is celery and instead of fish fillets, I got frozen fish sticks. And that's just the tip of the iceberg with this shitshow! Someone has to be pranking me, right?

This isn't cool. How the hell can I plan meals this week when my order's so fucked up?"

The feeling that something was very wrong—something much bigger than a simple food order—continued to make the hair on the back of Tiny's neck stand up.

Brick looked confused. Luna was standing off to the side, wringing her hands, not sure how to soothe her angry father. Then a noise behind him had Tiny spinning around.

Ryleigh was standing there, eyes big in her face—and she looked completely shattered.

He was moving before he registered what he was doing, approaching Ryleigh as he would a skittish colt. She was staring at the food strewn around the kitchen as if it was going to reach out and bite her.

"Ryleigh?" he said, taking a step into her line of sight, blocking Robert from her view.

She looked up, and the expression on her face almost made Tiny go to his knees. She looked lost. And so damn sad, it made his heart hurt.

"This is all my fault. I knew it was coming, but this is... it's not good."

"This isn't your fault," he told her. "There was probably a new employee packing Robert's order, and he or she just messed it up."

But Ryleigh shook her head. "No. It's not that. Tonka's insurance, the reservation, the fuel, the food...it's all him."

"Him who?" Tiny asked gently. He wanted to pull her into his arms, to comfort her, but she looked as if she would break into a million pieces if he touched her.

Her gaze cleared slowly...and Tiny could see the resolve transform her expression. "We need to talk."

"Okay," he said without hesitation, relieved that she was finally going to confide in him.

"Everyone needs to be there. The Refuge owners, that is."

Tiny wanted to insist she tell *him* what was bothering her first. But if she needed Brick and all the others to be there to hear whatever it was she had to say, he wasn't going to object. "All right. When Spike gets back from Albuquerque with Reese, we'll get everyone together and—"

But she was shaking her head. "No. Now. *Right now*, Tiny. It can't wait."

"Okay."

"What are we talking about?" Brick asked.

Ryleigh turned to him. "I know what's going on. And unfortunately, it's going to get worse."

"Worse?" Brick asked, a muscle in his jaw ticking.

Ryleigh nodded.

"You want to meet us in the conference room? I'll go get the others."

Tiny wanted to protest. Ryleigh hadn't eaten much before they'd been interrupted by the irate guest. And she looked pale. But Brick had already left the kitchen to gather their friends.

Putting his hand on the small of Ryleigh's back, Tiny led her out of the kitchen, leaving Robert still mumbling under his breath about the disaster of the food delivery.

He saw the others getting up from the tables and heading toward the conference room, as he followed Ryleigh inside. She didn't sit at the large table, instead began to pace back and forth.

Tiny eased himself down onto a chair but kept his gaze

fixed on Ryleigh. He didn't like this. Not one bit. Whatever was going on, he had a feeling he wouldn't be able to fix it easily. Not like he could while he was still on the teams. Whatever was happening wasn't something brute strength could resolve.

None of them were going to like whatever Ryleigh had to say. Of that he had no doubt.

CHAPTER SEVEN

Ry paced back and forth as her brain spun with how she was going to explain everything. How she was going to tell these men, who'd worked their asses off to make The Refuge successful, that everything they'd worked for was probably going to be destroyed, little by little.

Admitting that her name wasn't Ryan felt like *nothing* compared to what she was about to tell them. They'd accepted her, embraced her into their Refuge family. And now she had to tell them she'd brought an enemy right to their doorstep.

Stone was the last one to enter the room, and he closed the door behind him. The click of it latching seemed abnormally loud. Ry looked up and saw six pairs of eyes locked on her. She swallowed hard.

Stone walked toward the table and sat.

"Come sit down," Brick told her.

But Ry shook her head. She couldn't sit. She felt as if she was going to explode from the inside out as it was.

"Ry, come sit," Brick ordered in a low command that it was obvious he expected her to obey.

"She's fine where she is," Tiny retorted. "Breathe, Ryleigh. You're all right. You're safe. No one's gonna hurt you."

"Of course we aren't going to hurt her, Tiny. What the hell?" Owl asked with a growl.

"And she couldn't be any safer than here at The Refuge," Pipe added.

"The Refuge isn't safer than anywhere else in the world," Tonka disagreed quietly. "Evil has a way of finding its mark, no matter how safe someone might feel."

Ry had read the reports on what happened to Tonka and his partner, as well as their K9s. She'd been appalled and horrified, and understood perfectly why Tonka was the way he was. She wasn't surprised he understood that just because you were a badass special forces soldier, didn't mean you weren't vulnerable.

"Everyone chill," Brick ordered. "Ry, whatever you're going to say isn't going to change how we feel about you. But if you know something more about what's going on around here, we need that intel."

Ry nodded. Brick was wrong in thinking that what she told them wasn't going to change things. It would change *everything*. These men thought they knew what she could do, but they knew nothing. They only saw the tip of the iceberg.

She stopped pacing and faced the table. "I picked The Refuge because it was off the beaten path. I researched all of you, and you seemed like decent human beings. When I arrived, I immediately saw that I was right. You welcomed me, made me love it here, even though I'm not a huge fan of the outdoors. Even when I admitted that I'd lied about who I was and how I got this job, you didn't kick me out... so you'll never, *ever* know how sorry I am for bringing evil to your door."

"What evil?" Stone asked, his voice even.

"My father."

The two words seemed to echo in the space around them.

"I think you need to back up a bit, love," Pipe said. "Start from the beginning."

Taking a deep breath, Ry tried to organize her thoughts. She wouldn't go back too far, they didn't need to know about the hell that was her childhood, but she needed to give them *some* background so they'd understand the threat that hung over The Refuge now. To make sure they knew she wasn't understating the issue.

"My father is Harold Lodge."

When no one showed any recognition of the name, Ry mentally sighed. She'd hoped they would know who he was, just to speed this along.

"Is that name supposed to mean something to us?" Stone asked.

"He's on the FBI's most wanted list. He's stolen millions of dollars. And he hates me even more than he loves money. Nothing would please him more than to see me dead."

Saying the words out loud, for the first time ever, made Ry sway on her feet.

She'd spent much of her childhood trying to please him, trying to get even one speck of his love and affection. But he loved nothing but money. Couldn't get enough. It was only after she'd escaped from under his thumb that she even *realized* he hated her. Had tolerated her only because she was useful. But admitting out loud that her own father couldn't stand her...it hurt. She was thrown back to when she was eight, trying desperately to please him just so he'd smile at her instead of berating her.

"Breathe, honey."

Ry didn't even realize she'd slumped against the wall and was practically panting. She let Tiny lead her over to the table and get her seated. Minutes ago, she couldn't think about sitting, but now she was grateful for the chair. She didn't think she could stand on her own power.

"So your father is this Harold Lodge guy, and he doesn't like you. What does that have to do with The Refuge?" Tiny asked. He'd swiveled her chair and crouched at her feet, like he'd done the other day in the cabin.

Looking down into Tiny's turquoise eyes grounded her. They were something familiar in a world that had suddenly been thrown into chaos. She'd known this was coming, that she'd screwed up and her father had found her, but she hadn't realized how devious his machinations would be.

"When I left home, we...we weren't on the best of terms. I hated him for being such a jerk. For taking people's money. He wasn't happy that I left. Vowed to make me pay for leaving, actually."

"How old were you when you left?" Owl asked.

Ry jerked, so focused on Tiny she'd almost forgotten the others were in the room. She glanced toward Owl, but Tiny put his finger on her chin and gently forced her gaze back to his.

"Look at me, hon. Only me. How old were you when you left?" he asked, repeating Owl's question.

Ry had no problem looking solely at him. It made this less painful somehow. It was weird how this man who'd treated her like crap, who'd intimidated her, had mistrusted her so much that he took her computer away at night so she couldn't sneak online and do something nefarious, was now her lifeline.

"Twenty-one."

Tiny looked surprised. "You're what, thirty-one now?"

She nodded.

"So he's been looking for you for ten years? That's a long time."

Ry nodded again. "And now he's found me."

"How?"

"How what?"

"How'd he find you?"

"I messed up."

"I seriously doubt that," Tiny said gently.

"I did. I used an unsecured connection."

"When?" That question came from Pipe.

"It was when we were looking for Owl, Stone, and Lara. Brick wanted me to do what I do. We were here, in this room. He gave me his laptop. I knew better. I knew once I opened the smallest window, he could find me...but everyone was so upset and angry...so I used his computer instead of going to get my own, with a connection I knew was secure."

"Shit," Brick swore, his voice low. "I didn't *give* you my laptop. I shoved it at you. Yelled at you. Treated you like shit until you did what I wanted. *Fuck!*"

Ry didn't know what to say to soothe him. He wasn't wrong. He *had* done those things. She still could've insisted she use her own laptop. But she'd caved under the force of his displeasure. He'd reminded her so much of her father, when he'd used intimidation to get what he wanted.

She swallowed, refusing to look over at Brick. Staring into Tiny's eyes was safer.

"I'm sorry, but I still don't understand how that could allow your dad to find you," he said gently. His tone was so different than Brick's. It gave her the courage to continue.

"I have layers upon layers of encryption set up on my computer. The IP can't be traced, not without some serious effort and skill. I bounce the signals off IP addresses all over the country, and even some outside it."

"And our connection here isn't that secure," Tiny said, finally understanding.

Ry nodded. "But it's more than that. My dad taught me everything he knew—so he knows my patterns. Knows how I 'look' when I'm online. That's harder to explain, but it's like a signature. How I search, the words I misspell, the sites I use...he knows my digital footprint as well as he knows his own. He probably has alerts set up to ping him when one of my patterns shows up. So when I went online using Brick's computer, he was alerted. It wouldn't have been hard for him to trace the strings back to The Refuge."

"That was months ago. Why is he messing with you now?" Tonka asked.

Ry *did* turn her head then, but she felt Tiny's hand on her thigh, grounding her. Giving her the courage to answer Tonka directly. "He's not messing with me. He's messing with *you*," she said almost sadly.

"Why?" Brick asked.

"He's waited months to make a move because he's been studying The Refuge. Learning as much as he can. He's probably looked into the backgrounds of each and every one of you. And your wives. And all of your families. I wouldn't be surprised if he's hacked into the cameras. By now, he knows how much I like it here—if I didn't, I wouldn't have stayed this long. Knows that I've made friends. So he's going to do everything in his power to ruin the things I've come to love...just because he can."

"Ryleigh."

She turned to look at Tiny again.

"He's not going to ruin anything."

"You don't know him. Tonka's insurance snafu? The fuel? The food? That angry man out there? It's all just the beginning. He's going to continue to mess with The Refuge. Do little things that could be dismissed as people not doing their jobs correctly, or electronic glitches. But they aren't. It's all him."

"Now that you know what he's doing, can you stop him?"

Ry hesitated.

Tiny took her silence for uncertainty. "You're a computer genius. Even Tex has admitted that what you can do is nothing short of brilliant. Better than him. If anyone can stop your father, it's you."

His belief in her felt amazing. But she slowly shook her head. "I can't completely stop him. I mean, I can mitigate some things, but I can't control everyone else. Computers are used by everyone, everywhere. I can lock down communications here at The Refuge, but I can't lock down the grocery store, and the people who deliver gas, or individual cell phones. There will always be ways in that he can use to mess with us."

"So what do we do?" The question came from Pipe.

Ry closed her eyes. "I should've left. As soon as I screwed up, I should've left. Led him away from here."

Tiny's hand tightened on her thigh. "No."

That was all he said. One word.

Opening her eyes, Ry saw he was staring at her intently.

"If you took off, would he have left us alone?" he asked.

She wanted to lie. Tell him that, yes, if she wasn't around, her father would've moved on to find her, but that wouldn't be true. And even though she hadn't actually promised not to lie to him, he'd begged her not to. "Probably not," she whispered. "It's the only lead he's had in ten years for where I've been. He wouldn't have left The Refuge alone."

"Right. So we need to figure out what to do now," Stone said firmly.

Everyone was silent as they thought.

"I'll talk to him," Ry said, even though it was the last thing she wanted to do.

"And tell him what? To stop? I'm thinking that's not going to work," Owl said dryly.

He wasn't wrong.

"The thing I don't get is why he wants to find you so badly," Brick mused. "He's found you...now what? He just torments you until you disappear again? That makes no sense."

This was it. Ry had been trying to talk around this since she began opening up. Taking a deep breath, she turned to look at the other men. Amazingly, none of them were glaring at her. Instead, they all had various forms of concern in their expressions. For her.

"I have something he wants," Ry admitted.

"What?" Pipe asked.

"Money. When I left...I emptied his accounts. Took all the money he'd stolen for years. Sent tons of data to the FBI and gave them all the information they'd need to prosecute him. Where he stole the money from, and when, and how much. Not only does he want revenge on me for that, he wants his money back."

"How much?" Brick asked.

This was what she'd been dreading. Ry met Brick's gaze and tried not to flinch as she said, "Ten million dollars."

"Holy shit!"

"*Fuck*."

"Bloody Hell!"

The exclamations came fast and furious around her, but Ry didn't break eye contact with Brick.

"And I'm guessing you can't just give it back and he'll go away."

"I can't give it back because I don't have it anymore."

"You spent it?"

Ry flinched at Tonka's question. He didn't sound angry, but she still felt judged. "The original ten million? Yeah. And then some. Well, I didn't spend it, per se. I gave it away."

"Wait, wait, wait. The *original* ten million? And you *gave it away*?" Brick asked.

Ry nodded. "It's been a decade since I split, and since then, that stolen money has accrued interest...and I might have made some wise investment decisions."

"Okay, then how much with interest?"

Ry glanced at Pipe. "Thirty."

"*Million*?" he clarified.

"Uh-huh."

"And you've just given at least ten million away?" Tonka asked in bewilderment.

"Yes." Ry's chin lifted slightly. "Over twenty, actually." She was ashamed of her past, of the things she'd done. The people she'd ripped off. But she'd worked damn hard to atone for her sins. To give back tenfold to those who'd been stolen from.

"To who?" Owl asked.

"Humane societies, no-kill animal shelters, K9 training centers, GLAAD, American Foundation for Suicide Prevention, volunteer firehouses, prisons, veteran organizations like the Gary Sinise Foundation, women's rights organizations, Make-A-Wish, orphanages, St. Jude and other hospitals, homeless centers, drug addiction centers, halfway houses, wild horse organizations, the Red Cross, food pantries, Doctors Without Borders, the NAACP legal fund, Helen Keller Intl, boys and girls clubs, breast cancer research, Toys for Tots, Ronald McDonald House, the ACLU, National Audubon Society, The Christopher & Dana Reeve Foundation, RAINN, 4H programs...to name a few."

Ry didn't blink at the surprise on Owl's face.

"Wow."

She wasn't sure who said it, but she didn't break eye contact with Owl.

"Okay. All right then."

"Wait...have you given The Refuge money?" Brick asked.

Ry looked at him, but she didn't answer his query.

"You have. Shit, Ry, that's not cool."

"Why not? You guys are doing amazing things here. So many people have benefited from what you've built."

Brick looked flustered, and Ry had a feeling he wanted to insist she take back any money she'd donated, but that wasn't going to happen. And she'd never admit to *how much* she'd donated. The program running on her computer that regularly sent money through the donation button Alaska had added to the website would continue to do its thing until the account the money was coming from ran dry. Which wasn't going to happen anytime soon. And the money couldn't be traced back to her. She'd made dead sure of that.

"How much is left?" Pipe asked.

"Around eight million or so," Ry said. It was still a lot of money, and she'd worked her ass off to get rid of as much as she had. But it seemed as fast as she gave the money away, she made more.

"Right, so...this Harold guy wants his money, which he's not going to get. He's doing his best to wreak havoc on The Refuge until Ry does what?" Stone asked.

"It's not about me. I mean, it is, but it's not. Now, his goal is to destroy The Refuge. To get back at you for helping me. To make it impossible to work with vendors, or even to function," Ry said sadly.

"Can you find him?" Tonka asked. "If he's wanted by the FBI, can you track him down and turn him in, get him off our backs?"

"Maybe," Ry said. "But I doubt it. He's good. Not as good as me, but I'm guessing he's monitoring the FBI tip lines and emails. If I tell them where he is, he'll be gone before they get there."

"Even if we could get you an in-person meeting with someone in the FBI?" Brick asked.

"You can do that?"

"We know people with connections who can make it happen."

"Well...I think we could use all the help we can get. But the FBI is aware of what my dad can do. His skills. Any way we *do* communicate with someone, even if it's in person...it's possible he might have a way of knowing we're planning something."

"There has to be something we can do," Owl said. "I'm not ready to watch this place go under."

"Set a trap?" Brick suggested.

"Like what?" Tiny asked. "If it involves Ryleigh putting herself in danger, the answer is no."

"No, I'd never suggest anything like that," Brick retorted. "But what if she tells him via electronic channels that she's done hiding? Done running. That she wants to give him the money back and be done with him once and for all."

"But there's only around eight million left," Ry pointed out.

"Does he know that?" Brick asked.

She shook her head. "No. I've hidden the money. Like, buried it. There's no way he can access it or find it."

"Okay, then tell him you want to give it back and call it even. We come up with some way to set a trap...maybe set it up so he has to go into a bank and sign for it in person before the transfer will go through. Get the FBI to move in when he shows up."

Ry held her breath. She wasn't sure that would work. Actually, she was almost positive it wouldn't—her father was even more paranoid than *her*—but at this point, she was willing to try almost anything. Even talk to the man she'd never wanted to speak to again.

"What will keep him from screwing with us anyway?" Owl asked.

"Nothing," Brick said with a shrug. "But perhaps just opening up an avenue of communication will turn his attention away from destroying what we've built at least for a little while. Ry, can you lock down The Refuge's connection? Make it secure? Like you said, it won't keep your father from doing what he did this morning again... granting reservations when there aren't any available cabins, messing with our orders...but I'm going to contact Tex, have him see about getting us in touch with one of his FBI contacts. I'll use a burner phone, try to make it harder for your dad to trace and figure out who I'm calling."

"I can do that. It might take me a couple of days. And it might mean a few extra steps when connecting to the Internet...both for all of you and the guests," Ry warned.

"Not a problem. We'll just tell the guests it's for their own protection. If anyone complains, their other option is to go off grid while they're here," Brick said without any concern in his tone whatsoever. "Ry, I need to make something clear to you," he went on. "This is *not* your fault. This is the fault of your father. A man who stole millions of dollars that didn't belong to him. And now he's having a temper tantrum because he can't spend it. Understand?"

Ry nodded, even though Brick was completely wrong. *She'd* made the decision to come here. She never should've stayed as long as she had. But the lure of the friendship they'd offered so willingly was too tempting to deny. Especially when she'd never experienced it before.

Her father wasn't going to take the offer of returning the money in exchange with being done with her. He'd take the money, yes—but his anger toward her was too deep-seated for him to just disappear into the sunset. He'd do whatever it took to end her—because they both knew she was the better hacker. That she could turn around and steal everything back from him a second time.

No, the only way to make sure she couldn't screw him over again was to get rid of her once and for all.

She wouldn't mention that to these men, because she was pretty sure it would send them off the deep end. They'd lock down The Refuge faster than she could blink. Cancel all the reservations. Make the place a fortress. And that wasn't acceptable. That would go against everything this place stood for. The serenity of the forest, the getaway from the evils of the world for those who desperately needed it. The safety of the place would be forever marred, The Refuge's reputation tarnished, and she wouldn't be the cause of that.

Ry didn't want to die, not when she'd finally found a place where she felt as if she belonged. Not when she'd found friends who seemed to like her exactly for who she was, a nerdy computer hacker. Not when things between her and Tiny were finally starting to fall into place. She had no idea what might happen with them in the future, but she wanted to find out.

"All right. Ry will lock down our shit, but everyone needs to keep handwritten notes for the near future. Call the vendors and people you usually work with, tell them we're the victims of hackers and they should verify deliveries by phone in the short term, just to be safe. Stay on your toes. As Ry said, things might get even crazier before they settle down. Understand?"

Brick was a very good leader. Ry could understand why he'd gotten so many accolades while he was a Navy SEAL.

"I'll get in touch with Tex and see what he can do to help from the East Coast. In the meantime, as long as it won't put you in danger, Ry, see if you can reach out to your father. Start up an avenue of communication. Keep him occupied until we can dangle the money carrot in front of him. We want to lure him into a trap, and we can't do that if he refuses to talk to you."

"Okay," Ry agreed. The last thing she wanted to do was reach out to that man, but she'd do it if it meant keeping The Refuge and everyone on the property safe.

She stood as everyone else did, and Tiny took a step back, giving his friends room to approach her. To her surprise, everyone hugged her. Tightly. Told her they were on her side. Ordered her not to worry, promised they'd figure this out together.

She was overwhelmed.

It wasn't as if she'd expected them to scream at her and kick her off the property, but she didn't really think they'd be one hundred percent on her side either.

Brick was the last to approach. Tiny remained behind her, hovering protectively. Brick put his hands on her shoulders and looked deep into her eyes for a long moment. Then he shocked her by apologizing.

"I'm sorry for being a dick that day. I was worried about my friends and didn't have any idea about what to do to find them. When I realized you might be able to track them, I got impatient. I should've realized that someone with your skills would want to use your own computer."

But Ry shook her head. "No, I get it. I would've done the same thing."

"No, you wouldn't have," Brick said with a small smile.

"You would've made sure your shit was locked down, then done your thing. It would've taken five minutes, tops, for you to get your laptop. And in the end, nothing we found out made a difference. Lara was already kicking ass and taking names by flying that chopper off that island all by herself. I just want you to know, you *are not* expendable. Not now, not ever. Your dad is an asshole, but that doesn't make you one by association."

Ry wanted to cry. He was being so nice. And she might not be an asshole by association, but she definitely wasn't innocent either. The path to how they'd gotten to where they all were today was long and twisted, but for years, she'd blindly done what she was told, instead of what she knew was right.

He hugged her, holding on for long seconds, then said, "Alaska's gonna want you to look at the reservation system. I know she's aware the reservation was fake, but she's gonna think she did something wrong with Mr. Henderson anyway. If you could reassure her, I'd appreciate it."

"Of course," Ry agreed immediately. "I'll be right out."

"Thanks." Brick took her face in his hands and gently pulled her close. He kissed the top of her head before nodding at Tiny, then striding for the door.

The small growl of displeasure coming from Tiny surprised Ry, and when she turned to face him, the look of irritation on his face was easy to read. "What's wrong?" she asked.

"Don't like his lips on you," he said.

Ry couldn't help it. She laughed. It was more a tension-relieving chuckle than one of actual humor, but Tiny was being ridiculous. "He's madly in love with Alaska."

"And?" he asked a little belligerently.

She put a hand on his arm. "You know, I can't remember my father ever kissing me." She didn't know where the words were coming from, just knew that she wanted to reassure Tiny. "He never hugged me. Never kissed my boo-boos better. Not that I ever had any, because I wasn't allowed to play outside, and *inside*, he kept me in front of a computer, teaching me how to navigate the muddy waters of the dark web. Anyway...what Brick did? It felt nice. Like what a fatherly kiss might feel like. Not tingly-all-over nice, but heavy-warm-blanket nice."

She immediately felt stupid after her lame explanation. And talking about how much she liked Brick's platonic gesture probably wasn't the best move to make when Tiny was all riled up for some reason.

But to her relief, his expression cleared. Then he reached out and pulled her close. Ry went without hesitation. He put a hand on the back of her head and encouraged her to rest against his shoulder. She did, inhaling deeply, loving how his scent seemed to settle into her bones. Her very psyche.

"Tingly-all-over nice?" he asked after a minute. "You felt that before?"

Ry nodded without thought.

She felt a tug on her hair, realizing Tiny had wrapped the strands in his fist and was pulling her head back so he could see her eyes.

"When?" he asked.

"When *you* kissed my head," she admitted in a quiet whisper.

"Yeah?" he asked with a small smile. "Like this?" He

leaned in and pressed his lips to her head, like he had before.

A full-body shiver shot through Ry. "Uh-huh."

"Or maybe like this?" he asked, before moving his lips to her cheek. Then her nose.

Then he barely brushed her lips with his own.

Tingles? No. Flat-out electric bolts was more like it. She stared at Tiny in awe. Suddenly, she deeply regretted her lack of experience. She wasn't ashamed of it, just wished she knew more than she did so she could make him feel even a *fraction* of what she felt.

"You ever been kissed, Ryleigh?"

She didn't hear any surprise or mockery in his question, so she shook her head a little. When he didn't move, she frowned. "Is that bad?"

"No, not at all. On one hand, I'm disappointed, because it means I can't kiss you like I want to right now. This room isn't nearly private enough and our friends are all nosey little busy-bodies."

Ry's brain felt fuzzy. "You want to kiss me?"

"Very much so. What about you? Do you want to kiss *me*?"

"Oh, yes," she breathed.

"On the other hand," Tiny went on, "I can't help but feel overwhelmed with gratitude and pleasure that I'll be the first to show you how a proper kiss can curl your toes, make you desperate for more, and help you forget anything and everything but me."

Ry smiled a little at that. "You're pretty sure of yourself."

He didn't return the smile, just stared at her with an intense look. "And tingles? I don't know anything about those. What I felt when I put my lips on yours was a nuclear bomb. I've *never* felt the kind of connection with another woman that I do right now, simply holding you in my arms."

Ry's smile died. "You hated me not too long ago," she reminded him.

"I never hated you," Tiny countered. "I was confused. The connection we have is intense, and when I found out you'd lied, I fell back into my past. I couldn't stop thinking about Sonja and how badly she'd tricked me. I lost confidence in myself, in my observational skills and ability to see people for who they are. I painted you with a brush I had no business painting you with. But I came to my senses."

"Why? How?"

"You really want to know?"

Ry nodded.

"The night of Henley's baby shower, I finally heard you. When you told me you were terrified, I saw the fear in your eyes. I didn't understand it, but I finally took the time to look at you again, *really* look at you, and I realized I've been wrong about you all along. After that, it was only a matter of using my brain to think about the things you've done since you've been here. Not once have you done anything that would remotely hurt anyone else. Everything you do, with your computer or not, you do it with the best of intentions. My past clouded my vision for a while, but now I see better than ever. I see *you*, Ryleigh. And I like what I see."

Ry closed her eyes. She felt vulnerable right then. Had anyone ever bothered to take a second glance at her? Not that she could remember. She didn't totally love that Tiny could read her emotions so easily, but it was also a somewhat comforting realization. She wouldn't have to hide from him, he could look at her and know what she was thinking, feeling.

He proved her point by speaking again. "And while I appreciate you opening up to me and my friends, there's more you aren't saying. More than your dad simply wanting money. Isn't there?"

Ry wanted to deny it. Wanted to avoid his question entirely. But she was feeling too raw. Too exposed. She opened her eyes and gave him a tiny nod.

"Right. We'll talk later...if you're up to it. But I have to say this, and I need you to hear me." He waited for her to nod before he went on. "At no time are you to put yourself in danger to catch your father. Understand? My friends and I have each been through our own hells. Someone fucking with The Refuge isn't going to take us down. No way. We'll weather this latest storm one way or another, but not at your expense."

A tear escaped her eye, and Tiny shocked her once more by leaning in and kissing it away. "Tell me you understand and agree," he ordered.

"Okay."

"Say it, Ryleigh. I want to hear the words. I asked you not to lie to me, and if I let you be ambiguous with this, you'll claim that it wasn't a lie when you do something dangerous...like put yourself out there as bait."

She couldn't help but smile a little at that. It seemed Tiny's observational skills hadn't failed him, after all. "I understand and agree."

"Thank you."

Still...she couldn't help but think about what he'd said. About bait...

It wasn't a bad idea.

Yes, her dad wanted his money back, but he also wanted *her*.

She already knew Brick's vague plan would never work. Using her laptop, it would literally take minutes to transfer the money to a secure account for her father, something the man knew. He wouldn't need to go to a bank, wouldn't have to sign for anything. But more than that, her dad was far too paranoid to just waltz into a bank and assume there wouldn't be a building full of law enforcement waiting for him.

But he *was* desperate to get his hands on her. To make her pay for leaving him. For daring to steal from him. She'd seen comments he'd left on the dark web, where he knew she'd see them. He wanted her dead. It was the only way to truly end the threat to his way of life.

If she could lure him somewhere using not money, but *herself* as bait, and get the authorities to catch him, the world would be a safer place.

"Come on, I can see your mind spinning with who knows what. Alaska needs you to reassure her, you need to eat something, then we'll go back to the cabin so you can start locking down what you can. All right?"

"Okay." It sounded more than okay. Especially the part about going back to the cabin. Ry had been an introvert all her life. And while she enjoyed helping out around The Refuge and genuinely liked the people who lived and worked there, she was always grateful for her alone time.

As Tiny led her out of the conference room, Ry felt lighter than she had in a very long time. The threat of her father was as dangerous as ever, but she'd opened up to the guys and they hadn't rejected her. They hadn't looked at her with disgust. With disdain for bringing a threat to The Refuge. She would do what she had to in order to fix this.

There was so much to be happy about right now—the recent births, Lara and Maisy's babies coming before too long, Cora and Pipe's foster kid, the helicopter, the fact that everyone was healthy and in love...

Yeah. The Refuge was a place of happiness. It didn't deserve a cloud of evil hovering over it. She'd fix everything. After lunch.

CHAPTER EIGHT

A week later, Tiny was frustrated as hell, but he did his best to hide that from Ryleigh, who was already stressed to the max.

Things continued to go wrong at The Refuge, but nothing that the authorities would consider to be intentional. Tiny and everyone else knew better.

Hay arrived that was moldy, a slew of bad reviews suddenly showing up online, payments to vendors hadn't gone through, the trash wasn't picked up because the service was randomly canceled. Everyone knew this was all Harold Lodge's doing, but the frustrating part was, nothing could be proven. He'd covered his electronic tracks too well.

But the most alarming incident occurred earlier that morning.

The lodge had been surrounded by SWAT members who'd burst into the building, demanding everyone put their hands up.

The Refuge had been "swatted." Someone had called

into Los Alamos, insisting there was an active shooter at the lodge and people were in danger.

It was scary, and a few of the guests had pretty bad flashbacks that needed to be dealt with delicately. But the worst was the devastation on Ryleigh's face. They'd all seen it. Seen how she'd blamed herself for every little thing that was happening.

But Tiny had watched her work her fingers to the bone for the last week. She spent every available minute—when he wasn't insisting she take a break to go for a walk or eat something—staring at her laptop with a frown on her face as she did what she could to mitigate the things her father put into motion. She'd stopped many of them, but he'd still managed to work around some of the roadblocks she'd put up to cause mayhem at The Refuge.

This last stunt had gone too far. The call to the police couldn't be traced, of course, but Ryleigh had spent the last hour talking with the detectives from the local PD, explaining who she believed was behind the bogus call about the active shooter, and why. She'd been vague about the money, but hadn't flinched away from admitting who her father was, and why he was wanted by the FBI.

She was currently sitting on his couch, staring into space with a look so heartbroken, Tiny finally made a decision.

"Get up. We're going out."

"What?" she asked, frowning.

"You've been holed up in this house for hours on end for the last week. We both need some fresh air."

"I don't like fresh air."

Tiny couldn't help but chuckle at that. "I know, but you need it anyway."

When she got up without any more protests, Tiny realized how far down toward the end of her rope she *really* was. "I'll be right back," he said.

"Where are you going?"

"I need to grab something up at the lodge while you're changing. Hiking shoes and layers, Ryleigh."

She sighed. "How far are you going to make me go?"

"As far as it takes," was his response.

She frowned again but didn't protest further as she headed down the hall, toward her room.

It didn't take long to get what he needed from the lodge. Robert was happy to help. When he returned to his cabin, Tiny grabbed one more thing from the kitchen.

He had a backpack all ready to go when Ryleigh emerged from her room. He eyed her from head to toe and nodded in approval. She'd changed into a pair of cargo pants, a T-shirt under a sweatshirt, and she had a hat in her hand. He grabbed her waterproof parka and helped her into it. She'd be removing it sooner rather than later, as the weather was definitely too warm to exercise with it on, but he'd rather she have it and not need it, than need it later and not have brought it along.

He locked the cabin behind them and set out for Table Rock. They wouldn't be stopping there though. He had another destination in mind. It would take a couple hours all told, and the guests rarely went out that far.

They walked in silence until they passed Table Rock. Ryleigh had a slight sheen of sweat on her face, and her cheeks were pink.

"You aren't taking me into the woods to ditch my body, are you?" she asked.

He wasn't sure if she was kidding or not.

"That was a joke, Tiny," she mumbled, when he raised a brow at her.

"You know I'd never hurt you, right?" he asked.

"I don't understand you," she said after a moment. "Ever since you met me, things have been turned upside down."

"When I decided to accept a partnership in The Refuge, I was bitter and pretty much hated people," he said in response. He didn't talk about this. Ever. But he wanted Ryleigh to hear it. Wanted to share it with her.

"After Sonja tried to kill me, my trust in people disappeared in a puff of smoke. I didn't trust my teammates, my commander, civilians we came into contact with. I was paranoid and it affected my ability to do my job. I was an asshole to literally *everyone*. I had a hard time just going to the fucking grocery store because in the back of my mind, I knew someone was going to burst through the doors with an AK-47 and try to kill us all.

"So coming here, I had no confidence that The Refuge was going to succeed. In fact, I was completely sure it was going to crash and burn. Who the hell would come to the middle-of-nowhere, New Mexico? Hell, a lot of people think the state is part of Mexico, the country. And getting a bunch of people together who had PTSD sounded like a terrible idea to me. But I signed on anyway, because I needed to get away from my life.

"And a funny thing happened when I met Brick, Tonka, Spike, Pipe, Owl, and Stone...I saw six people struggling exactly like I was. The circumstances were very different, but the struggle was the same. And somehow, being around others who could admit they were just as fucked up in some way or another was oddly refreshing. Not a single one of them hid their demons. Which made it easier to deal with my own.

"And being out here in the woods...it felt right. The trees calmed me. The fresh air breathed new life into my body. It sounds corny as hell, but this place is magic. As the cabins were built, and we began to make plans for The Refuge to open, I reflected more and more on what happened with Sonja.

"I realized that it wasn't the fact that she'd tried to kill me that fucked me up so badly. It was that I'd thought she was *it* for me. I loved her. I would've done anything for her, given her anything. And when I was away on a mission, I counted the days until I could get back to her. I was a damn good SEAL, cautious but effective at what I did. And I did it for *her*. I thought we were going to get married, start a family, live happily ever after.

"Her betrayal totally blindsided me. Yes, the knife in my chest sucked. But knowing she'd thrown away the love I showered on her hurt way more."

"I'm sorry," Ryleigh said gently.

"It took me a while to bond with the guys. I expected them to throw me under the bus just like Sonja had. I kept them at arm's length for ages, but eventually they wore me down. Showed me day in and day out that they had my back. It was my idea to install the bunkers," Tiny admitted. "I wanted a place we could go to be safe."

"Safe from what?" Ryleigh asked.

"Everything. Guests who flipped out, strangers with guns, wild moose, storms...life."

"Are there moose in New Mexico?" Ryleigh asked.

For some reason, Tiny thought her question was hilarious. After everything else he'd just told her, she wanted to know if there were moose in the woods. "Seriously?" he asked, looking over at her.

"Yes! Moose are huge. They could stomp my head in a second flat!" she exclaimed. "I already know about the bears and coyotes and other dangerous wild animals, but moose? No. Just *no*. I can't deal with them being out to get me as well."

Tiny smiled. Then he chuckled. Then he bent over double laughing and couldn't stop. The thought that this woman was terrified of moose was hysterical. By the time he got himself under control and stood up straight, Ryleigh had her hands on her hips and was glaring at him.

"You're hysterical," he told her.

"I wasn't trying to be funny," she said with a pout.

"I know, which is why it *was* so funny," Tiny said. Then he reached out and grabbed her arm, yanking her toward him. She fell against him with a small *oof*.

"I'll protect you from any rabid moose."

"Damn straight you will. I expect you to sacrifice yourself and give me time to get away if we see one," she demanded.

"Deal."

Then she shocked the shit out of him by reaching a hand up to his face. She ran her thumb over his cheek before spearing her fingers into the hair at the side of his head.

"She was an idiot," Ryleigh whispered. "Sonja. If I'd ever had someone who cared about me even *half* as much as you loved her...I would've done everything I could to nurture that. To protect it. When you've never had anyone who cared if you slept, ate, got bullied at school...believe me, you treasure it all the more."

Tiny's heart broke for her. He couldn't imagine anyone *not* loving her. Not for the first time, he wanted ten minutes in a room alone with her father.

"Yeah...so...are there *really* moose in these woods?" she asked in a more normal tone, stepping away from him.

Tiny's hands itched to pull her back to him, but he resisted. He had a reason for opening up to her as they walked. He wanted to be an open book. She was becoming that important to him. It scared the shit out of him, but for the first time since Sonja's betrayal, he wanted something with a woman. More than friendship or a single no-strings-attached sexual encounter.

"There've been only a dozen or so confirmed sightings of moose in the last decade," he told her as he put a hand on the small of her back and encouraged her to walk again. "They require cool climates next to streams and rivers."

"It's cooler up here in the mountains," Ryleigh said. "And there are streams and rivers on The Refuge property."

Tiny grinned. He hadn't told her that the sightings were mainly in the north central part of the state...right where they were located.

"Well, in all the years I've been here, I've never seen one."

"Great, so now you're due," Ryleigh said with a sigh.

God, she was adorable. Even when she wasn't trying to be. They walked for another forty-five minutes before they reached the place Tiny wanted to show her. There were plenty of locations with beautiful views in the area. Places like Table Rock. But he'd come across this area a few years ago when he'd needed a break from the hustle and bustle of The Refuge.

He stepped off the trail, and when he didn't hear Ryleigh following him, looked back.

She was still standing on the trail, looking unsure.

He walked back to her. "What's wrong?"

"I'm not sure we should go off the path," she told him with a small frown.

"It's okay."

"What if we get lost?"

"We aren't going to get lost. I know where we are and where we're going," Tiny said.

She still hesitated.

"It's ironic that I'm about to say what I am—but trust me, Ryleigh. I'm not going to get us lost in the woods. Besides, I have a compass, a satellite phone, a flint, an emergency blanket, a first-aid kit, and even a small tent in my bag."

"You do?" she asked in surprise. "Why?"

"Because it's not smart to go hiking in the woods without any of that stuff. But we aren't going to need them. I'm taking you to a place I love."

Ryleigh took a deep breath, then nodded. "Okay."

Her trust in him meant the world. Especially after the way he'd treated her. As if she was the enemy. He couldn't have been more wrong. This woman had been through hell at the hands of the one person she should have been able to trust, and somehow still turned out compassionate and kind. More than a lot of people he knew who'd been through far less. He'd done her wrong, and he desperately wanted to atone for his actions.

Tiny spontaneously held out his hand. To his surprise, she didn't hesitate to take it willingly. Feeling as if he'd somehow crossed a major hurtle, Tiny turned and walked through the trees. It took about ten minutes for them to get to their final destination, but when they did, her reaction was everything he hoped it would be.

Ryleigh gasped and dropped his hand as she stepped forward with eyes wide open in wonder. "Tiny, it's...holy crap, it's beautiful!"

It was.

They were standing at the edge of a field of huge boulders. He had no idea why there were so many in this one place, but dozens were the size of SUVs or buses. They were weathered and smooth, and all around and among them grew trees that towered high above. It was as if the boulders had been dropped from a great height, scattered over this area and this area alone. He hadn't seen any other boulders this large in all his explorations of The Refuge's vast property. He'd been just as awed as Ryleigh when he'd first stumbled across them.

"Want to see something cool?" he asked.

She turned to him. "This *isn't* cool?" she asked with a smile, gesturing to the rocks.

"Cooler, then," he said, reaching for her hand again. The way she took hold so easily, without guile, hit him hard. He led her to the right of the boulder field. They had to step over logs that had fallen and climb over smaller rocks, but it would be worth it. Of that he had no doubt.

They rounded a particularly large boulder, and Tiny knew the moment Ryleigh saw what he wanted to show her by the huge intake of breath.

"Oh my God, is that...*stairs?*"

"Yeah."

"What...how...?" Again, she was as speechless as he'd been when he'd first found them.

"Come on," Tiny said, pulling her toward the crude steps that had been cut into the rock at some point many, many, *many* years ago.

He had no idea how old these rocks were, or when someone might have carved the steps, but it had to have been hundreds of years. Maybe when the indigenous people lived here. There were cliff dwellings in the area. He'd been to Bandelier National Monument, with petroglyphs and homes carved into the soft rock cliffs. He wanted to think maybe some of those ancestral pueblo people branched out into this area as well.

Tiny led her up the steps, going slow so Ryleigh wouldn't fall. When they got to the top of the surprisingly flat rock, he let go of her hand and watched as she looked around as if in a trance. The trees were thick, but he could imagine once long ago, the people who came here could probably see for miles around them. There was an indentation in the rock, probably also carved out, that was permanently blackened from what Tiny could only assume was soot.

"Wow," Ryleigh said as she turned to him. "This is amazing!"

"Yeah," he agreed. "I don't know much about this kind of thing, but I suspect this used to be some sort of lookout. A fire could be lit here." He pointed at the depression in the rock. "Maybe to warn his people of danger, or of game in the area. I bet there are other lookouts hidden in the forest, and the native people would send messages from these greater heights, before the trees grew so big."

"It makes you feel so small," she said quietly. "Like your problems are insignificant in the face of so much history."

"Never insignificant. Come on, let's sit," Tiny said as he

put down his backpack. He opened it and pulled out the emergency blanket. It wasn't the softest thing in the world, but using their jackets they'd wrapped around their waists when it got too warm would give them more padding.

Ryleigh watched as he arranged a little sitting area for them, then took his hand when he offered it and sat. Then he opened his pack and began to remove items.

"Holy crap, Tiny, I can't believe all the stuff you have in there," Ryleigh said with a small laugh, as he placed item after item on the blanket.

He had sandwiches, chips, bottles of water, and even a baggie of Robert's coveted chocolate chip cookies. They were in pieces, but Tiny figured they'd taste just as good.

He smiled as he pulled out another item with a flourish.

Ryleigh grinned. "A Christmas Tree Cake?" she asked incredulously.

"Yup."

"Do I even want to know what you did to get Robert to give you one of those from his secret stash?"

"Nope," Tiny teased with a smile. The truth was, he hadn't had to promise anything. Robert had offered one of his favorite treats without prompting, saying someone as special as Ryleigh deserved it. He couldn't disagree.

"Can I tell you something?" Ryleigh asked.

"You can tell me anything," Tiny said without hesitation.

She looked around as if trying to see if anyone might be eavesdropping. It was adorable. Then she whispered, "I can't stand those things."

Tiny burst out laughing.

"Seriously, they're gross. They have some sort of

coating on them that makes my mouth feel slimy. And they're too sweet. I always feel as if I need to eat something green and healthy to soak up the sugar coursing through my veins after I have one."

"But you always seem so excited when you get one," Tiny said.

"Yeah, because I know how precious they are to Robert, and if he's willing to give me one, I know it's because he really likes me."

Tiny's smile died. He didn't like that this woman thought she had to eat something she hated in order to be liked. "He's not going to be offended if you don't like them," he said.

Ryleigh merely shrugged.

"He's not," Tiny insisted.

"It's not a big deal. It's not as if he gives me all that many. It's the least I can do for everything he does for The Refuge."

That was another thing, Ryleigh did so much to help make The Refuge prosper. It was as if she had a personal stake in the success or failure of the place, but in reality, she gained or lost nothing if the retreat prospered. She simply wanted it to do well because she liked the people who lived and worked there.

Reaching into his bag, Tiny pulled out the last thing he'd stashed before they'd headed out.

Ryleigh's eyes got wide. "Is that...moonshine?" she asked.

"It is."

"But I thought alcohol wasn't allowed at The Refuge?"

"It's not," Tiny agreed as he unscrewed the cap. "But

every now and then, it's nice to have a swig or two." He held out the bottle to her.

Ryleigh stared at it for a beat, then lifted her gaze to his. "I've never had it before."

"You'll like it," Tiny reassured her.

"I heard it's strong."

"It is. You'll only need a few swallows to feel it."

"I'm not sure getting drunk is the best idea when we're sitting on a huge rock in the middle of the woods with a long hike to get home still."

"You aren't going to get drunk…just have enough to feel good."

She still hesitated.

"Trust me," Tiny cajoled.

To his joy, she reached for the bottle, sniffing the contents suspiciously. Her nose wrinkled at the pungent scent. Then she smelled it again and smiled. "It's watermelon?" she guessed.

"Yup. It's sweet, but not too sweet. It's really good over ice, but this'll have to do for now."

She took a cautious sip and winced as it slid down her throat. But after she'd swallowed the potent alcohol, she licked her lips and smiled wider. "The aftertaste is like I just ate a watermelon Jolly Rancher."

"You like it?"

"I think so."

"Take another sip," Tiny ordered.

She did. Then she handed the bottle back to him, and Tiny took a healthier swallow. He could feel the alcohol burning its way down his throat, a subtler warmth following in its wake. They passed the bottle back and forth a few times before he capped it and put it back in his bag. His intention was to get Ryleigh to relax, not get her blotto drunk.

"This isn't going to get me to like being in the wild outdoors," she told him after a moment.

Tiny chuckled. "I didn't think it would. But you have to admit, this place is nice."

"It is," she said without hesitation. "But it would be nicer if it was right outside our cabin and we didn't have to walk for miles and miles and hours and hours to get here."

Tiny laughed again. "But then it wouldn't be as peaceful as it is. There would be people climbing up here all day. Someone would probably fall off the top and we'd have to rescue them. Some asshole would probably sneak out here in the middle of the night and spray paint graffiti all over the place."

"Cynical, but you're probably right," Ryleigh agreed.

They sat in companionable silence for a minute or two, then Tiny mentally shrugged his shoulders and wrapped an arm around Ryleigh, pulling her against him. She came easily enough and rested her head against his shoulder, as he held her close.

"I feel as if I know nothing about you," Ryleigh said after a moment. "I mean, I know about that bitch Sonja, and that you were a SEAL, but that's about it."

Tiny had no problem opening up to this woman. Somehow with all the time they'd spent together, despite him resisting for so long, she'd snuck under his shields.

"I had a pretty good childhood. I told you about my brother. He was my best friend. My rock. We thought our lives were normal. But when I was twelve, I realized how *not* normal my life was. Our parents fought. A lot. I just thought that's how everyone's parents were. Then one evening, I was over at a friend's house, and his mom dropped the Crock-Pot with dinner in it, and it shattered. Food and shards of pottery went *everywhere*. There was soup literally on every cupboard and in every nook and cranny of their kitchen.

"I froze, knowing what was going to happen next. His dad would leap up from the table and start screaming at his mom. Grabbing her arm, hitting her over and over until she begged him to stop. But instead—he *laughed*. Yes, he leapt up from the table, but just to grab his wife around the waist and plunk her onto the counter, so she wouldn't step on the broken Crock-Pot and get hurt. And then they laughed together. Hard. When they finally stopped, my friend's dad cleaned up the kitchen, with our help, while his mom ordered takeout.

"I had normalized the yelling and fighting that my parents did. It was just the way things were, or so I thought. That evening at my friend's house was eye-opening. And confusing. From that day forward, I hated being at home, so I joined every sport and organization I could. Track, swimming, tennis, band, theater...you name it, I did it. Simply so I didn't have to go home after school. It meant less time with my brother, but he understood better than anyone. And I think my mom knew what I was doing, staying away from the house on purpose because I didn't want to hear them fighting.

"She loved me, told me all the time...yet she refused to leave him. He wouldn't leave either. They were so dysfunctional together. And my mom hit my dad as much as he hit her. It was an equal-opportunity abusive relationship. I didn't understand it then, and even today I don't get it."

"How's their relationship now?" Ryleigh asked. She'd

wrapped her arm around his waist while he was talking, and it felt...perfect.

"She's gone. Dead. One night they got into another fight, and my dad pushed her. Hard. She tripped over her feet and fell, hitting her head on the corner of the stone fireplace. Dad thought she was faking being more injured than she was, and he left the house in disgust. When he got back hours later...she'd bled out."

Ryleigh gasped. "Oh my God, Tiny... That's terrible."

"It's weird, because in their own way, I think they really did love each other. They were just no good together. Dad's in prison. Because of the history of abuse, the judge gave him the harshest sentence he could. Twenty years."

Ryleigh squeezed his waist and snuggled into him. But she didn't offer platitudes of sympathy or understanding. She simply sat at his side, supporting him, which Tiny appreciated.

"I was out of the house by then. A SEAL already. I think their relationship was part of the reason why I fell for Sonja so hard and fast. I refused to be anything like my parents, vowed to treasure any woman I ended up with. Which was why it hurt so bad when she betrayed me the way she did."

"Bitch," Ryleigh muttered under her breath.

Her hatred of his ex made Tiny smile.

"And your brother? Where is he? Do you still talk to him?"

"He died."

Ryleigh gasped again.

Tiny regretted being so blunt, but talking about his brother was still painful to this day. "He was a Marine. A damn good one. He was badly injured while I was on a mission. By the time I'd found out and made it back state-side, he was already gone."

"I'm so sorry," Ryleigh said, leaning against him.

"I miss him," Tiny admitted. "He was all the family I had left."

"No. Now you have your Refuge family."

She was right, of course. The pain of losing his brother would always be there, but time had dulled the agony. And his Refuge brothers had a lot to do with that.

They sat in companiable silence for a long moment. The birds chirping around them, the wind blowing slightly.

"My mom loved my dad. He wasn't physically abusive to her, but he was mean. So mean." Ryleigh's voice was soft, as if she was scared to speak too loudly about her past.

Tiny's arm tightened around her shoulders. He'd wanted her to open up to him so badly. Ever since she'd told part of her story to him and the others, he'd known there was a lot more to her history.

He'd tired her out by bringing her here, plied her with liquor to help her relax—and he didn't feel a bit guilty about that. Out of all the people he'd ever met, Ryleigh needed to talk to someone more than any of them. Purge the demons that plagued her, making her so desperate to help others.

He was glad she was talking, but he braced himself for what he was about to hear. His own story wasn't good, but he had a feeling hers was ten times worse.

He wasn't wrong.

CHAPTER NINE

Ry felt good. The moonshine was delicious, especially after those first couple of sips. The tart watermelon sparkled on her tongue and if she had her way, she could've drunk the entire bottle.

But Tiny had put it away. Had only let her take little sips, then tucked it back inside his pack before the bottle was even half empty. She felt pleasantly floaty, as if all her worries had taken flight in the breeze all around her. She knew that wasn't true. That her dad was still out there, doing everything in his power to ruin her life and the only good thing that had ever happened to her...The Refuge.

But for now, she felt amazing. Having Tiny's arm around her felt even better. She much preferred this nice Tiny to the man who used to glare at her and intimidate her with his harsh words.

She'd been shocked by the story of his childhood, and to learn that his dad had killed his mom...accidentally, but still. It made her feel not quite as alone. She never talked about her childhood. But out here, alone in the quiet with Tiny, she felt safe enough to speak.

"Your dad was mean?" Tiny asked, making Ry realize she'd started her story, then got lost in her head, the memories.

"Yeah," she agreed. "I don't remember much about my mom, only that she smelled really good. And gave the best hugs. Tried to encourage me to go out and play, but Dad wouldn't allow it. Then one day, she just up and left. My dad told me she didn't want us anymore. That I was too much trouble."

"How old were you?" Tiny asked.

"Maybe five or six," Ryleigh said.

"You ever try to find her?"

"Of course. It wasn't hard. She's dead. Heart attack."

"I'm sorry."

Ryleigh shrugged. "I had a fantasy that she'd come back one day. Apologize, beg for my forgiveness. Tell me that she never wanted to leave, but she'd had no choice. We'd hug and live happily ever after. But of course, that didn't happen. I *do* believe that my dad probably forced her to leave. But I don't have any proof of that. I never found any divorce papers on file, and she never remarried. She died in New York, and we were in Montana. She got away...but she left me there. Despite knowing how Dad was, she left me with him. I can't forgive her for that.

"My dad, he was...unbalanced. He started training me when I was still learning to read. He taught me what the dark web was and how to navigate it. When I messed up and did anything that could be traced back to me, he punished me. Locked me in a closet, hit my fingers with a ruler until they bled, took away food...you name it, he did it. Told me it was for my own good. But worse than anything physical was when he screamed and yelled. Told me how worthless I was. That I wasn't worth the money it took to care for me. That I was stupid and he couldn't believe he was wasting his time trying to teach me anything."

Ry took a deep breath. Now that she'd started talking, it felt as if she couldn't get the words out fast enough. Telling Tiny the hell that her childhood had been felt cathartic. He was rock solid beside her and didn't interrupt.

"When I was in the third grade, he took me out of school, saying he was going to home-school me. I wasn't upset about it, because I didn't fit in at school. I was the weird kid. The one others picked on. I was a nerd, even at that young age. I didn't want to play with dolls or watch cartoons. All I did in my spare time was stare at a computer screen and try to figure out ways to hack into websites.

"I have a brother. He's twelve or so years older than me. I'm honestly not sure how old he is or even when his birthday is. He was my dad's first prodigy. From what I understand he was good. Really good. But he ran away from home in his teens sometime. Done with my dad's bullshit. I guess my dad saw me as his second chance at having a partner in crime."

"Wow, do you know where he is today?" Tiny asked.

"No clue. Honestly, I'm jealous as hell that he got out... and a little pissed that he left me there...just like my mom did. I haven't tried to find him and he hasn't done anything to search me out either. He literally doesn't exist in my world anymore."

"Anyway, Dad was constantly bragging about the money he stole. Laughing at the despair of the people he took it from. He stole from *everyone*. Nonprofits, huge corporations, any company or organization that had a huge bank account was fair game. But his favorite thing to do was steal from individuals. He loved that they had fewer resources to try to get their money back. They never called the police or tried to get an attorney to fight the theft. Which might sound crazy, but in reality, if an account only had a few grand to begin with, those are exactly the kind of people who don't have the income to fight anyone in court. Even if they did, they wouldn't know who to go after, since Dad was so good at what he did. And, from the bank's perspective, the withdrawals looked exactly like the client's normal spending patterns.

"He was a ghost online. Could get into people's bank accounts and steal their money without any alerts being triggered. Sometimes he'd empty their entire account, and other times he'd only take like ten or twenty bucks at a time. Small amounts no one missed, because hardly anyone checks their account every day. He also designed a program that skimmed money from random accounts literally every minute. He'd get thousands of dollars in a day. He thought it was hilarious.

"And he taught me everything he knew. By the time I was thirteen, I was as good as he was at navigating the dark web. At stealing money. But I *hated* it. I couldn't help but think about what those people must've gone through when they realized their accounts had been hacked. Obviously the accounts that were skimmed probably didn't make much of an impact, except for people feeling violated or inconvenienced. But the ones who lost *everything*? Did they have to go without much-needed medicine? Did we take their rent money? Did their kids have to drop out of ballet or soccer because they didn't have the money to pay for it? Then there were all the nonprofits...good organizations doing important research and aiding thousands, sometimes millions of people. And he was stealing from them. Making *me* steal from them.

"So one day, I told my dad I didn't want to do it anymore."

The awful memories of that day were so visceral, Ry suddenly couldn't breathe. It was as if she was right back in that moment, when she'd told her dad she was done.

She felt herself being moved, but still she couldn't breathe.

"I've got you, Ryleigh. You're safe. Take a deep breath. That's it, again. Concentrate on what you hear and feel. The birds, the wind. Feel my hand on your back, good. I'm sure you can still taste the watermelon on your tongue. You're here at The Refuge. With me. You're okay."

Slowly, Tiny's words registered. Her face was pressed against his neck and he'd moved her so she was straddling his lap. She huddled against him as close as she could get and did as he ordered, concentrating on her five senses. Before too long, she was breathing normally again.

"Good girl," he praised, and those two words seemed to settle in Ry's soul. His approval was a balm, washing away all the harsh words her father had spewed in her direction all her life.

"He didn't take it well," she said, continuing with her story. She needed to get it all out. To finish. Ry had a feeling after this, she'd never speak of the hell she'd lived through again, but as Tiny had said, she was safe. Here. With him.

"He laughed and told me I didn't have a choice. That if I dared stop, he'd ruin my life. He knew people. Bad people. From the dark web. Told me he'd get one of them to kidnap me and sell me into the sex trade. Said no one would ever find me, and I'd spend the rest of my life with my legs spread for anyone who paid enough money to have me. And I believed him."

"How old were you?" Tiny asked.

"Fourteen. And to prove his point, a man came to the house the very next day. He smelled horrible, had rotten teeth, and he scared the living hell out of me. He sat with me on the couch and...and touched me."

"*Motherfucker*," Tiny swore.

Somehow his anger gave Ry the strength to continue.

"He put his hand under my shirt, held me down and laughed as I screamed and struggled. He stopped, but I had to sit next to him at the table as we ate lunch, like he was some family friend. I thought I was going to throw up. My dad gave him some money, and I thought that was it. That I was going to have to go with him and everything my dad threatened would come true. But the guy left, and right after, Dad sat me down in front of the computer and said I'd better add ten thousand dollars to his bank account by the end of the day. If I didn't, he'd call the man back and let him take me.

"So I did. I stole more money than ever before that day. And the next. And the next. But every single day that went by from that point on, I planned. I couldn't fight my dad physically. And I knew if he thought for a second I was doing anything that might get in the way of his money-making, he'd bring one of those scary men back in a heartbeat.

"Every day was a nightmare. I'd have to sit in front of the computer for hours. The days and years passed so slowly. But...I learned more and more. I got better at staying under the radar. My dad was impressed. But what he didn't realize was that I was getting better than *he* was. He'd taught me everything he knew about illegal hacking, and what he *didn't* know, I taught myself.

"I stayed too long, I know that, but the thought of striking out on my own was terrifying. Because I knew the second I left, he'd do everything in his power to get me back under his thumb. So I pretended to be cowed. I did what he asked without question, and he reveled in his power over me. Over the people he stole from. It had long since gotten to a point where he was letting me do all the work. He just sat on his ass and digitally counted his money.

"For years, I planned. I padded his account. Made it seem as if there was more money in there than he actually had...because for a few years, I was actually stealing from *him*. Moving the money he'd taken from others and putting it into various accounts all over the US and the world. When I left at twenty-one, he was broke. I'd taken it all. I left him twenty bucks. That was it."

"Good for you."

Ry blinked in surprise and looked up at Tiny. "Didn't you hear me? I stayed until I was twenty-one, way old enough to know better. And I stole money from people *all that time*. Millions of dollars."

"I heard you. And you might have been 'old enough to know better,' but your father had isolated you. You knew nothing about the real world. He'd threatened you, made you dependent on him. And yeah, you stole money, but you didn't enjoy it."

Ry couldn't stop the harsh snort that escaped. "I can see it now. I'm innocent, your honor, because I didn't like taking money from people. Yes, I used it to pay for a roof over my head, to fill my belly and travel all around the country. But it's okay because I didn't enjoy it."

"Listen to me," Tiny said as he took her head in his hands. She had no choice but to meet his gaze.

Ry was stunned to see no judgement in his eyes. He wasn't horrified that she was a thief. A damn good one. All she saw was compassion.

"I see you, Ryleigh. I know the kind of person you are."

"A thief," she mumbled dejectedly.

"The kind of woman who would single-handedly go after a serial killer to rescue a child. Who's donated millions of dollars to organizations that help the less fortunate. The kind of person who immediately orders food for her friends who are in the hospital because she's too far away to go to a restaurant for them herself. You cleaned Reese and Spike's cabin without help so they could come home to a fresh, clean space. You finished painting Dylan's bedroom without asking for help. You let three damn goats nibble on your clothes because you're too kind-hearted to push them away.

"Your father tried to make you like him—but he failed, Ryleigh. Spectacularly. Because you're nothing like him. *Nothing*."

"I'm not sure the courts would agree," she said sadly.

To her surprise, Tiny laughed. "Tell me this, you've

been away from your father for ten years. Have you stolen any money from anyone in that time?"

Ry's eyes widened. "No. No way."

"Exactly. And is there any *proof* of you taking that money before you left?"

Ry thought about that for a moment. Then shook her head. "No. I was good at what I did. I didn't leave any trace."

"So why do you think anyone will be able to come up with enough proof to charge you with anything? You've paid your dues, Ryleigh. Just as we all have. I've done things I'm not proud of. Things I wish I could take back. But you know how I'm atoning for those sins? With this place. By giving people a place to come to just *be* for a few days. The Refuge is my way of giving back. Yours is the money you donate. You could've given away the money you took from your father and then stopped. Lived off the millions in interest you made off of it."

"That money's tainted too," Ry protested. "No, it wasn't stolen, but it only accumulated because of the original money my father and I took. And I can't give away too much at one time or there will be questions asked, so it keeps accruing. I can't give it away fast enough."

Tiny chuckled again. "And that frustrates you."

"Yeah," Ry agreed.

"We'll figure it out. Give away every penny if that's what you want. So you can live free and clear."

Ry stared at him...and she suddenly realized how intimate their position was. Her legs were straddling his lap and he'd pulled her tight against him, so they were touching from their groins to their chests. She could actually feel his dick between her legs. But she wasn't embarrassed. Not in the least.

The truth was, she was still a virgin because of that terrifying man from so long ago, and her dad's threats. They'd turned her off wanting to be intimate with a man —ever.

But being with Tiny like this? She felt safe. She'd bared her deepest secrets to him, and he hadn't recoiled. Hadn't told her she was a criminal. He'd *defended* her. It was overwhelming. Deep down, she wasn't sure she was the kind of person he'd described, but for the first time ever, she felt a spark of hope well up deep inside. Maybe she wasn't such a horrible person after all. She'd done all she could to atone for her past sins, and her father's too. She wasn't sure she was anywhere close to wiping her slate clean, but maybe, just maybe, she was being too hard on herself.

"Ry? What are you thinking?" Tiny asked.

"I feel horrible that because of me, I've brought so much hardship to The Refuge."

"No," Tiny said. "It's not your fault. It's his. Your asshole father's."

She smiled a little at that. "Yeah. I don't know when or how this is going to end, but I want to be done with him. For good. And he never would've stopped looking for me. So in some ways, I'm glad he's found me. I want to live, Tiny. I want to have friends. To be normal. Well, as normal as a nerdy hacker can be. And that can't happen with him out there, roaming free."

"What are you saying?" Tiny asked with narrowed eyes.

Ry knew he was smart. "This isn't going to end without a confrontation."

"No," he said again, shaking his head.

143

"Yes."

"*No*," he said more firmly. "If you're telling me you want to invite him to The Refuge for a chat, that's not going to happen."

"I didn't ever want to see him again. But opening a line of communication, like Brick suggested, won't be enough. It's not enough to know what he wants. I have to know what it will take to get him to go away. To leave me alone. Leave The Refuge alone. And if that means seeing him in person, I'm not going to say no if he asks."

"And *I'm* not going to let you sacrifice yourself. We're in this together, Ryleigh. You, me, and everyone else at The Refuge. We aren't going to hang you out to dry. You're one of us."

Those words felt so damn good. Ry closed her eyes and let the warmth of them blossom inside her.

"Look at me, Ryleigh."

She opened her eyes and met his gaze.

"You're the expert in this situation. I wish like hell I could help, but no one is as good as you are at what you do. Your father already knows where you are, so I don't think it could hurt to see what the hell he wants. What his end game is. But whatever line of communication you open with him, I want it to funnel through me."

"What do you mean?"

"He's gonna say shit that's fucked up. He's going to try to get at you through the psychological crap he used while you were growing up. And I won't tolerate you having to endure that. He's hurt you enough. Let *me* filter what he says. I promise to pass on anything that *isn't* abusive."

Ry didn't have to think twice about his suggestion. "Okay."

One of Tiny's brows raised quizzically. "Okay? You agreed really fast, which makes me think you've got something up your sleeve."

Ry shook her head. "No. I don't actually *want* to talk to him. I don't want to be on the receiving end of his cruelty. I've lived through it long enough. I'm okay with you reading his messages first...as long as you can handle it. He'll probably say some horrible things. I don't want *you* to have to deal with that either."

"I can handle it for as long as it'll take to figure out how to take him down. And I have to tell you, your trust in me is humbling."

"I'm really doing it for myself. I'm being selfish," Ry felt obligated to point out.

"Good. You think about others way too much for my peace of mind."

Ry smiled at that. "Thanks for bringing me out here and plying me with alcohol to get me to talk."

Tiny blushed. Actually *blushed*. "You figured that out?"

She chuckled. "Wasn't hard. But I'm okay with it. The liquid courage was good. Thanks for not letting me drink too much."

"Never. I might've done a crap job of looking out for you until lately, but I promise that I'm a different person where you're concerned now. And now that I know about your background, remembering all the times you flinched when I raised my voice to you makes me feel like shit."

"It's okay."

"It's not. But I swear to you that's done."

Ry sighed and sagged against him, resting her head on his shoulder. His arms held her to his chest tightly and she felt as safe as she'd ever felt. "Can we stay here forever?"

she mumbled against his neck. "No fathers. No computers. Nothing to go wrong."

She felt more than heard Tiny chuckle against her. "I'm a decent cook, but I'm thinking with you not being an outdoorsy girl, you aren't gonna like pooping in a hole and using leaves to wipe."

Ry wrinkled her nose and sat up. "I'm with Jasna...can we not talk about pooping? That's gross."

"Part of life," Tiny said with a grin.

"I know, but still. Ew."

"Noted. No poop talk."

"You said it again. Stop it."

He laughed out loud that time. "Sorry."

Ry stared at him for a long moment, then she slowly leaned forward and pressed her lips to his. She couldn't have stopped herself if someone held a gun to her head. Tiny was everything she'd ever dreamed about.

His arms tightened as she leaned back. She stared at him for a beat, suddenly self-conscious. Had she done it wrong? She hadn't ever kissed anyone before. She wasn't sure what to do.

"What was that for?"

"Um..." Ry hedged, knowing her cheeks were a fiery red.

"Because if you wanted to thank me for listening, I'll say you're welcome and we can get up and head back to The Refuge. But if it was because you feel something for me, something more than gratitude, I need to know so I can kiss you back the way I've dreamed of for way too long."

Her heart was thumping so hard in her chest, she'd be surprised if he couldn't hear it. "I *am* grateful that you've been so understanding and nonjudgmental about every-thing. But that's not why I kissed you."

Tiny shifted under her, and Ry could swear his dick had gotten harder. But she was too nervous to move and find out.

"Why, Ryleigh? I need the words. Need to be sure we're on the same page. That you want the same thing I do," Tiny said softly.

"Because I haven't ever kissed anyone before. Haven't wanted to. But I want to with you. Want to experience everything I've missed out on because of my past. Because I've been too scared."

"You don't have to be scared with me," Tiny told her. "I'd never do anything that will hurt you. I'll only make you feel good."

Ry nodded.

Tiny smiled. "You've really never kissed *anyone?*"

"It's pathetic, huh? Thirty-one and not only a virgin, but never even had a first kiss."

"I'm so honored. I'm going to be your first, Ryleigh. In every way."

"Okay. But if I do it wrong, please don't yell at me."

"Never. And you won't do anything wrong. Promise. Kiss me, Ryleigh. Do it. Take what you want."

And with those words, Ry did as he asked. She leaned forward and put her lips back on his. But this time he didn't remain passive. His tongue peeked out and licked her lips, startling her so badly, she gasped. She wasn't an idiot, she knew what a French kiss was. She'd always thought the idea was kind of gross.

This was anything *but* gross.

He tasted like watermelon, and she couldn't wait to

sample more. Instinctively, Ry tilted her head and opened to him. His tongue didn't surge into her mouth, he licked and nibbled her lips, driving Ry crazy. He coaxed her tongue into following his, and the next thing she knew, she was inside his mouth. A moan left his throat, then she felt a hand at the back of her head as his tongue twined with hers.

She retreated, but he followed. The kiss was long, hot, and it made electric bolts shoot through her arms and down between her legs. Ry shifted against him, feeling as if she wanted...no, *needed* to be closer. Her nipples hardened and she regretted all her layers. She had the urge to feel them against his chest, skin to skin.

The thought was so carnal, she gasped again and tore her mouth from his. His hand was still on the back of her head, but he didn't force her to stay where she was. She was panting as she stared at him, surprised to find he was just as out of breath.

"Was that okay?" she asked.

"Okay? It was...life changing," Tiny breathed.

Ry relaxed. She'd been so afraid of this moment, of being intimate with someone, that she'd gone out of her way to keep her distance from men her entire adult life. But this kissing thing...she liked it. A lot. At least with Tiny.

"Was it okay for *you?*" he asked.

And it hit her then that Tiny was just as unsure as she'd been. It made him seem more human. More her equal. In her mind, he'd been this larger-than-life man for so long. But after today, after he'd opened up to her and she'd done the same, she felt as if they were on a more even keel.

"It was the best first kiss a girl could ever hope to have," she told him honestly.

She felt him relax under her. Yeah, he'd been just as nervous about this as she was. It endeared him to her all the more. Sighing, she let herself go boneless against him. This moment was perfect. He didn't insist on more kissing, was simply as content as she was to be in the moment.

They sat together for several more minutes before he sighed and said, "We should probably get back."

"Yeah," Ry agreed. She sat back up and said, "Thanks for bringing me here."

"Even though it was...*outside?*" he asked with a grin.

She rolled her eyes. "Yes. I'm not saying I want to go on another hike anytime soon, but after we figure all this out...I wouldn't mind coming back here."

"Deal. I'm thinking this is my new favorite place at The Refuge."

"I can't help but wonder who else sat right where we are now. Was it a single warrior scouting the land around him for threats? Was it a couple, kissing like we did? An elderly man or woman performing some sort of ceremony?"

"All of the above, probably."

"Yeah." Ry sighed, then did her best to climb off Tiny's lap. He helped her up then packed away the uneaten food —including the Christmas Tree Cake—and the blanket.

"You won't tell Robert that I don't like his favorite food in the world, will you?" Ry asked.

"Never. Besides, that leaves more for me."

Ry laughed. "You like those things?"

"Yup."

"They aren't good for you. As a former SEAL, you should know that."

"I do know it. I'm not saying I want to eat a box for dinner every night, but every now and then, they're a nice treat."

"Whatever."

He smiled at her, then took her hand in his and towed her toward the steps. They both stopped before they headed down, taking one last look around them. Then Ry thought of something. "Oh, wait! Can we take a picture?"

"We can do anything you want," Tiny told her.

Feeling the sincerity of his words down to her bones, she smiled as she pulled out her phone. There was no reception this far out in the woods, but she didn't need it in order to take a picture. She held up the camera and waited for Tiny to put his cheek against hers. She turned to look at him without lowering her arm, and smiled just before Tiny kissed her. She clicked the shutter as he kissed her hard and fast.

"Go stand back where we were sitting and let me take your picture," Tiny told her.

She handed her phone over and went to stand where he'd suggested. Ten minutes and almost twenty pictures later—of her alone on the rock, then Tiny, *then* a few more of them together—Tiny finally led her down the stairs. He told her he was going first in case she lost her balance and fell...so he could catch her.

He was being sweet and attentive, and Ry could hardly believe the change in their relationship in such a short period of time. She realized that it had happened when she'd opened up. Her lies and subterfuge had been a main reason why he'd kept his distance from her, and why he'd been so mistrustful. Knowing more about his past made her understand what made him tick, and why he'd treated her the way he had.

And being honest felt so much better than keeping secrets. She'd spent her entire life in the darkness, hiding from others, sneaking around. It felt glorious to know that someone, that *Tiny*, knew all her secrets now. And he didn't hold them against her. It gave her a confidence she wasn't sure she'd ever had before.

As they walked back to The Refuge to check on things, make sure her father hadn't done anything else crazy in the few hours they'd been gone, Ry made a vow to herself to always be as honest as she could be with Tiny. Even if it made her uncomfortable, she was done hiding. From herself, her father, her friends, other people. She was who she was, and for the first time in her life, she felt accepted as that woman.

CHAPTER TEN

"You seem...I don't know...different," Reese said. Ry was hanging out in Cora's cabin with all the other women. Reese was nursing Dylan, and Lara was holding Henley's baby.

"Is that bad?" Ry asked.

"No! Not at all. It's good. Great. It's just...you seem more sure of yourself or something."

Ry smiled at the other woman. She loved that she saw her that way. Ever since her walk with Tiny, and their kiss, she'd made a conscious choice to be as honest as possible with people. Instead of trying to please everyone by agreeing to anything they suggested, she only did the things *she* wanted to do.

Like when Robert offered her a Christmas Tree Cake that morning, she'd politely declined. Before, she would've accepted and eaten it, just so Robert wouldn't feel as if she was rejecting him. Or when Cora asked if she wanted to go with her to the grocery store in Los Alamos early one morning. Instead of agreeing and disrupting her schedule

—mornings were now the time Ry dedicated to scouring the dark web for anything her father might have set up the night before to mess with The Refuge—she'd told Cora that she had work to do.

Those were probably such little things to most people, but saying no, not doing something because she was afraid someone wouldn't like her, felt liberating.

"I wouldn't say I'm more sure," Ry admitted. "I just got to the point where I realized here at The Refuge, around you guys, I could be myself."

Everyone immediately agreed. Enthusiastically.

"Of course you can be you!"

"Good for you!"

"Go girl!"

"Awesome!"

Their acceptance felt great.

"Thank you for all the stuff you ordered for me and Spike when we were in the hospital, by the way," Reese told her.

"You're welcome. How're you feeling?" Ry asked, done talking about herself. It was one thing to turn over a new leaf by being exactly who she was, it was another thing altogether to talk about it with her friends. She wasn't *that* changed. It would never be easy for her to talk about herself. So she was more than ready to change the subject, put the focus on someone else.

"Tired," Reese said with a crooked smile. "Dylan's not exactly the best sleeper, and anytime he moves, I wake up because I'm paranoid something's wrong."

"But the doctors say he's doing okay, right?" Alaska asked.

"Yeah. For a baby born a few weeks early, he's doing

awesome. He's been having some issues with reflux, but overall, yes, he's healthy."

"He's adorable," Cora said, as she gazed at the infant in their friend's arms.

"I can't believe how close in age he and Elizabeth are," Lara said with a smile as she rocked Henley's daughter.

"Is it too early to hook them up?" Maisy asked. "You know, like pledge their troth or something."

Everyone laughed at that.

"Pledge their troth? You've been reading too many historical romances, girlfriend," Alaska teased.

"Nothing would make me happier than for my son to marry your daughter," Reese told Henley with a smile. "But of course, that will be his decision. He might prefer boys. Or maybe he'll want to stay single. Or maybe he'll be a computer genius like Ry and move to Washington, DC, to run the world."

Ry blushed. Once upon a time, she would've protested and insisted that she wasn't a genius, not by any stretch. But the truth of the matter was, she was damn good at what she did.

A dinging noise sounded in the small room, and it was almost comical how everyone looked down at their phones to see if it was theirs. Turns out Cora had been the one to receive a message.

Since Ry was looking right at her when she read it, she instantly knew something was wrong. "Cora?" she asked. "What is it?"

When the other woman looked up, she had tears in her eyes.

"What? Is Pipe okay?" Alaska asked.

All the women were frowning now, worried about their friend.

"He's good. But this is the *second* time that we were approved for a foster child and it was canceled at the last minute. I know these things happen, and it's better if the kid can stay with relatives instead of being removed completely from their situation, but we were *sure* this time that it would go through."

Uneasiness swam through Ry's veins. It was very likely that Cora was exactly right about what happened...but she couldn't help wondering if it was something else. Some*one* else who was manipulating the system.

Without a word, she stood up and went over to her bag that she'd left by the door. She didn't go anywhere without her laptop anymore. There had been too many instances of her father fucking with The Refuge for her to feel comfortable being away from the device.

She placed it on the table behind the couch a little too hard, and sensed more than saw the other women's heads turning her way.

"Ry?" Maisy asked.

She didn't answer. She was too upset. The more she thought about it, the more she knew this had to be her father's work. It *had* to be. Once again, her asshole of a father was doing everything to prove he was more powerful than she was. But it wasn't power he was showing —it was pure evil. Who messed with *foster children*? Her shitty dad, that's who. He didn't care about *anyone*. He was as unfeeling as a human being could possibly get.

She'd sent him messages through the dark web, but he hadn't responded. Not yet. But maybe this latest stunt of his was response enough. He didn't care about anything she had to say—but he would.

It had been years since she'd taken money from anyone. The day she'd left her father's home, in fact. Well...maybe it was time.

She understood now that her father couldn't be reasoned with. After all, how could you reason with a psychopath?

"Ry?" Maisy repeated, but again she ignored her. Her fingers were already flying over the keyboard. Logging onto the Internet with her secure connection. She needed to hack into the Los Alamos Social Services database and make sure Cora and Pipe's application was still correct. She wouldn't put it past her father to have messed with it. To make them look like less than desirable candidates.

A chair next to hers was pulled out, making her finally look up. Cora sat down. She had a small frown on her face and was studying Ry intently.

"You think he did it?" she asked.

Ry didn't have to ask who "he" was. "Yes," she said firmly.

When Tiny asked if it was all right if the guys shared with their wives what was happening with her father, she'd willingly agreed. Was relieved she wouldn't have to face the women herself and tell them how fucked up her childhood had been, and what a monster her own flesh-and-blood was. The next day, every single one of her friends had found her at some point to lend their support, along with much-needed hugs. Reassured her that they didn't blame her for anything, and to offer their help. It had felt amazing...and liberating. Their actions had reaffirmed that Ry was right where she was meant to be.

"Is it wrong that I'm relieved?" Cora asked.

Ry's brows furrowed. "You are?"

Cora nodded. "Yeah, I mean, I was beginning to think no one thought I'd be a good role model. That they saw something in our application that made them think Pipe and I wouldn't be good parents."

"That is *not* true," Lara said heatedly. The close friendship between the two women was something Ry envied. "You and Pipe would make the *best* parents. Ever. Any kid would be *lucky* to be placed with you."

Cora smiled at her friend. "Thanks. But I think you might be biased."

"No, she's not," Henley said. "You've been a huge help with Dylan already. The other day when you showed up on my doorstep, when he was crying his head off, I swear I was at my wits' end. You didn't say a word. You just gathered him up and walked right out the door. You knew I needed a break, and you didn't hesitate to give that to me."

"Some people would see that as kidnapping," Cora pointed out with a smile.

Everyone laughed.

"Not me," Henley said. "And you're even better with Jas. She can be a handful, but you never get tired of her questions. Of her constant babble about anything and everything. Even I have my limits on how many games of tic-tac-toe I can play. But not you. You'd sit with her for days if that's what she wanted."

Henley wasn't wrong. Ry had also noticed how patient Cora was with the young teenager. Her lips pressed together and she turned back to her computer. She was going to get to the bottom of why she and Pipe had been denied fostership, or whatever it was called, at the last minute. Again.

It didn't take long at all to find out why the latest foster had fallen through. Her dad wasn't even trying to be sneaky anymore. Social services had received an email that was extremely damning and derogatory. It claimed Pipe was abusive toward a former girlfriend in the UK. It included a police report that said Pipe had beaten and choked the woman until she was unconscious. Ry had never seen a British police report, but even *she* could tell it was bogus. It looked like a form a ten-year-old had made on his computer.

To mitigate the damage her father had caused, she created her own email, a perfect replica of correspondence from a police precinct in DC—where Cora used to live—informing social services that the report they'd received was a fake, and none of the allegations about Bryson Clark were true. The email indicated an ex-boyfriend of Cora's was attempting to sabotage her ability to foster by making false accusations against her and her husband.

"Did you find something?" Cora asked, obviously seeing Ry's satisfied smirk.

"Yup. But I fixed it."

"You *fixed* it?"

"Uh-huh?"

"What'd you do?" Cora asked.

"You don't want to know."

"Actually, I do. Wouldn't have asked if I didn't," the other woman said firmly.

That stuck Ry as funny, though she didn't know why. Cora was hardly afraid to say what she was thinking.

"What age range are you and Pipe interested in fostering?"

"Why? I thought you were going to tell me what you found and how you fixed it," Cora said, in lieu of answering her question.

"Are you opposed to a kid who's older, about to age out of the system? Like sixteen or seventeen? Or are you looking for someone who's seven, eight, nine, in that age range?" Ry asked, meeting Cora's gaze.

"It doesn't matter. We just don't want a baby or someone under, say, three. They're much easier to place and have a lot of options."

"And do you want one? Or is two or more at the same time acceptable?"

"What are you *really* asking?" Cora demanded, clearly exasperated.

Ry was well aware she and Cora had the attention of everyone in the room. Something that usually made Ry feel very uncomfortable. But she'd seen something else while she'd been searching the social services' records. Something important.

"There's a family. Their parents were killed in some sort of drug dispute. The oldest child is a girl. She's seventeen. The youngest is four. They have no relatives willing to take them on, which isn't surprising, since there are four of them. The seventeen-year-old quit school and is trying to get guardianship of her siblings, but it's not going well because she can't find a job. Not anything that would support a family of four. They were there when their parents were shot and apparently aren't dealing well with the violence they witnessed. Social services has been able to find foster homes for the four- and eight-year-olds. But the thirteen- and seventeen-year-olds haven't had any interest. They don't want to be separated, which is complicating matters."

"Yes," Cora said before Ry could add anything else. "You all know the entire reason we expanded our cabin was because we wanted to foster more than one child at a time. We've got plenty of room, now that we have a four-bedroom home."

"You should probably talk to Pipe," Alaska said hesitatingly.

"Don't need to," Cora said firmly. "We've talked about this a lot. Fostering. Who we'd be willing to accept. And we both decided that we'd take anyone who needed us. And it sounds like these kids definitely need us."

"They need The Refuge," Henley said with a sniff.

"You'd be wonderful with them," Maisy told Cora.

"And I'm sure I could help find a job for the oldest," Alaska volunteered.

Ry smiled. Her father's plan to sabotage Cora and Pipe's foster journey might have worked in the short-term, but in the long run, he'd done them a favor. She had a good feeling in her gut about this. "I won't manipulate the records by approving you outright," Ry warned Cora. "But I can put a note in that you and Pipe are very interested in fostering the entire family. Keeping them together. You'll still have to go through another interview, meet the kids, get their approval."

"I know how it works. And it's fine. I'd rather do it that way, have the children *want* to be with us than have you rubber stamp it on the back end," Cora said.

The excitement on the other woman's face was clear.

She wanted this. Those kids didn't know it, but their lives were about to change for the better.

"What are their names?" Cora asked.

Ry looked back at the computer screen. "The oldest is Joyce. The thirteen-year-old is Kason. Then there's Shannon and Max."

"Girl, boy, girl, boy," Cora breathed.

"Yup."

"We want them. Definitely."

"Good. Because it's done. Hopefully you'll get a call soon."

"Ry, this isn't a done deal yet," Alaska warned.

"It's not?" Ry asked, looking up with what she knew had to be a shit-eating grin on her face.

"Right. This is happening," Alaska said with a little huff of breath. "You're kind of scary, you know that?"

For some reason, Ry felt proud of her friend's words. "I'm not scary. I'm efficient," she countered.

Everyone laughed. And just like that, the mood of the room switched from one of worry and concern, to happiness once again. It felt amazing to have been the one to make that happen.

Suddenly, Ry felt very differently about her skills. She'd always been just a little ashamed of them, knowing that hacking, for the most part, was a bad thing. Something she had to keep hidden. But she wasn't a bad *person*. Yes, hacking into the government website wasn't exactly good, but her father had gone way over the line, and Ry was obligated...no, *honored* to help her friend.

Plus, she'd been honest with Cora. She wouldn't rubber stamp the approval. Wouldn't guarantee she and Pipe were automatically accepted. They'd still have to go through the steps to get the family. But was it really a bad thing, what Ry had done? When no one else had shown any interest in fostering all four kids together? Not in her eyes.

And that brought her back around to her original thought about her father. She needed to find a way to get him talking. If she didn't, this harassment would never stop. There would be many more days of frustration and worry for The Refuge and her friends.

What she did next was easy. Almost *too* easy. The things her father taught her, things she hadn't done since the day she'd left his house, came back as if by rote.

Hacking into his bank account was child's play. As was transferring out ten thousand dollars. It wasn't a ton of money, but it was enough to get his attention. She'd asked him to stop via the dark web. Begged. Had tried to open a line of communication, but he'd ignored her attempts to reason with him, refused to talk.

Fine. In his world, *money* talked. So she'd "talk" to him in a way he couldn't ignore.

She hit the enter button harder than she meant to, and it felt amazing when she saw his money—money he'd stolen from someone else—transfer into Padres Unidos's bank account. It was a local program that helped fathers become more engaged, committed, and responsible. Her own dad would hate that, and it felt appropriate, since he was, in her eyes, the worst father in the world. He could've done with a program like Padres Unidos, for sure.

"What was that?" Maisy asked.

"What was what?" Ry asked, trying to sound innocent.

"Whatever you just did."

"I didn't do anything."

"Uh-huh," Maisy said skeptically.

She sighed. "Okay, look—I have to end this. My dad messing with all of you. He's mad at *me*, and it's not fair that you're getting caught in the crossfire. I *need* this to stop." The last five words were whispered, and Ry realized she was on the verge of tears.

Cora reached over and closed her laptop, then grabbed Ry's hand and pulled her up from the chair. She towed her back over to the couch and sat, pulling Ry down next to her. Maisy sat as well, scooting closer until Ry was sandwiched between the two women.

"It's going to stop," Cora reassured her.

"We don't know that," Ry whispered.

"When I was in that basement," Lara said from the other side of Maisy, "I thought that was it. That I would die there. No one would ever find me. But I was wrong. Cora found me. Got me out of there...with *your* help."

"And when I was in that car on my way to Mexico, I had no idea how in the world it could ever end any way but badly," Reese added. "Even when I fell into that river, I thought I was a goner. But then Gus was there. The man I'd loved for what seemed like forever, and suddenly we were safe on the bank."

"Same for me. When I was shoved into that train car in Russia? I was sure I was a goner," Alaska added.

"And I was positive when Jack regained his memory, he'd hate me forever," Maisy said softly.

"Point is, we all survived our worst ordeals. And you will too. This *is* gonna end," Cora said firmly. "It'll work out. One way or another."

"And if you think Tiny is gonna let anything happen to you, or The Refuge, you're so wrong," Henley said. "That man is totally gone for you. Has been for months."

"Um, I'm not sure we're talking about the same Tiny," Ry protested, even though deep down, a blossom of hope bloomed at her friend's words.

"Yes, we are," Henley said. "Look, I get it. He's struggled with everything. But even when he was being...overly protective of The Refuge, he couldn't hide his concern for you. And lately, now that he knows your whole story? That concern is out in full force."

Ry couldn't deny it. "He's way out of my league," she said, admitting out loud something she'd been thinking for a while now.

"No, he's not."

"You're wrong."

"Are you kidding me?"

The immediate protests from her friends felt undeniably good.

"I don't know anything about having a relationship. I've spent my entire life as the weirdo. The outcast. The introvert. I've never had a boyfriend. Sex makes me nervous, and I literally just had my first kiss the other day...at *thirty-one*. It's ridiculous and pathetic."

"I got this, ladies," Alaska said, as she got up and came over to the couch. She knelt in front of Ry and put her hands on her calves. "I know a little about being an outcast. I didn't have many friends, spent all my time on the outside looking in. And here I am. With a man I've loved all my life. Engaged. Living a life I never could've imagined. Tiny is *not* out of your league, Ry. In fact, I'm willing to bet he thinks you're out of *his* league. You're a freaking genius, girl. Could probably take out Russia, China, and North Korea's nuclear programs with a few taps on your keyboard. So *what* if you haven't had a relationship before? If I'm interpreting what you said correctly, you just had your first kiss with Tiny. I bet he's thrilled, excited, and over-the-moon proud that he was your first. Was it awful?"

"Our kiss? No!" Ry exclaimed. "It was...amazing. I always thought touching tongues with someone would be gross. It was anything but."

Alaska was grinning from ear to ear. "My advice? Go with the flow. Continue doing what you're doing. Open up to Tiny, he needs that honesty probably more than any of our guys. Tell him what you're thinking, feeling. If something makes you nervous, tell him. He'll treat you good, Ry. I have no doubt."

"And he looks like Jake-freaking-Ryan. He was my first boy-crush," Reese admitted.

"I really don't think he looks much like him," Ry said, glancing at Reese.

"What? Seriously?" Lara asked with a gasp.

"Seriously."

"You need to watch *Sixteen Candles* again, my friend. And I dare you to tell me afterward that Tiny doesn't remind you of him," Reese ordered.

"The movie hasn't aged well, it's pretty misogynistic but...at the end...when he says, 'Yeah, you,' I melt every time," Maisy admitted.

Alaska squeezed Ry's legs a little. "In a year, we'll be sitting here, Lara with her baby, Maisy with hers, Elizabeth and Dylan toddling around getting into trouble, all of us reminiscing about how crazy things were, but how well they worked out."

"Promise?" Ry whispered. She wanted that. Oh, how she wanted that. If she could fast-forward time and have everything going on just be done and over with, she'd do it. In a heartbeat.

"Promise," Alaska said firmly.

Dylan began to fuss at that moment, and hearing the other baby's cries, Elizabeth joined in.

"I think this is our cue to head out," Henley said dryly.

"Same," Reese agreed.

Cora helped Reese to her feet, since she was still healing from giving birth, and walked her to the door, holding her arm. Henley headed out with Alaska at her heels.

Ry hugged everyone and walked toward the lodge. She wasn't ready to go back to the cabin yet. As much as an introvert as she was, at the moment, she didn't want to be alone. Tiny was helping Tonka with the animals in the barn, so she headed for the laundry room. Carly, Jess, and Joshua would most likely be there, folding towels and sheets.

The Refuge wasn't where she thought she'd end up, not in a million years. Living and working at a retreat that was in the middle of the woods, miles and miles from any kind of big city? No. But deciding to hole up here for a few months had been the best decision she'd ever made. It was now her home. And Ry would do whatever it took to protect it...and the people who lived and worked here.

CHAPTER ELEVEN

"Uh, Tiny?"

"Yeah?" He looked over at Ryleigh. She was sitting on the couch next to him and clicking away at her keyboard, as usual. She'd been out of sorts for hours.

Earlier that afternoon, Jasna had arrived back at The Refuge in tears. She'd discovered that her grades were all D's and F's. Which made no sense whatsoever, since the girl was actually a very good student.

Ryleigh nearly lost her mind, but Henley stayed calm. Told Ryleigh in no uncertain terms that *she* would take care of that one. That Jasna's teachers would realize immediately the electronically printed report card was wrong.

But everyone knew this was one more way Ryleigh's father was attempting to cause trouble. To pick on a child was unacceptable. Why Tiny thought the man would have any shred of compassion or empathy, and not drag a kid into his schemes, he had no idea.

While fixing the grade snafu would've probably been way easier than fixing most things Harold Lodge had done, it was a huge blow to Ryleigh. Tiny *hated* this. All of it. He could kill a terrorist intent on doing harm to him or his team members, could hunt down an HVT, high-value target, and take him or her out without any remorse. But he was helpless to fight against someone who hid behind a keyboard. Who used electronic means as his weapons.

Ryleigh was still doing her best to mitigate the damage her father was causing, but they were all on pins and needles, wondering what would happen next.

"You told me that if I heard from my dad, I should let you know. Well...he's messaging me."

"What?" Tiny asked, putting aside his phone and practically leaping for Ryleigh. She handed her laptop over to him without hesitation.

The message on the screen wasn't in a normal chat box. What looked like row after row of html code was slowly scrolling by, and it took Tiny a moment to pick out the message from Ryleigh's father.

Bitch dont mess with me. you'll give it back. all of it or else.

"Give what back?" Tiny asked.

"Um...I might have stolen ten thousand dollars from his account today," Ryleigh said.

"*What?* Why?"

"He made me mad! Messed with Cora and Pipe's foster application. And since he's refused to answer any of the messages I've sent him, I decided to talk to him in a language he couldn't ignore."

Tiny watched as more words scrolled past him on the screen.

The shit i've done, its nothing compared to whats coming.

Tiny had no idea how a father could talk to his own

flesh and blood like this. "How do I respond? Just type?" he asked.

"Uh-huh. But...what are you saying?"

You're a coward, Lodge. And a shit human being. Stop taking your patheticness out on innocent people.

ah the big bad seal speaks! enjoy her cunt, I'm sure its nice and tight considering what an uptight bitch my daughter is

Tiny ground his teeth together. He was doubly glad she'd let him screen the messages, as he'd asked. She didn't need to see this vitriol.

i shouldve sold her when I had the chance

Leave her alone. You've done enough to fuck up her life. We're going to find you, and when we do, you'll spend the rest of your pathetic life behind bars.

ha! no you aren't, and no I'm not

Be a real man and own up to your sins. Tiny knew that wasn't going to happen, but figured he might as well see if he could try to goad him into doing the right thing.

a real man like you and your buddies? fine i'll do that, i'll act in a way you can understand and appreciate. it'll be fun to watch the sparks fly

A chill went down Tiny's spine. He had no idea what Harold meant by that, but he knew it couldn't be good.

tell my darling daughter to give my money back, all if it, and all this stops. if not we'll see who wins in the end

Tiny began typing a response, but suddenly the entire screen went black. He lifted his fingers from the keys in surprise.

"What? What's wrong?" Ryleigh asked urgently.

"I don't know. Everything went black."

Ryleigh cursed and took the laptop from Tiny. She breathed a sigh of relief when words began scrolling on the screen once more. "He deleted the conversation. And I can't trace him because he bounced his connection off too many towers. What'd he say?"

Tiny sighed. "He wants his money back. All of it."

"I wouldn't give him a penny if he was drowning and the money kept him from going under," Ryleigh said fiercely.

"Come here," he said, not giving her a chance to respond before he pulled her against his side. He buried his nose in her hair as he tried to get control over his emotions. He wasn't surprised at how horrible her father was, she'd told him exactly what kind of man they were dealing with...and yet, he was still disturbed at how easily he'd talked about selling his own daughter.

To his relief, Ryleigh snuggled against him immediately. Her arms went around him and she pressed her cheek to his shoulder.

"Have you ever seen the movie *Sixteen Candles*?" she asked out of the blue.

Tiny stifled a groan. "Let me guess, the girls told you about Jake Ryan."

Ryleigh giggled, and the sound went straight to his dick. "Yeah, but I'd heard people say they think you look like him before today."

"I do not," Tiny insisted, although deep down, he had to agree there was a slight resemblance. On one hand, he couldn't believe he was having this conversation, but on the other, he was more than glad he wasn't trying to soothe Ryleigh after she was forced to read for herself all the shit her father had the nerve to say to her.

"Can we watch it?"

"*Sixteen Candles*?"

"No, *Alien* fourteen. Yes! *Sixteen Candles*."

"If I can find it on one of the streaming apps."

"Oh, it's there. I already looked it up," Ryleigh said. Tiny could hear the humor in her voice.

"Of course you did. What would you do if I'd said no?"

"Watch it with one of the girls. Maybe Reese, she seems to really love it."

Tiny reached for the remote. "Nope, that's not happening. We can watch it."

Ryleigh giggled again. He liked her like this. Relaxed. Happy.

She told him which app the movie was on and within minutes, the opening credits were rolling. Ryleigh looked up at him. "Tiny?"

"Yeah?"

"I'm sorry you had to talk to my dad. I'm sure it wasn't fun. And he probably said some awful things. But I'm going to stop him. If it's the last thing I do."

"*We* are going to stop him. And it won't be the last thing. I won't allow that. Not when we're just getting started."

"Started with what?"

"Us."

She blinked at him, then gave him the sweetest smile he'd ever seen. She put her head back on his shoulder and squeezed him tightly. Tiny kissed her head and relaxed against the cushions. Ryleigh had snuck under his shields as easily as she slipped into top-secret databases. But he wasn't sorry. He was tired of being suspicious of everyone and everything. He wanted what his friends had.

And he knew to the very marrow of his bones that Ryleigh was his chance. His chance to trust again. To love.

* * *

If Tiny thought Ryleigh would fall asleep halfway through the eighties movie, he was very wrong. She stayed awake and kept up a running commentary throughout. She rolled her eyes in disgust at the blatant discriminatory depictions of Asians, and how the supposed "hero" left a blind-drunk woman—one he was dating—in the hands of someone else, giving him carte blanche to have sex with her, even though she couldn't consent.

But at the end, when Jake Ryan appeared at the church where Samantha's sister got married and responded to her innocent, "Who me?" question with, "Yeah, you," Tiny still heard Ryleigh sigh.

The kiss over the birthday cake at the very end was cheesy as hell, but he could see how it would appeal to teenagers...and apparently Ryleigh.

She looked up at him when it was over, but she didn't speak.

"So?" he asked.

"So, what?"

"Does he look like me? That main dude?" Tiny asked.

Ryleigh studied him for a long moment before shrugging. "There's some resemblance, but honestly, you're much more..."

Tiny practically held his breath waiting for whatever she was going to say.

"Rugged. Less pretty-boy. More real."

He let out his breath. He could live with all of that. "What do you want to watch next? *Pretty in Pink*? *Say Anything*? *Breakfast Club*?"

She giggled. "How about *Under Siege*?"

Tiny groaned.

"What? It's manly. And has Navy SEALs in it," Ryleigh protested.

"It's awful."

She pouted. "I like it. I can picture you as the lead. Being all badass, blowing up microwaves, not shivering even though you've been locked in a freezer, caring about that poor low-ranking guy who was just trying to do his job, and vowing revenge when your friend the general was killed."

"Commanding officer," he corrected.

"Whatever."

Tiny couldn't help but like that she saw him that way. "Fine."

This time, Ryleigh did fall asleep halfway through the film. Instead of waking her up and sending her to bed, Tiny switched positions on the couch, lying lengthwise with Ryleigh dead to the world on top of him. One hand rested on the small of her back, and the other was under his head, acting as a pillow of sorts.

This felt good. *Amazingly* good. He hadn't slept in the same bed...er, couch...with a woman since Sonja. Hadn't been able to, mentally.

And yet with Ryleigh, he felt not one iota of doubt or trepidation. Even though she'd lied to him, even though he'd spent months trying to dislike her. It felt as if from the moment he'd met her over a year ago, they'd been working toward this point in time.

Was Tiny all of a sudden a different man? One who trusted everyone, and everything they said? No. Hell no. But he trusted this woman. She should be a complete mess, what with her background. Instead, she was compassionate and kind. She went out of her way to help others in any way she could. Tiny understood it was an attempt to atone for what she saw as her sins, but as far as he was concerned, they weren't *her* sins. They were her shithead of a father's.

She would no sooner stab him in the chest in the middle of the night than she would decide to go back to a life of crime at her father's side.

No, if she was going to do *anything*, it would be to slink off quietly, disappear like a puff of smoke.

Tiny was completely safe from Ryleigh attempting to inflict violence on his person. But not from damaging his heart. He wasn't safe from falling in love with her.

Shit. *Love...*

Yeah. He was a goner.

He'd have to go slow. For both their sakes. Prove to her that his assholery of the past was just that—in the past. That she could trust him with no reservations. More importantly, prove that he trusted *her* the same way.

With that thought, Tiny closed his eyes, a lightness he hadn't felt in years settling over him. He'd seen therapists, talked about his trust issues, about the things he'd seen and done as a SEAL, and yet, he'd never felt any different afterward. He'd remained the same messed-up guy he'd been before therapy. But now he felt a shift inside himself. As if he'd finally let go of the bitterness, the anger he'd held on to for so long.

Sleep came fast, for once. And it was a deep, healing sleep. Ryleigh in his arms, against his heart, was what he'd needed for years. Now that he had her, he wasn't letting anyone, including her asshole father, take what he'd waited for his entire life.

CHAPTER TWELVE

Ry was shocked when she'd woken up in Tiny's arms that morning. Knowing what his ex had done, and the fact he hadn't shared sleeping quarters with a woman since, she'd thought he would've woken her up and made her go to her room.

Instead, he'd stayed on the couch and held her all night long. And it felt incredible. Better than anything she could've imagined. Since she'd never slept with a man—or woman, for that matter—she'd expected it to be uncomfortable. But she hadn't woken up once during the night, like she usually did.

And when he'd finally opened his eyes, she'd expected *him* to be upset that they'd slept in each other's arms, but he'd simply kissed her forehead, mumbled something about his awful morning breath, and shifted out from under her, heading to his room.

She'd done the same, and when they'd met in the kitchen after showering, things had been better than normal between them. Ry wasn't sure what happened last night, but Tiny seemed even more different than he'd been lately—and that was saying something. All morning, he was way more affectionate. Touched her frequently... running a hand along her arm, touching her back, sitting closer at the table as they ate breakfast. And she couldn't say she hated it.

Tiny was going up to the lodge for his weekly owners meeting, and she was going to do her usual scan of the dark web, looking for more of her father's shenanigans. They planned to meet later for lunch up at the lodge.

They'd put their breakfast dishes away, and Ry was just about to sit at the table again and get to work when Tiny stopped her. He pulled her into his arms, and she looked up at him in surprise. Her hands rested on his chest, and she had to force herself not to caress him. The more she was around this man, the more curious she got about sex. It was a surprising feeling, because she'd never been concerned about it before. Hadn't really allowed herself to think about it. But now that Tiny wasn't glaring at her suspiciously anymore, and after that amazing kiss they'd shared, she couldn't seem to think about anything else.

"Is it okay if I talk to the guys about your father? About what happened yesterday, with the money you pilfered from his account and him reaching out?"

She nodded immediately. "Yes."

"You don't feel weird about taking his money?"

"Well, yeah. It's stealing, even if he took it from someone else in the first place. I don't want anyone to think I'd ever do anything like that to them. Take their money, that is."

"They don't think that," he told her.

Ry wasn't so sure, but Tiny knew the others better than

she did. Besides, hadn't she decided she was done hiding who she was? She'd done what she'd thought was necessary because her dad was ignoring her messages—and because he'd messed with Cora and Pipe. Screwing with Tonka's insurance was bad enough. Yesterday, he'd made things much more personal than they already were. And after learning about Jasna's grades, she felt even *less* guilty about taking the money.

"Okay," she said belatedly.

"He's escalating," Tiny said.

It wasn't anything Ry hadn't already thought. "Yeah."

"We need to step things up. See if we can track him down. Turn him in. Can I talk to Tex?"

"I already have," Ry admitted with a slight wince.

"You have?"

"Yeah. He's really good, and I thought maybe he might've thought of some way to find him that I haven't."

"And has he?" he asked.

"No."

For some reason, Tiny chuckled.

"What? Is that funny?"

"Kind of."

"Why?" she demanded.

"Because you thought Tex might know something you don't. Honey, you're way out of his league. He even said as much."

"That's not true," Ry said, feeling her cheeks heat.

"I have a feeling he'd love to sit down and pick your brain for, oh, about four days. And even that still wouldn't be enough. If you want a job, I'm sure Tex would hire you. Hell, anyone would. You'd be gold for an organization trying to lock down their security so hackers couldn't get in."

Ry blinked at him in surprise.

"You've never thought about that, have you? Using what you know to keep people like you *out*."

"No."

"You think you could do it? Lock down a system securely enough so hackers couldn't get in? Like credit card companies or government websites?"

"Probably. I mean, I could at least lock down how *I* would get in."

Tiny chuckled again. "Which means keeping out ninety-nine-point-nine percent of other hackers. We can talk about it later."

"Don't I need a degree for that?"

"No clue. But I'm guessing once some CEO realizes what you can do, he or she isn't going to care about a piece of paper. Thank you for letting me talk to the guys. We're going to figure this out. One way or another, I'm not going to let your father continue to harass you. Will you promise me something?"

"Depends on what it is," Ry told him.

"Smart woman, not to agree without knowing what it is. Don't run."

Ry frowned in confusion.

"We both know things are going to get intense. Your father isn't going to back off. But I don't want you to leave, thinking that will help the situation. It won't. I want you to promise me that you won't sneak off in the middle of the night. I'd never find you...but I'd spend the rest of my life looking."

"Tiny," Ry whispered.

"I slept with you in my arms last night, and I didn't feel a moment of hesitation. Of doubt. Of worry. I want more nights like that. I want it all with you. And if you leave..." His voice trailed off.

"I won't leave," Ry said, feeling overwhelmed. "Not now. I mean, if I wasn't going to leave before my dad started doing all the stuff he has, there's no way I'd leave now."

"Thank you. I didn't think so, but I wanted to be sure. I'd like to kiss you again. May I?"

Ry nodded.

His head lowered, and his kiss was soft and sweet. A brushing of his lips against hers. It felt...nice. He lifted his head, looked at her for a moment as if wanting to make sure she was okay. Then he kissed her again. Harder and deeper.

By the time he lifted his head a second time, they were both panting. Ry's fingers were digging into his chest, and one of her legs had actually come off the floor and was rubbing against the outside of his thigh.

Was this *her*? She wasn't like this. Wasn't this...horny. Ever.

Tiny grinned. "You liked that."

"Duh."

"Me too. If you want...and there's no pressure...maybe we can try sleeping in a bed tonight. I mean, the couch was okay but a little lumpy. I think we'd be more comfortable in my bed. But again, it's up to you. And when I say sleeping, I mean *sleeping*. Nothing more. Not yet."

"Not even if I want it?"

Ry wasn't sure where the words came from. Or who the hell she was anymore.

"I refuse to go too fast with you, Ryleigh. This is all new to you, and frankly, it's new to me too. I'd like some time to get used to this. Us. Baby steps."

When he put it like that, how could she refuse? Truth was, she couldn't. "Okay."

"Okay." Tiny kissed her forehead and stepped back, reluctantly. "If I don't go now, I'll be late and the guys will give me all sorts of shit," he said with a grin.

"They haven't ever been late to a meeting?" she asked.

"You have a point. When Brick moved Alaska in with him, he was late regularly. And come to think of it, *all* the guys have been late at one time or another." He stepped back to her, wrapped an arm around her back, and bent her into a dramatic dip as he lowered his head.

Ry was laughing when she flew backward, but soon she was lost in his kiss. The only thing keeping her from falling to the floor was his strong arm, and yet she felt no fear. This was Tiny. He'd never hurt her.

All too soon, he stood her up and grinned again. "Now I *really* have to go."

"Okay," Ry said dreamily.

"I like this look on you. Lips puffy from my kiss, dazed look in your eyes, cheeks flushed."

"Whatever," she murmured.

His grin widened. He tapped a finger to her nose. "See you at lunch. If your dad tries to communicate with you again, don't. Shut your laptop and come find me. Doesn't matter if we're still in the meeting. Okay?"

Ry sighed. She didn't know exactly what her dad had said the night before, though she could imagine. It was sweet that Tiny wanted to protect her from him. But she'd heard plenty of his threats in the past. She was sure he hadn't said anything much different than he'd already spewed at her. "Okay," she agreed.

"There are some apples in the fridge if you want a snack before lunch. Don't eat the Christmas Tree Cake that's in the freezer though. It's mine. I'm saving it."

Ry rolled her eyes. "It's safe."

It looked as if he wanted to say something else, but after a moment, he turned and headed for the door. "Lock this behind me," he ordered.

Ry wanted to roll her eyes again at how protective he was being, but since she secretly didn't mind it, she nodded.

"We're going to get through this," he said firmly, as if saying it would make it so. Then he was gone.

Ry immediately walked to the door and threw the dead bolt. Then she took a deep breath and went back to the table. She opened her laptop and got to work searching for more of her father's electronic signatures.

* * *

Tiny listened in frustration as Tonka explained how a woman in town had decided not to buy goat's milk from The Refuge after all. No one had any doubts it was somehow because of Harold Lodge. The man hadn't let up on his campaign to destroy The Refuge, and the strain was beginning to show with everyone.

On a lighter note, Pipe told them that he and Cora had received a call from social services that morning about fostering a family of four kids who had no relatives willing to take them in. Tiny knew all about it from Ryleigh, and he was happy for his friends that no time was being wasted in setting up meetings and getting the paperwork done.

But it didn't mitigate the threat they could all feel hanging over them.

"He's not going to stop, so what are we going to do to *make* him stop?" Brick asked.

It was the ten-thousand-dollar question. Or maybe the ten-million-dollar one.

"Ryleigh finally got a message from him last night," Tiny told the group.

"Could she trace it?"

"Unfortunately, no, but taking the money from his account definitely got his attention." He'd already told his friends about the ten grand she'd transferred to a charity to lure him out of hiding.

"So, what now?" Tonka asked.

"How can we leverage the fact that he reached out to her?" Owl added.

"What'd he say?" Stone asked, which was probably the better question.

"Lots of shit. Said he should've sold Ryleigh to the sex slaver when he had the chance."

"Bloody hell," Pipe swore.

In any other situation, Tiny probably would've laughed. Bloody hell wasn't exactly what *he* would've said; wasn't what he thought, for sure, when he'd seen the words on the screen the night before. But he wasn't in the mood to find anything about this amusing.

"He also said something about being a real man, after I taunted him with it, and that he'd do something we could understand. And something about sparks flying."

"Fuck, do you think he'd actually do something physical? Something other than hide behind his keyboard?" Spike asked.

"No clue. But I don't think we can ignore that possibility," Tiny said grimly.

"I'll contact the security company we contract with and tell them to be extra vigilant. We've already got a ton of cameras around the property, so I'm not sure adding more would do anything other than make it more difficult to monitor them all," Owl mused.

"There's more. He *did* say that if Ryleigh gave his money back—and I'm assuming he meant the original amount, not the ten k she took last night—that he'd stop."

"Do we believe him?" Stone asked.

"No way in hell. He's enjoying this. He's been stewing for years as he searched for Ry, and now that he's found her, he won't give up, even if she *does* give the money back," Tonka said.

Tiny agreed with him.

"What if we provoke him?" Brick asked.

"What are you thinking?" Pipe asked.

"Well, up until now, we've been on the defensive. Plugging holes as he makes them. Yesterday was the first time Ry fought back, by taking that money. And he responded. What if she does more? Takes *all* his money? Hits him where it hurts the most?"

"He could act even more batshit crazy than he is right now," Stone said with an unamused snort.

"If he gets too riled up, he could make a mistake. Open the door for Ry to find him. For the FBI to nab him," Brick suggested.

"Or he could come out of hiding with an AK and try to blow his daughter away," Tiny argued.

"Exactly. He could *come out of hiding*," Brick said. "Look at us. We're badass special forces. We've got two SEALs, a Coast Guard DSF, a Delta, an SAS, and two Night Stalkers. The day we can't take down a fucking hacker who's spent his entire life sitting behind a computer, making people's lives miserable, is the day I give up my Budweiser pin. We need to piss this guy off enough that he can't help but want to confront Ry in person."

"No. Absolutely not. No way in hell," Tiny growled. "We are *not* using Ryleigh as bait for this fucker."

"Then how do you suggest we get him?" Brick argued, voice equally hard.

Tiny leaned forward in his seat, pissed way the hell off now. "Would you be suggesting this if it was Alaska he wanted?"

"I wouldn't like it. I'd be scared as fuck. But *yes*, I would."

"Bullshit!" Tiny barked.

"If you have any other ideas, I'm listening. But this guy isn't fighting fair, Tiny, and we can't take down a ghost. We need him to show his face, and the only way I know how to do that is by sending him so far over the deep end that he tries to come after Ry personally."

Tiny and Brick were locked in a battle of wills. Never had Tiny felt more animosity toward a fellow SEAL, a *friend*, than he did right now. And what sucked was that Brick was right. Tiny knew it, but he didn't want Ryleigh to *ever* see her shithead father again. He'd done nothing but cause her pain, and Tiny didn't want him to cause one iota more.

"Maybe instead of grabbing all his money at once, she could take a little at a time. Let his anger really build.

When he's ready to explode, she can tell him she'll give it all back, but he has to come get it in person," Stone suggested.

"He's not going to be stupid enough to fall for that," Pipe insisted.

Tiny didn't take his gaze from Brick's. The other man stared back just as intently as the others talked around them.

"She could promise there won't be any cops, since she's also broken the law, stolen his money," Spike said.

"That excuse could work," Tonka said slowly. "We could have the meet here. Where it would be filmed by the cameras, so our own asses are covered if we have to take deadly action."

"No fucking way!" Brick said. "We've put our blood, sweat, and tears into this place. There's no way I want that psychopath anywhere near The Refuge. I don't care if we send all our women and kids away and shut down the place so there aren't any guests. It's still a horrible idea to invite him here."

"Tiny? Stop glaring at Brick. What are you thinking?" Owl asked.

Tiny glanced at his friend. "That I hate this."

"But?" Owl pressed.

"But...it could work. Not bringing him here, but having Ryleigh meet with her father in person. Harold Lodge is cocky as fuck. He thinks he's got this situation—and his daughter—under control. If Ryleigh continues to steal his money, little by little, it'll drive him insane. He won't be able to figure out how she's getting into his accounts because she's way better than him."

185

"You think she'll be able to do it? Because by now, surely he's locked them down," Pipe said.

"She can do it," Tiny said without a doubt in his mind.

"Will she *want* to do it?" Spike asked.

He sighed. "Unfortunately, yes. She'll do anything to make him stop. No matter how many times I tell her that this isn't her fault, she still feels that it is. If using herself as bait will ultimately lead to his arrest, she won't hesitate. But this is about more than the money. Yes, he wants his millions back, but at this point, it's a matter of pride for him. He can't let his daughter win. Not only that...I think he sees her as his only legitimate threat. I got the feeling from his messages last night that he wants her *gone*. That he's cocky enough to think he can kill her, tying up the few loose ends of his life in the process."

"If we set this up, we're going to be there the entire time. She won't ever be alone with him, no matter what," Brick said.

Tiny glared at his friend. "Nothing is ever that easy." He sighed. "And I'm scared." It wasn't something a SEAL would normally admit, but this wasn't a normal situation.

"I know. I am too," Brick responded. "But if we don't do anything, this place is going to go under. Maybe not tomorrow or the next day, but eventually that asshole will find a way to destroy us just like Ry said—a little at a time. No matter how good she is, the blows to our reputation will eventually wither away the confidence our guests have in us. They come here to feel safe, and if this kind of shit keeps happening, their trust will go away and our business will dry up. I'm not willing to let that happen.

"The Refuge is my safe place. It's where I found the love of my life, where I healed myself, and where my best friends have healed as well. We're starting a new generation here with Tonka and Spike's children, and I'll do whatever it takes to protect it. *Them*. Everyone here. Including Ry. She's one of us now, and I'm not going to let anyone hurt her, Tiny."

Some of Tiny's trepidation eased. Brick was right. This was their home. And he wasn't going to let anyone threaten that. Or the woman he loved.

He wasn't even surprised at his thoughts about Ryleigh. He loved her. It had taken him months to realize it, but it was the truth.

"Okay. You'll talk to Ry, let her know?" Brick said.

Tiny snorted. Just because he'd agreed to this plan didn't mean he had to like it. "That she's going to have to act as bait? Yeah, I'll tell her."

"Again, he won't touch her. I give you my word," Brick vowed.

Tiny nodded. He knew Brick had the best of intentions, but he also knew, just as all the men around this table did, that even the best-laid plans had a way of getting FUBAR'd in seconds.

CHAPTER THIRTEEN

Four days later, the plan to piss off Harold Lodge was working well. *Extremely* well. Ryleigh had kept her promise to not engage with her father, and she let Tiny do all the communicating with him.

The man wasn't happy.

Tiny winced every time Ryleigh passed her laptop over to him, but he didn't hesitate to take it. Her father was beyond angry. His messages were mostly swear words and threats. Tiny would've been amused if the situation wasn't so volatile.

The last thing he'd heard from the man was that Ryleigh would be sorry she'd messed with him. That they'd *all* be sorry.

It had been a full day since he'd last messaged, and even Ryleigh stealing everything but six dollars and sixty-six cents from one of his accounts hadn't made him message her again.

But he clearly wasn't sitting on his thumbs. Brick had just called an emergency meeting up at the lodge, and he wanted everyone to attend. By everyone, he meant all the women as well, and every employee who was currently on site.

Something had happened. Something bad.

As he walked toward the lodge with Ryleigh, Tiny's stomach churned. He looked at the woman at his side, and saw she was frowning as well. The stress of the last few days hadn't been good to her. She hadn't eaten much and wasn't sleeping well. He should know. He'd held her in his arms for the last four nights.

She'd agreed to sleep in his bed, and he wasn't ever going to let her go now, not if he could help it. Tiny had thought being in his bed with her might trigger some nightmares, but amazingly, it hadn't. He'd spent more time concerned about *her* than thinking about what had happened the last time he'd fallen asleep next to a woman.

Ryleigh tossed and turned, and *she* was the one suffering nightmares...and it sucked that Tiny couldn't do a damn thing about it. Her fucking father had a lot to answer for, and he prayed that everything would be over and done soon. That Brick's plan would actually work and they'd be able to flush the man out of whatever hole he'd been hiding in, so everything could go back to normal.

They entered the lodge and went straight to the conference room. Most everyone was already there. The women were all sitting at the table, and the guys were either pacing or leaning against walls. Everyone looked tense and unsure.

Brick didn't waste time telling them why they were there. "When Alaska logged in this morning, all the reservations for the next month had been canceled. Emails had been sent informing the guests, telling them they wouldn't get refunds, as per our cancelation policy."

"What? That's bullshit!"

"Oh my God."

"I'm sure there were a ton of complaints sent back in return."

"What are we going to do?"

Brick held up his hands to silence everyone. The room was so quiet, you could've heard a pin drop.

Tiny felt Ryleigh's hand tighten around his own. She hadn't sat at the table, but clung to her laptop with one hand and held onto him almost desperately with the other.

"She's already emailed everyone back, telling them there's been a computer error. That of course they'll get a refund, plus another 35 percent added on top of that. More importantly, we're going to have to deal with the fallout from this. Bad reviews are going to come in, and some people are going to have lost confidence in us, just as I feared would happen. We can rebound, we're just going to have to work harder."

"Are we rebooking them?" Luna asked.

"Yes," Brick said. "We've already rebooked those who still wanted their reservations. But after our current remaining guests leave—and the last is scheduled to be gone in two days—the following week is entirely unbooked. So...I think it's a perfect time to execute a plan to end this harassment once and for all. Without guests here, it'll be safer for everyone. Which means that anyone who doesn't live here will need to stay away too. Savannah, Carly, Jess, Luna, Robert, Joshua, Jason...that means all of you."

When the employees started arguing, saying they could

help with whatever plan was in motion, Brick stopped them. "I appreciate you wanting to help, but rest assured, if I could send everyone else away too, I would. But the asshole threatening our livelihood knows who our women are, how important they are to each of us, and I have a feeling he'd just go after them wherever they happen to be. So they're actually safer here than if we sent them to Los Alamos or somewhere else. I don't think he'll come after any of you, but you need to stay on your toes. Stay safe and smart until this is done."

He waited until everyone agreed.

Tiny had no problem with anything Brick decided. The man didn't need to consult with him or any of the other guys about this. He always had The Refuge's best interests at heart, this situation was no different.

"Also, if we can successfully execute Operation End This Shit, and if Harold Lodge is locked away where he belongs...I thought we could take the opportunity while there are no guests, and it's only family here at The Refuge, to have a wedding next weekend."

He turned to Alaska—and went down on one knee in front of the chair where she was sitting.

"I know I've already asked you to marry me, and you agreed to something small, but I was thinking maybe we could have our wedding here...and make it the celebration you've always wanted. Since we have the room, I thought we could invite some of our friends. My mom, maybe Reese's brother and wife, a few others. Let's make this a party...that is, if you still want one."

"Yes! I want!" Alaska almost screamed. "And yes! Invite *everyone*! All our friends. I want everyone to have someone here they love, not just us!"

It was weird to be both happy and pissed off at the same time. Ryleigh obviously felt the same, because after she hugged and congratulated both Brick and Alaska, she asked Tiny if they could go back to the cabin.

Once inside, she sat at the table and sighed. "This has to stop," she whispered.

"I agree. What do you want me to do?"

"Do?" she asked.

"Yeah. What should I tell your father to get him to agree to meet with you?"

Ryleigh sat up straighter. "It would be easier if I just did it."

"Not happening, hon. I don't want you to see one word of his venom aimed at you."

"I'm used to it," she said in a small voice.

"Don't care. And it's so damn wrong that you're used to it. No man should speak to *anyone* the way he has to you. Much less his own daughter."

"Okay. Let me just get this set up," Ryleigh said, pulling the laptop toward her and opening it.

But Tiny wasn't quite done with their conversation. He sat beside her, turned her chair around, and put his hand on her nape.

She stared up at him, looking exhausted.

"I appreciate you trusting me to talk to him and pass along what he says."

"It's okay."

"I don't know how you did it."

"Did what?" she asked.

"Survived living with that asshole for so long."

Ryleigh closed her eyes for a moment, then opened them as she said, "There was a lot of justifying his actions.

And I didn't have any friends, Tiny. Not one. No one to talk to. No one to tell me to get the hell out. No one to insist what he was doing was whacked. Most of the time he left me alone. I could surf the web, pretend my life was normal."

"Until he ordered you to steal someone's money."

"Yeah," Ryleigh agreed sadly. "I know I stayed too long. That someone looking in at my situation would be disgusted. Say that I was a grown woman, and that I must have enjoyed what I was doing at least a little, since I stayed as long as I did. But that wasn't the case. Not at all."

"I know. And everyone here knows it too. Has someone said something to you?" Tiny asked, getting irritated at just the thought of anyone belittling Ryleigh in that way. Especially when they knew nothing about her situation.

"No!" she exclaimed forcefully. "I just...sometimes I think this is all a dream. That I'm going to wake up and I'll be back in some dingy apartment, hiding from my father."

"You aren't. You're here, and you're so loved by everyone. Just yesterday, Lara came up to me and wanted to know what she could to do help you. She feels bad because you're taking the brunt of the shit from your father."

"It's okay," Ryleigh said.

"It's *not* okay. And we're going to stop him, but it's clear we'll have to force his hand. Tell me the truth, though—do you really think he's crazy enough to want to meet you in person? I mean, we probably need to come up with a secondary plan."

But Ryleigh was already shaking her head. "He'll do it. He's conceited enough to think he can outsmart me. All of us. I'm sure he's aware that you guys are going to be around when we meet, but he thinks he's smarter than everyone. But...what if we make him think he's already won? That he's broken us? *Me?*"

"What do you mean?" Tiny asked.

"What if we tell him that I'll give him his money back if he agrees to meet with me? Like...maybe I want to beg him in person to leave me and all of my friends alone?"

"And?" Tiny asked, thinking that she was on to something.

"We'll tell him that he can pick the meeting place. He'll love that. Again, because he'll think he can outsmart us. He'll assume we'll call the cops and FBI and whoever else, but he'll still think he's able to win—and my dad's *all* about winning. I just worry about any innocent people who might get caught up in all this."

"You're an innocent person too, you know," Tiny said.

In response, Ryleigh shrugged.

"You are," he insisted.

"I'm really not. I stole a lot of that money I ended up giving away. I was old enough to know better, and I did it anyway. Then I took it from my dad knowing he'd be pissed. That he'd want it back. And look what that led to. Tiny?"

"Yeah?"

"I'm scared."

"Of your father?"

"Yes, but also scared of what he might do to you. To The Refuge. To our friends."

"We aren't going to let anything happen," he said firmly. "If seven former special forces operatives can't protect one of their family members, there's something really wrong."

That earned Tiny a small chuckle. He was so proud of this woman. She'd had a hell of a life so far, and he was determined to make it better from here on out. He squeezed her nape, then leaned forward, resting his forehead on hers.

"Tiny?"

He smiled a bit as he lifted his head so he could look into her eyes. "Yeah?"

"I want you."

He blinked in surprise. But she didn't give him a chance to speak before she went on.

"I'm probably not going to be very good at first, but I'm a fast learner. The other day, when I told you that I was helping Tonka at the barn...I wasn't. I went to town. To the women's clinic. I'm sorry I lied to you but I was embarrassed to tell you what I was *really* doing, which is stupid because I'm an adult, but still."

She was babbling, and Tiny thought it was adorable.

"They gave me one of those birth control things they put under your skin. An implant. I'm nervous about having sex, but I want to try. With you. You won't hurt me, and I think you'll make it okay. Even my first time. As I said, I'll probably suck at it, but if you teach me what to do, I'll get better."

"Breathe, Ryleigh," Tiny ordered, even as every inch of his skin tingled with electricity. He was ready right this second to take her by the hand and drag her to his bed. But she was obviously nervous, and he hated that. "You're damn right I won't hurt you, and I have no doubt you'll be just as amazing in bed as you are with everything else you do. We can wait until all this crap with your dad is over and—"

"No!" she said with a frantic shake of her head. "I don't want to wait. We have no idea what he's got up his sleeve, and there's a chance he'll do something to mess this up too. He's already taken too much from me. I don't want him to take away the opportunity to show you how much you mean to me as well."

"We don't have to make love for me to know how much you care," he said gently.

"You...you don't want to?" Ryleigh asked uncertainly.

The fingers that were still wrapped around the back of her neck tightened. "I want to," he told her, his voice raw with desire. "There's nothing I want more. But you've waited a long time, I don't want you to rush into something that you might regret later."

"I won't *ever* regret letting you be my first," she said, honestly and firmly.

She humbled him. Tiny wasn't sure he deserved to be her first. He was sure he didn't deserve *her*, full stop. He'd been a dick to her, had mistrusted her, had actually been downright mean. And yet she still forgave him.

"I'd be honored to be the first man you make love to," he managed to say.

Ryleigh smiled. It was almost blinding. "When? Tonight?"

Tiny wanted to laugh. It was so like Ryleigh to want to schedule when she would lose her virginity. "Maybe," he told her. "Let's see how today goes. I want to make sure the mood is right. And if you're stressed out over whatever your father says, it won't be."

"I thought guys always wanted sex," Ryleigh said with a frown.

"Some do. But I'm not one of them. I want to make sure it's perfect for you. You'll only have one first time, and I want it to be a positive experience for you."

"Okay."

"Okay?" he asked, wanting to be sure they were on the same page.

"Yeah. But you should know, my dad has taken so much from me...a normal childhood, my mom, friends, a life... he's not going to take this as well."

She was so strong. Tiny admired her so much. "All right. How about a kiss to seal the deal?" he asked. He'd been staring at her lips for the last five minutes, and it was all he could do not to fall on her. Thinking about Ryleigh giving her virginity to him, being the first man, the *only* man, to see her naked, to get inside her...he was hanging on to his control by a thread.

"Yes. Please," she said with a smile, then she was leaning toward him. One of her hands landed on his thigh to brace herself as she lifted her head to his.

Their lips met, and this kiss felt different to Tiny for some reason. It felt like a promise of things to come.

His other hand came up to rest on the side of her head as he speared his fingers into her hair. He tilted her head slightly, so he could get deeper inside her mouth, and he showed her exactly what his cock was going to do when they got around to making love.

She moaned low in her throat, and her fingers dug into his thigh, making his cock press against his jeans painfully. All she'd have to do is move her hand a little to the left and she'd feel for herself how badly he wanted her.

Tiny lifted his head, and he loved the dazed look in her eyes. Her cheeks were flushed, her lips plumped from his kiss. She was as aroused as he was, from a simple kiss, and he could hardly believe she was willing to trust him with the gift of her body.

"You good?" he whispered, running his hand over her mussed hair.

"Yeah. You?"

He grinned. "I'm more than good."

She returned his smile.

They stared at each other for a beat before Tiny took a deep breath. "Let's get this over with, huh?"

Ryleigh nodded.

Tiny forced himself to drop his hands, but after she turned her chair back toward the table and had pulled the laptop closer, he put one hand on her thigh. He needed to touch her. Needed to stay close. He'd never felt this kind of need before. Not for sex. But to be as close as possible to another human being. Had he ever felt this way toward Sonja? The woman he thought he loved and was going to marry? No, definitely not.

Ryleigh's brow furrowed as she concentrated on logging into the dark web and pulling up the chat area she and her father had been using to communicate.

"Okay, it's ready," she said, pushing the computer toward him. Once more, Tiny was awed by the trust she showed him.

you bitch!

The two words seemed stark on the screen. Tiny had gotten used to the old-school look of the messages. He was relieved he didn't have to actually use html to communicate. The amount of other code around the messages that came in was jarring at first, but now he barely noticed.

i want my money

And I want you to leave me and my friends alone, Tiny typed as he pretended to be Ryleigh. *If I give it back, you have to promise to go away and stop harassing us.*

It was a ridiculous request. One that any battle-hardened soldier would never make. But at the moment, that wasn't who he was. He was pretending to be an exhausted daughter who wanted her dad to leave her alone.

give me my money, all of it, and i'll leave you alone

Tiny wanted to snort. As if he believed this asshole. But this was the first time in days he'd done anything but scream and curse at them in digital form. Time to put their plan into motion.

Fine. I'll transfer it and we can be done.

its not that easy, daughter dear. you owe me

I said I'd give the money back.

you owe me years of service. you agree to come with me, work with me like we used to, for say 10 years, then i'll call us even

Tiny's jaws were clenched together so hard, it would be a miracle if he didn't break a tooth. This fucking asshole thought Ryleigh would agree to go with him? To work with him for *ten years*? He was delusional. He took a deep breath to calm himself and typed out a response. Time to make this work in their favor. Clearly she wouldn't have to "beg" to meet with him. Not if Harold Lodge actually wanted his daughter back.

No way.

you want me to leave that pathetic motel you love so much alone you'll do it

Five

7

Five or nothing, dad.

fine. you agree to stay with me and work for me for 5 years, i'll leave your precious friends alone

Tiny's stomach hurt. The thought of Ryleigh going with this asshole made him want to puke. But he was doing exactly what Ryleigh thought he would. Agreeing to meet in person. Now to finish setting up the trap.

I agree. But if you do one thing against The Refuge, our deal is off. And you know I'll know, because let's face it...I'm the better hacker.

you've always thought you were so much smarter than you are. theres a green chile festival in los alamos tonight. meet me there and if i see one cop or anyone who looks like they are fbi, the deal is off and i'll take down the refuge for good

Tiny's heart was beating out of his chest. This was happening much faster than expected. Her dad had to be close by if he wanted to meet tonight. He could've been watching Ryleigh and The Refuge for days...or longer.

Deal.

and leave those special forces assholes home too

I don't know if I can get away without them wanting to know where I'm going.

figure it out. don't fuck me, daughter dear. you won't like the consequences if you do

The screen flickered and their conversation disappeared, just as it had every other time. No record of their messages ever remained.

"Well? What'd he say?" Ryleigh asked impatiently.

Tiny turned to her. He had things to do, details that had to be arranged immediately, but first he needed to make sure Ryleigh was aware of how much she meant to him. He took her face in his hands and kissed her. Hard. It wasn't nearly as long as he wanted it to be, because the clock was ticking.

"Tiny?" she asked nervously when he pulled back.

"He agreed to the meet. Tonight. In town at the green chile festival. We have shit we need to get done. *Fast.*"

Her eyes widened, and Tiny saw the moment panic struck.

"Tonight? Holy crap, we can't set this up that fast!"

"Yes, we can. It's not ideal, but we have no choice. You were right. He wants his money, but he's more concerned about getting you back under his thumb."

"What'd he say?"

"That if you agreed to work with him again for five years, he'd back off and leave us alone."

"Seriously?"

"Yeah."

"I'm never, *ever* going to work with or for him again. No way in hell!" Ryleigh spat.

"Shhhh, I know. And I have an idea he'd make you disappear for good if you *did* go with him. Not gonna happen. Meeting in town isn't ideal, as there will be a lot of civilians around, but he probably thinks you'll be more compliant in a crowd, that you won't want to cause a scene or get anyone else hurt. I'm also sure he thinks he can slip away easier with a lot of people about...but that also means the guys and I can blend in. Not sure we have time to get the FBI here, but we'll get with the cops in Los Alamos. Set up some cameras. We're going to get him, Ryleigh."

He saw her swallow hard, then nod. Tiny still had his hands on her face, and he said in a gentler tone, "We can still call this off if you want. I can message him back and say that you changed your mind. We can figure something else out."

Her shoulders straightened, even as her hands shook. "And have him cancel a year's worth of reservations? No. This needs to end. I need to see him. Need to watch him go down. He *is* going down, right?" she asked in a softer tone.

"He's going down," Tiny assured her.

"Okay, if you're sure."

"The one thing I'm *absolutely* sure about is that we're going to get this asshole. He won't be able to steal anyone else's money or ruin anyone else's life."

"He'll be watching for cops," Ryleigh warned.

Tiny was once more very impressed with this woman. She had to be stressed to the max, and yet she was still able to think like a soldier.

"I know. But the question is...will he be watching the skies?"

Tiny saw the moment it dawned on her what his plan was.

"No, I don't think he will be. But...crap, Tiny, we don't have much time."

"Right," he said. "Call Alaska, let her know what's happening. I'll get with the others. This is gonna be over tonight, sweetheart."

"I hope so," Ryleigh whispered.

CHAPTER FOURTEEN

Ry was nervous. No, she was scared to death. It had been years since she'd seen her father, and now here she was. Standing in a crowded festival in Los Alamos, waiting for him to arrive. She never liked the idea of her dad getting anywhere near The Refuge, and was relieved he chose the small town nearby. It still felt as if he was still too close to the one place she truly felt safe, but stepping foot on The Refuge property, he would've defiled it simply by his presence.

When she left The Refuge with Tiny earlier, she'd taken careful note of every detail...just in case. She'd heard Melba mooing in the barn, not happy she'd been brought into her stall early as a precaution, just in case her dad decided to make an unexpected appearance after all. The goats were probably eating their way out of their stalls already. The wind had blown gently through the trees, and the birds chirped merrily overhead.

It felt so surreal that things at The Refuge were as

normal as possible, when there was every possibility this meeting could go sideways and she'd never return.

Now, surrounded by so many people, she was damp with sweat, both from running around earlier, trying to get everything in place before going to meet her father, and from nervous energy.

The women and children were holed up in Alaska's cabin back at The Refuge, with Robert standing guard. The older man had volunteered, and when he'd brandished two of his cleavers from the kitchen, Ry wanted to cry. Everyone had been so supportive...and she was the one to bring this threat down upon them in the first place.

But no one saw it that way, which was baffling. If it hadn't been for her, there wouldn't be any cancelations, and none of the other shit that had happened in the last few weeks would've happened.

Well...this was her chance to fix it. And she needed to focus. Standing alone in the sea of people, she desperately studied the face of every older man she saw, looking for her dad.

Despite his warning that no cops be involved, Brick had arranged to fly in officials from the FBI office in Albuquerque. It was a risk, as her dad could be watching, but it was a *necessary* risk. The FBI wanted to get their hands on Harold Lodge almost as badly as Tiny and the rest of his friends did.

There were also officers hidden amongst the tourists and locals milling about, and Stone was standing by with the chopper, in case he needed to track her dad if he got away.

But what *really* allowed her to stand at the end of the

long street where vendors were set up and people were happily going about their evening, enjoying the weather and eating anything and everything that had to do with green chiles, was the knowledge that Tiny was also out there. Watching. Waiting. If her dad tried anything, she had no doubt Tiny would rush in to protect her. He wouldn't let her dad drag her away. He'd talked to her about what to do if her father pulled out a weapon. She wasn't to engage, wasn't to do *anything* but drop to the ground.

Tiny swore he'd kill him before he allowed Harold to hurt her.

And Ry believed him.

Though, she still couldn't quite believe she'd come right out and said she wanted to make love with him. It was bold, so unlike her. But the last few nights of sleeping next to him had her craving more. She wanted to know what she'd been missing. She wanted Tiny to be the one to show her.

The trip to the women's clinic had been embarrassing. No one had ever seen her...down there...in her entire life. She knew the appointment was way overdue, but the doctor had been kind and friendly, expertly helping Ry relax. She'd talked to her about her sexual history, or lack of it, and had a discussion about the pros and cons of different kinds of birth control. Ry had decided on the implant because it seemed like the most fool-proof method of contraception. Not that anything was one-hundred percent reliable, but there were a lot of things that could go wrong with pills or condoms.

Shaking her head, knowing she'd let her attention wander as a way of easing the stress she was under, Ry licked her lips and shifted, wishing her dad would just show up already.

Looking at her watch, she saw it was getting late. Her father hadn't given them a specific time to meet him, so they'd arrived shortly after sunset. They'd left as late as possible both to give themselves more time to prepare, and also to give Robert time to serve an early meal to the guests at The Refuge. It wasn't uncommon for guests to retire to their cabins after dinner on evenings when there wasn't a bonfire, which was a blessing tonight, given the circumstances. Otherwise, they hung out together in the lodge. Spike had been left behind to keep watch over the guests, and to help Robert guard the women, if necessary.

Now it was fully dark, and with every tick of the minute hand on her watch, her stress level increased.

It took another ten minutes of standing there, silently freaking out, before a man slowly approached. Ry would have recognized him anywhere. He was older, and his face was lined with deep wrinkles that hadn't been there the last time she'd seen him, but he still had that look of superiority he always wore. A look that told her without words how little he thought of her.

Her heart began beating a mile a minute. She was terrified of screwing this up. Terrified her father would somehow be able to grab her and spirit her away before Tiny or anyone else could stop him. The absolute last thing she wanted was to be alone with him, but she was doing this for her friends. And herself. So she could stop running and constantly looking over her shoulder. She wanted a life. A real life. And she thought she could have that here. At The Refuge. With Tiny.

Her father stalked closer and closer to where she

stood, taking his time, smiling at everyone he passed, even stopping to talk to a vendor for a moment. He probably wanted to intimidate her, but in reality he was giving her time to get her equilibrium back. Her nerves.

He finally came to a stop a few feet away, looking around carefully as he did. Ry held her breath, praying the officers and Tiny and his friends were well concealed in their hiding spots. Thankfully, her dad didn't seem to notice anything out of the ordinary.

"Good to see you, daughter dear. It's been a while," he said.

Ry swallowed hard. "Yes, it has."

"What? No hug? No happy reunion?" her dad sneered.

Ry didn't respond to the taunt, simply stared at him. That seemed to piss him off.

"We could've been unstoppable. We could be living in a mansion on the beach in Central America by now. Untouchable. Instead, you decided you were too good for me. I have news for you—you're just as bad as me, daughter dear. If you think you're above the law, you're wrong. You're *pathetic*. Nothing. You're less than worthless. Look at you...you're even uglier than you were when you left. I have no idea why anyone wants you, let alone *trusts* you. You're going to turn on them just like you did me. You've got these people snowed, but I know the real you. The girl I raised. I taught you what's important in life, and sooner or later you're going to remember it and do what you were born to do."

"And what's that?" Ry couldn't help but ask. She wasn't supposed to engage him, simply give law enforcement time to take him down...but his words made her feel like she was a little girl all over again. Desperate for his approval.

For even one kind word. Something she never got then, and figured she wouldn't get now. She knew that with absolute certainty...but the scared little girl who still lived deep inside her needed to know if she was *ever* anything other than a burden. A way to make money.

"You're a thief. A good-for-nothing, uneducated thief. All you're good at is *taking*. You're the most selfish person I've ever met in my life. You could've had the world at your fingertips, yet you double-crossed me. The man who raised you. Fed you. Put a roof over your head. When your mother left, I could've turned you over to the system. Let someone else deal with you. Instead, I taught you everything I knew. And what'd you do in return? Betrayed me."

Anger burned deep within Ry. She'd betrayed *him*? What a joke. For the first time in her life, she wasn't intimidated by this man. Didn't cower from his harsh words.

"I wish you *had* given me to the state. At least then I would've had a chance at a normal childhood. I'm beginning to think you *made* Mom leave. That she didn't want to, but you forced her away. You probably wouldn't let her take me either."

The look on her father's face told her everything she needed to know. She hadn't been sure what happened with her mother, but his look of surprise made it clear her guess was correct.

"I hate you," she growled. "I wish it had been *you* who'd left, not Mom."

To her surprise, her father laughed. Then his eyes narrowed, and Ry braced.

"She was weak! *Just like you!*"

Ry flinched. It had been so long since she'd been yelled

at like this, she'd forgotten how much she hated it. How it made her want to curl up in a ball and hide. Her face flamed, and with a quick glance, she saw a few people nearby staring at her father.

"She wanted me to stop training you. Wasn't going to happen, and I made that clear. Yeah, I kicked her out. Told her if she ever came back, she'd fucking regret it. That I'd take it out on *you*."

Ry's heart broke. No wonder her mom had a heart attack. She'd been forced to leave her child behind, knowing if she did anything to try to get her back, her daughter would pay the price.

"You were nothing but fucking trouble. I *hate* you. I've *always* hated you! You were only good for one thing— making me money. But I own your ass now. Five years is a fucking joke. You owe me double that. Quadruple. You'll stay with me and make me money until I'm good and goddamn ready to let you go, or everything you love and value will be gone. *Poof!* Gone! And don't even *think* of fucking me over, Ryleigh. You won't like the consequences."

He stepped toward her, and Ryleigh instinctively backed away.

Just in time too, because even as he reached for her, two SWAT members who'd been boxing him in were tackling him to the ground. They'd come up behind him and taken him down before he could blink.

The scream that left his mouth was chilling. It wasn't one of terror—it was frustration. Anger. And it made Ry's blood run cold.

More officers appeared from the crowd, surrounding her father and keeping dozens of curious onlookers back while also making sure Harold couldn't escape. Then Tiny was there. He and Pipe led her away, telling her what a good job she'd done, how amazing she was.

Ry could still hear her father yelling...threatening her, The Refuge, the officers who were handcuffing him.

She felt dizzy, glad that he was finally in custody, but scared to death that something would happen and he'd be released. Let go because the charges wouldn't stick or because he made bail.

If he got out, he really *would* kill her this time. Of that, Ry had no doubt.

"Easy, hon, you're okay."

Ry heard Tiny's voice as if she was in a long dark tunnel. She was moving by rote, not thinking about where she was being taken.

"She's in shock."

"I know. Let's get her back to The Refuge."

"FBI will want to talk to her."

"Then they can come find her there," Tiny growled.

"Got it. Send them to your cabin, I assume?"

"No, she needs her friends. I'm thinking the lodge. Will you call Alaska?"

"On it."

Ry didn't want to go to the lodge. She wanted to get in her car and drive. To get far, far away. Away from her father, from his threats. But Tiny ushered her into the back seat of his car and pulled her against him as Pipe drove them back to The Refuge.

When they arrived, Tiny led her through the front doors of the lodge, and she vaguely heard Spike telling the two guests lounging there that everything was fine. That *she* was fine.

Ry felt anything but fine.

She was urged downward until she was sitting. Forcing herself to focus, she saw Tiny crouched in front of her, looking worried, Pipe on the phone next to him. Then she realized where she was. In the kitchen.

For some reason, that struck her as funny. Tiny hadn't brought her to one of the conference rooms, or sat her in one of the comfy leather chairs in the lobby. No, he'd brought her to the kitchen, of all places.

"He's wrong, you know," Tiny said. It was the first thing he'd said in quite a while. They'd driven in silence, Tiny giving her time to come to terms with what had just happened, and she appreciated it.

Ry looked at him in confusion. She felt as if her head was stuffed with cotton.

"You aren't weak. Not in the least. You're one of the strongest women I've ever met. And one of the smartest. Even without any formal schooling, you're better than one of the best computer geniuses we know...and Tex has admitted that without any qualms. Your father tried to hold you down, and yet you were still able to fly. You're too good for me. For this out-of-the-way corner of the world, but I want you to stay so badly it makes my heart hurt. We need you, Ryleigh. All of us."

Before she could respond, tell him how much his words meant to her, the room began to fill. Then Tiny was brushed aside and Alaska was there, pulling Ry to her feet and hugging her. She was passed from one woman to the next, each one wrapping their arms around her and telling her how relieved they were that she was all right.

Then the others...Robert, Luna, Brick, Tonka...they all took their turn, as if they couldn't function without putting their hands on her, seeing for themselves that she was unharmed.

Their actions, more than any words, made Ry finally understand that these people genuinely liked her. Were worried about her. Wanted her around for more than her computer skills.

Her dad was wrong, Tiny was right. She wasn't weak. She'd not only beaten her father, she'd somehow found a home.

As happy as she was to have everyone there, she needed just one person right now.

Tiny.

Her eyes scanned the very crowded kitchen until she found him. He was standing by the door with Brick, watching her intently. Ry knew without a doubt if she gave the slightest indication she was uncomfortable, he'd be there, escorting her out in a heartbeat.

Licking her lips and offering a tiny smile, she tried to let Tiny know without words how much she appreciated him. How glad she was that he was there. How much she loved him.

The thought wasn't startling in the least. She'd loved him forever. From probably the first week she'd started working at The Refuge. That's why she hadn't left. Why she'd made excuse after excuse to stay, even when she knew it might mean her father could find her. She couldn't leave Tiny.

As if her thoughts drew him, he pushed off the wall and came toward her. When he reached her, he asked, "You good?"

"I am now," Ry said honestly.

The look of approval in his eyes, the spark of desire in

his expression, made Ry want to take his hand and drag him out of the kitchen and back to the cabin and insist he make love to her immediately. She'd held on to her virginity for this reason. To give it to someone she loved.

But she had obligations to take care of first. Talking with FBI agents, reassuring her friends, going online and making sure her father hadn't set up any booby traps to go off if he didn't return from his trip to escort her to wherever he was currently hiding out.

Later, all bets were off. Things might not work out between her and Tiny in the long run, but she'd make sure he knew how appreciative she was of everything he'd done for her. And the most valuable thing she had to give him... was herself.

CHAPTER FIFTEEN

Tiny had never been more proud of anyone in his entire life as he was Ryleigh. The evening had been long and stressful, and yet she'd handled it better than some of the newbie SEALs he'd been in charge of. Yes, she'd had a hard moment after her father had been taken down, but surrounded by her friends, she'd been able to get control of herself again.

She'd been amazing with the FBI agents. They already knew most of her part in her father's schemes, but she'd patiently answered the same questions over and over, without hesitation, for two solid hours. Then they finally reassured not only Ryleigh, but everyone at The Refuge that Harold Lodge's days of hacking and stealing money were over.

It was a huge relief.

Tiny was glad to be back home, where it was just him and Ryleigh. Robert had sent them home with a container full of chocolate chip cookies, and had even given Ryleigh a box of Christmas Tree Cakes. She'd looked at him and barely been able to hold back her laughter. She'd slipped the box to Lara later, with Tiny's approval, because she knew how much the other woman loved them.

If Tiny thought Ryleigh would relax once they got home, he was mistaken. She'd been sitting at the table on her computer for an hour and a half, fingers racing. Checking, double-checking, and triple-checking that her dad hadn't somehow scheduled some sort of electronic siege on The Refuge in case she double-crossed him.

To her surprise, she hadn't been able to find anything. He was seemingly as arrogant as he appeared, thinking he'd be able to intimidate his daughter into doing whatever he wanted. But Ryleigh was stronger than he'd thought.

When Ryleigh sighed for the tenth time, Tiny was done. She'd done everything she could for the moment. Tomorrow would be another day for her to scour the dark web for any sign of her father's despicable schemes.

"Come on," he told her, taking her elbow in his hand and encouraging her to stand.

"Oh, but there's one more thing I want to check," she said.

Tiny reached out and closed the laptop. "Tomorrow," he said firmly, before leading her down the hall. He brought her straight to the bathroom attached to their room.

Her mouth opened in shock. "Tiny...what?"

He'd filled the tub with hot water and bubble bath. Okay, it was the liquid soap he used in the shower because he didn't have any bubble bath on hand, something he planned to remedy as soon as possible. But he didn't think she'd mind, because he hadn't missed how much she liked to smell him at night when they sat together on the couch.

"Tonight was hard, and you were amazing. But I know you have to be sore from the tension you were under. I thought a long hot bath might do you some good."

She looked at him with tears in her eyes. "No one's ever done something like this for me before."

That made Tiny sad, and he vowed to do a better job at spoiling her. "Relax, Ryleigh. Take as long as you want." He kissed her forehead, then her lips, then he left her, closing the bathroom door almost all the way, leaving it open a crack so he could hear her if she needed anything.

He went back out into the cabin and finished straightening up. He wiped down the kitchen counters, washed her used glass, folded the blanket on the couch, fiddled around a little bit longer before heading to the guest bathroom to brush his teeth. After, he went into his bedroom. He could hear the water sloshing around in the bathtub, and it made him smile.

Tiny changed into the cotton pants he'd been wearing to sleep and climbed under the covers. He picked up a book but couldn't concentrate, especially not when he heard Ryleigh humming softly to herself.

He loved the sound. It was happy. Content. And Lord knew the woman hadn't had a lot to be content about lately. This thing with her father was stressing her out. Hell, it was stressing *him* out and it wasn't even his dad. She'd handled the pressure of facing him amazingly well. Tiny hadn't been thrilled to leave Ryleigh in that street by herself.

Oh, he knew she wasn't technically alone, there were lots of people watching her, and festivalgoers everywhere... but she'd had to confront Lodge all by herself, which he'd hated. Intellectually, he knew her dad was a piece of shit, but hearing the things he'd said to her had literally shaken his foundation.

You're pathetic. Nothing. Less than worthless.

All you're good at is taking.

You're the most selfish person I've ever met in my life.

I hate you. I've always hated you.

Tiny shook his head. Harold Lodge didn't know his daughter. At all. Ryleigh wasn't selfish. She was the most generous person he'd ever known. She didn't care about money. Not in the least. The donations she handed out like they were candy were lavish and the charities well thought out. She did her research to make sure they were legit, and all the good that money did couldn't be denied.

Yes, the money had been stolen in the first place, but she was doing all she could to atone for the things her dad made her do. In Tiny's eyes, she'd more than done so.

And for a father to come out and tell his daughter that he hated her...Tiny couldn't even understand that. Not for a second. His heart hurt for Ryleigh. Those words had to have stung, and yet she'd held her head up high and did what she had to do to help put the man behind bars for a very long time.

A noise interrupted his thoughts, and Tiny turned his head. His breath caught in his throat at the sight of Ryleigh standing in the bathroom doorway.

Her hair was damp, curling slightly around her temples. Her skin was dewy and there was a flush to her cheeks. She hadn't put on the pajama set she'd been wearing to bed, which he'd set on the vanity before starting her bath. Instead, she wore nothing but a blue towel. It was wrapped around her body, barely reaching her upper thighs. Her shoulders were exposed...and it was all Tiny could do not to throw the blanket off, stalk over to her, and bury his nose in the crook of her neck and shoulder.

His cock hardened in his pants and he licked his lips.

Ryleigh looked nervous and unsure, hands worrying the towel where it was tucked securely around her chest.

He opened his mouth to say something reassuring—when she shocked the shit out of him by letting the towel fall to the floor.

Tiny could only blink at the vision in front of him. If he'd been aroused by the sight of her in a towel, seeing her completely nude made him want to drop to his knees in worship.

"Ryleigh?" he managed to croak. He couldn't move. If he did, he'd lunge at her. Scare the crap out of her. He held himself stock still with the iron control he'd learned as a Navy SEAL.

"I don't want to wait. Today sucked. I was really scared. My dad could've done anything. He's paranoid and greedy and nothing will keep him from getting his hands on me. He could've hurt me today...and it would've kept me from finding out what sex is all about."

She was babbling, and Tiny wanted to kiss the lip that she was now biting in consternation. But he needed to make one thing clear before he did anything else.

"I want you," he said. "You're beautiful. So damn beautiful. It's taking all my control to stay in this bed right now and not throw you over my shoulder and take you on the floor right where you're standing. But I don't want to have sex, *just* to have sex. If all you want is someone to take your virginity, to experience sex finally, you can find that anywhere. Hell, I'm sure you know better than I do that all it'll take is an online ad and you'll have men lined up to do the honor.

"I want more than that. I want you to be standing there naked—looking so damn sexy I can't even stand it—specifically because you want *me*. Because you can't bear to go one more night without being as close as you can get... to *me*. Because you crave the emotional connection we have with one another, and you want it to go bone deep. If you don't want that, if you don't want a long-term relationship with me...as much as it'll hurt me to see, you should pick up that towel and head back to the room you were sleeping in before."

Tiny held his breath. He was practically panting, taking short, choppy breaths as he waited for her decision. Honestly, her being a virgin scared the shit out of him. He wasn't one of those men who dreamed about being a woman's first. There was a lot of responsibility that went along with that. He could hurt her, *really* hurt her, and that was the last thing he ever wanted to do. He'd done enough of that.

"If I have to sleep in your arms one more night and *not* have you inside of me, I think I'll die."

Tiny was moving before he could think. He *did* drop to his knees in front of Ryleigh, looking up at her in awe. His hands gripped her waist, immediately noticing that her skin was so damn soft. And warm. And she smelled like him. His cock got even harder. He needed inside this woman. Right this damn second.

But no...he had to go slow. Make sure her first time was good. Better than good—earth-shattering. Tiny closed his eyes and rested his forehead on her belly. Her hands came up and tangled in his hair. His dick twitched in his pants.

He was so fucked. If he was turned on simply by the feel of her fingers, he was doomed.

"Tiny?" she whispered.

He hated the uncertainty in her voice. He opened his eyes and met her gaze. At least, he *meant* to meet her gaze; her perfect tits distracted him. Her nipples were hard, probably from the cool air, and the fleshy globes were a gorgeous handful. Moving his hands up her sides slowly, he licked his lips as he stared at her chest. He gently palmed her breasts, and was rewarded by Ryleigh's small gasp as she arched into his touch.

She was incredibly responsive. And suddenly, Tiny was ravenous. He'd wanted this from the first time he'd seen this woman. Wanted her in his bed, under him. He hadn't admitted it back then, but that didn't make it any less true. Part of the reason her lies hurt so bad, and why he'd treated her like absolute shit, was because he'd been so drawn to her from the moment she'd stepped onto the property. And her deception had felt like a personal attack.

But it hadn't actually had anything to do with him. She'd simply been doing what she had to do in order to keep her father from finding her.

"Be sure," he said in a deep voice that didn't sound like him in the least. "Because if you give yourself to me, I'm keeping you. As long as you'll have me, I'm yours."

She nodded.

"Say it," Tiny ordered, not sure where this dominant side was coming from.

"I want this. You."

Thank fuck.

Tiny stood and shoved his pants over his hips. It wasn't a smooth move, and when her eyes widened as she got a glimpse of his rock-hard dick, he realized he probably should've eased her into seeing his body. She was a virgin, after all.

But then she shocked the shit out of him by reaching out a hand. Her fingers closed around his cock, and it was all he could do not to come right then and there.

"It's hard but soft at the same time," she said in awe.

Tiny wanted to laugh, but he couldn't do anything other than stand there and let her touch him.

"Does it hurt? It looks like it hurts," she said.

"Yes and no," Tiny told her honestly. "It's a good hurt."

Her hand fell from his dick, and Tiny wanted to cry. But then she brought her fingers to his chest. They brushed against the scar on his left pec, where Sonja had stabbed him. "So close to your heart," she muttered.

"Close, but not close enough," he told her.

Ryleigh looked up at him. "I did it, you know," she said, almost conversationally.

"Did what?"

"Found her. Took all the money from her prison account. Altered her records so it looks like she hasn't been a good prisoner. Took away her visitor privileges. And I'll *keep* doing it too." She sounded almost belligerent now.

Tiny would talk to her about that later. Make her undo the changes she'd made to Sonja's record. He didn't like the woman, but he'd finally moved on. Didn't want to think about her ever again. And while Ryleigh's anger on his behalf felt good, he didn't want *her* spending an iota of time thinking about the woman either.

"I'm thinking I don't want to talk about her right now," he said, taking Ryleigh's hand in his and backing toward the bed. Neither said a word as he brought them where they both wanted to be.

"If at any time you change your mind, it's okay," he felt compelled to say. This was a big deal, and he'd accept it if she decided she didn't want to give him her virginity after all.

"I'm not going to change my mind," she said with absolutely no hesitation in her voice, his ex seemingly forgotten. "I want you, Tiny. I want my first time to be with you because I know you'll make it good. Memorable. Amazing."

"Oh, no pressure, none at all," Tiny said a little sarcastically.

Ryleigh giggled. And the small sound made him smile. This woman was adorable, and sexy, and strong as hell. And he wanted to be the kind of man she deserved. He wasn't sure he could be, but he sure as fuck was going to try.

He let go of her hand and got on the bed, scooting over until he was lying in the middle of the mattress. He put one arm behind his head and the other stayed by his side. Ryleigh moved as if in a trance, climbing up and walking on her knees to his side. She sat on her heels and stared down at him.

Tiny was taking her in too. He couldn't get over how perfect she was. Perfect for *him*. His hands itched to touch her, to give her pleasure, but he forced himself to lie still as she studied him.

Her hand shook as she reached out. Tiny braced himself for her touch, and even then, he still jerked when her fingers made contact with his bare skin.

Ryleigh yanked her hand back, but he grabbed it gently

and brought it back to his chest. He pressed it flat against him, encouraging her to continue. It only took a moment before he was able to put his hand back at his side, and she was running her fingers up and down his chest. It was his turn for his nipples to harden. She brushed against one during a trip up his body, and she smiled.

"Yours get hard too," she said.

It wasn't really a question, but Tiny answered anyway. "Oh yeah."

Her fingers tweaked his nipples, and each touch made his cock twitch where it lay on his belly. Ryleigh didn't seem to notice, she was too fixated on his chest. Then she made his breath stall by leaning down and taking one of his nipples into her mouth.

Tiny let out a little grunt as his hand palmed the back of her head. She lifted her gaze and smiled again. "That okay?"

"More than okay. Stupendous," he told her.

In response, she once more wrapped her lips around his nipple. This time, she flicked it with her tongue, and another groan erupted from Tiny's throat. She was going to be the death of him, but he wouldn't dare deny her this. He'd let her explore his body as long as she wanted. He wanted her to be comfortable with him...and when he turned the tables and did the same things to her, he didn't want her to be surprised.

Her hand came up and pinched his other nipple lightly.

"Harder, sweetheart. You aren't hurting me. Pinch it harder."

Tiny felt a spurt of precome on his belly when she did as he requested.

Ryleigh lifted her head and studied her hands as she

played with his nipples. It was almost torture for Tiny, but the best kind.

"Kiss me," he ordered.

She leaned forward, bracing herself on his chest as she brushed her lips against his. But Tiny was too turned on for a chaste kiss. His tongue immediately pressed against the seam of her lips, demanding entry. She opened for him willingly, and he took what she so freely offered.

Had Tiny ever been this turned on by a kiss and a few tweaks of his nipples? No, the answer was definitely no. Ryleigh had him turned inside out, and he didn't think he'd ever be the same after this.

For a brief second, terror raced through him. If she betrayed him, it would destroy him. He thought he'd been irrevocably changed by Sonja's actions, but he'd be absolutely gutted if Ryleigh was using him for some reason.

But as soon as the thought registered that Ryleigh might be anything but exactly who he'd learned she was over the last few weeks, it dissipated. He could trust her. Tiny felt that down to his bones. She wouldn't screw him over. Wouldn't cheat on him. Would never attempt to kill him in his sleep.

He tore his mouth from hers and found he was having trouble catching his breath. He wanted nothing more than to roll over and take her, eat her out, ease his fingers into her pussy to get her ready for him, but he wanted to make sure she was completely comfortable with his body before he took over.

"Keep going, sweetheart," he told her.

She looked confused.

"Touch me. All over. Get used to me. See what's going

to be inside of you. Giving you pleasure. My cock. Because when you're done exploring, it's going to be *my* turn."

She blushed, but her eyes flashed with lust as she nodded. Sitting back on her heels, Ryleigh turned her attention back to his chest. Her fingers ran over his skin once again, but this time they didn't stop at his nipples. Her gaze went down to his toes, then back up, stopping between his legs.

"You're big," she said, but Tiny didn't hear any fear in her voice. Only matter-of-factness.

"I am, but you're going to be soaking wet for me. You'll take me without any problem, Ryleigh, I give you my word."

She nodded, as if that was all the reassurance she needed. Then she was touching him.

It was all Tiny could do not to come all over himself.

Her thumb brushed the tip of his dick, spreading the precome she'd already coaxed out of him over his skin. Then she shocked the shit out of him by touching her tongue to the head.

"Fuck!" Tiny muttered before reaching down and grabbing the base of his cock in a stranglehold.

Ryleigh sat back and lifted her hands to her sides, palms out. "Did that hurt?" she asked.

"No, it felt good. Too good. I almost came right then and there. And getting my load in your face isn't something you want for your first experience of a man's orgasm."

"Really?" she asked.

"Yes, really. I'm not a fan of doing that anyway. It's always seemed degrading to me. I'm sure some women totally love it, but you could actually get an infection from getting come in your eyes. At least, I've read some porn stars have."

To his surprise, Ryleigh giggled. "Yeah, that doesn't sound good. But I was actually wondering if you really were about to come. Just from me licking you."

Tiny groaned again. This woman was going to unman him. "Yeah, hon, just from that. You have no idea how sexy you are right now. Kneeling at my side, eyes devouring me, your tits begging for my mouth and fingers. I can even smell your arousal. So yeah, you touching my cock with your tongue almost made me lose it. What did you think?"

He loved that his dirty words seemed to turn her on even more. She squirmed, and even as he watched, her chest flushed a deeper pink.

"Would it upset you if I said I didn't love it?" she asked.

"Not at all. Some people enjoy it and others don't. It doesn't make any difference to me if you don't like the taste."

"Do you?"

"Do I what? Like the taste of your juices? I don't know. Why don't you touch yourself, then give me your finger and let me see?" He was pushing her, Tiny knew it, but he couldn't make himself stop. He wanted to taste her more than he wanted to breathe. Craved it. Craved *her*. He wasn't sure Ryleigh would be brave enough to do as he asked, but he shouldn't have doubted her.

She reached between her legs, and Tiny had to squeeze his cock harder at the sight.

"Go up on your knees. That's it. Like that. God, you're so beautiful. Touch yourself. Oh fuck, that's perfect. Ease your finger inside your pussy, sweetheart. Are you wet?" She removed her finger, and Tiny saw it glistening in the light. "Oh yeah, you're wet. Please, let me taste—give me that finger."

She sat back on her heels and shyly inched her hand forward. Tiny couldn't let go of his dick because if he did, he'd immediately come all over his belly, so he grabbed hold of her wrist with his other hand, lifting his head eagerly.

He took her index finger into his mouth and her musk practically made his taste buds explode. She tasted divine. He licked and sucked all the juice off her finger, trying to make it as sensual as possible for her.

He must have succeeded, because her gaze looked hazy and her breaths were coming out in pants. "Tiny..." she pleaded.

"For the record, I *love* your taste. Christ, it's like ambrosia...whatever the fuck that is. I want more. I want to lick your pussy until you're coming all over my face. Then I want to lick you clean and make you come all over again."

Yet again, Tiny didn't know where this dirty talk was coming from. He wasn't usually like this. He was more of a no-nonsense kind of lover. Made sure his partner was satisfied, but he didn't talk a whole lot. With Ryleigh, everything was different. Because she was made for him and he was made for her. "Are you done?" he asked.

"Done?"

"Exploring...for now. You can look and touch all you want later. I'm hanging on by a thread, sweetheart. I need you to give me permission to move. To pleasure you."

"Yes. Please. Touch me."

That was all Tiny needed to hear. He had her on her back before either of them took another breath. The feel of her body under his was what he'd been waiting for all his life. He felt not one speck of doubt.

"In case I forget to tell you later, thank you."

"For what?"

"For giving me your body. For trusting me to make this good for you. For letting me be your first."

"You're welcome," she said shyly.

Then Tiny was done talking. He kissed her briefly before moving his lips to her ear. Then her neck. He inhaled deeply, loving the smell of his soap on her skin. He continued to her chest and finally got his mouth on the tits that had been tormenting him ever since she'd dropped her towel.

He was going to devour her, one inch at a time. When he was done, she'd be delirious with pleasure...and hopefully the pain of taking a cock for the first time wouldn't be overwhelming.

CHAPTER SIXTEEN

Ryleigh couldn't think. Couldn't do anything but feel. She'd touched herself over the years, but nothing had ever felt as good as Tiny's hands and mouth on her skin. He ate at her breasts as if he was a starving man and she was a three-course meal. She felt electricity go from her nipples down to her pussy, and it made her shift restlessly on the bed under him.

She needed something. Needed *more*.

As if Tiny could read her mind, he shifted down her body, pushing her legs farther apart, making room for his shoulders. He reached up and grabbed a pillow, stuffing it under her butt. She was on full display to him, and it made her a little nervous.

But when he spoke, saying more dirty things that made all her inhibitions disappear, need welled up once more.

"Look at you, so damn pretty," Tiny whispered as he stared between her legs. "And it's mine. *All mine*."

Some women might have been irritated by the owner-ship and possessiveness they heard in a man's voice as he said something like that. Ryleigh couldn't help being turned on by it.

One of his hands came up and brushed against her pubic hair. It tickled, making Ryleigh squirm against him.

He smiled up at her as he continued to pet the small strip of hair.

Ryleigh dropped her head, then immediately picked it up again when she felt Tiny's breath against skin that hadn't seen the light of day in another person's presence. Her gaze met his.

"Grab another pillow and put it under your head," he ordered.

Ryleigh frowned. "Why?"

"So you can watch what I'm doing without getting a crick in your neck. I just got you relaxed in the tub, the last thing I want is you pulling a muscle."

Ryleigh wanted to be embarrassed by her obvious curiosity to see what he was doing, but she was quickly learning that Tiny didn't feel uneasy about *anything* that went on in bed. She should have realized that when he'd licked her finger, after she'd put it inside her body.

Since she really *was* curious, and she desperately wanted to watch him, she did as he requested and stuffed another pillow under her head. Now she was propped up and could see what he was doing between her legs without strain.

"You've orgasmed before?" he asked, as he began to gently caress her clit. It felt good, but the touch wasn't nearly hard enough to make her come.

"Of course."

"There's no 'of course' about it. Some women aren't comfortable with masturbating."

The word made Ryleigh's cheeks heat.

Tiny grinned wickedly. "Oh, we're going to have so much fun." Then he seemed to be done talking. His gaze went back to her pussy and his tongue came out, licking her outer lips. It felt nice.

He did it again. And again. Then he pushed her legs farther apart, almost uncomfortably so, lowered his head and covered her clit with his mouth. His gaze moved up to hers...and he watched her as he began to lick and suck the bundle of nerves.

Now, *that* felt good. Really good! The muscles in Ryleigh's belly contracted, and she tried to close her legs, to no avail.

Tiny's hands came to rest on her inner thighs, and he kept her spread open for him.

All of a sudden, looking into his eyes seemed too intimate. Ryleigh closed her eyes.

His mouth lifted from between her legs. "No, watch me. I want to see you go over the edge. I want to see you reach orgasm for the first time under my mouth."

She couldn't. But when he said, "Please," Ryleigh was helpless.

Her eyes opened, and she met his gaze.

"Thank you," he whispered. Then he kissed her clit before once more taking it into his mouth.

This time, his touch wasn't light. He sucked strongly, making her ass come off the bed. He smiled but didn't pull away from her as he concentrated on making her come.

Ryleigh barely felt his finger easing into her body, but when she clenched down, it felt different...fuller.

"Tiny!" she gasped.

He didn't respond, simply held on as she bucked under him...used his tongue almost like a vibrator against her clit.

She felt the orgasm rising, but it was different than anything she'd felt in the past. Bigger. It was almost scary, and she wanted to beg Tiny to stop. But as soon as she had the thought, she dismissed it. He wouldn't let anything happen to her. He'd keep her safe.

She'd had the same thought earlier, when she was waiting for her father to show up. She'd been scared then too, but knowing Tiny was out there, watching over her, gave her the courage to stay the course. Just as she would now.

The feelings inside her welled up, consuming her, just like Tiny was doing.

The orgasm surprised her. One second she was nearly desperate, the next she was flying over the edge. She'd never felt anything as good in her entire life. Every muscle tensed, and she shook as pleasure overwhelmed her. Through it all, she kept her gaze locked onto Tiny's. It was more intimate than she ever could've imagined. Which made the experience all the more mind-blowing.

She thought Tiny would back off once she came. She felt his finger sliding out of her body, which made another jolt of pleasure shoot through her, but then he lowered his head farther and licked her pussy. He did it again. And again. He ate at her as if he'd never get enough.

"Tiny!" she said breathlessly.

In response, he simply grunted as he continued to lick up every drop of pleasure he'd wrung from her. To Ryleigh's surprise, she felt another orgasm building. Watching him, seeing how much pleasure he was getting from tasting her, was a massive turn-on. He hadn't lied when he'd said he enjoyed her taste.

He must've felt how close she was, because he finally lifted his head from between her legs and scooted up a little on the bed. His shoulders still kept her legs parted around him, but now he brought one of his hands up to her clit. He used his thumb to strum the bundle of nerves firmly. The other hand went between her legs and he eased a finger inside her.

Ryleigh reached down and grabbed his wrist with one hand.

"Am I hurting you?" he asked softly.

"No, it's just...I...I don't know." Ryleigh couldn't describe the feelings coursing through her body. She felt as if she was having an out-of-body experience. Like this was happening to someone else.

"Just feel, hon. That's all you need to do."

That was the problem. She was feeling too much.

He eased his finger in and out of her body, and soon, it didn't feel like enough. She needed more, but she had no idea what she actually needed or wanted.

Tiny did. He added a second finger to the first, and while she felt a slight pinch of pain, it quickly receded as pleasure bloomed in her pussy. She felt full, and her inner muscles clamped down on him, his cue to stroke her clit harder and faster.

"That's it, Ryleigh. You're stretching around my fingers just like you will around my cock. You're going to take me so deep. You're soaking wet, and you taste so damn good. I could spend every night drinking you down. So damn responsive, so beautiful. And mine. All fucking mine."

She smiled at that, then gasped as his pinky brushed against her ass.

"You like that?" he asked. "Anal isn't my thing, but there are a ton of nerve endings back there. Close your eyes. Just feel."

She immediately did as he requested, glad for the reprieve. Swirls of color swam across her eyelids as she neared her second orgasm of the night. She was hot, burning up, and strained to reach the pinnacle once more.

"I've got you, hon. I'll make you feel good."

And he did. His fingers played her like a priceless instrument. A low keen escaped her lips as she flew over the edge once again. She gripped his wrist as tightly as she could, fingers still deep inside her body. Yet it *still* wasn't enough. She humped his hand, out of control, and the pleasure almost overwhelmed her.

She felt him moving between her legs, but she didn't have the energy or mind space to try to figure out what he was doing.

"Open your eyes. Look at who's going to be inside you. Look at the man who's going to make you his, just as you make him yours. Look at me, Ryleigh."

She pried her eyes open to see Tiny looming over her. His turquoise eyes seemed to be even brighter than usual. She felt something between her legs, and she looked down.

He was nestled between her knees, his cock resting on her pussy. But something was wrong. She couldn't feel his heat. And his cock didn't look like it had earlier. Then she realized...

"You're wearing a condom," she blurted.

"Yeah."

"But I'm on birth control," she said in confusion. "The lady said it was okay to have sex without one."

"I'm protecting you, sweetheart," he said tenderly.

Ryleigh was sick of being protected. She wanted wild, messy, out-of-control sex. She wanted to feel all of Tiny. She shook her head. "No. Take it off."

"Ryleigh," he started, in a conciliatory tone.

"No!" she repeated more firmly this time. "I want all of you. I don't want any barriers."

"I haven't been with a woman in more than a year, but I can't prove that," he told her.

"I trust you, Tiny. Hell, you've done more for me than anyone in my life ever has. I trust you completely." Then something occurred to her. "Oh...but if you don't trust *me*, I understand. I mean, I—"

She didn't get to finish what she was saying before Tiny growled low in his throat and ripped the condom off his cock. He stroked himself a few times, until a bead of precome formed at the tip. Then he looked her in the eyes and said, "Last chance to back out. I said this before, but I'll say it again. Once you let me inside, that's it. I'm yours."

Ryleigh liked that. Liked that he hadn't claimed she was his again; frankly, that was a given as far as she was concerned. Instead warning her that if they had sex, he'd belong to *her*.

In response, Ryleigh reached between them and brushed his hand off his cock, placing the tip at her opening. "I'm ready."

"Look at me. Again, don't look away. This will probably hurt, but I swear I'll make it good after."

Ryleigh nodded. She couldn't lie. She was nervous about this.

But he didn't draw out the anticipation. He pressed into her slowly, but surely.

Ryleigh felt a pinch, then she gasped as he continued to push inside her. It *did* hurt. A lot. Tears sprang to her eyes, but she did as Tiny asked and didn't look away from him.

"It's over. It's done. I'm in. Breathe, Ryleigh. I'm not moving. You're okay."

She wanted to push him away. He was big, huge. Enormous. And it felt as if he was tearing her in two. A small whimper escaped her lips.

"I know, I'm sorry. God, I'm so sorry. Give it a moment. If it still hurts, I'll pull out and we'll be done for now. But this is the only time it'll hurt this much, I promise."

Even as he spoke, the pain lessened. It didn't disappear, but instead turned into a throbbing ache.

Tiny shifted up carefully until he was bracing himself on one hand above her. Then he moved the other between their bodies. Without a word, he began to caress her clit gently. Ryleigh was relieved when pleasure began to override the pain.

"Better?" he asked.

Ryleigh couldn't speak, she could only nod.

"Good. This orgasm probably won't be as intense as the other two, but it'll help loosen your muscles. Yeah, like that."

With every caress of his finger on her clit, Ryleigh could feel her inner muscles—previously clenched as tightly as possible, as if that could prevent him from going deeper—relaxing more and more. And as they did, his length inside her began to actually feel good. Better than his fingers. More substantial.

Her breaths came faster, and while she was aware she was digging her nails into his biceps, she couldn't seem to make herself let go.

"God, you have no idea how good you feel. You're so hot and tight. Nothing in my life has felt better than being inside your pussy. I'm going to make this up to you. Next time it won't hurt. I swear. You'll feel nothing but pleasure. I can feel you fluttering around my cock. It's like you're caressing me from the inside out. Come for me, Ryleigh. One more time, then you can rest."

Resting sounded great. Perfect. But the orgasm that was just out of reach felt more important. She experimented by pushing her hips up into Tiny. It felt good. *Really* good. She wanted more.

But Tiny refused to budge. "No, stay still. I know you want to move, but I don't want to hurt you. You can orgasm like this, I know you can. Do it, Ryleigh, come for me. Come on my dick. Bathe me with your juices. I want to feel it on my bare cock. Claim what's yours."

That was all it took. The thought of Tiny trusting her enough to make love to her without the condom made her careen off the edge once more. He was right, the orgasm wasn't as intense as it had been the last two times, but with him deep inside her body, it felt very different. She gripped his dick hard as she came.

Then, to her surprise, he collapsed to his elbows and moaned into her ear. She was confused for a second. Had he come? No, he couldn't have. He hadn't moved inside her at all. Didn't guys have to thrust in order to orgasm?

She felt stupid that she didn't actually know. Only recalled what she'd seen in movies and read in books. In every case, the guy needed the stimulation of thrusting to come.

After a moment, he lifted his head and smiled wryly down at her.

"Did you...was it okay?" she asked.

"Okay? I've never come so hard in my life," Tiny said. A bead of sweat dripped down his temple, and Ryleigh was fascinated by that small sign of his exertion.

"But you didn't...I thought men had to move to come."

He laughed. "So did I."

"I'm so confused."

"Honey, I was on a hair trigger even before I entered you. Feeling you come around my bare dick? I've *never* felt that before. Ever. I've always worn a condom. I got a little control back after I saw how much pain you were in, but the feel of you fluttering around me...then when you squeezed my cock as you came, it milked my orgasm right out of me. I didn't *need* to move, the pleasure I got from simply being inside you was enough."

He grinned and ran a finger down her nose when she gaped at him.

"Your blush is adorable," he said.

Ryleigh shifted under him and realized he was still inside her body. Her Kegels tightened, and he groaned.

"*Fuck* that feels good."

"What? This?" she asked, tightening her core around him again.

"Yes! That," he agreed, sitting up and pulling out of her.

Ryleigh couldn't stop the small whimper of pain from escaping.

"I know, sweetheart. Give me a second. Don't move."

Ryleigh watched as Tiny leaped out of bed—he looked damn fine, wandering around butt-ass naked—and headed for the bathroom. He returned a moment later with a damp washcloth. She tried to take it from him, but he shook his head and climbed back onto the bed.

He gently wiped between her thighs, and looking down, Ryleigh saw a smear of red on the cloth.

"You know, I never thought much about what a woman goes through when she has sex for the first time. But now I'm understanding why the men of olden times hung the bloody sheets out their windows. I want to pound my chest and declare to the world that you're mine. That you chose me for your first. It's an honor, sweetheart. I won't ever forget this moment."

"It's just a bit of blood," Ryleigh felt obligated to point out.

"No, it's you trusting me not to hurt you more than necessary. It's you letting me take you without a condom. It's you giving me something you held on to for thirty-one years."

She wasn't sure what to say about that. And then she recalled the look on his face when he realized how much pain she was in. He looked terrified. But he hadn't panicked. Had immediately done what he could to mitigate her discomfort by staying absolutely still. By giving her pleasure to work through the pain. She couldn't have chosen a better man to give her virginity to. This was why she'd waited. To give it to him. To Tiny.

When he was finished cleaning away their combined orgasms from between her legs, he got back up to put the washcloth in the bathroom. As he approached the bed, she

239

noticed that he hadn't cleaned himself. Even though he was flaccid, she could see tiny streaks of her blood on his cock, along with evidence of their orgasms.

It wasn't until he'd situated them in their usual sleeping positions that she found the courage to say, "Won't you be uncomfortable? With that...stuff, drying on your skin?"

He chuckled against her. "Maybe. But I don't care. I want you on me. Don't love the blood, but since it's evidence of you taking me for your own, I'll be okay for a night."

"It's kind of gross," Ryleigh whispered.

"You want me to clean up?" he asked, lifting his head, his muscles flexing as if he was preparing to get off the mattress once more.

"No! I mean, not if you don't want to. I just want you to be comfortable."

"Smelling you on my skin, my soap on your body, holding you in my arms...I'm comfortable."

"Okay then."

"Okay," he agreed.

They lay in silence for a moment, before Ryleigh asked tentatively, "Next time...you're going to move though, right?"

He chuckled. "No clue. I lose all control when it comes to you. You think you'd like that?"

"Um, yeah. I liked how it felt there at the end, but I think having you moving would feel even better."

Tiny groaned, and he shifted next to her. She smiled, loving that she could affect him. Could turn him on.

"What else do you want to try?"

"Try?"

"Yeah, in bed."

"Everything?"

"I'm going to need you to be more specific. I know you enjoyed when I touched your ass, and as I said, anal's not my thing, but if you want to try it we can. But not right away. It'll take a while for us to get you ready for that."

"I don't think so...but I did like you touching me there."

"I liked it too."

"And I want to give you a blow job. And maybe you can take me from behind? I've heard that feels good."

"You're killin' me, sweetheart. Anything you want, you can have. Don't be embarrassed to ask. Between us, in this bed, nothing's off-limits. Okay?"

"Okay," she said with a smile. To be honest, she was relieved her first time was behind her. It had felt like this huge *thing* hanging over her head. And now that it was gone, she was...free.

Her dad was behind bars, The Refuge was safe, she was free to be exactly who she was. And she could be that person with Tiny. She'd never been happier.

CHAPTER SEVENTEEN

Almost a week later, The Refuge was in a whirlwind. Even though there were no guests, there *were* still people at the retreat. Now that Harold Lodge was behind bars and the threat to their livelihood was gone, everyone was throwing themselves into the preparations for Alaska and Brick's wedding.

As far as Tiny was concerned, the couple was the cornerstone of this place. The people who'd made the rest of the owners see for themselves that love was possible. After Ryleigh's dad had canceled an entire month of reservations just to be a dick, they'd rescheduled most of the stays, but kept a week clear and were going ahead with the decision to throw one hell of a weekend party for the couple.

Tiny and the rest of the guys had also discussed it, and decided that since there were no guests, they wanted to serve alcohol at the reception. Not enough for everyone to get completely drunk, just so that those who wished could have a glass of wine or two, or a beer, and of course, toast to the married couple's happiness with a glass of champagne.

The mood around The Refuge was almost giddy. The staff members were happy to relax before getting back into the swing of having paying customers once more. And all of Brick and Alaska's friends had been encouraged to invite whoever they wanted to the wedding.

Henley asked her previous neighbor, Cheri Singleton, and her daughter to come up from Albuquerque. Jasna was allowed to invite Sharyn, a friend she'd made in art camp, and her mom. Reese had of course invited her brother Jack —also known as Woody—and his new wife, Isabella, to come back. Maisy invited the cook in her previous home, Paige, who'd been more like a mom to her. Brick's mom was attending; Tonka had asked if it was all right for him to invite his former partner, Raiden, and his wife, Khloe. They were coming to New Mexico from the small town of Fallport, Virginia.

And Tiny invited someone he'd actually only met a couple of times, but chatted with via phone and email plenty. A man named Matthew Steele, otherwise known as Wolf, and his wife, Caroline. Wolf was a retired SEAL very well known in Navy circles. He and his wife had been through their own hell, and Tiny couldn't wait for her to meet his Ryleigh. From what he knew of both women, they'd be like two peas in a pod. Sweet, considerate, and strong as hell when things went sideways.

Most guests had already arrived and were having a great time. It felt right to give Brick and Alaska this huge celebration for their wedding ceremony. Robert was outdoing himself in the kitchen, cooking up a storm, and

Stone and Owl had been busy giving aerial sightseeing trips to their friends and family.

Cora and Pipe also had their hands full with their new fosters. Joyce, Kason, Shannon, and Max had arrived two days ago, and were still adjusting to life at The Refuge. They seemed like good kids, just unsure and shy, which hopefully would fade as they realized they weren't going to be separated. Jasna was in the same grade as Kason and it helped that the two already knew each other.

Tiny had been busy himself...with Ryleigh. After taking a couple days to recover from her first time, she'd been insatiable. Almost desperate to know everything she'd been missing out on when it came to sex, and Tiny was more than happy to oblige her curiosity. She was his perfect match, both in and out of the bedroom.

She gave him space to do the things he enjoyed, like hiking with their friends, but made sure he knew how much she missed him when they saw each other again. And she'd been busy as well, babysitting for Reese and Henley, entertaining Jasna after school, helping make sure the cabins were ready for everyone's arrival, and generally pitching in wherever and whenever she was needed.

But when they arrived back at their cabin at the end of each day, Tiny had her complete attention. They made love over and over, deep into the night, and she was thrilled to learn that he'd been right. Sex hadn't hurt since that first time. Of course, Tiny made sure she was soaking wet each and every time before he entered her. They'd already made love in every position he knew, and some he'd never even heard of. But since Ryleigh was a master at all things computer, she'd unearthed some kinky things that Tiny was happy to try. Some worked, others hilariously didn't, but adding laughter to their lovemaking was another bonus, and something Tiny hadn't experienced before.

He loved her. So much it was almost scary.

Ryleigh tried to hide her continued worries about her father, but she wasn't very successful. Tiny didn't begrudge her the few hours in the mornings when she obsessively searched the web for signs that Harold had left behind any last-minute surprises, but now, nearly a week after he'd been taken into custody, she still hadn't found anything. Which was a relief for everyone.

They'd just finished with some wedding prep and were back in their cabin, making a quick lunch. Wolf and Caroline would be arriving in about an hour, and he couldn't wait to introduce them to Ryleigh. She'd heard a little about them from Tiny already, but Tex had actually reached out when he heard the couple would be coming to The Refuge, and he'd told Ryleigh even more. Everyone was a little disappointed when Tex himself couldn't come, but they understood. One of his daughters had a ballet recital he didn't want to miss. Family first, always.

"What if they don't like me?" Ryleigh asked nervously.

"They're going to love you," he reassured her.

She rolled her eyes. "I'm thinking you're biased."

Tiny chuckled. "Maybe, but I'm not wrong. You're likable, sweetheart." He didn't like the doubt on her face, or the fact she looked away from him.

He stepped in front of her, giving her no choice but to look at him. "You are," he insisted. "The first day you were here, you had Jess and Carly wrapped around your little finger. You won over Alaska in your interview, and no, don't even try to tell me you somehow managed to sway

Alaska's opinion of you with your internet skills. You might have gotten the interview with some fancy finger work, but you got the job on your own. The guys all respect and love you, and don't think I've missed how close you and Jasna are."

Tears filled Ryleigh's eyes, but he went on.

"And you know how hard I tried *not* to like you…and failed completely. Even when I was trying to convince myself you were here with bad intentions, I still couldn't keep my distance. I didn't *need* you to move in here to keep my eye on you. There were a dozen different ways I could've done that…but I *wanted* you here. Under my roof. Even when I was mad at you, there was something about you that I just couldn't resist. Didn't want to."

"A dozen different ways?" she asked with a small sniff. "Like what?"

Tiny's lips twitched. "I don't know, but I could've figured something else out. My point is…Caroline and Wolf are gonna love you. With my luck, they'll probably try to get you to move to California so they can see you more often. Set you up with one of the SEALs they work with out there—which isn't happening, by the way. I hope it doesn't embarrass you, but they know the gist of your story, why you're here, about your dad. Wolf was pissed and Caroline wasn't much better. They're going to adore you, hon. You just need to be yourself."

She still looked skeptical—and Tiny made a decision.

He put down the spoon he'd been using to stir the tuna salad he was making and placed his hands on her shoulders. He pushed her backward until she was leaning against the counter. "Jump up," he ordered.

"Why?"

"Because. I want to eat you out, then fuck you from behind right here in our kitchen."

And just like that, their previous serious conversation was forgotten and anticipation filled the air.

"I have a better idea. Why don't *you* take a step back and let me give you a blow job? Every other time I've tried, you've gotten impatient and haven't let me finish."

The thought of her mouth around his dick had his erection pressing against his jeans. His woman may have been a virgin a week ago, but she'd certainly been making up for lost time—fast.

"You sure?" he asked.

In response, she reached for his belt. Tiny took a step back, as she'd requested, and watched as she went to her knees in front of him, taking his pants and boxers down with her as she went.

The sight of her fully dressed, kneeling at his feet, made Tiny so hard, he hurt. And when she took his cock in her hand and opened her mouth, it was all he could do not to haul her up and have his wicked way with her. But she wanted this, and he'd already denied her more than once. Not because he didn't want it, but because he didn't think he'd have enough restraint to let her explore him for very long.

He figured because it was the middle of the day, and he was standing in his sunny kitchen, maybe he'd have more control.

He was wrong.

The sight and feel of Ryleigh touching his cock with her fingers and mouth was way too much. She wasn't skilled, her movements were sloppy and uncoordinated as she figured out a rhythm, but her enthusiasm alone made it all the more erotic.

Still, Tiny thought he might be able to keep himself in check—until she took him deep in her mouth and moaned. The reverberations caressed his cock in a way he'd never felt before. And he was done.

Reaching down, he pulled her off his dick and spun them both, practically shoving her toward the table.

He wrenched her leggings and underwear down, more than thankful he didn't need to fumble with a belt or zipper, then pressed her upper body down. He'd fantasized about this more than once, taking her from behind at the very table where she'd spent so many hours fiddling with her computer. His cock dripped precome impatiently as he used his hand to make sure she could take him without pain. He never wanted to see her flinching the way she had when he'd entered her that first time.

"Do it!" Ryleigh coaxed, her cheek resting on the table and her hands gripping both sides as he played with her pussy.

Tiny was beyond words. He lined his cock up and pressed inside her with one long push.

They both groaned in ecstasy. After that, their lovemaking was hard and fast. With Ryleigh encouraging him and holding on for dear life as he pounded into her like a madman. Her ass jiggled with each of his thrusts, and nothing he'd experienced before had ever been this good.

Colors exploded behind his closed lids as Tiny desperately fought off his orgasm. He wanted, *needed* her to come first. Hunching over, he sought out her clit with his fingers, and he could feel his cock sliding in and out of her soaking-wet pussy as he stroked her.

Ryleigh bucked back against him, not content to simply lie there and take what he gave her.

"Come, Ryleigh. *Now.*"

She didn't, not right away, which made Tiny have to desperately hold off his own orgasm even longer. But soon enough, he felt her inner muscles fluttering around him. Immediately after, she clamped down on him so hard, it almost hurt.

Tiny flexed his ass and planted his cock as deep inside her as he could get, which felt deeper than usual in this position, and let go even as her muscles were still spasming around him.

He saw stars, then could've sworn his vision went dark for a moment. When he came back to himself, he realized he was probably squishing Ryleigh by lying against her back on the table. He eased upward and found his arms were shaking.

"Holy crap," he mumbled. "I think you just turned me inside out."

"That's my line," she panted.

As soon as he pulled all the way out of her body, Ryleigh turned, practically throwing herself at him. Tiny caught her and held her against him. He mentally chuckled at the picture they probably made. Shirts on, pants and underwear around their ankles, stopped by their shoes.

"I want to say something, but I don't want you to freak out," he said.

Ryleigh pulled back and looked up at him with a quizzical and worried expression.

"I love you," he blurted. "You don't have to say it back, but I hope you'll give me a chance to prove that my asshole days are behind me, and I can be a man you both trust and love back. I never thought I'd be here again, not after my ex and what she did. But not once have I been afraid to fall asleep next to you. In fact, I'm not sure I can sleep all that well without you anymore. You've ruined me for any other woman, and I want to spend the rest of my life by your side. But I'm not telling you all this to pressure you. I just needed you to know."

Her eyes were huge in her face and her fingers were digging into his biceps as she clung to him.

"Ryleigh? Am I freaking you out?"

"Yes. No. Maybe?"

He chuckled. "Sorry. Probably not the best timing, huh? Let's get you cleaned up and finish making our lunch. Then we can go to the lodge and meet Wolf and Caroline. Tonight, we're all eating up at the lodge, as a kind of rehearsal dinner thing and so everyone can visit." Tiny was babbling, and he knew it, but he didn't want Ryleigh to feel awkward about his confession.

She lifted a hand and placed it over his mouth. "I know about dinner, I helped organize it, remember?" She didn't give him a chance to respond, and since her hand was over his mouth, he couldn't talk anyway. "I love you too," she told him softly, blushing slightly. "I have for quite a while."

Tiny grabbed hold of her hand and tore it from his mouth. "Don't say it if you don't mean it. I can't handle you saying it then taking it back."

"No take-backs," she whispered.

"Damn, now I want you again," he said with a pout.

Ryleigh giggled.

Tiny loved the sound. *Loved* it. She hadn't had nearly

enough opportunities to laugh, to be carefree in the time she'd been here. He made a mental vow to change that.

"You didn't let me finish giving you a blow job," she told him in a mock annoyed tone.

"Sorry, but the second you touch me, I lose all control."

"Whatever," she said with a roll of her eyes.

"Come on, shuffle your beautiful ass over to the sink so I can clean us up."

That made her giggle again, but she let Tiny hold on to her as they both made their way to the sink. It was Tiny's turn to kneel at Ryleigh's feet as he ran a wet paper towel up her inner thighs, wiping his come that had leaked out of her. He'd never done this for any woman before—hadn't needed to, since he'd always worn condoms—but he found it unbearably intimate and extremely erotic, seeing their combined juices on her skin.

He also loved the slight blush on her cheeks as he cared for her. It was just one more reason why he swore to always make sure this woman knew how precious she was to him.

They managed to get their clothes back on and finish preparing lunch. Sitting at the table he'd just fucked her on was difficult, just made him want to repeat the process immediately, but he promised himself he'd do so as soon as feasibly possible. The juxtaposition of taking her from behind, bent over the table, with the similar image in his head of her hunched over her laptop was a kinky turn-on for him. She was a nerd...but she was *his* nerd. His sexy-as-hell nerd.

"What are you thinking about so hard over there?" she asked when they were almost finished eating.

"I was just wondering if I got you a pair of black librarian glasses, if you'd wear them while I fucked you on this table."

His love for her grew when, instead of calling him weird or a pervert, she simply rolled her eyes and chuckled.

"Is that a yes?" he pushed, suddenly desperate to make the fantasy in his head come true.

She shrugged. "Sure."

Tiny had to adjust his cock in his suddenly too-tight jeans.

"You're so weird," she told him, reading his mind, but since she was smiling when she said it, Tiny didn't take offense. Then again, he didn't think he could be offended by anything she said.

"Yup," he agreed. Then he sobered. "Did you mean it? You weren't just saying it because I did?" Where this uncertainty was coming from, he had no idea.

"Did *you*?" she countered, looking uneasy.

And *that* was unacceptable. "I've never meant anything more in my entire life. I love you, Ryleigh. Always will."

"I love you too."

Hearing the words for the second time soothed something deep inside him that Tiny didn't realize needed soothing.

They smiled at each other. There was nothing he wanted more than to take her into their bedroom and make long, slow love to her, not like the quickie they'd just had on the table.

As if she could read his mind, she said, "We should go talk to your friends."

"Yeah," he agreed with a sigh.

They cleaned the kitchen and headed up to the lodge twenty minutes later. Tiny immediately saw Wolf and his wife and headed toward them.

Wolf was taller than Tiny by a few inches, and older by about a decade or so. He had gray hair at his temples, and even though he was big and muscular, anyone looking at him might think he was nothing but a middle-aged accountant or something, but Tiny knew better. The man might be retired from the Navy, but he was still a SEAL through and through.

As if he could feel Tiny looking at him, Wolf turned, and a grin formed on his face. He leaned down and said something to the woman standing next to him, and she turned in their direction as well. Then Wolf was striding toward him.

He held out his hand to Tiny, and they shook before Wolf gave him a man-hug and pounded on his back in greeting.

"Damn nice to see you again," Wolf said.

"Same," Tiny agreed with a smile. The first time he'd met the former SEAL, they'd hit it off immediately.

Caroline smiled at Tiny from beside her husband. Wolf immediately wrapped his arm around her shoulders and drew her against him. She was almost a foot shorter than her husband, but seemed to fit against him perfectly. Her light brown hair wasn't done up in any special hairdo and it didn't look as if she was wearing any makeup. Her jeans and blouse were casual and comfortable-looking. When she looked up at Wolf, her eyes came to life and she seemed to shine from the inside out. This was a woman who was deeply loved, and blossomed as a result.

"This is my wife, Ice."

Caroline mock-slapped his chest and shook her head in exasperation. "Caroline. My name is *Caroline*. It's very good to meet you, Tiny. And you too, Ryleigh. It is Ryleigh, right?"

"Most people call me Ry," she told the other woman.

"Ry it is, then."

"You have a chance to look around yet?" Tiny asked.

"Just got here, so no," Wolf said.

"I'll be glad to give you a tour," Ryleigh volunteered.

For all her nervousness at meeting the couple, Ryleigh seemed completely at ease, and Tiny was so proud of her. She might think she wasn't a people person, or that she couldn't make friends easily, but that definitely wasn't the case.

"I'd love that!" Caroline said. "Matthew, you go and do your thing with the guys. I'll go with Ry. She can show me around."

"Sounds good to me. I'll bring our stuff to our cabin later," Wolf told her.

"I'm sure it's probably already there," Tiny informed him.

"And I'll show Caroline which cabin you guys are in during our tour," Ryleigh said.

"You guys run a smooth ship," Wolf said with a grin.

"Hell yeah, we do," Tiny agreed.

Wolf dipped his head to his wife and said something softly, and Tiny took the opportunity to sidestep with Ryleigh. "You good?" he asked.

"Yeah."

He couldn't stop himself from saying, "Told you that you'd be fast friends."

Ryleigh rolled her eyes. "I've known her for like two seconds. I think the jury is still out."

"Nope. You're in. Besties. I wouldn't be surprised if she was inviting you for a visit to Riverton before the evening's out."

Instead of rolling her eyes again, Ryleigh whispered, "This place never fails to surprise me. People don't usually like me when they first meet me."

Tiny hated that for her. "Then you've simply been meeting the wrong people."

She considered his words for a beat. "You're probably right."

Tiny kissed her forehead gently and squeezed her hand. "Have fun, but be careful walking around."

"We will."

"Meet you back here in an hour or so? Is that enough time?"

"Plenty. The Refuge isn't *that* big," she told him with a laugh.

"Right." Tiny squeezed her hand as they turned back to Wolf and Caroline.

"Ready?" Ryleigh asked the woman.

"Definitely. I can't wait to see this place. I couldn't believe it when Wolf said we were coming here. I've heard all sorts of wonderful things. Is the cow really named Melba?"

Tiny smiled as Caroline and Ryleigh walked toward the kitchen side-by-side. He almost forgot where he was for a minute...because he was staring at his woman's ass, remembering how it looked as he pounded into her from behind less than an hour ago.

Wolf cleared his throat, and Tiny glanced over at him with an apologetic look.

"How long have you two been together?"

"Ryleigh and I? *Together*-together, not long," Tiny admitted.

Wolf's eyebrow rose. "Really? You two have a connection, it's easy to see. I'm surprised it's been that short of a time."

"We've known each other for over a year now, but I had to get my head out of my ass before anything could happen."

"Ah, yeah, I've seen that more than once. Well, for what it's worth...you guys seem like a great match. She's the computer genius that has Tex's panties in a twist, yeah?"

Tiny laughed. "Yup. The things she can do..." He shook his head. "It's pretty scary. She told me the other night that she used to hack the CIA firewalls just to see if she could do it—at fourteen."

Wolf whistled.

"Right? I'm torn between not wanting to know and *needing* to know," Tiny said.

"A bit of advice? You don't want to know," Wolf said.

"You're probably right."

"I'm always right, just ask my wife," Wolf said.

Tiny chuckled. "You want a tour too?"

"Absolutely. The reputation of this place is legendary. I've recommended quite a few sailors and people I know spend a few nights here. I hear your psychologist is top-notch."

"She is. Henley's a miracle worker. If you'd known

Tonka before and after he got together with her, you'd agree with me," Tiny said.

"I don't have to, the reviews online say it all. Happy for you, man. I wish all our veterans had this kind of place to fall back on when they need it."

"Me too. We're working on a no-fee program for those who can't afford the prices. And we've had enough donations to make something like that happen sooner rather than later."

"Good news. I'll definitely keep recommending this place on my end too," Wolf said.

"Appreciate it. Come on, let's get this tour started. I'm sure you and Caroline will want to freshen up or rest before dinner tonight. Warning, the next couple of days are gonna be kind of crazy."

"Can't be any crazier than when my crew all gets together. I can't keep all the kids straight anymore."

Tiny knew Wolf was full of shit. The man was sharp as a tack; there was no way he'd ever forget whose kid was whose and what their names were.

"We've only got two babies now, but there are two more on the way, and Cora and Pipe just had their first four foster kids move in. Plus, Jasna and the pets. So things will just get more crazy around here. We used to think having children around would be a negative thing... because some people are triggered by babies crying or screaming children. But honestly, it's been okay, at least in the short time we've had to observe before Harold Lodge started messing with our reservations."

"I'm sorry about the trouble he's caused, but can I admit that I'm not sorry we're here now as a result?" Wolf asked.

Tiny chuckled as they headed for the front doors. He gave Brick a chin lift as he headed out with Wolf. His friend returned it and pointed at his watch, then held up four fingers. Tiny nodded, acknowledging the reminder about when dinner would start. He didn't need it, but he realized Brick was under some stress, wanting to make everything perfect for Alaska.

"Only if I can admit that it's kind of nice to be able to relax a little, not worry about tiptoeing around the guests while we have a celebration for our friends. We've had a couple of weddings here, but since we don't want to disrupt people's vacations, or make it seem as if we aren't paying the kind of attention to them that their money has bought with their stay, it's nice to not have to worry about that kind of thing this week."

"I understand. It's a delicate balance...making sure your guests are doing all right mentally, but living your lives as well, since this is your home."

"I suppose it's what we took on when we decided to live on the property," Tiny said with a shrug.

"Again, you've all done an amazing job. The Refuge is the perfect place for those with PTSD to come and unwind. To live without having to worry about the world judging them."

Wolf's praise meant a lot to Tiny. He and his friends had worked their asses off to make this a safe place for anyone who needed it. Hearing from a third party, another vet, that they'd succeeded made him feel proud.

As he took Wolf around and showed him The Refuge, a part of Tiny was always thinking about Ryleigh. Hoping her own tour was going well. He had no reason to think it wouldn't be, but he knew she always stressed about meeting someone new. He was counting down the minutes until he saw her again. She centered him. Grounded him.

And he couldn't wait to hear how things with Caroline had gone. Couldn't wait to see her smile. Hear her laugh.

He was completely besotted, and he didn't feel an ounce of trepidation about it.

CHAPTER EIGHTEEN

Ry smiled at the chaos all around her. The tour of The Refuge with Caroline had gone really well. The other woman was funny and down to earth. She'd loved meeting all the animals at the barn and had even gotten down on her knees in the dirt to meet one of the new goats that had been born recently.

By the time Ry dropped her off at the cabin where she and Wolf were staying, it felt as if they'd been friends for years rather than just meeting an hour earlier.

They were now sitting at tables in the lobby of the lodge, eating dinner, while everyone laughed and talked loudly. Tiny was on her right, and they were sitting with Tonka, Henley, and his friend he'd served with, Raiden, and his wife, Khloe.

Raid, as he'd asked to be called, was huge. He towered over everyone. He said he was six feet, eight inches tall. Khloe was tiny compared to him, but somehow her personality made her seem much bigger. Raid's bright red hair made him stick out almost as much as his height. But he was so gentle, and when he'd taken Tonka's tiny daughter into his arms, Ry's eyes actually teared up.

She knew all about what these two men had been through with their service K9s. It was horrific, and so damn sad. But both seemed to be happy now, which Ry was grateful for. She silently swore to do a search as soon as she could for anyone associated with the asshole who'd hurt the two men and their dogs, and make sure karma was taking care of them.

This bloodthirsty side of her was new, but she was discovering that the thought of anyone messing with those she loved was unbearable.

Jasna was sitting at a different table with her friend Sharyn and the little girl's mom. Brick's mom was also at that table, along with Lara and Owl.

Cora and Pipe were sharing a table with their four foster children, and Cheri Singleton and her daughter. Cheri used to babysit Jasna. The older woman had four-year-old Max on her lap and was entertaining him with games on a piece of yarn she'd woven through her fingers.

Wolf and Caroline were sitting with Reese and Spike, and her brother and Isabella.

Stone and Maisy were at a table with Brick and Alaska, and Paige. Paige was the woman who'd basically raised Maisy, and was the closest thing she had to a mother.

All in all, the mood in the room was joyous. Alaska had insisted that Robert make this meal a buffet, so he could sit and eat with everyone else and wouldn't have to be running back and forth to the kitchen all night. All the other Refuge employees were there as well, although they'd be heading out to their homes after dinner.

A big bonfire would take place once it got dark, so

everyone could continue to hang out before heading to bed and meeting back up for brunch the next day, then Alaska and Brick's wedding ceremony. Afterward, they would have another buffet dinner, then dancing. All the tables and chairs would be pushed toward the edge of the lobby, and Jason had volunteered to be their DJ. Apparently, he was more than just their maintenance man; he worked as a DJ in a small club in Los Alamos on the weekends.

"You look happy," Tiny said in her ear.

Ry took a moment to reflect on his words, before turning to him with a smile. "I am. I think this is the first time in my life I'm not worrying about what tomorrow will bring. I used to stress about what my father would ask me to do, who he'd want me to steal from, and then after I left, I was constantly on alert and on the move, always afraid he'd find me. But now? I'm not thinking about anything other than how fun this is. How happy I am for Alaska and Brick. And how being around so many happy people makes *me* happy by osmosis."

Tiny squeezed their clasped hands, resting on his thigh. "I'm glad."

"Me too," she agreed.

Talk at the table turned to Khloe, and her job as a veterinarian in their small town in Virginia. She talked about some of her clients—the ones with fur, not their human owners. Then she bragged about her husband, how Raid had started a Dungeons and Dragons club at the library he managed, and how popular it was.

Ry wouldn't have pegged the man as a D&D nerd, but then again, most people wouldn't ever guess that she could hack into the President of the United States' email without anyone being the wiser. It drove home the fact that everyone had hidden talents and passions...it didn't make them more or less likable. It just *was*.

Slowly, people began to leave the lodge after eating. The plan was for those who wanted to attend the bonfire to reconvene at the firepit around sunset. Ry had volunteered for kitchen duty, making sure Alaska was nowhere near any dirty dishes. This was her wedding week, and everyone was determined she'd work as little as possible and enjoy every second of her unplanned vacation.

Tiny—along with Luna, Maisy, and Paige—helped. Ry had tried to shoo Paige out, but she told Ry and the others in no uncertain terms that she'd spent her life in a kitchen, and it was one of the places she felt the most comfortable. After that, no one had the heart to make her leave.

The dishes were cleaned in no time, the lobby of the lodge swept and the tables and chairs straightened for brunch in the morning. As Ry was walking to the firepit to assist before the others arrived, she once more reflected on how different her life was now, than when she was on the run from her father.

Choosing The Refuge had been a stroke of luck. She'd not only found a place to hide out—and money she'd earned legally—but she'd inadvertently discovered the place she was always meant to be. She'd never be an outdoor girl, but she'd learned to appreciate the silence, the fresh air...and was *learning* to tolerate the bugs.

"What's that smile for?" Tiny asked as they walked hand-in-hand toward the property's designated bonfire area.

"It's weird how life works, isn't it?" she said somewhat cryptically.

"Absolutely," Tiny agreed. "If anyone had told me when I'd first stepped foot on this property that years later, this is where I'd still be, I would've laughed in their face. There was nothing here but trees. I thought it was beautiful, but also kind of lonely. I didn't think in a million years that The Refuge would actually work. Sure, I wanted it to succeed, but I didn't think anyone would pay big bucks to come out to the middle of nowhere, where there were no fast food restaurants nearby, and not even internet at the time, to try to heal their souls.

"And never, *ever* would I have believed us confirmed bachelors would be married. And Tonka and Spike with babies?" Tiny shook his head. "Nope. I would've laughed like crazy at anyone who'd suggested there was the possibility."

"I know. I feel the same. I mean, not about your friends, but about myself. When I left my dad, I was scared to death. I was naïve and had no idea how to live on my own. He was a horrible person and father, but he paid the bills, ordered the food...he did everything. And I was so scared. Scared that he'd find me, hurt me for stealing his money, but more than that, I think I was scared of *people* in general."

She stopped on the path and turned to Tiny. She leaned against him, looking up into his eyes. "All my life, I'd been told I was stupid. Pathetic. That I couldn't do anything right. I had no friends, and no clue how to make them. I was the weird kid, and I grew into a weird adult. I didn't make eye contact with anyone, stuck to myself. But eventually that got lonely. I mean, I liked being on my own for the first time ever...eating what I wanted, *when* I wanted, reading whatever books I wanted...all the things adults do when they live alone. But I also began to crave companionship. I didn't want to get a pet, because I moved too much and that wouldn't be fair to the animal. It's one of the reasons why I wanted this job. I could talk to people a little during the day, then go back to my apartment at night.

"I never expected people to actually like me. To want to be around me. First it was Jess and Carly. Then it was the other employees. Including Alaska. And Henley. And as the others came to The Refuge, them too. Then there was you...

"I was drawn to you from the start. But I knew I wasn't a good person. Didn't deserve you. You were a hero, this larger-than-life SEAL, and you already know I hadn't spent any time around men before. I had no idea how to be the kind of woman you might be attracted to."

"I wanted you too," Tiny told her. "There was something about you that drew me in the second I saw you. I could tell you were hiding something, but I convinced myself I was imagining it. That I was letting my past color my feelings. And when I found out my instinct was not only correct, but your secret was something bigger than I ever could've dreamed, I closed myself off. I'm sorry for that, hon. So sorry."

But Ry shook her head. "Don't be. I think we had to go through what we did for us to end up where we are now."

"No," Tiny disagreed. "There was no reason for me to be a dick to you for as long as I was. I treated you like shit, and you didn't deserve that."

"Tiny," Ry protested, but he pulled her closer, until their upper bodies were plastered together.

"You didn't," he said firmly. "Your father was wrong. You aren't stupid, you aren't ugly. You aren't *anything* he said you were. He was purposely trying to make you feel worthless, keep you under his thumb, doing what *he* couldn't do. You're a shining light, Ryleigh. The type of woman anyone would want to be friends with. Unselfish, giving, and so damn kind it makes me feel like an ogre."

Ry chuckled. "Whatever, Jake Ryan."

It was Tiny's turn to roll his eyes. "Look at you, sweetheart. You haven't slowed down for a minute. You gave Caroline a tour, helped Robert and Luna set up the buffet, cleaned the kitchen, straightened the lodge, and now here you are, going to help make sure things are all good to go for the bonfire. And that's just today. I'm sure tomorrow you'll be just as busy, running around making sure everyone else is happy and comfortable."

"Well, of course. It's Alaska and Brick's day. I want it to be perfect for them."

"It will be. Even if a freak snowstorm blows through, the chairs all break, and the food suddenly goes bad. Because they'll be together. Because Brick will get to marry the woman he loves, and Alaska will finally get to call the man she's loved her entire life her husband. All the other stuff...it's just noise. It doesn't matter. Except for being surrounded by friends. That's the best gift they could have."

Ry loved that he thought that way. She'd learned the hard way that money didn't buy happiness. Her father proved that. She smiled up at Tiny and nodded.

"I'm going to marry you," he said bluntly. "One of these

days, we're going to go down to the courthouse and do it. A small ceremony, no frills, no fuss. Unless you want a big party, then I'll give you the biggest party The Refuge has ever seen."

Ry smiled up at him. "No, I don't want a party. I just want you."

"So, you'll marry me?"

Ry blinked. "Wait, was that a proposal?"

Tiny smirked. "It was if you say yes."

"And if I don't?"

"Then it wasn't a proposal. Yet."

Ry loved this man. So damn much. "I'd marry you today if I could," she admitted. "But it's only been a week."

"Wrong. I think we've both known we were headed here from the first time we saw each other. It's been months. We've just had to work through some stuff before we got our heads out of our butts."

Ry snorted. "Stuff. Yeah." Then she sobered. "I don't know how to be a wife."

"Do you love me?" Tiny asked.

"Yes." There was no hesitation in her response.

"And I love you. I'm not sure I know how to be a husband, but together, I think we can figure it out. I'm sure we'll make mistakes along the way, but that's part of life. Of being a couple."

She liked that philosophy. If he'd said their lives would be perfect, she probably would've felt uneasy. But knowing he expected there to be bumps in their road made her feel less stressed about the whole thing. "Okay."

"Okay what?" Tiny asked with a small furrow in his brow.

"I'll let you marry me."

He chuckled at that, and his eyes seemed to sparkle. She felt him grow hard against her belly. "Maybe we should go to our cabin and celebrate our betrothal."

She giggled. "Our betrothal? Who says that?"

"I have no idea," he admitted.

"We said we'd help with the fire," she reminded him.

He sighed dramatically. "Fine. You're such a hard taskmaster."

Ry's smile grew. "Yup."

The grin faded from Tiny's expression. One hand came up to cup the side of her face. "I love you, Ryleigh Lodge. Exactly how you are. Genius computer hacker, generous friend, protector of everyone here at The Refuge. I want to spend the rest of my days learning everything there is to know about you and watching you blossom."

"Tiny," she murmured, trying desperately to hold back the tears that had welled in her eyes.

"Don't cry," he ordered. "This is a happy moment."

"Sorry, I know," she said with a wobbly smile. "I love you too. And I have no idea why in the world you want to marry me, a weirdo who would rather sit inside in front of a computer than anything else, but I'll always put you first. I'll be a woman you can trust to sleep by your side and protect you from anyone who might dare to touch one hair on your head."

Tiny leaned down and kissed her lips lightly.

They stood like that, wrapped in each other's arms for several minutes, until Jasna went running past them yelling, "Hurry up, slowpokes! We're gonna have s'mores!"

Tiny chuckled and pulled back. "Guess that's our cue to get our butts in gear."

"Guess so," Ry agreed.

As they started for the fire grounds, Tiny said nonchalantly, "We can go shopping for a ring next week."

"I don't need a ring," Ry said.

"Well, I'm getting you one, so get used to it. I want everyone who sees your finger to know you're taken."

Ry wanted to point out that it wasn't as if people were beating down her door to date her, or that anyone other than him had *ever* shown the slightest interest in her. *And*, she didn't want anyone but him...but she couldn't deny she wanted to wear his ring. "Will you wear one too? I mean, when we get married?"

"Hell yeah, I'm wearing one. I want everyone to know I belong to you."

It was a good answer. No, it was an awesome answer.

She squeezed his hand as they walked. He glanced over and gave her a loving smile. "This is gonna work," he said firmly. "I'm gonna make sure it does."

They reached the ring of logs that sat around the property's firepit.

"Over here!" Jasna called, gesturing them toward her. "We need to put the small sticks down first, then the bigger logs on top. Once it's going, we can add more wood." It was obvious the girl had absorbed everything about fire-starting from the camps she'd attended, and from all the bonfires they'd held at The Refuge.

"Go on, I'll carry the logs so you don't hurt your hands," Tiny told her.

Ry went up on tiptoes and kissed him. "Thanks."

"You don't have to thank me for doing anything that might keep you from being hurt," he returned, kissing her hard, then heading for the woodpile.

He was wrong. No one else in her entire life, including

her father, had ever done anything to keep her from harm. Harold had actually *put* her in harm's way. It was hard to get used to Tiny's protection and care, but she liked it. A lot.

CHAPTER NINETEEN

Ry stood in front of Tiny, his arms wrapped around her, his chin on her shoulder as they watched Brick and Alaska enter the lodge. Brunch that morning had been lively, everyone in excellent moods. Robert had a huge spread ready and waiting when they'd all wandered up to the lodge. Spirits were high, and Ry hadn't felt as relaxed as she was now in years.

Her dad was behind bars, Tiny had made long slow love to her the night before, and not only was she watching one of her friends marry the man she'd been in love with forever, she herself was basically engaged.

The latter was hard to believe. Actually, as far as Ry was concerned, it was a miracle.

The furniture had all been pushed to the side, and Brick and Alaska had bucked tradition and entered the lodge together, walking toward where Owl was standing. Since he'd gotten certified to marry Cora and Pipe, Brick had asked if he'd marry him and Alaska as well.

Alaska was wearing a white floor-length dress with cap

sleeves. It skimmed her torso and flared out at her hips. It wasn't a wedding dress, per se, but was completely appropriate in Ry's eyes. Even if it wasn't, no one would've cared. She could've worn a hot-pink dress with orange polka dots and no one would've blinked. This was her day, her wedding, and she could wear whatever she wanted.

Her shoulder-length brown hair was pulled back in a simple upsweep, her makeup was modest yet elegant...and she looked radiant. The smile on her face was bigger than Ry had ever seen.

And Brick looked just as happy. He had on a pair of pristine black jeans and a white button-down shirt with no tie. He looked relaxed and confident, and he couldn't take his gaze off of Alaska.

Brick's mom had tears in her eyes as she watched her son walk toward Owl with Alaska by his side. From what Ry had heard, she was the one who'd fished the cross-stitch Alaska had made for Brick out of the trash all those years ago, giving it to him before he'd headed off to boot camp. A high school graduation gift that he'd kept with him for nearly two decades, until tragedy had brought him and Alaska together again.

And now, several more years later...here they were.

"Welcome to all the friends and family who've come together today to celebrate the joining of Drake Vandine and Alaska Stein," Owl said with a smile. "This isn't the start of a new relationship, but a continuation of many years of support and love they've both given to each other. Alaska and Brick have spent decades getting to know each other as friends, and we all get to witness how they've come full circle to stand before us today.

"Out of all the owners of The Refuge, Brick has truly

been our leader. Our rock. He was the one who had a grand vision for this place. Who encouraged us to keep going forward when we wanted to quit. Who always had the utmost confidence that we'd succeed. Honestly, it was kind of annoying."

Everyone in the room chuckled. Ry looked back at Tiny. "Is that true?" she whispered.

"One hundred percent," he said. "He was always positive. We wanted to throw him off Table Rock sometimes."

Ry giggled, then turned her attention back to the ceremony.

"But you know what? He was right," Owl said. "The Refuge became so much more than any of us could've imagined. More than a business. More than a money-making venture. It became our home. Our own refuge from a world that seemed overwhelming and too harsh at times. It was a place for us to heal our own wounds while we did the same for those who trusted us enough to come all the way to our small corner of New Mexico, to see what The Refuge could do for them.

"But honestly, it wasn't until Alaska arrived that we realized something had been missing from this place. We built it, kept it going, hired the best people we could to help it run like a well-oiled machine...but it lacked heart. Love. And Alaska brought that tenfold when she arrived. She not only worked her way into Brick's heart—which wasn't hard, because the man had been a goner for her ever since she'd brought him back from the brink of death in that hospital in Germany—but she embedded herself into all of our hardened hearts too.

"Alaska, Brick. You two are the backbone of this place. You've unselfishly let some of us have our wedding ceremonies here, while putting off your own. You've celebrated our successes, and suffered with us through our trials and tribulations. I can't imagine a more perfect start for your marriage than this one. Than standing before our family and friends, surrounded by everything we've all built. I have no doubt your marriage will be just like the trees around us...steadfast and strong. Blowing in the wind, but never breaking."

Ry's eyes filled with tears. She had no idea Owl had such a way with words. What he'd said was perfect. Absolutely perfect. Alaska obviously thought so too, because she sniffed and turned to Brick. "I need a tissue. I'm about to snot all over myself."

Everyone laughed at that, mostly because just about all the other women in the room were crying, as well. Once Alaska got herself under control, she nodded at Owl.

He smiled at her and said, "Brick and Alaska will mark their transition to a married couple by celebrating the love between them, but they also want to acknowledge the love that surrounds us today. The love of between couples, siblings, old friends, and new friends.

"They'd decided to exchange their own vows...so ladies, keep those tissues handy because I have a feeling we're all going to be a little teary-eyed by the time they're done."

Once again, everyone chuckled.

Brick turned to Alaska and took her hands in his. "Hi, Al," he said with a small grin.

She beamed up at him.

"To be honest, I planned out in my head this long speech about how much you mean to me, and how I'm the luckiest guy in the world, but standing here before you today, I realize that's not true. Seeing all our friends and family here with us, I know they all think *they're* the luckiest people in the world too. And that's amazing to me.

"We've all found partners who see beyond our faults. See beyond our warts and the parts of ourselves that we hate. We all deserve to be loved like that, to love someone like that in return. And with you, I can be exactly who I am. I don't have to pretend to love broccoli, or like wearing ties, just because it's what's good for me or what society thinks I should do. You've set me free to be the man I've always been, but a better version of myself.

"With you, I'm not the decorated Navy SEAL, I'm not the guy everyone looks to for answers, I'm not a problem solver, or the garbage-taker-outer, I'm simply Drake. The man you love. Who you've always loved. I'm not sure I'll ever feel as if I deserve to *have* your love, but I'm not giving it back.

"I promise to always love you. To cherish you. To come when you need me, whether that need is a glass of water because you're thirsty, or because you're locked in a speeding train in a country thousands of miles away. You own me, Al. You've owned me since I was a kid.

"During the long years when we were apart, every morning I'd look at the gift you gave me when we were eighteen, and I felt grounded. When my world was shifting around me, all it took was seeing that cross-stitch, knowing how much effort you put into it, for *me*, and I was able to find my purpose again. I feel like that every morning now, when I wake up and see you lying next to me. You're my purpose, Alaska, and in sickness and health, good times and bad, richer and poorer, I give myself to you. Today and every day that follows for the rest of our lives."

The room was so silent, you could hear a pin drop... until Brick's mom sobbed. That was followed by several sniffs around the room.

But Alaska wasn't crying. She was smiling at her almost-husband with a look of such love on her face, it made Ry truly believe in soul mates for the first time in her life.

"Wow," she whispered when Brick was done. "I totally should've gone first."

Her words broke the heavy emotion in the room, and everyone laughed.

"Get it, girl!"

Ry wasn't sure who said it, but it made her laugh harder.

Alaska took a deep breath before speaking. "Drake, I love you. I've always loved you. From that first bus ride when you sat next to me and asked if I wanted to play war with you. And yes, I remember that conversation, just like I remember all of them. You befriended me when I needed a friend the most.

"I was yours before I even knew what that meant. And when I needed you, you came. Without question. Without hesitation. I don't think you truly understand what that meant to me. How completely unusual that was. And then you continued to be there for me. Whatever I needed, you gave to me. But the only thing I *truly* wanted was you.

"I never thought it would happen. I would've been content with a lifelong friendship. But then somehow, someway, you decided that you liked me as much as I liked you. I felt like I was that little girl on the school bus all over again. I felt giddy, and excited, and scared to death.

Terrified I'd do something to mess it up. To make you not want me anymore.

"But...I've realized something since I've been here. We're not perfect. None of us are. And you know what? I'm glad. Because being perfect would be exhausting. You let me be grumpy, eat the last Pop-Tart, be selfish and sleep in when you're just as tired as me. You deal with the toughest customers so I don't have to, and you don't flinch when I wear my ugliest fat pants and huge T-shirts around the house, because you know that's what makes me most comfortable. You don't judge me, don't want me to be anyone other than who I am.

"And I feel the same about you. I never want you to change who you are because you think it's who I want you to be. You're Drake Vandine, ex-SEAL Brick, Refuge owner. And I love you so much it hurts sometimes. I'm totally rambling now and I have no idea what else I wanted to say, so I'll add one more thing then shut up so we can get on with this party...with our friends.

"You know what? I never really *had* friends. Ever. Except for you. I'd convinced myself that I was an outcast." Alaska looked around the room as she spoke. "But you all accepted me. Embraced me. Made me feel as if I was truly a part of something for the first time in my life. You came to me when you needed help, had questions, or simply wanted to talk. You'll never know how much that meant, *means*, to me."

Everyone was crying now, and Ry was no exception. It was as if Alaska had looked into her brain and pulled out exactly how she felt. She'd been that same person, the one without friends, who never thought she'd fit in anywhere. And now she was surrounded by men and women she'd felt as if she'd known her entire life. And Ry would gladly protect each and every person standing in this room. No matter what it took, no matter how many laws she had to break. She'd keep them safe from whoever or whatever tried to take them down.

As far as she was concerned, this was her family.

"Right, now we're all crying. Sorry," Alaska said with a small sniff. Then she looked up at Brick. "I take you, Drake, for my own. I'll love you if we win the lottery—which we don't play—and have a hundred million dollars in the bank, or if we're down to our last dollar. I'll love you when you're sick with a man cold and complaining that you're dying, and when we're completely healthy. When times are good, like now, and when the shit hits the fan, I'll stand by your side and love you. There will never be anyone else for me. Ever. You're it. And as far as you deserving me, or me deserving you...I think we deserve each other. We've been through hell, and we're each other's reward."

To Ry's surprise, a tear rolled down Brick's cheek. It wasn't as if she didn't think men cried, but seeing how moved Brick was by Alaska's vows was as heartwarming as anything she'd ever seen.

Alaska reached up with the tissue in her hand and dabbed Brick's face as she smiled.

"Right, now that Alaska made us *all* teary eyed," Owl said with a huge smile, "let's get this done so we can party. Before these witnesses, you have pledged to be joined in marriage. You have sealed this pledge with your vows and the rings you wear on your fingers. By the power vested in me by the state of New Mexico, I pronounce you man and wife. You may kiss the bride—but don't forget that you're in the presence of minors and we're all ready to dance and have a beer or two, so don't take all day."

Once again, everyone laughed, lightening the mood. Ry smiled as she watched Brick take Alaska's head in his hands and tip her chin up. Then he leaned in and kissed her. It was a sweet kiss. Beautiful. Until he wrapped an arm around her waist, put another behind her head, tilted her backward and kissed her long, hard, and deep. *That* definitely wasn't a chaste, innocent kiss. It was a claiming. And it curled Ry's toes simply by watching. She could only imagine what Alaska was feeling.

"You want that?" Tiny asked in her ear.

His warm breath wafted over her skin, making her shiver in delight. "Want what? Brick to kiss me? No."

"Smartass. No," Tiny said. "As if I'd let him get his lips anywhere near yours. You want a ceremony like this? With friends and family? A party? Because I'll give it to you. I'll give you whatever you want. Just say the word."

Ry turned in Tiny's arms and shook her head. "No. I've never dreamed of a big wedding. Honestly, I never thought I'd ever get married. I want what you said, a small civil ceremony. I have everything I've ever dreamed about already. You, everyone here at The Refuge. I don't need or want something big like this."

"You think this is big?" Tiny said with a grin.

"It is," Ry insisted.

"You're adorable," he told her. "Fine. No big wedding shindig. But I'm gonna want a honeymoon. I want to take you somewhere. Warm, cold, doesn't matter to me. Somewhere you've always wanted to go."

"Hawaii," Ry said without hesitation. "I want to go to Hawaii, eat malasadas, climb Diamond Head, go to the

North Shore, eat snow cones...which aren't called snow cones over there, but I forget at the moment what they're called. I want to buy a hula girl and put it on the dashboard of our car, go to a luau, and have a room with a balcony that looks out onto the ocean. I want to make love with the ocean breeze coming in through the door of that balcony and revel in the knowledge that I've got the handsomest, bravest, most Jake Ryan-est husband in the whole world."

Tiny's pupils dilated as she talked about making love, but he chuckled at her last remarks. "I love you," he told her.

"And I love you back," she said without hesitation. The truth was, she didn't need to go to Hawaii, didn't even need to leave their cabin. Wherever Tiny was, she was happy.

"Every day that goes by, you get more and more beautiful," he whispered before his head lowered. He kissed her sweetly, with only a hint of tongue, but Ry could still feel the passion in his touch. In the way his hands held her, the way he breathed unsteadily when he lifted his lips, the way he stared at her as if she was literally the only woman in the world.

"We'll go to Hawaii. I know some SEALs there. We'll get them to show us all the best places to visit on the islands. Where all the best malasadas are. We'll watch surfing competitions on the North Shore and make love every night, all night long. I can't wait to see you in a bikini."

Ry snorted. "Not happening, Tiny. Sorry, but no. Just *no*."

"Why not?"

Ry rolled her eyes. He might find her irresistible, but she wasn't comfortable in a bikini.

"Champagne for a toast!"

Turning, Ry saw Luna standing next to them with a tray filled with glasses. They were plastic, as The Refuge had no need to own champagne flutes, but it didn't seem to faze anyone around them, who were all eagerly waiting for a chance to toast the new couple.

Ry took one and smelled the drink, then wrinkled her nose.

Tiny laughed. "Never had champagne before?"

"No. I'm thinking it's not going to be for me."

"It's an acquired taste. But if you don't want to drink it, don't. No one is gonna care. Especially not Alaska or Brick."

Ry knew that. It was one more reason to love being here.

"To Brick and Alaska!" Stone said, holding up his plastic flute.

"To cross-stitch!"

"To meddling mamas!"

"To friendship!"

"To babies!"

Everyone kept calling out toasts, and everyone took sips of champagne between each one. But after her first swallow, Ry only pretended to drink. Champagne *definitely* wasn't for her. It was bitter and it made her eyes water.

Eventually, Brick held up his hand and stopped the multitude of toasts. "I don't know about you guys, but I'm ready to eat something. I know Robert and Luna made an amazing spread for us, and as much as I like being toasted as if I'm king of the world, my feet hurt."

Everyone laughed.

"But, I think we can do one last toast," he added. "To friends!"

The cheer that rose in the room was almost deafening, but Ry found herself yelling her agreement along with everyone else.

Brick and Alaska were immediately surrounded by everyone congratulating them. Ry held back, watching with a smile on her face.

"You're happy," Tiny said.

"No," Ry said with a shake of her head.

"No?"

"Nope. I'm ecstatic. Overwhelmed at how lucky I feel to be here. To be a part of this."

"You and me both," Tiny told her, wrapping an arm around her waist once more and pulling her back against him.

Ry rested against his chest and watched as the people she loved most in the world, people she never would've guessed would become her *entire* world, celebrated the joining of Brick and Alaska. She still felt the need to pinch herself now and then to make sure she wasn't dreaming. That she still wasn't in some dingy apartment trying to hide from her father.

"Come on, Ry! Come try the punch Robert made. It's delish!" Jasna exclaimed, grabbing Ry's hand and trying to drag her toward the table against the wall that held huge bowls of red liquid.

"Go," Tiny urged. "Have fun. I'll catch up with you later."

Smiling at him over her shoulder, Ry let the teenager drag her over to the punch. There were big signs in front of each, making sure guests knew which had alcohol and which didn't. Between the kids and the pregnant women, Robert didn't want anyone to accidentally imbibe.

Jasna scooped a ladle of alcohol-free punch into a glass and handed it to her. Ry cautiously took a sip. Then smiled as the flavor hit her taste buds. "This is good!" she exclaimed.

"Yup," Jasna said happily. "Maybe Elizabeth would like it."

Ry chuckled. "I'm thinking she's a little young for punch, but it won't be long before she's following you all over this place."

"I know, I was kidding! And I can't wait for her to walk," Jasna breathed. "I love her so much." Then she saw one of Cora's new foster kids across the room. "Oh! Kason needs to try this!" And with that, Ry was standing by herself in front of the punch table, but not for long.

"That looks good," Isabella said.

She smiled at Reese's sister-in-law. "It is. Although I think I might want to try the leaded variety."

They both put some of the alcoholic punch into a cup and sipped.

"Wow, this has alcohol in it?" Isabella asked as she took another swallow.

Ry was amazed herself. It tasted almost exactly like the alcohol-free version Jasna had given her. She wondered if Robert was playing a trick on everyone. Making them think they were imbibing when they weren't. But after drinking an entire glass, and feeling the effects, she decided he wasn't tricking anyone...he was simply that good at making punch.

Ry walked around the room, talking to everyone, for

once in her life not feeling out of place or too timid to strike up conversations with people she might not know all that well. Like Paige, the cook in Maisy's previous home. She was sweet and obviously very fond of the woman. She kept talking about how excited she was for the baby to arrive...which would be quite a while yet, as Maisy wasn't that far along.

She also chatted quite a bit with Khloe, who seemed intimidating at first, but once she'd talked to her for a while, Ry realized the woman felt a little out of place, and that was probably why she came across as a little stand-offish at first.

Everywhere she looked, Ry saw people having a good time. When the music started, the kids were the first ones on the makeshift dance floor. The finger food had been a genius idea, as everyone could eat and drink at their leisure while still mingling and talking. Brick and Alaska stayed together, holding hands, as they made the rounds throughout the room.

The day was perfect. Everything Ry could have wanted for her friends. A day to remember, made even better because they didn't need to worry about guests or anyone complaining about the loud party.

Ry's gaze met Tiny's across the room. He was standing with Wolf and Owl. As soon as their eyes met, he mouthed, *You good?*

Warmth filled her. It felt nice that he was concerned about her. She nodded and gave him a smile.

She was still looking at him when a loud *BOOM* sounded from outside.

Whatever it was shook the entire lodge. One of the

huge lobby windows broke into thousands of pieces as it shattered.

Jason immediately cut the music as everyone froze in place. One of the babies started crying, which seemed to break everyone out of the weird collective trance.

Tiny's eyes widened in his face, and Ry saw him start across the room toward her.

He didn't make it before another loud explosion blasted from outside. This one even louder and more powerful than the last.

Instead of getting down, like all the men were yelling for everyone to do, Ry headed for four-year-old Max. He was standing in the middle of the dance floor, crying as everyone dashed around him. The first thought in her head was to protect the kids...

The second was that somehow, someway, her father was responsible for whatever was happening. And it would be up to her to stop him.

CHAPTER TWENTY

The first explosion had Tiny freezing where he stood, but he'd started moving and was halfway to Ryleigh when the second one went off. He had to make sure she was safe! He had no idea what was happening, but it was serious, whatever it was. Explosions like the ones going off outside the lodge weren't accidental. One, maybe. But two?

No, something bad was going on, and he had to get to Ryleigh.

Instead of getting down, as he'd hoped, she'd run toward the dance floor. For the youngest of Cora and Pipe's foster kids. Max was standing stock still, crying. Ryleigh reached him just before he got to them both. Tiny didn't hesitate to snatch them up in his arms, and rush them away from the windows.

Scenarios shot through his head. Snipers. RPGs. Gas leaks. He had no idea what the threat was, only that there *was* a threat.

He went to his knees and huddled against the wall, putting his body between Ryleigh and Max and the nearest windows. He felt, more than heard, Ryleigh's phone ring-ing. It was in her back pocket, and her ass was pressed against his leg where he held her tightly.

Her head came up and her gaze met his. She took one arm from around Max and reaching for her phone.

Everything moved as if in slow motion for Tiny. He wanted to tell her not to answer it. That they were in the middle of an unknown situation, and besides, all their friends were already here. No one should be calling her. Not right now. It was too much of a coincidence, and Tiny knew deep in his bones that whoever was on the other end wasn't calling to say hello.

Pandemonium reigned around them. Babies were bawl-ing, his friends were trying to calm the invited guests, and pretty much every adult was trying to figure out if anyone was hurt. What had happened. But Tiny's attention was focused on Ryleigh.

Max squirmed in her grasp. He'd seen his sister and wanted to go to her. Ryleigh let go of him, but kept her eyes on the boy as he ran across the room to his oldest sister, Joyce, who was in a huddle with her other siblings, Cora, and Pipe.

The phone in Ryleigh's hand continued to vibrate. Whoever was on the other end wasn't hanging up. He or she wanted to talk to her with a determination that made the hair on Tiny's arms stand up.

"Unknown," Ryleigh whispered, turning the phone to show Tiny.

He wanted to take the phone from her, throw it across the room, but whatever was happening needed to be played out. And if the person on the other end was somehow responsible, they needed to know.

"What if it's him? My dad? What if he did this?" Ryleigh whispered.

"He's in prison. It can't be him," Tiny said, not really believing his own words. There was only one person he could think of who wanted to do harm to The Refuge.

Harold Lodge.

But Ryleigh shook her head. Her eyes no longer held the excitement and happiness that had been there just minutes ago. That Tiny had loved seeing so much. She once more looked like the paranoid and wary woman he'd watched over after she'd admitted lying to everyone to get the job at The Refuge.

Tiny wrapped his hand around her nape, the only thing he could think of at the moment to show her that she wasn't alone. That whatever was going to happen when she answered the phone would go down with *him* by her side. He and Ryleigh may not have exchanged vows that day, but everything Brick had said, he'd felt. And he thought Ryleigh felt the same way.

Ryleigh took a deep breath...and answered the phone. She put it on speaker, and she and Tiny bent over the phone so they could hear what was said over the voices of their friends.

"Hello?"

"Hello, daughter dear."

Ryleigh's eyes widened and her pupils dilated in fear. Tiny tightened his grip on her nape, doing what he could to reassure her.

"What...how...where are you?" she asked.

"That's not important. It sounds as if things are kind of crazy there," Harold Lodge said with a small laugh.

"What did you do?" she demanded.

"Nothing much. Just blew up two cabins. I made sure no one was in them first though. Doesn't that give me some brownie points?"

Ryleigh's horrified gaze met Tiny's. "Blew up two cabins?" she asked.

"Yup," her dad said, sounding completely unaffected. "C4 is amazing stuff. It can blow up buildings but there's not a huge fireball after. Really, daughter, you should be thanking me. That entire forest could be burning down around you right now. Instead, you just have a shit-ton of new kindling for those bonfires you all seem to like so much."

Ryleigh was shaking so violently in his grasp, Tiny had a hard time holding on to her. It was a good thing they were already on the floor, otherwise he had a feeling her knees would've given out by now.

"Why? Why can't you just leave me alone?" she asked, the agony easy to hear in her tone.

"Because you have something I want," Harold said in a hard voice. "You double-crossed me, *again*, and you already know how I feel about that. No one fucks with me, and you've screwed me over more times than I can count. I want my goddamn money, Ryleigh."

"It's not your money. It's *never* been your money," Ryleigh told him.

"I stole it. It's *mine*."

"You didn't steal anything. You made *me* steal it. So it's doubly not yours!"

Tiny was glad to see a little color coming back into Ryleigh's cheeks, and that she seemed to be getting over her shock about what happened, what her father had done. But he wasn't sure antagonizing the man was smart right about now.

"It's my money!" her dad yelled, making the people nearest them look over in surprise and curiosity.

"If you think I'm giving you anything when you're hurting my friends, you're insane," Ryleigh told him.

"I didn't think you'd simply hand it over, not when you already had that chance and failed," Harold Lodge said almost conversationally. "That's why we're going to play for it."

Tiny didn't understand what he meant, but it was obvious Ryleigh did. Every muscle in her body tensed. "No," she said firmly.

"Yes," her dad countered. "I'll give you twenty minutes to go check out my handiwork, to see that I'm serious about this. That I'm not going to fall for any more of your tricks. There's nowhere you can hide. You have no idea what building might explode next. It might be that lodge you and your so-called friend are holed up in. It might be the barn with all those adorable animals. Maybe a vehicle. Or maybe another cabin. But which one? *Nowhere* is safe from me. No *one* is safe. You play my game, or everything you've come to love is gone."

"How'd you get out of prison?" Ryleigh asked, actually sounding calm.

Harold chuckled. "It wasn't hard. All I had to do was steal a cell phone from one of the guards and I had everything I needed. I altered my records to indicate I was scheduled to be released immediately. It took like half an hour."

Tiny pressed his lips together in irritation. Someone would definitely get fired for that. For allowing a prisoner who was known for being a world-class *computer hacker* to gain access to anything electronic. And the fact that he'd allegedly just walked right out of prison irked him to no end.

Then something else occurred to him. Harold Lodge was a free man. Was out there somewhere—and he knew they were all "holed up" in the lodge. Did that mean he was hacking their cameras even at that very moment? He doubted the man would be stupid enough to step foot onto their property...but if he was pissed enough at Ryleigh, he could do anything.

"I'll give you what I can of the money. I don't have it all," Ryleigh told her father, clearly trying to do anything she could to protect everyone at The Refuge.

"Too late. We're playing. Oh, you'll give me my money, but I want to have some fun. You know my favorite game too. Twenty minutes, daughter. I'll see you online."

Ryleigh stared at Tiny with tears in her eyes.

Without a word, he stood, taking Ryleigh with him. He wanted to comfort her. Wanted to take her in his arms and tell her that everything would be okay. He had a million questions for her as well, but he didn't have time for any of that. Ryleigh apparently needed her laptop. And he needed to assess the damage, see if what Harold Lodge had said about the cabins exploding was correct, and get with his friends to come up with a plan.

As Harold had said, there could be more bombs anywhere. And he wouldn't put it past the man to torture Ryleigh by killing her new friends just because he could.

Tiny walked Ryleigh over to the blown-out window and blinked at the destruction in front of him. Two cabins had been blown to smithereens, just as Harold claimed. They were the two guest cabins closest to the lodge. Wolf and Caroline had been staying in one, and Brick's mom had been in the other. If they'd been inside...

He took a deep breath. But they weren't. They were safe...for now.

Small flames could be seen between the trees, but again, like Harold had said, the forest itself wasn't on fire. The C4 had done what it was designed to do, blow things apart, not cause a huge fireball.

Still...Harold Lodge had followed through on his threat. Tiny couldn't help remembering the asshole's last words during their first online chat and they made a lot more sense now. *It'll be fun to watch the sparks fly.*

"What the fuck is happening?" Spike asked as he joined Tiny and Ryleigh. He held his baby in his arms, the boy looking so tiny in his grasp.

"It's my fault," Ryleigh said in a small voice.

"No, it's not. It's your asshole father's fault." Tiny recounted what Harold Lodge had said, what he'd threatened.

"Meeting. *Now*," Spike said, turning to head back to where the other owners of The Refuge were standing with their wives. Their family and friends were gathered not too far away, most looking scared and confused, with the exception of Wolf and Raid. The carefree and happy wedding reception had turned into a nightmare.

Tiny followed Spike over to his friends, his hand in Ryleigh's. As far as he was concerned, she wasn't leaving his side. No way in hell.

"Sit rep," Brick barked.

Tiny once again repeated what Harold Lodge had threatened.

"What's this game he's talking about?" Pipe asked Ryleigh.

"He used to make me play it with him before I left. We'd basically battle via computer. See who could hack faster and outsmart the other to prevent an entire electrical grid from being taken down in some random city."

Everyone stared at her in shock.

"What? Is that even possible?" Henley asked.

Ryleigh nodded. "Unfortunately, yes. My dad always wanted to play the 'bad guy,' of course. He'd try to out-hack me to take down the grid, and I'd have to do what I could to prevent it. I was better than he was, so I could've stopped him, but he hated losing and would take out his anger at me by stealing more money than usual from the people in those cities who needed it the most. From government programs that helped the homeless, the poor, kids, things like that. So I learned to let him win, let the electrical grid fold. He could gloat that he beat me, then he'd usually get drunk to celebrate, and I'd bring the grid right back up again as soon as he passed out."

"So that's what he wants to do now? Play this insane game with you again? Why? What's the end game?" Stone asked.

"And what city is he targeting? Or does he want to mess with The Refuge's power supply?" Tonka asked.

"I don't know. It doesn't make sense," Ryleigh said with a small shake of her head.

"I agree. Why threaten to blow up everything at The Refuge, only to make her play a game?" Brick said.

"Does he *need* a reason? He's sick," Owl pointed out.

"What matters now is getting everyone somewhere safe," Pipe said. "If Ry makes a mistake, this wanker could decide to punish her by blowing up another cabin. We have no idea what he might strike next."

"We could all go to Los Alamos," Alaska suggested.

Spike shook his head. "Tiny said that Lodge mentioned the vehicles. He could have put a bomb in one or all of them, for all we know. The second we try to get everyone out of here, he could blow them up."

The women's faces all leached of color.

"So what do we do?" Cora asked, gaze going to her foster kids, who were standing with the other guests, huddled around their sister Joyce, who was holding onto them as tightly as if she was their mother.

Tiny met Brick's gaze, then looked to his other friends. They'd made a vow years ago never to disclose their secret to anyone. But that promise seemed pointless in the face of the current threat.

Brick cleared his throat. "The bunkers," he said.

Immediately, the owners of The Refuge all nodded.

Ryleigh squeezed Tiny's hand. He returned the pressure but didn't look at her.

"Bunkers? What bunkers?" Maisy asked.

"When we had this place built, we had seven bunkers installed. Out in the woods. Underground. One for each of us. As a precaution. When we first arrived, we were all paranoid and still dealing with our own versions of hell that we'd been through. I stashed Alaska in one when I was hunting a man who was here to kidnap her, and it was where Ry stashed Jasna when she'd gone missing, until we could get to her," Brick told the group.

"Holy crap," Reese said.

"You knew about them?" Cora asked Ryleigh.

She nodded but didn't elaborate.

"Ry found evidence of the bunkers easily enough, maybe her father did too," Tonka said.

"Maybe. But I swear I erased any mentions of them on the web that I could find," Ryleigh countered.

"It's a chance we'll have to take," Brick said. "They're our best option. The bunkers aren't huge, but they should be large enough to fit everyone. We can make an even split between women and men, keep everyone safe for the time it'll take us to search all the buildings and make sure there aren't any more bombs. While Ry does her thing, that is."

Ryleigh straightened. "No, you *all* need to go to the bunkers. There's no telling what my dad has up his sleeve. He could set off one of the bombs right when you go into a cabin to search it. *No one* is safe. You have to go with your wives and friends to the bunkers." Her voice was hard and unbending.

"I'm not sure the Wi-Fi will reach the bunkers," Tonka said. "Sometimes it gets flaky even down at the barn."

"That's okay, because I'll be right here," Ryleigh said.

Everyone immediately protested. Loudly.

But she held up a hand. "We don't have time for this," she hissed, looking at her watch. "My dad gave me twenty minutes to get online. There's only twelve minutes left. You guys have to get everyone to those bunkers. I need to get my laptop from the cabin. You go. I started this, and I'm going to end it. I've put each and every one of you in enough danger. I won't do it anymore. *Please*. Get everyone to safety."

Tiny's friends weren't happy. They were used to taking control of any kind of dangerous situation. They were used to action, not hiding. But Ryleigh was right. No one could do what she did. They couldn't pretend to be her, couldn't go online and face down her father.

Their lives were, literally and figuratively, in her very skilled hands.

"She's right," Tiny said. "Take the others to safety. I'll stay with Ryleigh."

"No, Tiny, you can't."

He ignored her protest. If she thought he was leaving her here to face Harold alone, she hadn't been paying attention to the kind of man he was. He might not be smart enough to go toe-to-toe with Harold Lodge on a computer, but he damn well could have Ryleigh's back while she was fighting for all their lives.

As the others began to plan who would go to which bunker, Tiny pulled Ryleigh to the side. "I'm going to go run to our cabin and grab your laptop. Stay here. Do *not* go anywhere, do you hear me?"

"Tiny, please! Go to one of the bunkers."

"Not happening."

"I won't be able to live with myself if you're hurt because of me," she told him.

"And I won't be able to live with *myself* if I'm hiding away in a damn bunker while you're up here battling your dad. I've got your back, sweetheart. For better or worse, in sickness and health. I'll never leave your side."

She sniffed, but thankfully nodded. "Be sure to get the power cord too, I don't know how long this will take."

Tiny kissed her hard and fast, wanting to say so much more, but the clock was ticking. He could feel it in his bones. It was a risk to leave the lodge, her father could've planned for this exact thing. He could blow him up the second he stepped inside the cabin.

But he didn't think he would. No, Harold Lodge wanted this showdown. Was cocky enough to think he could win.

Tiny would put his money on Ryleigh every day of the week. Somehow, someway, she would come out on top. She had to. Because if not, everything he'd ever wanted, everything he and his friends had worked for, would be destroyed in front of their eyes.

Tiny had never run so fast in his life as he did when he left the lodge. He was on high alert, but nothing seemed out of place...except for the slats of wood, bricks, and other debris scattered everywhere from the two destroyed cabins, of course. He grabbed the laptop and power cord from the kitchen table and was back at the lodge in under three minutes.

Ryleigh grabbed her laptop from Tiny and placed it on the reception desk. Her fingers immediately began moving over the keyboard almost frantically as she set up whatever she needed in order to play her father's "game."

While he was gone, Brick and the others had obviously explained to everyone what was going on. That they were going to evacuate to the bunkers located around the property. It would be a bit of a hike to get to them, but nothing too strenuous or that anyone couldn't handle.

Everyone looked a little freaked out, but no one was panicking. They were ready to go, split into groups...

Bunker 109 with Brick, Alaska, their dog Mutt, Brick's mom, and Robert and Luna. Bunker 110 with Tonka, Henley, Jasna, baby Elizabeth, Cheri Singleton and her daughter. Bunker 111 with Spike, Reese, baby Dylan, Woody and Isabella. And bunker 112 with Pipe, Cora, their four foster kids, and Jess and Carly.

At the one o'clock position to the lodge, bunker 101 would hold Owl, Lara, Sharyn Vogt and her mom, and the property's landscaper, Hudson. Bunker 102 included Stone, Maisy, Paige, Jason, and Savannah. And the last bunker, the one that Ry had put Jasna in for safekeeping after rescuing her, 103, would be Raiden, Khloe, Tonka's dogs Beauty and Wally, and Wolf and Caroline.

The animals in the barn would have to stay where they were, and everyone prayed they'd be all right, but with such a short time frame in order to get to safety, there wasn't a minute to spare to go down and open all the stalls, letting them escape if there was an explosive planted in the building or nearby.

Even as worried and stressed as Tiny was, he still appreciated each and every one of the women telling Ryleigh they loved and believed in her as they hurried toward the doors. He could see her shoulders relax a fraction. Knowing no one blamed her for this fucked-up situation, even if she blamed herself, did wonders for her mental health.

Soon, the lodge was empty except for Ryleigh and himself. It was eerie to look around at the food on plates, discarded on tables around the room. The half-full cups of punch. It was obvious a party had been interrupted, and if he didn't know what happened, Tiny would wonder what in the world had made everyone disappear as if into thin air.

As it was, knowing his friends would be safe in the bunkers allowed him to turn his complete attention to Ryleigh. She was hunched over her computer at the reception desk, a furrow in her brow.

And she was crying.

Tears fell from her eyes onto the desk, and every few seconds she impatiently wiped them away with her arm.

"Ryleigh?" Tiny asked in concern as he stepped closer.

"I can't believe you stayed," she whispered, but her fingers never stopped typing. "You should've gone with them."

"I told you before, I'm not going anywhere."

"I saw a movie, a long time ago. Toward the end, Sandra Bullock's in trouble. Handcuffed to a pole on a moving subway car. The hero couldn't get her out of the cuffs and they were going to crash. But instead of leaving, getting away safely, he stayed with her. Sandra Bullock couldn't believe he chose to stay with her instead of jumping off the train." Ryleigh looked up at him then, her fingers going still on the keyboard. "You stayed. No one's ever chosen me over...*anything* before."

Tiny couldn't stay away from her. Not then. He pressed against her side and lowered his forehead to her temple. "If I had to choose between a life without you and certain death—I'd choose death. Every time." He picked up his head, stared into her eyes and said sternly, "But this isn't me choosing death. No way in hell have we gone through what we have and found each other, only to die now. You're going to beat him, Ryleigh. I have absolutely no doubt about that."

She sighed. Then took a deep breath before turning her attention back to the screen in front of her. "I can beat him at this stupid game of his. He always wanted to be the bad guy when we played in the past. And I let him win. Every damn time. Because if I didn't, he was even more horrible. But it wasn't hard to figure out what he was going to do before he did it. He's predictable...or at least, he used to be. Now? I don't know. I'm positive I can beat him at games on the computer, but it's what *else* he has up his sleeve that freaks me out."

"Like what?" Tiny asked, giving her some space but staying right at her side.

She didn't look up from the screen. "He didn't set those bombs, Tiny. He's simply not that smart. I mean, sure, he could look up how to make them, but physical stuff just isn't his jam. He doesn't like getting his hands dirty...literally and figuratively. So who *did* set them? Who'd he hire to do that for him and how did they get onto the property without being seen? And are they still out there now?"

Tiny pressed his lips together. She was right.

"I've still got," she looked at her watch, "three minutes before it's time for his stupid game to start. I'm looking into the camera feeds. The ones around the cabins he blew up first. I want to see if I can find anyone lurking around."

Tiny held his breath as she scanned the camera footage. He wasn't sure what she was looking for, but he trusted her. He didn't need to be the one to study them, Ryleigh would find what she was looking for.

It didn't take long. "Son-of-a-bitch!"

Leaning forward to see what had her sounding so concerned, Tiny saw that a message had popped up on the computer screen. He had no idea who it was from, assumed it was her dad fucking with her. All it said was, *Camera 3; 10/16; 2:26am.*

Without hesitation, Ryleigh began to click on the keys,

pulling up the link to camera three on the property and pulled up the time and date indicated in the message.

"Holy crap! Look, Tiny! See that?"

He did. All he saw was trees. The footage was from one of the cameras facing the woods. One of the cabins that didn't exist any longer was in the right-hand corner of the screen. "What am I looking at?" he asked when he didn't see anything out of the ordinary. No one skulking through the woods. No birds or other animals. Nothing.

"There, *that*? See it? That branch falling? It shouldn't be there. It fell two minutes earlier. He looped the footage so it shows the same thing over and over. And since all we're looking at is trees, it was easy to miss. Shit, shit, *shit*!"

She hit a few more buttons on the screen, and the current view from the camera came up on the screen. The cabin was no longer there, just the foundation and some burning debris in the middle of it.

She switched to another camera, and they both watched as Spike helped Reese climb down into bunker III. She pulled up all the bunker cameras—of *course* she knew which ones were placed so they could see the bunkers—and they saw all their friends entering, the doors closing behind them. All that was left once they were inside was a pretty forest scene, nothing anyone who saw the feeds would think twice about.

"I need to look at the other cameras. I also have to see if I can find the missing footage. See if I can figure out who placed the bombs after he looped the footage," she muttered. But then a digital timer popped up on her screen, over the camera feeds. It started with the number twenty and began counting down.

"Take a breath, sweetheart. I believe in you. You've got this," Tiny said, feeling helpless. He hated this. Almost wished this was a mission where he could use bullets and knives to protect his teammates. Because Ryleigh *was* his teammate. His everything. But he couldn't do a damn thing other than stand next to her and let her know he was there.

"Bring it on, Dad," she muttered.

The numbers counted down to zero, then line after line of code began to scroll on Ryleigh's laptop screen.

"Fuck! That asshole! He's targeting Albuquerque," Ryleigh said as she frantically typed code Tiny couldn't even start to understand. Her fingers were pounding the keys as she muttered under her breath.

"Oh no you don't," she mumbled as she hit the return key extra hard. "That hole's closed, find another way in, assjack."

In any other situation, Tiny would've smiled at her ferocity. But not now. Every time she swore, he held his breath. Praying she'd be able to get the better of her father.

"Shit, what now?"

He saw another message had popped up on her screen. It was another time and date.

"This can't be my dad," Ryleigh mumbled with a small shake of her head.

To Tiny's amazement, the lines of undistinguishable code disappeared when she brought up the camera views again.

"What are you doing?" he asked quietly.

"Someone's feeding me intel, and it's not my dad.

302

There's no way he would've told me exactly what time and camera to look at to figure out that the camera feeds were looped. Whoever it is wants me to see whatever is on this specific time and date. While Dad's working to get through the latest hole I plugged, I have a minute or two to check out this video," she told him.

Tiny was in awe all over again. She was multitasking. Fucking *multitasking*. She was amazing. No, *scarily* amazing.

She went back and forth a few times, from the camera to the game. Then she swore. "I just sent you a video," she said, going back to the code scrolling by. "See if you recognize the guys in it."

Tiny's phone vibrated in his pocket. Clicking on the link she sent, he squinted and enlarged the video. There were two men dressed in camouflage walking through the woods. Try as he might, he had no idea who they were. He didn't recognize them at all.

"Their names are Archer and Arthur Anderson. And yes, those really are their names. It looks like they were kicked out of the Army. Dishonorably discharged. My dad found them by hacking into government files. He probably looked for the most assholey guys he could find. Offered them money, then killed them."

Tiny knew he was staring at her with his mouth open, but he was completely shocked at what she was saying. He knew she was good, but *this*? Finding all that out while playing a mental game of chicken with her father? It was fucking unbelievable.

"Are you *surmising* what he did, or telling me?" he asked her.

"Telling," she kind of grunted. "I'm in his system. He's

more worried about winning this stupid game than protecting the back doors into his hard drive. I see where he transferred ten thousand dollars into Archer's bank account. Then he did a search for their names three days later and hacked into the coroner's reports. Their deaths were ruled a murder/suicide, and the day they died, that ten thousand dollars was transferred back out of the account."

Tiny couldn't believe what he was hearing. "And he killed them himself?"

"Probably not. I don't know how long he's been out of jail, but he wouldn't get his hands dirty like that. He most likely hired someone from the dark web. Or even someone who was behind bars with him. Maybe got them released early as the form of payment. He doesn't like loose ends. Like me. But the good thing is, at least we don't have to worry about those two skulking around The Refuge, planting more bombs."

Tiny couldn't keep himself from reaching for Ryleigh. He needed to touch her. Reassure her that he wouldn't let anyone hurt her. Ever.

Looking around, watching for the slightest threat to the woman he loved, who he'd protect with his own life if necessary, Tiny felt goose bumps pop up on his arms. He suddenly felt very exposed where he and Ryleigh were located at the front desk. The slight smell of explosives was in the air, coming from the shattered window. He could hear the wind in the trees outside, but otherwise everything was deathly silent. The click of her fingers on the keyboard the only other sound.

He didn't miss how Ryleigh leaned into his touch. Even though she was focused on the screen in front of her, she was still allowing herself to take comfort in his presence.

Several minutes went by as Ryleigh continued to battle her father in the online game of wills. Then she gasped. "Oh no. No, no, no, no!"

"What? What's wrong?"

Her breathing sped up until she was almost hyperventilating. "He knows! He knows about the bunkers! I swear I removed mention of them everywhere I could find, but I obviously missed something. And now he's taunting me. Telling me that we did exactly what he wanted. That he *knew* we'd send everyone to the bunkers if he told us he'd planted bombs around The Refuge."

"And? What did he do? Talk to me, Ryleigh."

"He says the second the doors to the bunkers closed, the bombs he placed on all of them were activated."

Tiny's blood ran cold.

"If they open one, they'll all go off. Every one of them. They're connected somehow. Remotely. I don't know how. And he has the detonator." Ryleigh's hands were shaking, and Tiny could see she was having a hard time typing.

"Is he bluffing?" Tiny asked, hoping against hope she'd say yes.

"I don't know! I don't think so. He's telling me that if I send him the ten million dollars, he'll disarm them and let everyone live. But Tiny—*he won't*. Why would he? He killed those guys he hired to plant the bombs. He won't hesitate to kill everyone I love. He's *always* wanted to win. Wants me to know I'm incapable of loving. He's a *psychopath*. And he wants me to suffer."

Her hands suddenly dropped from the keyboard and fell to her sides. Ryleigh slumped forward and put her forehead on the desk in defeat. "What's the point?" she said brokenly. "He's going to win. He *always* wins!"

"Fuck that," Tiny growled. He took her shoulders in his hands and pulled her upright. Then kissed her. A hard, punishing kiss. A kiss to get her attention. "He's not going to win. No one's going to die. And you're going to figure out where he is, and *this* time he'll be put away for good. Got it?" He wasn't sure what he was saying, or even if he believed it himself. But he couldn't let Ryleigh give up. Not now. She was literally everyone's only hope of getting out of this clusterfuck alive.

She blinked. Then nodded and turned back to her laptop.

Tiny let out a small breath of relief. He wasn't sure which of his words lit a fire under her, but he was glad something had gotten through.

Then she stopped typing again. "Tiny...I've locked down The Refuge's Wi-Fi. Changed the password every week. It's encrypted to the max, and you know as well as I do that the sixteen-character password is annoying. The guests hate it, and many don't even bother trying to go online because it's a pain in the ass. I didn't change it this week, because we didn't have any paying guests..." Her voice lowered. "He's *here*, Tiny. I know it. He's using The Refuge's own Wi-Fi to play this stupid game. To taunt me. He wants to watch me suffer in person. Wants to see my face when he wins. Wants me to know he's gotten the better of me."

Tiny's heart raced. "He's here? On the property?"

"Yes. I'd stake my life on it."

This was his chance. His chance to get rid of the threat to The Refuge and his friends. Just as he opened his mouth to tell her that he was going hunting, the front door to the lodge opened.

Tiny spun, making sure his body was between whoever was entering and Ryleigh. He didn't have a gun, but he'd spent his life training for this moment. He'd do whatever it took to take down Harold Lodge, giving his life in the process if necessary.

CHAPTER TWENTY-ONE

Ry thought her heart was going to beat out of her chest. She was terrified. And pissed. It was a weird combination. Never in a million years had she imagined her father doing what he was right now. If she had, she would've left The Refuge, no matter what the consequences. But it was too late for that.

She was locked in a battle of wits with a man who'd never loved her. Had never seen her as anything but a means to an end. Even this game was a setup. He didn't care if Albuquerque lost all its power or not. He just wanted money. As it always did with Harold Lodge, everything came down to money.

He was here. She knew it in her bones. He wanted to see her lose. Wanted to see her cry, beg, promise to do whatever he wanted. He was arrogant enough to want to see her pay for her supposed sins against him in person. That would be his downfall. She hoped.

The door to the lodge opened, and she flinched. But she didn't miss the way Tiny immediately turned and put himself between her and whatever new threat had entered the building. She hated and loved that he'd done that at the same time.

But the person who entered wasn't her father. Or some other corrupt former military commando come to kill them.

It was Tiny's friend. Wolf.

"Easy, it's just me," he said, lifting his hands, showing he was unarmed.

Ry wanted to laugh. Even though the man was long since retired, she didn't think he'd ever be the kind of guy anyone *didn't* assume was a threat. Yes, earlier, when he was relaxed and happy, he'd looked pretty mild-mannered. But now? He oozed a kind of menace that she'd only witnessed in Tiny and the other Refuge owners, when one of their own had been threatened. The menace that seemed to fill the room after the cabins exploded.

It had felt overwhelming then, almost choking her with its intensity. But now she welcomed it. Embraced it.

Her dad thought she was helpless. A sitting duck. Didn't respect Tiny or anyone who lived at or came to The Refuge. Thought anyone who couldn't handle "a little adversity"—his term for PTSD—was a wuss. This coming from a man who'd spent his life hiding behind a computer, sitting on his ass in his house.

Harold Lodge was a pathetic human being. And Ry believed in karma. Sometimes it took its sweet time making people pay for their evil deeds, but eventually they got what was coming to them. And she fervently prayed that today was the day her father would come face-to-face with karma itself.

But she couldn't stop working while she waited for that

to happen. She had to continue with his sick mind games. Continue to read his taunts that popped up on the screen between the lines of code as they went back and forth. Her dad taking advantage of the power grid's security system, and her patching holes as fast as he opened them. Eventually he'd run out of holes to poke, and she'd win.

But then what? Ry had no doubt he had something planned.

As he'd said, he held all the cards. As long as he had a detonator for the bunkers, as long as he controlled who lived and who died in a fiery blast, he had the upper hand. They both knew it.

"Wolf, what the hell are you doing here?" Tiny asked.

"If you think I'm going to sit my ass in a bunker while you have all the fun, you're not the SEAL I thought you were."

Ry wanted to roll her eyes. Fun? Wolf thought this was *fun*? But then she shook her head. Of course he didn't. It was just a phrase. She was actually glad he was here. Not for her sake, but Tiny's. He wouldn't let the man she loved take any insane risks. He'd have his back, while Tiny had hers. After all, he'd been a SEAL too. They could work together.

"What's the situation?" Wolf asked.

"Not good," Tiny admitted. And the fact that he didn't sugarcoat anything made Ry respect him more. He quickly explained what was happening. Ry kept sneaking glances at the older man, and wasn't surprised at the way he frowned and looked extremely concerned. His wife was in one of the bunkers. He had every right to be worried.

"I have a friend, he was on my team," Wolf said. "He's an ordnance expert. Maybe I can call him. Go out to one of the bunkers and have him talk me through how to disarm it."

Ry wasn't so sure that would work. But she wasn't sure it *wouldn't*. She was completely conflicted. She wanted to get everyone out of those damn bunkers, right this second, but not if it meant causing all those bombs to go off—and her gut told her that Harold wasn't bluffing.

"If you want to do something," she blurted, "take Tiny and go find my asshole of a father. He's here somewhere. Watching. Waiting for the right time to blow us all to pieces. Find him and kill him before he has a chance to do the same to us."

She couldn't believe she'd just said that, had encouraged anyone to kill another person. But enough was enough. Her father was an evil man. He had to be stopped. Even if she agreed and somehow found ten million dollars to give him, he wouldn't go away. He'd come back. Wanting more. Blackmailing her, threatening her friends, doing anything necessary to get his way. The only way to make him stop, was *permanently*.

She was probably going to go to Hell for wishing for the death of her father, but at this point, Ry didn't care. As long as Tiny was safe. The Refuge was safe. She'd take whatever punishment she earned if the people she loved were protected.

"That won't be necessary, daughter dear. I'm right here."

Ry froze and her hands dropped from the keyboard.

Her father stepped out of the kitchen with a shit-eating grin on his face.

Her mouth fell open. She couldn't believe he was

stupid enough to show himself willingly. *Here*. With Tiny and Wolf by her side.

He was as good as dead, he just didn't know—

Suddenly, Wolf moved...

Turning and running straight for the front door.

Ry watched in stunned disbelief. He was literally running away! So much for her thought that he was a big bad SEAL.

Her father laughed hysterically as the door swung shut behind Wolf. "He's not going to be able to save his precious wife. I'm in control here."

Tiny shifted and sidestepped out from behind the reception desk.

"No, don't," Ry whispered.

He didn't listen. He stepped out in full view of her father, who wasn't holding a gun, but she still didn't trust him. Not in the least.

"So, you're the man who finally made my daughter a real woman, huh?"

The question was rude and crude, but Ry wasn't surprised.

"You have a choice, Ryleigh," her dad said, almost conversationally.

Ry could feel her hands shaking, but she forced herself to look at the man who, before last week, she hadn't seen for years. The man who'd done his best to make her exactly like him. Amoral. Evil. With no thought for anyone other than himself.

"Don't you want to know what the choice is?" her dad asked, clearly enjoying himself. He obviously thought he had the upper hand, but Ry would literally bet on Tiny any day of the week. She had no idea what he could do, but there was no chance at all that he'd simply stand there doing nothing for long.

"What?" she finally asked, knowing if she didn't, her father would likely start yelling.

"You can save yourself—or your friends," he said almost gleefully. "These detonators in my hands are remotely connected to two different series of bombs I've placed around this godforsaken place. When one goes off, it'll set the next one off, and so on. You can save yourself and your fuck toy, and I'll take out all the bunkers with the press of a button. Or you can choose the people out in those good-for-nothing bunkers—why anyone thought they'd be safe is beyond me—and I'll blow up this lodge with you in it. And that fancy new hangar. And the barn with those adorable...*barf!*...animals."

Ry blinked at him once. Twice. Then she couldn't help it—she laughed.

And once she started, she couldn't stop.

She probably looked and sounded like a lunatic, but she didn't care. Her father was delusional. Ridiculous. And so *stupid*.

"What are you laughing at? Stop! I mean it, stop it *right now!*" her dad yelled.

"Ryleigh," Tiny said in a low voice.

She didn't risk looking over at the man she loved more than anything else in the world. If she did, she'd probably fall into a heap on the floor. She was barely hanging on by a thread as it was. She couldn't believe her father, a man she'd once looked up to—a long, *long* time ago, before she'd realized he was a piece of shit—was threatening to blow up not only her, but dozens of innocent people. He was so much worse than she'd ever imagined, it was impossible to wrap her brain around.

"I'd give you all the money in the world if I could," she told her dad when she could speak again. She didn't recognize her own voice. She'd never talked back to him like this. But she was done cowering. Done doing everything he demanded simply because she was scared. "But I can't. It's gone. All of it. Every dime."

"What?" Harold asked. "No, it's *not*. I know you have it hidden away. Just like I taught you. Transfer it back to me, now!"

"I've given it away. To charities all over the country and the world. A little at a time. I gave it back to the people you stole it from. Veterans groups, homeless organizations, orphans, animals...you name the charity and I supported it. All the money you stole from hardworking and innocent people, from fledgling businesses that didn't have security on their accounts, even the cash you were so proud of taking from our government...it's gone. Like the wind. Given back to those who deserve it. And you know what? It felt *amazing*. So much better than stealing it in the first place."

"You're lying. You bitch, you're *lying*!" Harold shouted.

"I've even given a big chunk of it to The Refuge. The very buildings you're threatening to blow up were built with that money. The hangar? Built with donations. The cabins you already blew up? They'll be rebuilt with the money I donated."

"No! No, no, no!" Her dad screamed, his face turning dark red. "That's *my* money! I stole it fair and square!"

"Wrong!" Ry yelled back, feeling more and more confident. "You didn't steal shit! You made *me* steal it. I was a kid! All I wanted was your love, and I did everything you ever asked in the hopes you'd even so much as *smile* at me. Tell me 'good job.' Tell me that you loved me! But instead, you belittled me, told me I was worthless. That I wasn't fast enough. Wasn't sneaky enough. Wasn't *good* enough. So I worked harder. Learned as much as I could, so you'd maybe love me one day. But nothing was ever enough.

"The laughable thing is, if you'd shown me even a scrap of affection? I probably would've become just like you. I'd still be at your side today, stealing money. But because you were so cold, so heartless, you're *responsible* for everything I did. For me leaving—and taking that money with me."

It was as if she and her dad were the only two people in the world. Glaring at each other. She didn't feel intimidated, like she usually did in her father's presence. Didn't flinch. She kept her chin up as she told her father the things she'd always wanted to say, but never had the guts to voice.

"I *never* loved you," her dad barked. "Never wanted kids. Your mother was even more worthless than you. Gave me two ungrateful brats and beyond that, was barely useful for getting my rocks off. I kept her around until you were old enough to take care of yourself, then she was fucking gone."

"I was *five!*" Ry screamed. "I couldn't take care of myself! I needed my mom. My *dad!*"

"You act like you're so much better than me," Harold sneered. "But as you just pointed out, it was *you* who stole that money. *You* were the one who hacked into the coffers of the very charities you pretend to support now. And you loved it! I watched you, daughter dear, you got off on sneaking around online and taking what didn't belong to

315

you. That's why I wanted you back, working at my side. You're good at what you do because you love the power that comes with it! I might be wanted by the FBI, but you're just as bad as me. *Worse!*

"You've got everyone snowed. Everyone here thinks you're so sweet and kind. You're actually a viper in a pit of cuddly kittens. They have no idea how dangerous you are. But one day they'll figure it out, and you'll be gone. Kicked in the face. All these people you're protecting, they'll turn their backs on you faster than you can blink. You're *stupid*. You've *always* been stupid. And because of you, all of this is gonna be gone. *POOF!* Gone with one goddamn press of the button on these detonators!"

At any other time, his words would've crushed Ry. She would've taken them to heart. Internalized them. Believed what he said. But she stood tall and proud. He was wrong. About her, about her friends. And about what was going to happen here.

Because what she knew, and her father didn't, was that Wolf hadn't run away from the lodge in fear...he wasn't running to a bunker to try to save his wife.

He'd circled around the lodge and was now—even as her dad ranted and raved, completely focused on trying to belittle and demoralize her—stealthily moving out of the kitchen.

"You think I won't do it?" her dad yelled. "I will! I'll blow this entire place sky-high! It'll fucking rain body parts! And it'll be your fault. *All your fault!* I'll give you one more chance to give me my money. Ten seconds, Ryleigh. Put your fingers on that keyboard and give me my money. Otherwise...*KABOOM!*"

Ry wasn't sure how he thought he'd blow *her* up, and

not himself in the process, but it didn't matter. He wasn't going to get a chance to press the buttons on the detonators. She had no doubt of that.

As soon as she had the thought, Wolf made his move.

He lunged at her father and wrapped a muscular arm around his neck.

It was almost comical the way his eyes widened, how fast he dropped the detonators to grab Wolf's arm, trying to dislodge it from around his neck so he could breathe.

Ry winced as the plastic devices bounced on the hardwood floor of the lodge. She held her breath, half expecting to hear the horrifying sound of bombs exploding out in the forest. But nothing happened, allowing her to breathe once again.

Tiny leaped forward and grabbed the detonators as Wolf held her dad, but Harold Lodge apparently wasn't going down without a fight. As Ry watched from her safe spot behind the reception desk, Harold pulled out a knife from somewhere.

"Wolf! Knife!" she yelled—but it was too late. Her dad managed to plunge the blade into Wolf's thigh. In the next instant, the floor beneath them was slippery from what she assumed was blood coming from the wound in his leg.

Still, Wolf didn't let go of her dad. Instead, his hold around his neck tightened, her father's face turning almost purple.

Tiny quickly placed the detonators on a table and joined the fray.

Now Ry was scared. Her heart was in her throat as she watched her dad battle for his life. He wasn't an accomplished fighter, not like the two former SEALs he was grappling with, but he was desperate...and he still had a solid grip on the knife.

The fight was surprisingly quiet, the only sound grunts as her father fought to get free. The men slipped in the blood on the floor, struggling for balance. Ry saw a flash of the knife, then all three men went down, *hard*.

She ran out from behind the reception desk, ready to... what? Help? There wasn't anything she could do other than get in the way. But the urge to do *something* was overwhelming.

Then Tiny straightened to his knees. Wolf did the same.

Her father remained flat on the floor. Unmoving.

Tiny stood, holding a hand out for Wolf, who took it and got to his feet as well.

Looking back down at her father, Ry saw the knife he'd used to stab Wolf, sticking out of his neck. Blood rapidly pooling around his unmoving body.

She should've been shocked. Horrified. Instead, she felt numb.

"Sit," Tiny ordered Wolf, reaching for his arm.

But Wolf shook his head. "I'm good. Didn't get an artery. Hurts like a bitch, but I've had worse. We need to figure out how to disarm the bunker bombs."

Ry blinked. How could she have forgotten? Just because her father was dead didn't mean they were in the clear. It was possible that, as he'd threatened, he had bombs planted all over The Refuge, and if they didn't figure out how to disarm them, he could still win. Which was unacceptable.

Turning, Ry raced back to her laptop behind the reception desk.

"Ryleigh?" Tiny asked.

"Bring the detonators over here," she ordered, her voice shaking. "He said they were connected. That if one went off, they'd all explode," she muttered. "So we need to figure out which was placed first. Maybe if we can disarm that one, the others will all go offline too."

"Breathe, Ryleigh," Tiny ordered.

She jerked, not realizing he'd come up next to her. He placed one hand on her hip, and his touch grounded her. Taking a deep breath, she forced herself to relax. The bombs hadn't gone off yet, she still had a chance to save everyone.

The thought of her friends dying because of her father was abhorrent...the kids, Brick's mom. The dogs. All of them could be gone in a flash if she didn't concentrate and do what she did best.

Her father wasn't wrong. She *had* broken the law. Had stolen money. But she'd worked her ass off in the last decade to repent, to give back. She wasn't sure a court of law would care that she hadn't wanted to take that money, that she'd been trying to earn the love of a man who wasn't capable of caring about anyone other than himself, but she'd be damned if she let dozens of innocents pay for her sins.

She pulled up the surveillance cameras once again. It was an impossible task. To scroll through hours of video to try to find the men her father had hired to set the explosives. She wasn't even sure which camera to watch. Which of the bunkers was the first, let alone which day they'd been rigged to blow.

"Which one do you think it is, Ryleigh?" Tiny asked calmly from her side.

Ry's breaths came out in pants now. She couldn't do this. "I don't know," she said, sounding pathetic and defeated even to her own ears. "I don't know!" she repeated as she looked up at Tiny.

"Yes, you do. You can do this. I trust you, Ryleigh."

His trust was everything. This was a man who'd been broken by a woman's betrayal. Had spent years of his life keeping everyone at arm's length. Who couldn't even stand to fall asleep next to anyone for fear they'd try to kill him while he rested. And yet, he'd moved her into his cabin. Had slept like a baby with her in his arms. He not only trusted her, he loved her.

Her.

She'd found what she'd spent her life craving. Love. And it wasn't just Tiny's love. It was everyone's love. Brick, Alaska, Tonka, Henley, Spike, Reese, Pipe, Cora, Owl, Lara, Stone, and Maisy. And everyone else who worked here at The Refuge. She wasn't going to let them down. No way.

Closing her eyes, she took a deep breath. Then another. Her hands still shook, but she felt much more centered. She thought about the bunkers. The first time she'd learned about them. And the first time she'd used them...

"Bunker 103," she said, more to herself than anyone else. "I think he somehow knew that's where I took Jasna. If he found that archived footage, he would have picked it on purpose. It's the only bunker I have a connection to."

"Caroline's in 103," Wolf said, his voice cracking.

Determination welled up inside Ry.

"Can you disarm it remotely?" Tiny asked, holding one of the detonators. "Using one of these?"

Ry took it from him and turned the small device over in her hands. She was afraid to take it apart, even though that had originally been her plan. See if there was a microchip inside she could plug into her computer that she could deprogram. But the thought of making even the tiniest misstep made her want to throw up. This wasn't a computer game. This was real life. And real live humans would die if she messed up.

She reluctantly shook her head.

"Right, so we go to the source then," Wolf said, sounding like the take-charge Navy SEAL he was.

"The bunker," Tiny agreed.

"I'll call Dude on our way. He'll know how to disarm it and make sure the connection to the others is broken. There's no way your father found anyone better than Dude."

"I should check the videos...see if that really was the first bomb placed," Ry protested.

"No time," Tiny told her with a shake of his head. "You stay here."

She snorted. "Not happening. One, you aren't leaving me here with a dead body. With my luck, my father will come back to life and sneak up behind me, or his evil soul will possess me and you'll have a girlfriend whose head spins around at odd times. I'm coming too."

Tiny's lips didn't inch up even a fraction. "I want you safe."

"And I want my friends to not be blown up!" she cried almost hysterically. "Please, Tiny. Don't leave me here. I'm safest by your side. That's it. Nowhere else."

He stared at her for a second or two, then nodded.

The relief that flooded through Ry made her light-headed, but she didn't hesitate for a moment when Tiny turned toward the door. While they'd been talking, Wolf had made a makeshift bandage out of a couple of cloth napkins sitting on tables around the room. He limped toward the door with Tiny and Ry at his back, his phone to his ear.

This had to work. It *had* to. Wolf's buddy had to come through. If not, Ry wouldn't be able to forgive herself, ever. No matter what Tiny or anyone else said, she'd brought this threat to The Refuge. It was *her* father, *her* baggage that had brought them to this point. She needed to be there...either when everything was literally blown to bits, or to see years of running and fear come to an end.

Either way, the next few minutes would change her life once and for all.

CHAPTER TWENTY-TWO

Tiny jogged through the trees and didn't dare let go of Ryleigh's hand. Wolf was ahead of them, acting as if he hadn't just been stabbed in the thigh. But he supposed adrenaline and fear for his wife was a powerful motivator. If they lived through this, if Wolf's teammate was able to disarm the bombs, he'd make sure Wolf got medical treatment as soon as possible.

But at the moment, time was of the essence. One wrong move and a little scratch on Wolf's thigh would be the least of anyone's worries.

Tiny had been surprised when Wolf ran out of the lodge, but he didn't for one second think the man was actually leaving them behind. He knew what the former SEAL was capable of. His and Caroline's story was legendary. Not to mention all the other missions Wolf and his team had been on. They might not be public knowledge, but SEALs talked. Sometimes the gossip network from SEAL to SEAL was embarrassing. But it was thorough.

Wolf wasn't the kind of man to run from a confrontation. But he *was* smart enough to know when stealth was more practical.

Ryleigh's father hadn't gone down easily, even with both him and Wolf trying to subdue him. That knife was also damn sharp, and after Lodge attempted to swipe at Wolf's throat while they'd been grappling, Tiny had wrestled it away from him—and was hit with sudden clarity.

Ryleigh was right. Harold Lodge would never stop trying to hurt his daughter and everyone she loved. He couldn't be contained in a regular prison. All it would take was one illegal cell phone, and the man would be out once more. He'd proven that. So Tiny did what he had to do. He didn't enjoy killing, but in this case, it felt damn good.

Never again would Harold bother his daughter. Never again would he make Ryleigh feel as if she had to disappear to protect him or anyone else. She could live her life free and clear from the monster who'd raised her.

Tiny hated that she was with him now though, headed toward the rigged bunkers. But if her father had been telling the truth—and he had no idea if he was—she was probably no safer in the lodge or anywhere else on The Refuge than she was with him. And...he couldn't deny he felt more steady with her at his side.

She'd been amazing. He'd always known she was good at what she did. He'd seen her in action. But watching her single-handedly save an unsuspecting Albuquerque from a major blackout was crazy impressive. Tex had been right all those months ago when he'd admitted that Ryleigh was a better hacker than he was. She was one of a kind.

They approached bunker 103, the one that was in the three o'clock position from the main lodge. "Where is it?

It can't be near the opening, it would've been spotted," Tiny mused.

"Right, the guys would've known something was off and wouldn't have gone inside the bunkers if they thought there was any kind of danger. I know I didn't see anything when I was helping Raid get the dogs inside this one," Wolf said.

Tiny's gaze ran over the ground where the bunker was buried, then he pointed to a disturbed plot of earth near where the back side of the bunker would be. "There."

The three of them crept forward, and Wolf awkwardly went to his knees about a foot away from the disturbed ground. He held up his phone to Tiny. "Hold this? Put it on speaker so I can hear Dude."

Nodding, Tiny took the phone. He felt Ryleigh's fingers curl into the waistband of his pants. Knowing she was there made him practically vibrate with nerves. If this bomb went off, they'd all be dead. Immediately. He clicked on the speaker button of the phone.

"Dude?" Wolf asked.

"Tell me what you see," the man on the other end of the line ordered. He was no-nonsense, which Tiny appreciated.

"Can we use FaceTime?" Tiny asked. "It would make this easier, I think."

"The cell signal isn't strong enough out here," Ryleigh said softly from behind him.

Tiny swore. He'd forgotten. The first thing he was going to do when they got out of this was see about getting more cell towers in this area of their forest. Even if The Refuge had to pay for every cent of getting it done, even if they had to bribe someone at the phone company, he'd make that happen.

"Don't worry, Dude can walk me through it. He doesn't need to see the bomb to know what to do," Wolf said, sounding completely calm.

"Wolf, talk to me," Dude said, his tone irritated now.

"Dirt. The bomb was buried. I'm afraid to clear it because I don't want to set it off."

"From what you told me, I don't think that'll happen. If the scumbag had a detonator, it won't blow from dirt being removed around it. Just go gentle."

"Ten-four on that."

Tiny watched, hating the helpless feeling that was almost overwhelming as Wolf slowly uncovered the bomb.

"What's it look like?" Dude asked.

Wolf described what he was seeing, what color the wires were, how they were hooked up.

"Seems like a pretty crude apparatus to me," Dude said.

"My father said they were all connected. That if one went off, they'd all go," Ryleigh interjected.

"I don't think that's true," Dude said. "I mean, what Wolf described seems to be amateurish. And if your father found soldiers who'd been dishonorably discharged, that wouldn't surprise me. They probably didn't get through bomb-making one-oh-one, much less the more advanced techniques."

Tiny felt Ryleigh lean against him as she whispered into his ear, "Was that a joke?"

His lips twitched, but it was more from nerves than humor. "I think so," he said with a nod.

"Wolf? You said there's yellow, purple, and red wires, right?"

"Yeah."

"Figures the assholes couldn't even use the correct color wires. And there's an electronic box strapped to the top of it? The light is blinking, yeah?"

"Uh-huh."

"Right. So all you need to do is pull the purple wire out from the bottom of the blinking box."

Tiny tensed. That seemed *way* too easy.

But Wolf didn't hesitate for even a second. As soon as Dude finished speaking, he pulled the purple wire. It came out of the electronic device with a simple tug.

Tiny held his breath, bracing himself for an explosion.

"Wolf? Did you do it?"

"Yup, and the light's not blinking anymore."

"Right. Then it's done."

"That's it? *Really?*" Ryleigh asked.

"Yes. C4 is actually a very stable explosive. It's why it's so popular in the military. We can stuff it in our ruck sacks and not worry about it going off simply by being jostled around."

Wolf painfully got to his feet and headed for the hidden door to the bunker.

"What about the other bombs? Can they be disarmed just as easily?" Tiny asked. On the one hand, he was very relieved the bombs weren't all linked, after all. And it didn't seem as if the bomb could be triggered from someone opening or closing the bunker doors, otherwise they all would've gone off when their friends and family entered them. But on the other hand, there could very well still be six active bombs ready to explode.

"I don't know. They'd need to be described to me before I could tell you that for sure."

Tiny looked at Wolf, who now had his wife clasped in a bear hug. "Wolf, can I take your phone? I want to check those other explosives."

Wolf waved him on.

"Stay here," Tiny told Ryleigh.

To his amusement and irritation, she rolled her eyes. "Not happening. Come on, we need to get moving."

The next thing Tiny knew, he was running toward bunker 102 with Ryleigh at his side. When they arrived, they cautiously looked around and found another slightly disturbed area of dirt. Tiny carefully unearthed the bomb and, to his relief, it looked exactly the same as the first. Just to be safe, he described it to Dude, and once again his recommendation was to simply pull the purple wire out of the electronic box strapped to the top of the C4.

Ryleigh opened the door to the bunker. Tiny briefly explained to Stone everything that had happened, then told him to head back to the lodge and find something to cover Harold's body, to make sure none of the women or kids saw it. He also asked him to keep everyone out of the lodge to preserve the scene. The cops needed to be called. But first, they had more bombs to defuse.

He and Ryleigh jogged through the trees once more, toward bunker 101. In total, they repeated the process of disarming the bombs Harold's accomplices had planted five more times.

When they opened the last bunker, 109, with Alaska and Brick inside, Tiny was exhausted. He felt like he did after a particularly grueling two-week mission to Iran when he was a SEAL. They'd had to sneak into the country over the mountains, then leave the same way after killing their HVT. He felt as strung out and shaky as he had back then.

"Thank you," he told Dude. "You have no idea how much your assistance means to me and my friends."

"I'd advise that you check out every other building on your property. See if you can bring in a bomb-sniffing dog. Wait, I think I have a contact, I'll see if he can get out there ASAP. You don't want to risk thinking all is well, only to have some hidden bomb go off."

"Yeah, I agree. Although, the asshole lied about these being connected, he probably lied about the rest of the bombs too. But I'm not willing to take that chance."

"Tell Wolf to call me later when he has a moment. Want to make sure he and Caroline are good. My Cheyenne will want to talk to Ice, as well."

"Will do. Anytime you and your family want a vacation, The Refuge is open to you. At no charge...no pun intended."

"Thank you. Have any cabins away from the others? I'm thinking my wife and I will need some privacy."

Tiny chuckled. "Yes. We'll make that happen." He watched Ryleigh embrace Alaska as she reassured her that everything was all right. Luna was crying as she joined the others in a three-way hug.

"Tiny?"

"Yeah?" He barely remembered he was still on the phone with Dude.

"She did good. Your woman. Stayed right by your side. Not sure you could ask for anything more from a partner."

"Except for her to stay where it was safe," he murmured.

"She's safe with *you*. She knows it, and was smart enough to stay where she needed to be in order to feel protected."

Dude wasn't wrong. But the funny thing was, Tiny felt just as protected by her. It wasn't about him being a man, a SEAL, it was about knowing if the shit hit the fan, she was smart enough to help him figure out what their next steps should be. They were a team, and it felt amazing. "Yeah."

"Right, gonna let you go. Don't forget to tell Wolf to call me later."

"I won't. Thanks again, Dude. Seriously, I don't know what we would've done without you."

"Your woman would've looked up how to disarm bombs and figured it out," he said with a chuckle. "Later."

Tiny clicked off Wolf's phone and stuck it in his pocket. Dude wasn't exactly wrong. Ryleigh totally would've researched how to disarm a bomb, or she would've found someone on the dark web who'd know how to do it. Anything The Refuge needed, any kind of expert they needed, he had no doubt Ryleigh could find.

Once upon a time, the power she had would've scared him. But now? After going through what they had? He embraced it. His Ryleigh was amazing. A treasure. He could no more be afraid of what she could do than he was the skills of his fellow special forces friends. They were all scary in their own right. And yet, their women didn't cower from them. Didn't expect them to suddenly start using the skills they'd learned in the military to harm others. Why would he think Ryleigh would do any different?

A hand clasped his shoulder, and Tiny turned to find

Brick standing there. Before he knew it, he was hugging his friend. Hard.

"Thank you," Brick said huskily.

Tiny pulled back and nodded at him. Today had been a roller-coaster of emotions. Both men were well aware they could've lost everything. The Refuge, the loves of their lives, their friends and family. Today had been way too close of a call, but Harold Lodge was no longer a threat. Hopefully now everyone could relax and live happily ever after.

Tiny grinned a little at the thought. Who was he kidding? He had no doubt there would be a ton more ups and downs as they all raised families and continued serving the PTSD community. But together, they could conquer anything. They'd proven it time and time again.

"Come on, we need to get back. Check to make sure the lodge is safe, then deal with the authorities," Brick said.

Tiny pressed his lips together and nodded. There would be questions about what happened, how a dead man came to be on the floor with a knife in his neck.

He felt Ryleigh's arm go around his waist and his anxiety quieted. "The cameras were running. It's all on video. As much as I would like for the things my father said never to be repeated again, I'll face whatever consequences I have to face to make sure you and Wolf don't get in trouble for killing him."

Tiny leaned down and kissed the top of her head. "There will be no consequences."

"But—"

"No. Consequences," Tiny enunciated. "We have connections, sweetheart. And you're too good to leave a trail. You're fine. Besides, who will believe the rantings of a demented man? A man who was wanted by the FBI and broke out of prison?"

"And who planted nine bombs—that we know of—and blew up two buildings?" Brick added.

"You're one of us," Alaska said as she sidled up to her brand-new husband. "And we protect what's ours."

"Damn straight," Brick agreed.

Ryleigh smiled and snuggled against Tiny. He was still exhausted, and wasn't looking forward to dealing with the authorities back at the lodge, but nothing felt as good as his woman at his side.

Mutt barked once, as if to tell them to stop talking and start walking. Brick chuckled and patted his dog on the head. "Sorry, we're going," he told him. Then he took Alaska's hand on one side, and his mom's on the other, and started heading for the lodge.

Luna and Robert were behind them, and before Ryleigh could follow, Tiny held her in place.

She turned so she was against his front and looked up at him. "Tiny?"

"I love you," he said.

She smiled. "I love you too."

"I'm also proud of you. And in awe. What you can do… it's extraordinary. You're way too smart for the likes of me. To be out here in the middle of nowhere. But I'm not giving you up. You can do whatever you want, work for whoever you want, I know for a fact our government would love to have you on their payroll, or you could work as a security consultant teaching companies how to avoid being hacked. I don't know. But I'm not letting you go. I'm yours, sweetheart. For now and always."

She smiled up at him. "How about The Refuge? Can I work here?"

"As I said, you can work wherever the hell you want, as long as you let me stay by your side. Because I'll tell you one thing, the safest place I've ever felt is right here. All you need is a cell phone and you can do anything. Take down terrorists, save the oceans and planet, make the world a better place."

"Tiny," she whispered, clearly overwhelmed.

"No, don't cry. I'm just stating facts. We need to go make sure the lodge is safe, give statements to detectives, you need to download security footage to give them so they can see that your father was a threat and we were defending ourselves." He kissed her then. And not a brief kiss either. He put all the love he had for her into the embrace. Showing her without words his love, his trust, and his pride in all she could do.

When they parted, they were both breathing hard.

"Is it bedtime yet?" Ryleigh asked. "The only thing I dislike more than bugs and being in the great outdoors is exercise. And we had to have jogged for miles and miles."

Tiny chuckled. He looked at his wrist. "Actually, it's not even dinnertime."

She blinked. "Seriously? It feels as if hours and hours have passed."

"I know. But it actually hasn't been that long. If we hurry and get through the rest of the crap stuff, maybe we can even finish out the reception."

Ryleigh smiled. "I'd love that. And I know Alaska would too. It would be just what we need to put this shitty day behind us."

"Amen to that," Tiny said. Then he took her hand in

his and they started after the others, through the trees. There was a lot of work to be done. Cabins to be rebuilt, holes in their security to be patched, the C4 had to be removed...but first, they needed to see their friends. See for themselves that everyone was safe and unharmed.

Then their future lie ahead of them. The possibilities were endless, and Tiny couldn't wait to experience every moment with this woman at his side.

CHAPTER TWENTY-THREE

When Ry and Tiny got back to the lodge, everyone was pretty keyed up. The police and fire department were already there. The cabins exploding had been heard—and felt—all the way to Los Alamos and people had called 9-1-1 immediately.

Two hours later, her father's body had been removed, the evidence of his death scrubbed away, and all the buildings had been searched for additional explosives—with no more found. The bomb squad from the Los Alamos Police Department was working to remove the C4 and the bombs at each of the bunker locations.

"I'm sorry your bunkers are no longer a secret," Ry told Tiny when they had a moment to themselves in all the chaos.

"It's okay. They've served their purpose. Once upon a time, we needed them for our own peace of mind, but as time has passed, and as we've all found our soul mates, I think we've outgrown them."

"That's good," Ry told him, squeezing the hand she still held.

"Yeah. And I'm thinking after today, we'll probably have them dug out. Maybe sell them. The thought of what could've happened to everyone if Wolf wasn't here to call his friend..." Tiny shuddered.

Ry hugged him. Hard. He returned the embrace just as fiercely. Then he pulled back. "How are you doing? That was a pretty intense scene you went through."

"I'm fine."

"Ryleigh, don't shut me out," Tiny said with a frown as he looked down at her, his hands clasped at the small of her back as he held her against him.

She shrugged. "My dad used to do that kind of stuff all the time. Tell me I was under a time crunch...which, I might've been, because I wasn't always as good as I am now at hacking, so if someone had caught me mucking around in their files, it could've been bad."

"I didn't mean the power grid thing, though that was truly awful. But also...you shouldn't have had to see your father like that."

"What? Crazy? Money-hungry? Fucking insane?" Ry said, a little harsher than she intended. She took a deep breath. "Sorry. Tiny, any feelings I had for my dad had long since died. He wasn't a good person. No, that's an understatement. He was a monster. Absolutely no empathy for anyone other than himself. He didn't care what *anyone* else was thinking or feeling.

"What happened today *had* to happen. You know as well as I do that if he was taken into custody again, it would only be a matter of time before he got free. Here's the thing...the world revolves around computers. My father might not have been as good as I am at manipulating code, but he was still very knowledgeable. What happened today, him dying, is best for everyone."

"Still...he was your father."

Ry shook her head firmly. "No. He stopped being that a long time ago. Now...can we please talk about something else?"

"All right. But Henley is always here if you need to talk, and me too, of course."

"I appreciate it, but honestly, Tiny, I'm good. Promise."

"Okay."

Just then, her cell phone rang. Surprised, because pretty much everyone she cared about or knew was there with her, Ry pulled it out of her pocket and glanced at the screen, only to see the number had been blocked. She was about to ignore it...but something made her answer instead. "Hello?"

"Don't hang up. It's Bryce."

Ry blinked in surprise. Then panic hit.

She hadn't heard from her brother in...*years*. She'd known her dad still talked to him very infrequently, and the last thing she needed or wanted was to get rid of one threat, only to find out the relief she felt at her father's death was premature.

"Ryleigh? That *is* the name you're going by these days, right?" her brother asked.

Obviously seeing her distress, Tiny took her arm and pulled her off to the side, out of earshot of everyone else, taking her phone out of her hand. He clicked a button to put it on speaker and asked in a low, harsh tone, "Who is this?"

"Who's *this*?" Bryce countered.

"Ryleigh's man. And someone who will do whatever it fucking takes to protect her. Now who the hell is this?"

"Bryce. I'm her brother."

Ry took a deep breath and nodded her head at Tiny. She hoped Tiny remembered her telling him about her brother. How Bryce was older than her and wasn't around when she was growing up. He'd left the house even before her mom, and didn't exactly get along with her father. Ry barely knew him...but she could never take the chance that he wouldn't tell their dad where she was hiding if she'd reached out to him while on the run. From everything her dad had told her, thrown in her face, he was a computer genius...so it wasn't hard to understand how he'd found her. But she had no idea why he was contacting her now.

"What do you want?" Tiny clipped.

"Ryleigh? Are you still there?"

"I'm here," she said.

"When we're done talking, I won't contact you again, and I'd appreciate if you did the same. We're free now. Both of us."

"Both of us?" Ry asked, intrigued.

"Dad's been unhinged for a long time, but even more so lately. Bitching about you and that place where you've been hiding out. I ignored him, the way I have for years, until he decided to blackmail me into helping him get you back into the fold, so to speak. He figured with my...*experience* with Army databases, I had connections. Dad didn't find Archer and Arthur Anderson. I did. They were total morons. They knew about explosives only because they fancied themselves preppers or some such shit. Anti-government, the whole shebang. I recommended them to Dad because I knew they'd do the

338

minimum they could to get paid, and they'd screw up even that much."

Ry couldn't believe what she was hearing. "Are you serious?"

"Deadly. And I was right. They only placed half the bombs they were paid for. And those bombs on the bunkers were easy to disarm, weren't they?"

"Yeah," Ry said softly.

"Good. Then everything went as it should."

"You sent those messages, didn't you? Telling me what parts of the videos to watch?" Ry asked.

"Yes. It would take too long for you to find what you needed to know, so I pointed you exactly to what you needed to see. I knew your SEAL boyfriend and his friends could handle the bombs, and I'd hoped they'd take Dad out as well. We're both free. He's been a thorn in my side for years. Blackmailing me, threatening me, basically making my life a living hell. And now it's done. For both of us."

Ry had mixed feelings about what she was hearing. She never knew Bryce really, had no idea their dad had been using threats to control him much as he'd done with her. Since he'd never attempted to reach out, had left her to suffer alone for decades, she figured Bryce was probably cut from the same cloth as their father. That he was just as bad. Hearing differently, that he'd done what he could to help her, to rid them both of the black cloud hanging over their heads, was a huge surprise.

"Be well, Ryleigh. Have a good life. I know I will."

Then the line went silent.

"Bryce?"

But he didn't answer. He'd hung up.

Ry looked up at Tiny, at a loss as to what to say.

"*Fuck me*!" Tiny exclaimed as he pulled Ry into his arms. She snuggled against him, feeling better knowing that her man seemed just as surprised as she was by the entire conversation.

Eventually, she pulled back. "Should we tell the police what we just learned?" she asked.

Tiny sighed. "Probably. But I'm thinking we should let it go. We have no proof that what he said was true. And do you want them tracking your brother down to find out more information?"

"No," Ry said without hesitation. Bryce had never been a part of her life, merely one more person in the background that may or may not want to do her harm. If he was telling the truth, he'd done her a huge favor. And she wasn't going to repay that by dragging him into their father's misdeeds or legal trouble.

"Right. So, I feel as if I need to ask this again. And I'll probably keep asking you for a while, just to make sure. Are you good?"

Looking up at the man she loved, Ry realized she was more than good. A huge weight had been lifted from her shoulders. Her dad was dead, her brother wasn't waiting in the wings to take up where he'd left off. She could truly live now. Move on with her life...with Tiny. "I'm good," she reassured him.

Looking around the room, Ry saw, to her relief, that no one was freaking out. Everyone was talking quietly amongst themselves. It didn't seem as if anyone had left either. They were all still gathered together, supporting each other. "Everyone else seems to be handling what happened all right too," she mused.

"The guys are pissed I didn't tell them what was happening and call them in for backup," Tiny said with a shrug.

Ry frowned. "It wasn't as if we had time to casually give them a call and tell them what was going on. Besides, we thought if they'd left the bunkers, they'd set off the bombs."

"I told them that, but they still aren't happy."

"Well, they just need to get over it," Ry said a little huffily.

Tiny chuckled. "They will. They just need some time. Uh-oh, incoming."

Ry turned and looked at where he indicated with his head, and saw all the women coming her way. Tiny let go of her. "I'm going to go talk to Wolf, but I'll be watching. You need me to run interference, let me know and I'll get you out of here."

"Thanks, but I'll be fine," Ry told him, loving that he was both giving her space *and* keeping watch over her.

He kissed her briefly before heading toward where Wolf was standing with his wife, talking to Woody and Isabella.

Ry braced herself for whatever it was her friends wanted to talk to her about, because it was more than obvious they had something on their minds. But Alaska didn't give her a chance to say anything, she grabbed Ry and hugged her so hard it almost hurt.

"We're so glad you're okay," Alaska said when she pulled back.

"I'm fine," Ry reassured her and the others.

"You aren't leaving," Reese blurted.

"What?" Ry asked in confusion.

"In case you're feeling all guilty, or like you're somehow tainted because of what your dad did...we don't want you to leave," Reese said a little more calmly.

"Oh," Ry said, surprised.

"We know you. You're probably feeling as if maybe we don't trust you because of what Harold did. Or we might hold a grudge, but that couldn't be further from the truth," Henley said gently.

"We need you," Cora told her.

"Yeah, who else will fix the Wi-Fi when it goes out?" Maisy asked.

"Or get rid of the viruses on our computers?" Reese added.

"Or give me the Christmas Tree Cakes Robert slips you because you're his favorite?" Lara said with a smile.

Ry felt so blessed to have these women as friends. She suddenly felt overwhelmed with emotion. "You all could've died. Your kids, husbands, friends and family..." She couldn't continue.

Alaska pulled her into another hug. Ry felt Henley hug her from behind, then the other women joined the group squeeze. Ry was in the middle of all her friends, and she'd never felt so content, so loved.

"We didn't," Alaska said. "Besides, we didn't even know we were in any danger, so if you're thinking us being in those bunkers was traumatic, you're wrong. You were the one who had the horrible experience, not us. And you saved us."

Ry shook her head. "No, I didn't. Wolf's friend Dude did."

But Alaska pressed her lips together stubbornly. "No, *you* did. I don't know everything that happened, but I'm positive that you and your super computer skills figured out exactly what information the guys needed to do their thing. Us women, we're stronger than society gives us credit for. We somehow form tiny humans in our bodies then squeeze them out our vaginas. We feed them, raise them, manage our husbands, work, and maintain friendships. We're *awesome*. And you...Ry, you've overcome so much. And you're so *smart*. I'm sure you could go anywhere, work for anyone, but we want you to stay. With us. Here. Please tell us you won't leave."

"Leave?" Ry said, a little overwhelmed. "Why would I want to leave the only family I've ever known? The only friends I've ever had? Besides, there's a lot of work to do around here with rebuilding the cabins, the bunkers have to come out, and so much more."

Everyone cried out in glee, then they were in a huge group hug once more.

"Do you think we can get the party going again?" Henley asked with a smile. "I don't know about you guys, but I think we need to relieve some of the tension still hanging over everyone. Maybe with some more dancing."

"Yes!" everyone said, almost in unison.

When everyone had wandered away, Alaska hung back.

"I'm sorry my father ruined your wedding day," Ry told her.

But the other woman shook her head. "Made it a little more memorable, maybe, but ruin it? Nothing would ruin the day Drake finally made me his, officially. I feel as if I've waited my entire life for this day, and nothing, *no one*, can ruin it." She put her hand on Ry's arm. "Seriously, thank you for saving all our lives."

Ry felt herself blushing. "As I said before, I didn't."

"You can go on thinking that if you want, but everyone here knows differently. You're a vital part of The Refuge, Ry. Don't ever think otherwise. And it's not because of your amazing computer skills. It's because you're *you*. Your kindness, the way you're always there when someone needs you. How down-to-earth and practical you can be. The Refuge needs you as much as you need it."

"Thanks," Ry murmured.

"You're welcome."

The music started, a little softer than it had been before everything happened, but Alaska beamed. "Come on! It's the electric slide, we have to do it!"

"Are you kidding me? The electric slide?" Ry asked with a laugh.

"Yup. It's mandatory, and it's my wedding day, so you have to do what I want."

"You're going to go all bridezilla on me *now*?" she joked.

"Yes!" Alaska said, pulling her toward where the other women had lined up in the middle of the floor.

Ry let herself be led to the makeshift dance floor, but she caught Tiny's gaze as she went. He lifted a brow at her, clearly wanting to make sure she was okay. Ry smiled at him, and she actually saw his muscles relax at seeing she was all right.

This might be a celebration of Alaska and Brick's marriage, but Ry felt as if it was somehow her own party. A culmination of years of heartache and terror. Her reward for not having to run and hide anymore. Her father would never threaten her or the people she loved ever again. And while she couldn't erase anything she'd been through, Ry was determined not to let her past rule her life. She was responsible for her future, and from what she could tell right now, surrounded by friends and so much love she could feel the air vibrating with it, she was going to have an amazing life. Here. At The Refuge. A place where broken people came to heal. To be themselves. To not be judged.

The Refuge was a miracle. It had brought Ry everything she'd ever wanted. She had no idea what the future might hold, but she had no doubt whatever it was, it would be chaotic, messy, and full of enough love for anyone who stepped foot on the property.

EPILOGUE

Tiny winced at the loud screaming coming from the large play area behind the owners' cabins. One of Cora and Pipe's newest foster kids was being chased by Rebecca, Maisy and Stone's third child...who, at just five, thought she was in charge of everyone.

"What's the princess screaming about now?" Stone asked as he joined Tiny.

The small, proud fatherly smile on his friend's face made Tiny chuckle. "She's a holy terror," he said.

"Yup," Stone agreed without hesitation.

"You guys seen Patrick?" Spike asked.

"He's inside with Josiah and Samantha," Pipe said from behind them.

Glancing over his shoulder, Tiny grinned when he saw Pipe—holding *his* daughter. He immediately turned and held out his arms for his baby girl. "Thanks," he said.

Pipe smiled, handing the freshly changed, sleepy baby over to her father.

Tiny stared down at Miracle. She was perfect. It had

taken almost nine years for Ryleigh to get pregnant. And many tears and disappointments. She'd had three miscarriages, and the doctors hadn't thought little Miracle would make it to full term either. And yet, here she was.

Elizabeth, Dylan, Matthew, and Max ran out of the building behind them, into the yard, adding to the chaos. Brick, Tonka, and Owl joined Tiny, Stone, Spike, and Pipe on the porch. They all watched over their children as the ladies had one of their weekly "women-only" breaks.

The last ten years had been full of good times and bad. There had been a lot of changes to The Refuge, changes Tiny could never have imagined when he and his friends had started this place so long ago.

It hadn't taken long before the guys realized having The Refuge remain a child-free retreat wasn't something they could continue. Not with the number of babies that were being born. So they'd updated the website, made it clear that there were babies and children who lived on the premises, and if kids were a trigger for anyone's PTSD, they encouraged guests to find another place to visit.

They *did*, however, build new owners' cabins a good distance away from the main lodge, both to maintain their own privacy and make sure the guests still had as relaxing a stay as possible. The new cabins were much bigger, and set in a massive circle around a central play area and a mini-lodge, where they could all gather and hang out.

That's where Tiny and his friends were now. Standing on the covered porch, watching their children play.

Tonka and Henley had only had one child together, Elizabeth. Jasna was currently in Albuquerque, finishing up her degree. Reese and Spike had the three kids they'd always wanted—Dylan, who was ten; Patrick, who'd arrived three years later; and little Joyce, who'd just turned four.

Lara and Owl also had one, a little girl they'd named Samantha Jean. She was nine and a half going on eighteen. They'd wanted more, but when Sam's birth had almost killed Lara, Owl put his foot down and refused to even consider risking the love of his life's health with another pregnancy.

Cora and Pipe had adopted their original foster children. Their Joyce was twenty-seven now, living in Los Alamos with her husband and two children; Kason was twenty-three and had moved to Los Angeles to pursue an acting career. He'd just gotten a huge part in a big-time crime show on TV. Shannon was eighteen and planning on staying at The Refuge, working part-time while going to community college. And Max was fourteen and the high school's basketball star, even though he was only a freshman.

The couple had fostered almost two dozen children in the last ten years, making a huge difference in each and every one of the kids' lives. They currently had two fosters living with them at The Refuge, a ten-year-old boy and a sixteen-year-old girl.

Maisy and Stone had four kids, Matthew, Josiah, Rebecca, and Luke. They were spaced two years apart, with their oldest being nine. So they'd had their hands full for almost a decade, and had decided they were officially done with having children.

Alaska and Brick didn't have any children of their own. They'd thought about it, but since Alaska was forty when they'd gotten married, they'd decided together that they were content to run The Refuge and help care for their friends' babies and children.

With all the kids, The Refuge was a lively place. There was always something happening. Hikes, bonfires, scavenger hunts. And Tiny and his friends reveled in the chaos. Sure, there were times Tiny missed the serenity The Refuge used to offer. But it was worth it when he lay down at night next to Ryleigh, with their little Miracle snuggled between them.

"Who would've thought this is where we would've ended up?" Brick mused as they watched all the kids run and play in the yard.

"Not me," Tonka said with a shrug.

"Me either," Spike agreed.

"It's funny," Owl mused. "It wasn't too long ago when we were deciding what kind of place we wanted The Refuge to be, and we were all in agreement that it should be an adults-only retreat."

Tiny chuckled. He'd just been thinking the same thing. "And that we wanted it to be simple, with only a few cabins and employees."

Everyone laughed at that. They'd certainly expanded the place, adding cabins and hiring more full-time staff. They now had twenty full-time employees. From housekeepers and admins, to cooks and animal wranglers. They had an expanded barn full of animals that were constantly being visited by the guests, a helicopter that kept Owl and Stone more than busy. Between aerial tours, helping out with searches for missing people and with wildfires, they were in constant demand in their area of the state.

They had Girl and Boy Scout weeks, where they donated the cabins to groups to have jamborees and learn about outdoor safety. The Refuge had become a place not only for those with PTSD to come to heal, but for all sorts of groups to learn various survival skills.

The changes were extensive, but in Tiny's eyes, they made The Refuge more well-rounded. And none of it would've been possible without Ryleigh.

He was the only one aware of *exactly* how much money she'd donated to The Refuge.

The FBI had spent eight hours with her in an interrogation room not too long after her father was killed. Eight hours that had almost broken Tiny. He'd wanted to protect her from their questions. Wanted to storm into the room and steal her away. If they'd thought for one second they'd charge her for her father's crimes, or make her do time for what they perceived was her part in the thefts, he'd been ready to flee the country with her. There was no way he'd have let her spend one day behind bars for something her father had forced her to do.

But in the end, the FBI never wanted to incarcerate her—they'd wanted to hire her. They weren't stupid. They'd realized immediately that having someone with her skills on their payroll would be a huge boon.

The money she hadn't been able to give away at the time of her father's death—around eight million—continued to grow through interest and smart investing, and Tiny was well aware his wife was still funneling a steady stream into The Refuge, as well as the other charities she liked to support. But he never said a word. Simply let her do what she needed to do in order to exorcise the demons she still had from her past.

She still worked for the FBI. Digitally tracing cybercriminals. Tracking down fugitives using their online and cell phone activities against them. Tiny was sure there were many things she did that weren't exactly legal, things that would give him a heart attack if he knew more details...but then again, hadn't he done the same thing when he was a SEAL? Missions that were top secret that he'd never talk about?

Tiny trusted his wife without reservation. Trusted her to know when to say no to something her superiors wanted her to do—because she'd said no plenty of times. She had a sharply honed moral code. She had no problem bending the law to find child molesters and murderers, but drew the line at spying for her country. Tiny loved her even more for her integrity.

They'd gotten married in a small, private ceremony, just as they'd planned. It was a day Tiny would never forget. Just the two of them, and the witness and officiant, vowing to love and cherish each other for the rest of their lives.

And now, here he was. A decade later, his daughter in his arms, his best friends living a stone's throw from his front door. The saying was that it took a village to raise a child, and he and his friends had made their very own village right here at The Refuge.

"We're lucky," Pipe said. "We have everything we could ever want. Soul mates, children, best friends, and a safe place to raise them."

Tiny nodded as his friends agreed. They were getting mushy in their old age, but he didn't even care.

Just then, Rebecca fell, landing hard on her hands and knees. She immediately started to cry. Luke, who wasn't sure why his sister was crying, joined in. Joyce looked worried, and she pulled her older brother Dylan over to where Rebecca was crouched on the ground.

Stone stepped forward, prepared to go soothe his daughter, but Brick caught his arm. "They've got it," he told his friend.

"They" meaning the kids. Everyone gathered around the more startled than hurt little girl, calming her. Elizabeth got her to her feet, Patrick brushed the dirt off her knees, while Max did the same to her hands. The younger kids simply patted her back and arms, telling her that she was all right. Within two minutes, everyone was running around again, all hurts forgotten.

Their kids had made their own tribe, were their own best friends. And once more, Tiny's heart swelled in his chest. This was their future. The future of The Refuge. This second generation would never know what it meant to be an outcast. They'd never be bullied because they had a tribe of "brothers and sisters" who'd have their backs.

Looking down into the face of his daughter, he smiled. She was the youngest, the baby. She'd probably be spoiled rotten, but he was all right with that. Every little girl should feel as if she was a princess. He sighed thinking about his wife's upbringing, how horribly she'd been abused by the very person who was supposed to love her the most, and he vowed that Miracle would always know she was loved. By her father most of all.

Ryleigh could've let her father break her. Just as all the other women here could've let their experiences destroy them. But they'd all been determined to be happy. To put their pasts behind them and live the best lives they could. It hadn't always been easy. They'd had to deal with the negative emotions and trauma that popped up now and then. But with the support system they'd created here, everyone was thriving.

Tiny had no idea what was in store for the next decade and beyond. For Miracle, his wife, or the rest of his friends. But one thing he knew without a doubt was that what they'd built here, in their corner of New Mexico, would last for generations. The children they were raising, the people they were helping, the friendships they'd solidified in the last decade, they would all continue to flourish.

"What do you think they're talking about in there?" Owl asked, referring to their wives, who were inside the mini-lodge, shut into a room with a "do not disturb unless there's blood and guts" sign on the door.

"Food. Sleep. Sex," Spike said with a shrug.

Everyone laughed. He probably wasn't wrong.

Leaning down, Tiny kissed Miracle's forehead, and her little face smushed up in response. Probably in irritation; his daughter loved her sleep and didn't like to be interrupted for any reason.

"Gonna go shoot some hoops with Max," Pipe said. "He'll beat my ass, but that's okay. One day he'll be a big NBA star and I'll brag that I taught him everything he knows."

"I think I'll go see if Sam, Dylan, and Elizabeth want to play hide and seek with me. Anyone else in?" Owl asked.

"Sure."

"Sounds good."

Spike and Stone joined Owl, heading for the yard.

"I'll go corral the younger kids and maybe we can play tag," Brick said.

"I want to check on the animals. I'll grab the rest of the middles and see if they want to help," Tonka said.

And just like that, Tiny was alone on the porch with Miracle. He sat on one of the dozen rocking chairs they'd put on the porch, grinning as he watched his friends and their kids run around in the fresh mountain air.

The door to the lodge creaked, and he looked over, smiling when he saw Ryleigh.

"You okay?" he asked.

"Yeah. It was my turn to get more snacks from the kitchen, and I thought I'd check on everyone at the same time."

His wife was still one of the kindest people he'd ever met. It was more likely she'd volunteered to get more snacks, and while she and the other women had no problem leaving their husbands in charge of the kids, Tiny knew she was still a little traumatized by the three miscarriages she'd had and the trouble she'd had conceiving. She didn't like letting Miracle out of her sight for too long.

"She's fine," he whispered, holding out a hand to his wife.

Ryleigh came to his side immediately. She leaned down and caressed Miracle's face with a finger, then turned and kissed him. And just like that, Tiny's cock hardened. Even after ten years, his wife never failed to turn him on. She wasn't even trying to seduce him, she was simply showing her husband how much she loved him.

"You need anything?" she asked.

"No."

"Sure? Water? A snack?"

"What, am I three?" he teased.

Ryleigh rolled her eyes. "I seem to remember the last time you got a freaking cold, you acted like you were dying and wanted me to bring you ice chips and sit by your side, holding a compress on your forehead...like you were a toddler."

Tiny chuckled. She wasn't wrong. "I don't need water or a snack. I'm good."

She grinned. He couldn't get enough of her smiles.

"Tiny?"

"Yeah, sweetheart?"

"I'm so happy. Whatever sins I did in my past, I've more than made up for them. I just wanted you to know that I wouldn't want to be anywhere else in the entire world than right here with you. And our daughter. And our friends and all this craziness."

Tiny had worried now and then that he was holding her back. It was more than obvious she could be working with the finest minds in the world. She could be working to advance technology, to do amazing things with computers. Instead, she was here at The Refuge, living a life that some scientists and engineers might claim was a waste of her talents. So hearing her say she was happy, content, meant the world to him.

"I love you," he said, emotion making his words wobble.

"And I love you," she replied. "And when our Miracle goes to sleep tonight, I'll show you how much."

Her words didn't help the situation with his dick. It got even harder thinking about exactly how his wife might show her love later. "Looking forward to it," he said as calmly as he could.

"You should be. Because I'm going to rock your world."

"Shit, you've been talking with the girls about sex," he mused.

Ryleigh smiled a secret little smile, then leaned down and kissed him once more. "Maybe," she said coyly, before turning and heading back inside.

Tiny chuckled, making Miracle squirm in his arms, not liking another disturbance of her nap. "Sorry, beautiful. Didn't mean to wake you. Go back to sleep, but just sayin', you need to give Mom and Dad a good couple hours tonight without interrupting us. Okay?"

His daughter didn't reply, not that he expected her to.

Tiny leaned back, slowly rocking as he watched his friends and their kids run around the yard.

Yeah, it was safe to say he was a lucky man. He and his friends had made a life in New Mexico that their families deserved. One filled with love, friendship, and the knowledge that no matter where they went, The Refuge would always be a safe place they could call home.

* * *

Thank you for reading The Refuge series. I've always thought it would be an ideal place for anyone who'd suffered any kind of trauma in their life and needs a 'safe' place to hole up for a while. I also loved bringing back some of my 'OG' characters from my SEAL of Protection series. If you want to check out more from Caroline & Wolf and Dude, their stories are *Protecting Caroline* and *Protecting Cheyenne*.

I've also started a *new* series with Navy SEALs called

SEAL of Protection: Alliance. The first book is *Protecting Remi* and you'll see some of Caroline, Wolf and the gang as well.

Thank you all for your support over the years. I couldn't do what I love if it wasn't for you.

Scan the QR code below for signed books, swag, T-shirts and more!

Also by Susan Stoker

The Refuge Series
Deserving Alaska
Deserving Henley
Deserving Reese
Deserving Cora
Deserving Lara
Deserving Maisy
Deserving Ryleigh

SEAL of Protection: Alliance Series
Protecting Remi
Protecting Wren
Protecting Josie (Mar 4, 2025)
Protecting Maggie (Apr 1, 2025)
Protecting Addison (May 6, 2025)
Protecting Kelli (Sept 2, 2025)
Protecting Bree (Jan 2026)

Rescue Angels
Keeping Laryn (July 1, 2025)
Keeping Amanda (Nov 2025)
Keeping Zita (Feb 2026)
Keeping Penny (TBA)
Keeping Kara (TBA)
Keeping Jennifer (TBA)

SEAL Team Hawaii Series
Finding Elodie

Finding Lexie
Finding Kenna
Finding Monica
Finding Carly
Finding Ashlyn
Finding Jodelle

Eagle Point Search & Rescue

Searching for Lilly
Searching for Elsie
Searching for Bristol
Searching for Caryn
Searching for Finley
Searching for Heather
Searching for Khloe

Game of Chance Series

The Protector
The Royal
The Hero
The Lumberjack

SEAL of Protection: Legacy Series

Securing Caite
Securing Brenae (novella)
Securing Sidney
Securing Piper
Securing Zoey
Securing Avery
Securing Kalee
Securing Jane

Delta Force Heroes Series

Rescuing Rayne
Rescuing Aimee (novella)
Rescuing Emily
Rescuing Harley
Marrying Emily (novella)
Rescuing Kassie
Rescuing Bryn
Rescuing Casey
Rescuing Sadie (novella)
Rescuing Wendy
Rescuing Mary
Rescuing Macie (novella)
Rescuing Annie

SEAL of Protection Series

Protecting Caroline
Protecting Alabama
Protecting Fiona
Marrying Caroline (novella)
Protecting Summer
Protecting Cheyenne
Protecting Jessyka
Protecting Julie (novella)
Protecting Melody
Protecting the Future
Protecting Kiera (novella)
Protecting Alabama's Kids (novella)
Protecting Dakota

Delta Team Two Series

Shielding Gillian
Shielding Kinley
Shielding Aspen
Shielding Jayme (novella)
Shielding Riley
Shielding Devyn
Shielding Ember
Shielding Sierra

Badge of Honor: Texas Heroes Series

Justice for Mackenzie
Justice for Mickie
Justice for Corrie
Justice for Laine (novella)
Shelter for Elizabeth
Justice for Boone
Shelter for Adeline
Shelter for Sophie
Justice for Erin
Justice for Milena
Shelter for Blythe
Justice for Hope
Shelter for Quinn
Shelter for Koren
Shelter for Penelope

Ace Security Series

Claiming Grace
Claiming Alexis
Claiming Bailey
Claiming Felicity
Claiming Sarah

Mountain Mercenaries Series

Defending Allye
Defending Chloe
Defending Morgan
Defending Harlow
Defending Everly
Defending Zara
Defending Raven

Silverstone Series

Trusting Skylar
Trusting Taylor
Trusting Molly
Trusting Cassidy

Stand Alone

Falling for the Delta
The Guardian Mist
Nature's Rift
A Princess for Cale
A Moment in Time- A Collection of Short Stories
Another Moment in Time- A Collection of Short Stories
A Third Moment in Time- A Collection of Short Stories
Lambert's Lady

Special Operations Fan Fiction

http://www.AcesPress.com

Beyond Reality Series

Outback Hearts
Flaming Hearts
Frozen Hearts

<u>Writing as Annie George:</u>

Stepbrother Virgin (erotic novella)

ABOUT THE AUTHOR

New York Times, USA Today, #1 Amazon Bestseller, and #1 *Wall Street Journal* Bestselling Author, Susan Stoker has spent the last twenty-three years living in Missouri, California, Colorado, Indiana, Texas, and Tennessee and is currently living in the wilds of Maine. She's married to a retired Army man (and current firefighter/EMT) who now gets to follow *her* around the country.

She debuted her first series in 2014 and quickly followed that up with the SEAL of Protection Series, which solidified her love of writing and creating stories readers can get lost in.

If you enjoyed this book, or any book, please consider leaving a review. It's appreciated by authors more than you'll know.

www.stokeraces.com
www.AcesPress.com
susan@stokeraces.com

facebook.com/authorsusanstoker

x.com/Susan_Stoker

instagram.com/authorsusanstoker

goodreads.com/SusanStoker

bookbub.com/authors/susan-stoker

amazon.com/author/susanstoker

Made in United States
Cleveland, OH
06 January 2025

13142898R00207